To Dolores —

THE DRAGON'S SONG

BLACKTHORNE FOREST - BOOK 3

CLAIRE FOGEL

With happy memories of Elm Street, and thanks for your friendship for so many years!

Love,
Claire
xoxo

Copyright 2016 by Claire C. Fogel

All rights reserved except as permitted under the U.S. Copyright Act of 1976, no part of this publication may be reproduced, distributed or transmitted in any form or by any means, or stored in a data base or retrieval system without prior written permission of the owner of this book.

This book is a work of fiction. Names, characters, places and incidents are either products of the author's imagination or are used fictitiously and any resemblance to actual persons, living or dead, business establishments, events or locales is entirely coincidental.

Please do not participate in or encourage piracy of copyrighted materials in violation of the author's rights. Purchase only authorized editions.

August 2016 First Edition
Printed in the United States of America

Print ISBN: 978-0-9908923-5-9
Digital ISBN: 978-0-9908923-4-2

Editor: Laurie A. Will
Cover Design: Alexandre Jose Cardoso Rito
Formatting by Elaine York, Allusion Graphics, LLC
www.allusiongraphics.com

DEDICATION

To Neil,
Who's always there for me,
With thanks for your enthusiasm
and encouragement!

CHAPTER 1

There were three possible explanations for the anxiety I'd felt for weeks. One, I might be psychic; two, I might be paranoid; or three, I'd finally cracked. Probably because people kept trying to kidnap or kill me.

And then there was that strange, haunting little tune that seemed to be embedded in my brain. Number three was beginning to seem the most likely explanation.

It would be extremely inconvenient if I were really cracking up. I was starting my senior year at Thornewood High next week. Right. No pressure.

Nevertheless, I was packed and ready to leave for the beautiful Elven village where my father and his community of Elves lived, completely hidden from the human world.

I was sitting on the back porch enjoying my view of the deep green forest when, just before noon, my father rode Smoke out of the woods with the smaller Pigeon tied to his saddle. The sight of the beautiful grey Elven horses usually raised my spirits, but not today. The familiar feeling of dread hovered over me.

There were goose bumps up and down both arms. I had that feeling of being watched, even though I saw no one around in any direction. I shuddered slightly.

My father fastened my bags to Smoke's saddle, gave me a quick hug, and we left for Elvenwood. When he gave me an encouraging smile, I knew he was fully aware of my mental state. Having a telepathic father made certain explanations unnecessary.

When we rode through my father's camp, Kelly O'Rourke, my best friend Kevin's dad, walked out of one of the tents and waved at me. I waved back.

The camp varied in size, depending on the current threat. Today there were about a dozen tents situated in a semi-circle around a large fire pit used for cooking. A wooden lean-to had been built behind the tents for the greys stabled there.

My father chuckled. "Cara, Kelly was hoping that you and Kevin were future mates. I explained that you two are more like brother and sister. I think he was disappointed."

I couldn't help snorting when I thought of what Kevin would have to say about his father's hopes for us. Romance was simply not a possibility.

We were riding side by side at a leisurely pace, so we were able to talk.

"How was your night out with Sean?" he asked.

"It was fine, Dad. Since we were by ourselves, with no bodyguard listening in, we had the chance to talk about a lot of things. Sean was always great to talk with, and I've missed that."

Smirking, I added, "He wanted to know when I got so stubborn."

My father chuckled. "Cara, you're becoming more like your mother all the time."

"Really?"

"Sweetheart, I've never met a woman as stubborn as your mother." He shook his head, looking resigned about the many things that were beyond his control, which included my mother.

Fifteen minutes later, when we approached the gateway to Elvenwood, that solid looking illusion of boulders and pine trees, he said, "Are you ready to learn a little Gaelic? Now that you can ride, you may want to ride to Elvenwood by yourself occasionally."

I agreed and he said, "Repeat after me." He spoke three strange-sounding words, and I repeated them several times.

"In English it means green home," he said. I wouldn't mention it to my father, but it sounded a lot better in English.

When we got close to the impenetrable barrier, I said the Gaelic words out loud and the boulders and trees turned to mist and disappeared. Immediately I felt magic in the air. Sweet, welcoming magic.

My father beamed at me. "Very good. Don't ever write the words down; you must commit them to memory."

As we rode into Elvenwood, we passed picturesque thatch-roofed cottages, all with colorful gardens, and the flower-scented air mixed with the familiar feeling of Elven magic welcomed me to my second home.

When we reached my father's cottage, we dismounted and untied my bags from Smoke's saddle. After we thanked the greys for a good ride, they nodded to us and trotted off to the stable. As I approached the front door, a brown streak flew around the corner of the cottage, leaped in the air and licked my face. Laughing, my father bent down to scratch Roscoe's ears. "He's tried to jump up and lick my face many times, but he's always about a foot short." Roscoe was my dad's beautiful fawn and white Boxer, the father of my dog Ralph at home.

My father took my bags into my bedroom and returned to the sitting room where I sat on the floor with Roscoe, rubbing his belly. He was overjoyed to see us, judging by the madly wagging tail.

I loved the warmth of my father's cottage. The sitting room, equivalent to a living room in the modern world, held a large couch and several deep, cushioned chairs facing the stone fireplace. The largest chair faced a drawing of mine that my father had framed and hung over the fireplace. It showed my mother trimming her roses in our flower garden a year ago. The rest of the walls were covered with a large number of landscape paintings, which my father loved and had collected for years.

There was a large wooden table along with eight chairs placed at the rear of the large room. That table was where business was conducted and meals served when my father was home and invited friends in for a meal. I especially enjoyed the private meals we shared occasionally. My father was always more relaxed when it was just the two of us.

I was glad to see that a doggy door had been installed at the cottage's back door. My father saw me checking it out. "Adam said you suggested it, so he designed one and installed it. He thought it would make you happy."

I snorted. "I think it makes Roscoe even happier. How did Adam find time to build a doggy door with all the furniture building he's been doing?"

"You can ask Adam that yourself, Cara. As soon as he knows you're here, I'm sure he'll be over to see you." There was a knowing smile on his face as he winked at me. Ten years older than me, Adam had been my full-time bodyguard until his carpentry skills were needed in the village's wood shop. Admittedly, I was fond of Adam, and my father was aware of it.

"Cara, you haven't had lunch yet, have you?"

"Nope. Where will we be eating today?"

"I heard a rumor there would be baked ham and roasted potatoes in the dining hall today. And apple pie, if you're interested."

THE DRAGON'S SONG

That put a smile on my face.

While my father looked at some papers that had been left on his table, I unpacked my clothes and washed up. When I got back to the sitting room, he looked up with a smile.

"Ready for lunch?"

My growling stomach let me know I was more than ready.

As we walked to the dining hall, I was again humming that persistent melody that had taken root in my head.

"Where did you hear that melody?"

I shrugged. "No idea, Dad. It's been stuck in my head for days."

He shook his head, frowning slightly. "I know I've heard it before, probably a long time ago. Keep humming it. Maybe it'll come to me."

The large, stone dining hall consisted of two huge rooms, one for cooking and one for dining. The dining room was furnished with a dozen long wooden tables and benches, where meals were served family-style. The other side of the stone building held the cooking area where one wall was lined with fireplaces so big, a person could walk into them and stand up. At mealtimes, more than a dozen Elves were in the kitchen area preparing food.

When we walked into the dining area, at least fifty people were already seated and all heads turned to smile at us. My father was the popular leader of Elvenwood. His family had owned Blackthorne Forest for more than two hundred years.

I spotted Conor waving at us so we headed in his direction. I hadn't seen him since my last visit to Elvenwood, when I was agonizing over the fact I now had defensive skills that could kill. Conor had given me good advice, as he always did.

He stood and gave me a warm hug. "I don't get to see you enough these days." He was right. I was rarely in the woods now looking for scenic spots to draw, as I'd done for years. There were too many other things going on.

Within minutes, platters of ham, bowls of roasted potatoes, and several salads were placed on the tables by boys from the kitchen.

My father handed me a plate and I filled it with a little of everything. He looked at my plate, frowning. "Is that all you're eating?"

"Dad, I gained enough weight the last time I was here. I don't want to get any fatter."

Conor chuckled. "No need to worry. You look wonderful. In fact, there are at least a dozen young men who would line up at your door if your father would allow it."

Surprised, I looked at my father. He was shaking his head. "Not for at least a couple of years. She's only sixteen, and she's already growing up too fast."

When I thought of growing up too fast, my thoughts immediately went to Adam who had just walked in, heading for our table with a smile on his handsome face. In my opinion, I wasn't growing up fast enough.

My father looked up when he saw me begin to smile. "Have a seat, Adam. Join us for lunch." He sat down next to me, greeting my father and Conor and winking at me.

"Couldn't stay away, could you, Cara? I know someone who will be very happy to see you. Ian asks every day when you're coming back. Have you seen him yet?"

"No, not yet. I'll stop over there later."

More softly, Adam asked, "Are you feeling any better since we last spoke?"

"Uh, not really. I hope I can relax while I'm here so I can start school next week without feeling like the sky is about to fall on my head." We were speaking in low tones, but Conor overheard us and asked, "What's wrong, Cara?"

My father answered. "She's been having frequent anxiety attacks. She's convinced something big is about to happen."

Conor's silvery eyes showed concern. "Nothing bad will happen to you here. Do you have any idea where this anxiety is coming from?" I shook my head, and he turned to my father. "Brian, has there been any news from the Thornewood police?"

"No, nothing new there. Gaynes hasn't been seen anywhere in the past month. Police throughout the northeast are looking for him." Gaynes was my father's enemy and I seemed to be his favorite target.

Just the mention of Donald Gaynes made me shiver. My throat got so dry, I couldn't swallow. I closed my eyes for a few seconds and took a couple of deep breaths. This was Elvenwood. I was supposed to be safe here, although I was beginning to doubt I'd be safe anywhere.

Conor and my father didn't seem to understand what I was feeling, so I tried again to explain.

"I have this feeling that something really big is going to happen, something unavoidable." I was having nightmares again, waking up covered in sweat and terrified, but I didn't want to talk about that.

Conor asked, "You mean like a premonition?" I nodded and he looked at my father.

"Didn't you tell me once that your mother would have premonitions occasionally?"

My father looked undecided. "Yes, but her premonitions weren't always accurate. Sometimes nothing came of them."

"But sometimes her premonitions did come true, didn't they?"

My father looked away, frowning. It didn't seem like something he wanted to talk about.

When we'd finished eating, Adam stood up. "There are half a dozen chairs waiting for me at Garrett's wood shop. Cara, if you'll walk over there with me, I can show you what I've been working on."

"Would that be okay, Dad?"

"Of course, dear. I have a few meetings scheduled this afternoon. Go ahead and I'll see you both later this afternoon for tea."

I said goodbye to Conor, who leaned down to hug me. "Don't be such a stranger, Cara. I've missed you," he said with a smile. I'd missed him too. Conor was the first Elf I'd met, although he'd been "glamoured" and I hadn't known he was an Elf at the time. He had appointed himself my "big brother" and quickly became a close friend.

As we walked out of the dining hall, Adam said, "Your father mentioned to me that you were going out with Sean the other night. How did that go?"

I snorted. "You men gossip as much as girls do. My father asked me the same question this morning." I shook my head as I saw that familiar amused look on Adam's face.

"Well, it went fine. We're friends again."

"Do you really think Sean will be satisfied just being your friend?"

"Maybe not. But he knows that's all I'm willing to offer. He seemed to be happy that we're speaking to each other again. I think we both missed that part of our relationship."

"And the way you behaved at that party, Cara?" He arched one eyebrow as he glanced at me.

"How was I to know the fruit punch was spiked with vodka?"

I sighed. "I called Sean the next day and apologized for the way I'd acted. Thankfully, he understood and wasn't mad." Adam shook his head, looking amused as usual.

When we arrived at Garrett's workshop, Adam led me inside. Garrett was almost finished sanding a large table.

He looked up and put his tools down with a warm smile for me. "Welcome, Cara. It's good to see you." He took my hand between his rough, calloused ones. "I guess I should apologize for stealing your bodyguard. Adam's the best wood worker I've found in many years. I was so swamped with furniture orders I didn't think I'd ever catch up. Adam, show Cara those chairs you're working on. I think she'll be impressed."

Elvenwood's hand-made furniture, as well as other crafts, were sold in the human world, providing most of the village's income.

Adam led me to the rear of the workshop where there were six chairs in various stages of construction. One was almost finished and it was a thing of beauty. It appeared to be a period piece with gracefully curved legs and a high back, slightly rounded at the top. The wood looked like maple. I had no idea what period it represented, but it had a graceful look.

"This is beautiful."

"Thank you. I'm glad you like it, but I'm afraid I have to get back to work now. Can I join you and your father for tea later?"

"Absolutely. See you later."

As I was on my way out, Garrett stopped me. "I think Arlynn would like to see you while you're here. She'll be stopping by your father's cottage." I tried not to grimace. He smiled and winked at me. "I think you'll notice a definite change in her attitude."

Arlynn and I had been friends until she let me know she didn't trust Adam and thought I might get hurt because he was so much older. We'd never resolved that issue.

I left the shop and walked to Kathleen's to say hello. When I got there, I was surprised to find Gabriel there, again with a dressing on his injured leg.

He looked a lot happier than the last time I'd seen him, when we feared he might lose that leg.

"Hey, Cara. Couldn't stay away, could you?"

Kathleen smiled at me. "Welcome back, dear. I'll be through with Gabriel in a few minutes. His leg is coming along so much better now. I don't hold with most modern medicine, but that antibiotic Dr. Costello gave him has cleared up the infection beautifully. It's just a matter of allowing the leg to finish the healing on its own. My herbs can help."

I sat down to wait, happy to see Gabe looking like himself again.

"How's your archery coming along?" he asked. "I heard from Ryan that you've been concentrating on what you're calling non-lethal training. I'd like to see a demonstration while you're here."

We arranged to meet at the practice field the next day, and I went outside to wait until Kathleen was free. I sat down on her bench, absent-mindedly humming that same melody. There was a sudden shadow overhead like a low cloud passing over Elvenwood. I looked up but didn't see anything. A few minutes later Kathleen and Gabe walked out of her cottage.

"I've got half a dozen children for archery training now." Gabe smiled. "They're still enjoying the targets you painted for them. See you tomorrow morning." I was relieved to see him walking toward the practice field without a cane.

Kathleen sat down next to me. "What was that tune I heard you humming?"

I shrugged. "Everyone keeps asking me that, but I have no idea where it came from. It's been stuck in my head for days."

"Well, it's faintly familiar, but I can't remember where I heard it before." She shook her head.

"Your father tells me you've been anxious and tense lately. Are you still drinking that tea I gave you?"

"Yes, but maybe I should be drinking more of it."

She nodded. "Do you have any idea why you've been so anxious?"

"I'm not sure. Nightmares, a sudden feeling I'm being watched, that kind of stuff."

She took my hand and held it. "Your grandmother was a great one for premonitions. You should talk to your father about it. I'm sure he remembers. Of course, she wasn't always right, but the things she predicted often came true." She sighed. "You've certainly inherited a great deal from the Blackthornes already, dear. A little psychic ability wouldn't surprise me."

I sighed. Swell. One more Elven gift I'd rather not have.

Time to change the subject.

"Kathleen, have you seen Kelly O'Rourke yet?"

Her face lit up. "Of course I have. Now you know why your friend Kevin looked so familiar to me. When I opened my front door and found Kelly standing out here, I couldn't believe my eyes. It's so good to have him back. He thanked me for sending your father in the right direction. He was living in the White Mountains, as I suspected. Kevin looked so happy to be here with his father, it was a delight to see."

"I'd better be going. I think you've got a new patient." I pointed to a young boy heading in our direction, his arm in an unnatural position. His mother was with him, shaking her head when she saw Kathleen.

"My son will not stay out of the trees. I think his arm is broken."

Kathleen gave me a quick hug and led mother and son into her cottage. The boy was doing his best to be brave, lips clenched together, and only one tear visible on his cheek. I whispered, "Good luck," and left for the stables.

I was walking alone when I got that being watched feeling again. The hair on my arms was standing straight up as I whirled around, looking for anything threatening. No one was in sight. The air was barely moving, but I knew with certainty that I was being watched. That same shadow passed over me again and I shivered.

The greys always made me feel safe. I hurried to the stable.

After Will greeted me by lifting me off my feet, I made the rounds in the stable, apologizing to all the greys for arriving without any apples for them. I promised to bring apples on my next visit. Their whinnying and snorting sounded like laughter, calming my nerves.

Judging by the position of the sun, I thought it was time to head back to my father's cottage. There were so many things I wanted to talk to him about, so many magical things that I knew nothing about.

Whenever I visited Elvenwood, I could feel magic in the air. Sometimes I felt I was breathing it in.

CHAPTER 2

As soon as I walked in the door of the cottage, Roscoe came running. I could have sworn he was smiling, his tongue hanging out and his little tail wagging like mad. I leaned down to rub his velvety ears. My father looked up from the papers he'd been reading and smiled.

"Get all your visiting done?"

"Well, all except Ian. Is it too late for me to stop at his cottage now?"

My father looked out the sitting room window and chuckled. "You won't have to. Here he comes!"

I turned toward the doorway just as the little boy dashed in and practically tackled me. Ian grinned. "How long are you staying, Cara? Not just for a few hours this time, I hope."

He was so happy to see me, I couldn't resist leaning over and dropping a kiss on his cheek. He blushed but there was a big smile on his face.

"I'll be here for the rest of the week. I'll be going back to school next week, so I won't be able to visit as often when school starts. We can spend time together this week and make some good memories together." His face fell.

I could hear Ian's mom, Doreen, calling him so I walked him outside and told him to come over after breakfast in the morning so we could walk over to the practice field together and meet Gabriel. He looked more cheerful as he ran home. Doreen waved at me and I waved back.

When I got back inside, Dad had put away his papers and was waiting for me.

"Ready for tea?" He nodded and I got to work filling the kettle with water and putting it on the hook in the fireplace.

He sat down on the couch with me. "Sweetheart, I know you're still curious about your Elven heritage, so I thought this would be a good week for you to learn more."

I handed him his tea just as Adam walked in the door, smiling. "Am I in time for tea?"

My father looked up and nodded. "Have a seat. You'll probably be interested in what we've been discussing. Cara has always wanted to know more about Elven talents, the kind that the human world considers magical. Since she'll be here with me this week, I thought this would be a good time."

When Adam looked at me, I quickly handed him a cup of tea before I got lost in his amazing cobalt blue eyes. Those eyes would be the death of me. I took a deep breath to get myself under control. The way his lips turned up slightly at the corners, I was afraid he was reading my mind.

My father broke the spell. "There are several Elves you know who have wonderful gifts, but some of them are not unknown in the human world. Your cousin Jason is one example. He's never had a music lesson, but he plays the flute beautifully."

"Why haven't I heard him play?" I asked.

"Jason's not a showoff. He doesn't thrive on attention the way his brother Justin does. But I'm sure he'll play for you if you ask him. I've been keeping him so busy running errands in town, he hasn't been home much. He enjoys the human world, and everyone likes him wherever he goes, which is an enormous benefit for us. He always asks for you, Cara. Jason feels he formed a bond with you when he rescued you after you were kidnapped."

He smiled. "I know he'd like to spend more time with you. Perhaps I'll give him some vacation while you're here. Would you like that?"

"I'd love it. I was wondering why I haven't seen him. Although Amy told me she had often seen him at the bakery. Everyone there was madly in love with him."

My father chuckled. "I think Jason has a sweet tooth. Amy's family's bakery was his favorite place in Thornewood. Does Amy know when they will reopen?"

"The Fire Chief is sure it was arson. Amy's parents may not reopen. Amy said they were so freaked out when they heard it was arson, they started talking about retiring."

My father and Adam both looked shocked. My Dad asked, "Do they have any idea who would do such a thing?"

Suddenly I had a disturbing thought. "They have no enemies. Amy's parents are really nice people; everyone loves them. I can only think of one person who might wish any of our friends harm." I looked at my father.

There was a sudden silence. Frowning, my father stared at me, nodding slowly. "I hope you're wrong, but I have to admit, it's possible." He turned to Adam. "Is Neal still acting as Amy's bodyguard?"

Adam nodded. My father looked thoughtful. "Perhaps we should keep a close eye on Amy and her family for the time being. Send two more men to Amy's house with instructions to keep an eye on the house. If our suspicions are correct, their home might be the next target." He shook his head, rubbing his forehead. "I hate to think that Gaynes would stoop that low."

"Don't forget what he did to Gavin's mother."

My father just closed his eyes and nodded.

"You're right. I'll speak to Tommy O'Donnell about it."

Police Chief O'Donnell was a Halfling too, and had been fully aware of all the trouble Donald Gaynes had caused over the past several months. He'd given us all the help he was able to, since Blackthorne Forest was not exactly his jurisdiction.

"In the meantime, Jason will be at home most of this week and the two of you can spend some long overdue time together," my father promised. He glanced over at Adam, a gleam in his eye. "That way Adam can get those chairs finished."

There was a slight flush on Adam's cheeks. From the look on his face, I wondered what he'd been thinking about. Having a telepathic father wasn't always a good thing. I gave Adam a sympathetic look. He gave me a faint smile and an unobtrusive wink.

My father looked at me. "On another subject, your mother discussed with me your need for transportation, and we decided we would buy you your first car. We'll share the expense, but if you manage to put another mailbox out of its misery, that expense will be yours."

I leaped off the couch and threw my arms around his neck. "Thank you! It means a lot to me to know you have faith in me. But I'm not planning on taking out any more mailboxes, honest. So when is this going to happen? And what kind of a car are you getting me?"

"When you arrive home at the end of this week, your car will be waiting for you."

Taken aback, I said, "You mean I won't be picking it out for myself?" He could see how disappointed I was. "Is Mom picking out my car?" That was even worse. Mom was a huge fan of plain, boxy economy cars.

"Not entirely, dear. Harry Callahan will be with her since he knows how to pick out a good used car. And your mother will ask Kevin to join them since he knows what you like. Is that acceptable?"

That was a relief. I knew that Kevin wouldn't let her buy something too uncool, and Mr. Callahan, Dad's business manager, wouldn't let her buy a lemon.

"That's okay. There's a good chance they'll pick out something I'll like. Thank you." I leaned down and kissed his cheek. I would be starting my senior year driving my own car. I was thrilled!

Adam stood up. "Congratulations on your new car-to-be. Thanks for the tea. I won't see you at dinner, I'm afraid. Garrett and I have so much work, Arlynn has been bringing dinner over to us to save us time. But I'm sure I'll see you soon."

He turned to my father. "Thanks for letting me stay for tea."

My father smiled. "You know you're always welcome here." I thought I could see something unspoken pass between them. When I looked at my father, the warmth of his smile showed me how much he liked Adam. One more thing that ran in the family.

We both watched the tall, slender man walk out the front door. This seemed to be the perfect time to ask my father what he knew about Adam.

"Dad, sometimes when you speak about Adam, you wink at me, and I get the impression I should be reading between the lines. What am I missing?"

He turned sideways on the couch so we could look at each other. "We've talked about your feelings for Adam before."

I nodded. He had actually asked me once if I was in love with Adam. I couldn't deny I had feelings for him. I just didn't know what to call those feelings.

"Sweetheart, I think a lot of Adam. He's a fine young man. I would be proud if he was my son, and I've told him so. I trust him, Cara. But I also understand that he has feelings for you, and you for him. He's promised me to keep his feelings under control because you're so young." He sighed. "The age difference doesn't bother me, but it bothers your mother a great deal." He looked into my eyes. "You can probably figure out why."

"How old were you when you met Mom?"

He hesitated for what seemed like a long time. Then he seemed to come to a decision. "Your mother has never told you about our relationship, has she?" I shook my head.

"When I met her, she was only seventeen." He was silent for at least a minute. "I was thirty-five, but I looked much younger. You know, of course, that Elves don't show their age." He hesitated. "Our relationship didn't end well, as you know. It had nothing to do with the difference in our ages, but I'm afraid that's what your mother saw when she met Adam. She could see how interested he was in you." It was clear he wanted me to understand Mom's reaction.

"I've told you I don't even know what falling in love feels like, Dad. All I know is that I like and respect Adam. I trust him, and I enjoy being with him. We have good talks and believe it or not, I actually take his advice most of the time. Even though he's older and wiser, he doesn't treat me like a stupid kid. He seems to understand me. I think he just wants to see me happy."

"And that's why I trust him. He wants you happy, whether that happiness includes him or not." He sighed. "All young men should be so unselfish." Shaking his head, he said, "I wasn't at all unselfish when I fell in love with your mother. I wish I had been."

He stood up abruptly and went to the fireplace to pour himself another cup of tea. When I looked up, I realized there was someone standing just outside the front door. I went to open the door, surprised to find Arlynn standing there, holding a large, covered tray.

She smiled a bit nervously. "Dinner delivery. Your father said he wanted to spend more time with you this week."

I gestured her in and she walked to the long table at the rear of the sitting room and set the tray down. My father greeted her with a smile and then turned to me with one eyebrow arched. Apparently, he thought I'd stayed angry with her long enough. And, of course, he was right.

Walking over to her, I said, "How are you?" I meant it. I'd missed her.

She smiled that breathtaking smile. I'd forgotten how Arlynn could light up an entire room with her smile.

"I'm fine. Thank you for asking. I've been wanting to talk to you for the past few weeks."

"Yeah, me too." My father returned to his easy chair, and I led Arlynn to the couch.

She looked a little embarrassed. "You may be young, but you're an excellent judge of character. Better than I am, I'm afraid. Since Adam has been working with my cousin Garrett, I've had a chance to get to know him. You were right. He's a good man. Good enough not to hold my past behavior against me."

She shook her head. "I was such an idiot. We all care about you and worry about you. Why shouldn't Adam feel the same way? I know he would do anything for you; we all would, you know. I've already apologized to him for my lack of trust. He said he hadn't been angry, that he understood my concerns."

She grinned. "He also said he thought it was time for you to get over it!"

I was trying not to laugh, but Adam's remark was so human, I couldn't hold it in. "I usually take Adam's advice. I'm over it," I said laughing. I leaned forward and hugged her. She hugged me back with a look of relief on her beautiful face.

"I hope we can spend some time catching up this week. We have a lot to talk about." I had a feeling she was referring to Conor and their growing relationship.

"Okay, just let me know when you have some free time, and we'll get together. And I still want you to model for me, okay?"

"I'd be happy to model. Now I've got to get back to the kitchen. Dinner's in another half hour. The tray I brought you doesn't have to be warmed. I made your favorites and they're good cold. Enjoy."

My father stood up and walked her to the door, hugging her before she left. I thought I heard him murmur, "Thank you."

When she was gone, he walked over to me, placing a finger under my chin to tilt my face up. "Happier now?" I smiled, nodding. "Good. I don't want any of my people angry at each other, especially when one of them is my daughter.

"We can talk over dinner, dear. I'm ready to eat if you are."

I went into the kitchen to bring in plates, cups and silverware, along with a jug of water from the cold pantry, and Dad sat down and uncovered the tray of food. There was fresh baked bread, a green veggie salad, a fruit salad, a whole roasted chicken, and half an apple pie. We looked up at each other and I said, "Wow." My father chuckled. "I'm certainly glad that you and Arlynn are on good terms again."

After we served ourselves, I said, "I'd like to know more about the magical talents your Elves have. To begin, Conor seems to be gifted in many ways. I know he plays caretaker in the Eastern end of the forest, and he seems perfectly comfortable with humans, but I've always had a feeling there's more going on behind those silvery eyes than he admits."

"Yes, Conor McKay is multi-talented. There is virtually nothing he can't handle. You've probably never seen him taking care of the forest's wildlife. The wild animals will come right up to him, even if they're injured. An injured animal will usually try to hide from us. But when Conor approaches any animal, it will walk up to him and wait for his help. That backpack you see him carrying is full of medical supplies for our wildlife. They seem to recognize him as one of their own. I don't know of anyone else with this ability. And you know how easy it is to communicate with Conor. His personality is the main reason I asked him to keep an eye on you while you were growing up. I knew he'd be a good friend to you if you ever met him. He loves children." He smiled. "Of course, we all do."

After we'd finished eating, I took the dishes into the kitchen and cleaned up while my father started the fire and made tea. I left the apple pie on the table, hoping we'd have room for it later.

Now was my chance to ask a question that had really intrigued me. "Dad, several people have mentioned your mother's premonitions, but you never seem to want to talk about them. If I'm actually having a premonition, I'd like to know more about your mother. After all, she's my grandmother."

He sighed. "Of course you have a right to know about your grandmother." He gave me a sad smile. "She would love you. Your resemblance to her is truly amazing."

"Is she small too?"

Smiling, he said, "No. You inherited your size from your mother. My mother is quite tall, like all Elves. You're like a miniature Rebecca Blackthorne."

"Rebecca Blackthorne. What a beautiful name. But tell me about her premonitions. I'm really curious. I'd also like to know why you're so reluctant to talk about them."

He began running his fingers through his long hair. Finally, he nodded. "My parents were still living here when I met your mother. Elven relationships with humans weren't uncommon, although my father completely disapproves of them. He's an extremely rigid and old-fashioned man, still living in the Middle Ages in his mind. Fortunately, my mother is far more open-minded and compassionate. You'd like her."

"I'm sure I would. But what about her premonitions?"

He ran his hands through his hair again. "My mother knew I was seeing a human girl, and she knew I had given my heart to Alicia. I finally sat down with her, describing your beautiful mother excitedly, and watched my mother's eyes become sad. She said, 'I'm sorry, Brian, but this girl will not make you happy. She will give you a wondrous gift and then withhold it from you. It will be many years before you will find happiness.' I've never forgotten her words. My parents left for Scotland a month later."

I was amazed. My grandmother had really nailed it.

"Her premonition was accurate. Of course, at that time I didn't believe her. I was convinced it was just another one of my mother's arbitrary predictions." He sighed. "It was a few years later before I realized how accurate she'd been."

I reached out to touch his hand. "You never talk about those years, but when I needed you last spring, you were there."

Smiling, he squeezed my hand. "Sweetheart, you were worth waiting for." He added, "And so's your mother. I haven't given up on her, you know."

We shared conspiratorial smiles. "I think you're making progress."

"Getting back to your 'premonition,', I found one of my mother's diaries recently. It's one of the last ones she wrote in before they left for Scotland. I only had time to skim through it, but you might like to read it. Maybe you'll learn something there.

"By the way, I finally remembered where I heard that tune you keep humming. It was a song my mother would sing occasionally when I was very young. I don't remember the words, but it's the same melody. There might be something about it in her diary."

"Thanks. Maybe it'll help me get to know my grandmother a little. I'll read some of it before I go to bed tonight."

When I looked out the window, it was almost dark, so I knew it was probably the time my father usually went to sleep. We'd been talking for so long, he had to be tired, but when I looked at him, he seemed awake and perfectly content.

"I know it's late, but you don't look tired."

He smiled. "I want to spend as much time with you as I can this week. I'll have to go into Thornewood once, but this week will be one I hope we'll always remember. You're growing up so fast, I feel I'm running out of time to make up for all the father-daughter moments I missed."

He chuckled. "You have no idea how much I enjoy the talks we have, even though they're not usually long enough to suit me. Getting to know you over the past few months has been an absolute joy. I couldn't be any prouder of the young woman you're becoming. You probably don't realize it, but everyone in Elvenwood feels the same way. They don't think of you as a Halfling. You're simply one of us."

His words touched me. I couldn't think of a single thing to say.

But then he stood up with a grin on his face and said, "I think that apple pie is calling our names. Let's go finish it off." So we did, with more tea, and more talk about talented Elves until we were both too tired to stay awake any longer.

Reading my grandmother's diary would have to wait until tomorrow.

I usually slept well whenever I spent the night at my father's home, but not that night. I tossed and turned. My subconscious must have been working overtime.

CHAPTER 3

I dreamed of my grandmother that night. Rebecca Blackthorne was a taller, older version of the girl I saw in the mirror every day. In my dream, I was alone in the woods, surrounded by mist. The tall woman walked toward me. "There's something I have to tell you, dear."

We walked toward the orchard, hand in hand. She stopped and turned to me. "You will be meeting an old friend of mine soon. Whenever you sing the dragon song, she'll appear. Her name is Rowenna. She has always been a friend to the Blackthorne women. Please give her my love and tell her I miss her."

When I turned to ask her what she meant by the dragon song, she had disappeared in the mist.

The dream was still vivid in my mind when I woke the next morning. I would definitely have to find time to read my grandmother's diary.

I got up, washed and dressed, and found my father already gone. I knew he was still in the village, but I had evidently slept past breakfast. He'd left a plate of muffins and some fruit juice on the table for me with a brief note: "Taking care of some village business this morning. See you at lunch. Love, Dad."

Remembering that I was supposed to meet Gabriel this morning, I ate quickly and walked outside to find Ian waiting for me across the road. I waved and he came running over, tackling me a bit more gently this time.

"I'm meeting Gabriel to show him the kind of archery I've been working on. Want to come?"

"Yes! I can't wait until I can start training with Gabriel, but I have to wait another year."

When we reached the practice field, Gabe was practicing while he waited for me. His skill didn't appear to have been hurt at all during the months since his leg was injured. Ian was clearly impressed, watching Gabe shoot his arrows with such fast precision. When he'd finished his practice, he brought me one of the smaller bows and a pouch of arrows. "Let me see what you've been working on."

Using the grizzly bear as my target, I began aiming carefully for the bear's arms and knees. At first I concentrated on accuracy rather than speed. Gradually, my shots got faster until I felt I was performing to the best of my ability.

When I finished and went to retrieve my arrows, Gabe was smiling. "I see what you're doing. Excellent technique. You'll stop your attacker without killing him, if you're lucky." He winked at me. " You realize this technique wouldn't have helped you when we were attacked, right?" I closed my eyes briefly, then nodded. He added, "But I think I'll still add this approach to my classes. Was this Adam's idea?"

"Yes. If Adam hadn't come up with this approach, I think I would have given up training altogether."

He frowned. "I remember how upset you were when I told you that you'd killed that dark Elf." Looking me in the eye, he said, "I'm glad you didn't give up. There was nothing else you could have done to save yourself and Ryan. But in a less extreme situation, aiming for knees or hands probably would be effective."

Ian had been watching, wide-eyed. He turned to Gabe. "Will I be able to shoot as well as Cara?"

"It just takes a lot of practice, Ian." He smiled and ruffled Ian's hair. "I'm due at Kathleen's now. See you at lunch?"

He left for Kathleen's and I could see he wasn't even limping. He seemed to be completely recovered, which was a huge relief. Gabriel had had a rough couple of months.

Ian and I walked over to the stable to see Will and the greys. After we'd greeted Will and made the rounds of the beautiful grey horses, we walked back to my father's cottage. I was anxious to begin reading my grandmother's diary, so I sent Ian home with a promise to take him with me when I went out to do some drawing later.

In the sitting room, I curled up on the couch with Rebecca Blackthorne's diary. Roscoe curled up at my feet. Within minutes he was snoring, which felt just like home.

Reading my grandmother's diary felt like reading a letter from a friend. Her style of writing was simple and direct. She wrote about the people in her life, her husband, her son, her stepson, and several friends, two of whom I knew—Kathleen and Conor. She described Kathleen as highly intuitive and gifted in the herbal arts, despite being very young. I guessed Kathleen was in her teens when this was written. She spoke fondly of Conor McKay, saying that her son

Brian was lucky to have Conor as his closest friend. She also predicted that Conor would be a bachelor for many years, but would be happy in his work. Her prediction about my father's future didn't go into detail, but she didn't believe he would find lasting happiness until he reached middle age. Well, that was accurate. It was hard for me to see my handsome father as middle-aged, but he'd admitted last night that he was now past fifty. Not that he looked as old as forty.

She described my grandfather as "too stubborn for words, but I do love him." That made me smile. She wrote about other relatives I knew nothing about, but she did say that she wished her stepson, father of my twin cousins, Jason and Justin, could be "more like my beloved Brian, who has brightened every one of my days since he was born." It sounded like my father's half-brother had been a thorn in her side for years.

My father walked in, smiling when he saw me curled up on the couch, and I put the diary down. It was fascinating reading, and I felt as though I was actually getting to know my grandmother.

"Ready for lunch?"

I laughed. "You probably heard my stomach growling before you walked in. Are we going to the dining hall for lunch?"

"Yes. I don't want to make too much extra work for Arlynn and the other cooks, because I planned to have dinner at home tonight. I asked Adam and Jason to join us. Jason was really excited when I told him that I was giving him most of the week off from his normal duties. Your cousin is really looking forward to spending time with you."

We both washed up and left for the dining hall. As we walked, I started humming that same persistent tune again. My father said, "Now I'm sure. That is the same melody my mother used to sing occasionally. I think she mentioned that it was a favorite of one of her friends, but I don't know who the friend was."

"I think I do." There was a definite look of surprise on his face.

"I had a dream about my grandmother last night. She said that I'd be meeting an old friend of hers. She said her friend would appear whenever I sang the dragon song. I have a feeling that's the tune that's been stuck in my head. Do you remember her calling it by that name?"

He shook his head. "No, I never heard her mention a dragon song. There were some old tales of dragons living in the forest hundreds of years ago, but I think it was simply myth. Dragons may have existed a long time ago in Elven lands, but as far as I know, they became extinct long before I was born."

"But they really did exist at one time?" I asked.

He shrugged with a smile. "It's hard to tell. I've never heard anyone talk about any personal experience with dragons, not even the Elders." With a laugh, he added, "One more Elven myth from the old days, I guess."

A few months ago, I'd discovered that some myths were surprisingly real. Based on recent experience, in the Elven world anything was possible.

Inside the dining hall, we sat down with Gabriel and my father asked him about his health. "You gave us all quite a scare, Gabe. Kathleen has been keeping me updated, but I'm happy to see you looking so well." In a softer voice, he told Gabe he would always be grateful for how well he and Ryan had protected me during the attack we'd experienced in June.

Looking embarrassed, Gabe said, "Cara did an excellent job of protecting herself. Ryan and I are both proud of her."

Suddenly, I felt a pair of arms being wrapped around my shoulders, almost lifting me out of my seat. I heard a happy voice exclaim, "It's so good to see you, cousin! Move over a little so I can sit next to you." I turned around to return Jason's happy smile. I hadn't seen him in at least a month.

He still looked more like an angel than an Elf, with his green eyes, perfect features, and black hair curling around his face. It was no wonder he was welcomed everywhere he went. And he was as good-hearted as he was beautiful, unlike his twin who had virtually disappeared after I'd been kidnapped. I had never asked my father what he'd done with Justin; I was just glad he wasn't around anymore.

"Jason, I hear you play the flute. I hope you'll play for me while I'm here this week. My father says you play beautifully."

Naturally, he turned beet red, but he nodded and said, "I'll do anything you ask. It's such a treat to have time to spend with you. Your father has been keeping me busy all summer, but I'm actually on what he called 'vacation' right now." He leaned over and whispered, "I'm sure I have you to thank for that."

"Jason, there's one more thing I hope you'll do for me. I've been working on a series of what I'm calling 'Elf drawings.' I've hidden an Elf in each landscape just for fun, and many of your friends have modeled for me. Would you be willing to appear in one of my drawings?"

He grinned. "Of course I would. Your father told me about those drawings, and they sound wonderful. I've been looking forward to seeing what you've been working on. One day this week we'll take a picnic out into the apple orchard. I'll bring my flute, and you can work on your Elf drawings. We'll make a day of it."

"Sounds great," I said, smiling.

Conversation slowed down as we ate thick ham and cheese sandwiches spread with homemade mustard dressing, a butter lettuce and tomato salad, and more apple pie. Since the orchard was now full of ripe apples being picked daily, I was happy that we wouldn't run out of apple pie any time soon.

I didn't see Adam at lunch, and then I remembered that he and Garrett were taking their meals in the workshop in order to save time. Whenever I didn't see Adam, it always seemed as though something was missing. I knew he'd become too important to me, but there really wasn't anything I could do about those feelings.

After we finished lunch, Jason disappeared to take care of some last-minute chores, and my father said he wanted to visit with several of Elvenwood's artisans who were already working on orders they'd received for the upcoming holidays. He told me that more than half of the village's income was earned from filling Christmas orders from the outside world for handmade furniture and other goods. Which, of course, reminded me again that so many Christmas gifts actually were being made by Elves, a fact that delighted me.

I walked back to my father's cottage, again humming that haunting little melody, to collect both my art supplies and young Ian, who was waiting impatiently on our front step.

"Ian, where else can we go besides the orchard? I'd like to find a different setting for my next drawing."

"Well, past the orchard is where the West side of the forest begins. You can see mountains from there, and it looks kind of wild, not as pretty as the orchard. I'm not supposed to go that far by myself, but if I'm with you, I don't think I'll get in trouble."

"Do you think it would make a nice picture?" I asked him.

"I think it might look a little scary, but I like the mountains. They turn kind of purple when the sun starts going down."

That sounded good to me, so we hiked to the orchard and walked through it until we reached the end. The scene beyond the orchard was fascinating. A mixture of tall Pines and ancient apple trees with twisted trunks led us to the edge of the mountains. I could see scrubby pines growing up the sides of the lower mountains, with higher peaks tinged with lavender in the distance. The lower mountains looked climbable, but the taller mountains were too steep, probably only suitable for mountain goats.

The rugged mountain view was one I would definitely draw another time. It was a little too stark for one of my Elf drawings, so I found a place to sit under one of the tall pines, facing the group of ancient, gnarled apple trees.

"Do you think you can climb that apple tree?" I pointed to the largest of the old trees.

Laughing, Ian shouted, "Sure," as he ran to the tree and quickly climbed up to one of the higher branches. He was partially hidden by the thick leaves, which was perfect. The only parts of him that were visible were his big smile and his feet hanging from the thick branch he sat on.

"That's perfect. This will be one of the best Elf drawings I've done." I was sketching as quickly as I could as I spoke to him. I didn't know how long he'd be comfortable sitting on that branch, and I realized that he was at least fifteen feet above the ground, not the safest place for a six-year-old.

My hands flew over the paper, rushing to get all the important details drawn quickly. I would add the colors and shading once Ian was safely on the ground. I found myself humming that same melody as I worked, thinking only of what I was drawing. I looked up as a large shadow passed overhead, surprised because there didn't appear to be a cloud in the sky.

I decided that my imagination was working overtime because I thought I heard the word *Sing* in my mind, spoken in a soft, gravelly voice. I looked around, listening carefully, but heard nothing more.

"Can you climb down now? Carefully, please." As I watched Ian scramble down the gnarled trunk, I thought the same shadow passed overhead one more time. I looked up, but again saw nothing.

Ian came running back to me, anxious to see the drawing I'd done. I asked him if he'd noticed the shadow that had passed over us twice. He nodded. "Something very big flew over us, but the leaves were in the way and I couldn't see what it was."

Something flew over us? "I thought it was a cloud passing overhead. Are you sure it was something flying?"

He nodded. "I thought I saw something with wings. Clouds don't have wings."

Surprised, I said, "You're right. I wish I'd looked up sooner."

He shrugged. "I liked that song you were humming. What's it called?"

I put my pencil down, stretching my fingers and hand. "I don't know. It's just a tune that's been stuck in my head for the past few weeks." I smiled. "I can't seem to make it stop."

"Well, it's pretty. I like it. Do you know the words?"

"I'm afraid not. My father told me he thinks his mother used to sing it, but he doesn't know the words either."

Ian curled up next to me as I picked up my pencil again. He watched as I added more detail and all the colors to the drawing. With Ian safely on the ground, I took my time. This picture was quite different from the other Elf drawings I'd done. The setting had a wilder look, contrasting with Ian's happy smile peeking through the upper branches of the old tree. When I was finally satisfied, I put the last pencil down and asked, "What do you think?"

He was wide-eyed. "This is the best one yet."

"Thank you. I like it too." I looked up at the sun, much lower in the sky than it had been. "We should probably go back now." With a smile, I added, "It's late and you missed your nap, didn't you?"

"I think I'm too big for a nap now. I'm almost seven, you know."

"Well, I hope your mother won't mind. I don't want her to be mad because I kept you out too long."

He grinned. "Mom would never get mad at you. When I'm out with you, she knows she doesn't have to worry about me." I tousled his hair and we got up to hike back through the apple orchard.

I found myself humming that same tune again. Suddenly, inside my head, I heard, *Sing. Please.* I stopped short, looking around. I wondered if Rebecca Blackthorne's friend was somewhere nearby, speaking to my mind the same way my father did. That thought gave me goose bumps up and down both arms.

I was beginning to feel that familiar sense of urgency again.

CHAPTER 4

When we reached the cottage, I sent Ian home, after thanking him for his help this afternoon. My father was still out and it wouldn't be dinnertime for at least another hour. I made myself a cup of tea and curled up on the couch again with my grandmother's diary, hoping to learn more about her mysterious friend.

I skimmed through more pages of family activities and comments about friends, but found nothing about anyone named Rowenna, and nothing at all about a song. Rebecca Blackthorne's handwriting was so small, it took quite a bit of time to read each page.

After reading for a while, my eyes grew tired. Reluctantly I put the diary down, leaned my head against the couch's cushioned back and closed my eyes. I must have dozed off because I thought I was hearing that gravelly voice in my head saying, *Sing. Please.*

I felt a warm hand on my arm and sat up suddenly, totally disoriented. Adam was bent over me, shaking me gently. "You must have been dreaming. I heard you mumbling something. Are you all right?"

Shaking my head to clear my mind of that voice and what must have been a dream, I looked up into Adam's worried, deep blue eyes and felt better immediately. "Have a seat. I'm glad you're here. Something strange has been happening since I got here."

He sat next to me, wrapping one large, warm hand around one of my small, surprisingly cold hands. "What's going on?"

I explained about the song that had been stuck in my head, about my father's memory of his mother singing it, about the dream of my grandmother, the "cloud" that apparently had wings, and the voice I was now hearing in my head. He frowned and shook his head slowly.

He was silent for a few minutes. Finally, he squeezed my cold hand and gave me a wry smile. "Well, I think we now know a bit more about this premonition of yours. My guess is that one of the things you've been worried about is right here in Elvenwood, which should mean it's not something that will hurt you."

"I think I'm beginning to understand. My grandmother's old friend is somewhere nearby. Her name is Rowenna, and she wants to hear the dragon song that Rebecca Blackthorne used to sing to her. She hasn't heard the song since my grandmother moved away, and that was before I was born."

I picked up the diary and showed it to Adam. "I've been reading Rebecca's diary, trying to find out more about Rowenna and this dragon song. But so far, there's been no mention of either. Her writing is so small, it's slow reading, but I think Rowenna is depending on me somehow." I hesitated. "And maybe my grandmother is too."

"Does anyone here know of Rowenna?"

"I don't think so. My father's not familiar with the name, which is surprising since she was supposedly a good friend of his mother's." I shrugged. "I'll just have to keep reading." Adam continued to hold my hand until my father arrived with Jason.

Adam let go of my hand as my father leaned down to kiss the top of my head. Jason again hugged me so hard, I gasped and almost came off the couch. My father leaned over us and said softly, "Your emotions have been all over the place for the past few hours. Are you all right?"

"I'm okay, Dad. I'll tell you more about it later."

He nodded. "I'm glad Adam was with you, dear." He looked down at Adam, who was still sitting close to me. "If holding Cara's hand comforts her, I have no objection." My father spoke softly, but Jason heard every word and simply winked at me with his usual sweet smile.

Thanks to the three of them, my stress level was now more bearable.

I looked at my father, my cousin, and my favorite bodyguard and said, "Thanks for your support. I feel better than I've felt in weeks."

There was a tapping at the front door and my father opened it to let in two ladies carrying the familiar, heavily loaded trays. I'd lost track of time, as usual. It was dinnertime. Jason and I went into the kitchen to gather up everything that would be needed for the table, and my father got a large jug of water from the cold cellar.

My improved mood seemed to be contagious. There was a lot of good-natured teasing and joking over dinner, which was, as always, delicious. I managed to save enough for the next day's breakfast and maybe even lunch. I planned to do a lot more reading the next day, comfortably curled up on the couch as I searched for answers.

After everyone left, I told my father what I'd experienced during the afternoon. He looked as surprised as Adam had.

THE DRAGON'S SONG

"I don't remember ever hearing the name Rowenna. It's a shame my mother is too far away to explain these things to you. But I do remember her speaking to me in my dreams now and then, mostly when she had advice she wanted to give me privately." He gave me an apologetic smile. "It's a family talent, I'm afraid. And now she's speaking to you. I'd advise you to pay careful attention to whatever she said."

He spent time telling me more about his parents until it was time for bed. "Are you going to stay up reading tonight, dear?"

"I think so. I keep hoping I'll find something about Rowenna or the song."

"Well, feel free to sleep in again tomorrow if you're up late. I'll be in and out all day, but if you need me just send me a message and I'll come home."

We said good night and he left me with a hug. "I'm relieved you're feeling calmer now, sweetheart. Sleep well."

I stayed up reading my grandmother's diary until my eyes started to close. I'd managed to read quite a bit further into her diary but still hadn't found what I was looking for. This was a mystery I was determined to solve.

Except for Roscoe, the cottage was empty when I woke in the morning. The sky was cloudy and dark, making me glad I'd planned to stay in and read. And thanks to all the leftovers from last night's dinner, I wouldn't go hungry. I took a shower in cold water again, but with this morning's humidity, it was actually refreshing.

I lit several of the oil lamps, and their soft glow immediately transformed the cottage into a warm inviting oasis despite the light rain hitting the windows softly. After enjoying a few of last night's leftovers, along with a basket of fresh muffins some thoughtful person had left on our table this morning, I made a pot of Kathleen's herbal tea and settled myself on the couch with my grandmother's diary.

More entries about village activities, a little gossip about the young, single Elves, a recipe for apple-cinnamon muffins, which sounded heavenly, but nothing I had hoped to find. I poured myself another cup of tea just as Jason rushed in, a big smile on his face. I poured him a cup of tea, and he planted himself next to me on the couch.

"I have it on good authority that tomorrow will be a beautiful, sunny day, and I have the entire day to myself, so would you like to spend the day with me? We can picnic, you can draw, I can model if you like, and I'll play my flute for you." He smiled apologetically. "I hope tomorrow's a good day for you, cousin. I guess I should have asked."

"Tomorrow's a perfect day. It'll be fun."

As he sat back to drink his tea, he saw the diary. "Is that our grandmother's?"

"Yes, my father gave it to me. He thought it was the last one she wrote in before she left for Scotland with our grandfather. I'm trying to find some answers to some strange things that have been happening to me lately."

He nodded. "Uncle Brian told me about this premonition you've had. You know, I was near the orchard yesterday afternoon, and I think I heard the same voice you were hearing. She wanted you to sing for her."

"Then I'm not losing my mind! You thought it was a woman's voice? I wasn't sure."

"Definitely. But I'm guessing she's a very, very old woman who must have hidden herself away years ago. That's probably why no one knows of her today."

I hadn't realized that my cousin was telepathic too. That was a relief.

"Jason, do you think we can find her?" The prospect was exciting, but it made me nervous too.

He tilted his head to one side with a faint smile. "Perhaps, but only if she wants to be found." At that moment, my cousin looked quite fey, even more than most Elves did.

Finishing his tea, he took his cup into the kitchen and I could hear him rinsing it under the tap. When he came back into the room, he said, "If you ever need someone to talk to, about anything at all, I'll always be here for you." His cheeks colored. "I just wanted you to know that, cousin. Sometimes I can feel what you're feeling. I'd like to help, if you'll let me."

He dropped a kiss on my cheek and dashed out the door. I couldn't help thinking that the difference between Jason and his twin brother Justin was one mystery that I would never be able to solve.

THE DRAGON'S SONG

I picked up the diary again and read until lunchtime. I made myself a sandwich and continued reading while I ate.

My father came in while I was eating, helping himself to some of the leftovers, and asked if I'd found any answers yet.

"Nope. Lots of gossip, but no Rowenna and no dragon song." I sighed deeply, closing the diary. My eyes burned. I glanced out the window. It was still dreary, still raining. "I think I need a nap. My eyes are really tired."

"Did you see Jason this morning? He said he was coming by to see you."

"He was here before lunch. He said he has it on good authority that tomorrow will be a sunny day, so we're going out to picnic, draw, and enjoy his flute. We were also talking about this mystery I'm hoping to solve. Jason was near the orchard yesterday and heard the same voice in his head that I heard. He thinks it was this Rowenna, and that she's a very old woman who's been in hiding for years. What do you think, Dad?"

He shook his head. "I find it hard to believe that there could be anyone living in Blackthorne Forest who I've never seen. How would an old woman survive out there by herself? No, it really doesn't make any sense." He hesitated. "Unless . . . no, it's just not possible." He chuckled. "Pure fantasy."

"What were you thinking?"

"It's too crazy," he scoffed. "Forget I said anything." He stood up and took his dishes and mine into the kitchen. I heard the water running for a few minutes. My father was actually washing the dishes. I don't know why that surprised me, but it did. I smiled. He was considered a Prince in the Elven world. A Prince who washed dishes. I couldn't help smiling.

He walked back into the sitting room. "I'll be visiting Francis Sullivan this afternoon, as well as our weavers and our jewelry designer. I want to make sure they've stocked up with all the materials they'll need to fill their holiday orders." He raised one eyebrow. "Some creative people aren't too well organized, you know."

I giggled. "Santa's workshops, right?"

He chuckled and headed for the door. "Right you are, sweetheart. Now go take your nap. I'll be back in an hour or two."

I went into my bedroom with Roscoe at my heels. Apparently, it was time for his afternoon nap too. It was warm and humid indoors, so I lay down on top of the quilt and Roscoe curled up in his usual spot at the foot of the bed. My eyes closed.

I knew I was dreaming again. I couldn't see my grandmother, but I heard her voice. *You must sing for Rowenna, dear. She needs you.* She sounded sad. *I hated to leave her. She will protect you as she always protected me.*

Abruptly, the fog lifted and I found myself near the ancient apple trees where I'd been the day before, staring toward the Western peaks where the tallest mountains were shaded with purple.

I heard a soft voice close to my ear. "Wake up, Cara. You're talking in your sleep." Opening my eyes, I found my father kneeling next to my bed, looking worried.

"Who were you talking to? You were having a conversation with someone."

I was finally awake enough to remember my dream. "What was I saying?"

"Something about singing and being protected. I couldn't make out everything. You were speaking too softly."

"Those were your mother's words. She was talking about Rowenna again."

He looked at me, frustration clear in his face. "Sorry, sweetheart. I wish I could help."

"It's okay, Dad. Something tells me I'm getting closer."

But closer to what, I had no idea.

CHAPTER 5

My father left for the sitting room, leaving me sitting up on my bed. I had goose bumps up both arms and I heard that now familiar rough voice in my head. *Sing. Please.* Then, more faintly, I thought I heard, *Rebecca* ...

That sense of urgency I'd been feeling for weeks was now telling me to hurry! I felt I was running out of time, or maybe it was Rowenna who was running out of time.

I got up, splashed cold water on my face, and returned to the sitting room and my grandmother's diary. My father looked up from his paperwork and smiled at me as I curled up again on the couch with the diary in my lap. I had to find more information if I wanted to help Rowenna.

An hour later, my father asked me if I was hungry, but I felt I had to keep reading. There were still a few leftovers in the cold cellar if I got hungry. He left for the dining hall, promising to bring back a piece of apple pie.

I kept reading, skimming sections occasionally when they didn't appear to have what I was looking for. Finally, when I got close to the end of the diary, I found something. Rebecca Blackthorne had written down the lyrics to what she called, *"The Dragon's Song,"* saying she wanted to be sure the song *"wouldn't be forgotten and lost to future generations."*

I was beyond thrilled! Grabbing a piece of drawing paper, I printed out the words as she had written them.

"Soaring above clouds,
Across sky so wide,
Almost touching the sun,
Here no reason to hide.
Air so clear, below so green,
A perfect new world
No others have seen.

Sweet song from below,
Drawing me down.
Beautiful lady,
Beautiful sound.
Singing of love,
So sweet to hear,
She smiles as she sings,
Showing no fear.
She beckons me closer,
Welcomes me home.
Peace so sweet,
No longer alone."

I repeated the words, singing them along with the melody I'd been humming, and they fit. Perfectly. Curiously, Rebecca had called it, *"The Dragon's Song."* But my father had assured me dragons were extinct.

I decided to spend the rest of the night finishing Rebecca Blackthorne's diary. If I could just find any information about Rowenna, Jason and I might be able to find her tomorrow.

It was definitely time to take a break. My eyes burned and my stomach growled just as my father walked in the door with Adam at his side.

"Your timing is perfect, Dad. I found the words to your mother's dragon song, and I'm starved. What did you bring me?"

He grinned as he uncovered an entire apple pie and handed it to me.

I laughed. "This isn't all for me, is it? I have to share, right?"

Adam smiled. "We're doing you a favor. You did say you didn't want to get any fatter, remember?"

I muttered, "I knew that statement would come back to haunt me."

Grinning, Adam pulled another plate from behind his back. "Arlynn said this was one of your favorite salads. So, salad first, then we'll help you eat your pie. But please don't take too long." My father tried to stifle a laugh.

"So have you had any success with the diary this afternoon?" my father asked.

"Yes! I found the words to that song I've been so fixated on. And they fit the melody perfectly."

My father smiled. "Excellent. You may solve this mystery after all. Right now, I think you should have something to eat. Put the diary down and come over to the table. I'll make the tea."

While I ate, Dad and Adam sat with me and talked business over cups of tea. Garrett's woodshop would have to be expanded to make room for his growing business, and they were looking for another carpenter trainee as well.

My father turned to me. "I stopped by to see Francis Sullivan today. He said he's looking forward to seeing more of your Elf drawings while you're here."

"Okay. I'll stop by and see Francis before I leave." I was surprised and flattered that the well-known artist still remembered my drawings.

When I finished my salad, I cut into the huge apple pie and served three large pieces. After my first bite, I decided it was definitely worth gaining another pound or two. When I couldn't resist cutting myself a second piece, Adam and my father both smiled. Adam shook his head and arched an eyebrow.

Saving me from temptation, my father picked up the rest of the pie and took it into the kitchen. A wise decision.

When he returned, he said, "Okay, tell us about this song you've spent so many hours searching for."

They followed me over to the couch where I picked up the lyrics I'd copied. "I'm not much of a singer, but I think I can stay on key. Here's what I think it's supposed to sound like."

I sang the words softly along with the familiar melody, and they simply felt right. Adam and my father were silent for a few seconds after I'd finished the song.

I didn't know how to interpret the expressions on their faces. Adam smiled, looking thoughtful, and my father looked stunned.

Adam spoke first. "That was beautiful, Cara. Beautiful and sad at the same time. You have a lovely voice."

My father finally said, "I remember it now. My mother used to sing that song when we'd go out to the apple orchard to pick up apples that had fallen on the ground. I don't think I was more than four years old. I can remember that she always insisted I sit on her lap and stay quiet while she sang." He shook his head sadly. "But I don't remember anything else, or anyone named Rowenna. Is the old orchard where you and Jason plan on picnicking tomorrow?"

"I think so. Especially now that we know that's where your mother used to sing this song. I'll ask Jason to play it on his flute. Maybe that will draw Rowenna out from wherever she's hiding."

"If she's even out there. Don't get your hopes up."

I knew my father was trying to shield me from disappointment, but I felt I'd been pulled along in this direction for weeks. That sense of urgency I'd had weeks ago, the song that wouldn't leave my mind, and finally dreams of my grandmother speaking of someone named Rowenna. I was certain I'd been set on this quest by a woman I'd never met, a woman named Rebecca Blackthorne, who was thousands of miles away.

Before Adam left, he asked me to stay in touch with him the next day. "I'll be thinking of you." He might be building furniture now, but he was still my devoted bodyguard. When I walked him to the door, he bent down and whispered, "Good night, love," pinning those dark blue eyes on me for a few breathless seconds.

My father stood up, stretched and yawned. "It's bed for me. I'll be waiting for your message tomorrow. I won't be far if you have any need of me. Please tell Jason the same thing. To be honest, I'm a little nervous about this quest of yours, so I'm glad you won't be alone."

After a hug and a kiss on my cheek, he went off to his bedroom. I was tired too, but excited about what we might find the next day. I hadn't quite finished the diary, so I took it into my room to read in bed for a little while. I knew I wouldn't be able to stay awake much longer. I snuggled under the quilt and opened the diary.

The last thing Rebecca wrote concerned Rowenna. She said that if she didn't hear her song again, her friend might never be seen in Blackthorne Forest again. I had the feeling that if Rowenna still existed, she was my responsibility now.

CHAPTER 6

I slept like a rock and woke up to the promised sunshine, feeling well rested and strangely relaxed. I felt I was moving in the direction that was meant for me.

My thoughts were abruptly interrupted when I heard Jason calling to me from the sitting room. "Rise and shine, cousin. Places to go and things to do today!"

Laughing, I jumped out of bed, and stuck my head out of my bedroom door. "Would you make tea for us? I'll be ready in just a minute."

"Okay. Someone left a basket of muffins for us." He laughed. "I'll try to save one for you."

I quickly threw water on my face, brushed my teeth, and got dressed in a hurry. At least two of those muffins had my name on them.

Jason was sitting at the long table, biting into a muffin. Pushing the basket over to me, he grinned. "Good thing you and Arlynn made up. She doesn't deliver fresh baked muffins for just anyone, you know."

After biting into one, I realized it was an apple-cinnamon muffin, like the kind I'd found written down in my grandmother's diary. I groaned in pleasure and Jason laughed at me. We had our tea, and I was wondering where the promised picnic basket was hiding.

"You did promise me a picnic today. So where have you hidden it?"

"One of my younger friends works in the kitchen. He's promised to deliver a picnic basket to us around lunchtime. In exchange, I had to promise to take him with me the next time I go into Thornewood to your friend's bakery."

"Uh, Jason, I'm afraid I have some bad news. There was a fire at Amy's bakery last week. The police say it was arson. Amy's parents are so upset, they may not reopen the bakery."

Jason was obviously shocked. I think this was the first time I'd ever seen him frowning.

"Arson? Doesn't that mean the fire was set deliberately? Who would do such a thing to such nice people?" His voice had taken on a hard edge.

"As far as we know, everybody loves Amy's parents. They have no idea who would have started the fire. It's a police case now." I didn't mention my suspicions.

Jason shook his head, still frowning. "Please tell Amy I'm available if she needs any help. Everyone at the bakery has been so nice to me, I want to help if I can."

"I'll let her know. She'll appreciate the offer of help, although I'm not sure what you can do. Her parents aren't even planning on repairing the kitchen."

"That's a real tragedy. They're such good people. And they make such wonderful donuts. That's the reason Aron wanted to go there with me. He'll be disappointed too."

I took a large bottle of spring water from the cold cellar, and Jason and I set out for the old orchard, my messenger bag of art supplies over my shoulder. Jason wasn't saying much while we walked. I was sure he was thinking about Amy and her parents. I could tell when he decided it was time to think about happier things.

Unlike our other bodyguards, Jason hadn't been part of our Thornewood High bodyguard crew last spring, and he was curious about what high school was like.

"Patrick, Neal, Gabriel and Ryan talk so much about how much fun they had while they were in school with you back in June, I've always wished I'd had a chance to join them."

"Jason, I've never understood why they enjoyed high school so much. I realize it probably made a nice break from their normal chores, but high school is just a large group of teenagers rushing from one class to another for six hours a day. What's the big deal?"

Jason shook his head. "There are probably only about twenty teenagers in Elvenwood, and we've known each other all our lives. And the boys greatly outnumber the girls." He looked at me with one eyebrow raised.

The light dawned. "Ah. I get it. New blood!"

"Yes, exactly. Before Neal got so friendly with Amy, he'd spend every evening talking about all the pretty girls at Thornewood High. And we'd hear the same from Gabriel and Patrick. The rest of us were all quite jealous."

He sighed. "I wish I could enjoy your senior year with you, Cara. I've heard Amy talking about all the parties and other fun you'll be having, and it sounds wonderful. The closest I'll get are the errands I run for your father, and they don't involve teenage girls."

It had never occurred to me that Elvenwood's teenagers would feel deprived once they'd been exposed to human high school. Maybe something could be done. I'd have to talk to my father about this.

"Will Adam be taking you to your parties and other activities when school starts?"

"When he has time, I think he will. Of course, Ryan will probably have to fill in when Adam's busy, but I may be able to go out with my school friends too. I'm hoping I won't need a bodyguard all the time."

"Cousin, can I volunteer when you need an escort? Your father told me that Sean isn't your boyfriend anymore, so I'd be glad to join you when you need someone."

"Sure, I'd enjoy your company. Sean and I are friends again, so we may go out in a group to things like ball games and maybe parties. But you'll always be welcome to join me, no matter who I'm with. I want you to have fun this year too. After all, next year I'll either be in Art School or college, and I won't be in Thornewood very often."

For a few seconds, he looked sad. "You're lucky. There's a whole world out there for you to explore."

At that moment, I realized that I hadn't been the best possible influence on the Elves I'd become close to. Their eyes had been opened to the attractions of the world outside Blackthorne Forest, maybe for the first time.

When I finally looked away from Jason, I saw lavender shadows decorating the highest peaks in the distance, and the old grove of antique apple trees was just ahead.

"I haven't walked out here in years," Jason said. "Where would you like to stop?"

"It's a warm day, so let's see if we can find a comfortable place under one of these old trees." I chose a tree that offered the most shade, and Jason and I set our things under its low hanging branches.

Jason chuckled. "Cozy under here, isn't it?"

I nodded and pulled my bag off my shoulder. I had tucked an old quilt inside my bag so we wouldn't be spending all day sitting on the hard ground. Jason helped me spread it out and we sat down, more comfortable than we'd expected to be.

He pulled a slender silver flute out of his shirt and practiced for a few minutes. "You'll have to hum the melody for me before I attempt to play it."

"I found the words to the song yesterday, so I can sing them for you." I began humming the tune as Jason listened to the melody and began to follow it. He picked it up quickly.

"You have a great ear for music," I told him. He smiled, blushing. He played the melody through again, and then I began to sing the words.

I was so intent on reading the lyrics, I barely noticed the shadow passing overhead. Jason seemed oblivious to it as well. His eyes were closed as he played his flute.

As I sang, I could feel the air moving heavily above me, more like a caress than a breeze. His eyes still closed, Jason swayed slightly from side to side. His flute was almost unbearably sweet. I sang the last few lines feeling as though my grandmother was sitting beside me.

> "She smiles as she sings,
> Showing no fear.
> She beckons me closer,
> Welcomes me here.
> Peace so sweet,
> No longer alone."

I could feel the magic in the air. I was sure Jason could feel it too. He finally opened his eyes, looked at me strangely, and then looked over my shoulder, his mouth dropping open.

The magic in the air was electric, shimmering all around us. I heard that same soft, rusty-sounding voice in my mind. *Blackthorne young. Beautiful.*

I turned around slowly, excited but nervous. She rested on the ground not more than twenty feet away, watching us with large golden eyes, her gray-green scales gleaming in the sun.

I suppose I should have been shocked, but I wasn't. I'd known in my heart that I wouldn't find an Elf or a human when I found Rowenna. And I now understood why Rebecca wrote the title as *"The Dragon's Song."*

A little nervously, I smiled. "Hello, Rowenna. Rebecca sends her love."

My father was wrong. Dragons weren't extinct, not in Blackthorne Forest.

CHAPTER 7

I couldn't take my eyes off the beautiful, glittering dragon sitting in front of us. It was like being in the middle of a surreal fairy tale.

Then I heard her rough voice again. *Thank you for my song. You've made me very happy. Rebecca is gone and I haven't heard my song for many years. It's been a sad time.*

"Are you alone, Rowenna?" Could there be other dragons in Blackthorne Forest?

Alone, yes. I have one egg that won't hatch. A Dragon needs a song and a friend. She couldn't hatch her egg because she was alone and unhappy.

"Rowenna, I'm Cara, and this is my cousin, Jason. We'll visit and sing for you as often as we can. I hope that will help."

She lowered her head, and her golden eyes looked moist as she stared at us. *Thank you, Cara. Thank you, Jason. I called and you came. You gave me my song. I have always been a friend to the Elves.* Then it sounded as though she was chuckling.

Cara, you are a very small Elf. You only think you're human. Rowenna knows.

She raised her head, looked over my head and bowed. Lifting her huge glittering wings, she rose into the air gracefully. As she rose, the moving air all around us shimmered with magic, and we watched her turn toward the mountains in the distance until she disappeared behind the purple peaks.

Behind us I heard someone exhaling slowly. I turned to see my father standing just a few feet behind me, looking at the distant mountains in amazement. I realized that he was the reason Rowenna bowed as she left. I stood and handed the jug of water to him, although he looked as though he could have used something stronger.

Jason looked amazed but relieved. His eyes wide and a slight smile on his lips, he said, "I think we've solved more than one mystery today."

I must have looked confused. He said, "Many of our Elves have been wondering exactly what you are, cousin. We just got an answer straight from the dragon's mouth." He shook his head and began to laugh.

My father sat down between us, handing the bottle of water to me, and started laughing too. Wrapping one arm around my shoulders, he said, "There are no words for what we've seen—and heard—today. But you don't seem surprised." He looked at me with both eyebrows raised.

"Yeah. I don't know why, but I didn't expect to find an Elf or a human when and if we found Rowenna. I had a feeling she was something else. Didn't your mother ever tell anyone that her friend was a dragon?"

"Not as far as I know. If Rowenna has been a friend to the Blackthorne women, then none of them ever talked about her, or there would have been some history of it."

"Well, she didn't seem upset when she met Jason, and I saw her bow to you just before she left. Maybe she only feels connected to the Blackthornes. Do you think we have to keep this a secret?"

He nodded. "I think that's probably a good idea, dear. The news would be safe with Conor and maybe Adam, but Rowenna might not appreciate the attention if everyone in the village knew about her."

"What about Mom?" My father looked at me with one raised eyebrow, and I knew exactly what he was thinking.

"Yeah, Mom's too protective already. I'm not sure how she would handle news of a dragon." I heard Jason chuckling.

"Not to change this intriguing subject, Uncle Brian, but my friend Aron promised to bring a picnic basket to us at lunch time. Do you have time to join us?"

"I'll make time. I have to admit, I was a bit nervous about what you and Cara might find out here today. After I visited Francis Sullivan, I decided to walk out here and keep an eye on you. That song was so lovely, both the flute music and Cara's singing, I was glad I'd come, even if nothing else happened. But when the dragon landed so close to you, I was furious with myself for not bringing my bow. It was a huge relief when she started speaking in our minds." He chuckled. "A telepathic dragon. And I thought I'd seen everything."

I heard someone approaching just as Jason hopped up and went to meet Aron who was loaded down with a large, heavy-looking basket. My father stood and greeted the boy, who looked about twelve. He looked strong but the basket he carried was half as big as he was.

"Thank you, Aron. It was very kind of you to carry such a heavy

The DRAGON'S SONG

burden so far." The boy looked surprised and somewhat awed to see my father, apparently only expecting to see Jason and me.

"It's my pleasure, Mr. Blackthorne," he said, nodding respectfully. "Enjoy your lunch." He backed away and then turned to jog back the way he'd come. I heard him say something to someone else heading our way.

I had just opened the basket when Adam came into sight. I had to smile. He must have been as nervous as my father.

"Good timing," my father called to him. "Join us for lunch. We have some news."

Adam looked relieved to see me smiling. "You found Rowenna?" he asked me.

"We did, but here, have a sandwich." I grinned at him. "You can relax; we're fine. Rowenna was happy to meet us. She's a friend." My father looked amused, his lips turned up at one corner.

When Adam looked over at my Dad, my father said, "Have your lunch, Adam. Cara and Jason can fill you in after we've eaten." Since my father was smiling, the tension visibly eased in Adam's shoulders. He looked at me, nodding in a relieved way, and unwrapped a sandwich.

Adam and my father talked about the planned expansion of Garrett's wood shop while we ate. Jason continued smiling, winking at me occasionally. I realized that Jason's life had probably been less eventful than mine for the past two months. He was enjoying himself today.

Jason and I finished our lunch first. He picked up his flute, playing a simple melody that reminded me of the kind of music Mom played in the bookstore. When he looked at me with a smile, I knew exactly what he had in mind. I nodded, and he began playing Rowenna's song. I sang the words softly, but I was fairly sure she would hear us. As I sang, I looked toward the mountains and saw her soaring into the sky. When I looked over at Adam, his mouth was slightly open. His sandwich had just hit the ground.

We watched her gliding in our direction, but when she spotted Adam, she changed course and flew in ever-widening circles until the music stopped. I heard her voice in my mind. *Thank you.* And she headed back to the purple peaks in the distance.

We were all watching Adam, who still looked shocked. He looked at me. "I'm guessing that was Rowenna."

I nodded. "She's been alone since my grandmother moved away. I don't know what put that melody in my head, but when she heard me humming it, I guess she realized there was another Blackthorne who might become a friend." I shrugged. "Without my grandmother's diary, I don't think I would have figured it out and she'd still feel alone."

Jason told Adam how surprised we were when Rowenna heard the music, landed in the orchard, and sat down with us. "Although I don't think Cara was nearly as surprised as I was," he added with a laugh. He looked at me with a smile. "Rowenna told Cara something else you may or may not find surprising."

Adam looked at me curiously. I sighed. "Well, Rowenna insists that I'm all Elf, although a small Elf, and that I only think I'm human. Dad, how could that be?"

He shook his head, taking hold of my hand. "Sweetheart, the only thing I can think of is that because of all the Elven traits you've inherited, that part of your nature is obscuring the human part." He shrugged. "We know your mother is all human; she has no Elven blood at all. I only know this because when I tried to bring her to Elvenwood before you were born, the gate wouldn't open." He glanced down at me. "Elvenwood's gateway won't open if there's a human nearby. That's the only way I know to determine whether a person has any Elven blood."

He stood. "I have to get back to the village now. There are still a few of our artisans I need to check in with. Thank you for sharing your picnic with me. Are you and Jason going to stay for a while?"

"I think so. I wanted to do some drawing, and Jason agreed to be my model today." Jason rolled his eyes and smiled.

"Well, now that I know you're both safe out here, I can get back to work with a clear mind. How about you, Adam? Do you have to get back?"

"Actually, we're caught up in the wood shop so I thought I'd keep Cara and Jason company this afternoon. Unless there's something else you need me to do."

"No. Enjoy an afternoon off. You deserve one. Cara, we can have tea together when you get back. Enjoy your afternoon." He kissed the top of my head and ruffled Jason's curly hair as he headed out of the orchard.

"How are you feeling now? Any anxiety?" Adam asked.

I had to think about it. Surprisingly, I was relaxed. "Maybe Rowenna was the reason for all that anxiety. I must have been sensing that she needed me, or someone in the Blackthorne family, to sing her song and be a friend to her. If my grandparents moved away before I was born, she's been alone, feeling friendless, for a very long time."

Adam smiled. "It's a good thing you paid attention to that premonition you had. I'm guessing you have a great deal of sensitivity to the strong emotions of others, even if they're dragons."

That reminded me how I used to hear Sean's thoughts when he was feeling emotional. Emotion was the key. Although I could communicate telepathically with my father and Adam, the only time I would hear someone's private thoughts was when they were feeling extremely emotional.

I must have been quiet for too long. Adam was asking Jason if he wanted another sandwich or some fruit. Jason grinned and took an apple out of the picnic basket, stretching out on the quilt with one hand behind his head. It was perfect! That was exactly how I would draw him.

"Don't move, Jason. The way you're stretched out under this tree will make a wonderful picture."

Adam packed up the leftovers in the picnic basket while I pulled my drawing pad and pencils out of my bag. Jason was chuckling. "I hope you won't be offended if I fall asleep, cousin. I ate a lot, and I'm very comfortable here."

"No problem. A stationary model makes my job easier." I had to smile at the picture he made. He was long and slender, with black hair falling over his eyes, and the face of an angel. I started sketching as he munched on his apple. Finally, his arm fell to the side, the half-eaten apple rolled away, and I heard him snoring softly. Adam and I smiled at each other, and I went to work on my drawing. Adam sat to my left, slightly behind me. He'd always said he enjoyed watching me draw.

I drew the quilt Jason was lying on as if it were grass, matching his green tunic and pants, to make him less noticeable. The mountains in the distance were visible from this angle, so I played up the beautiful shades of mauve and purple on the tallest peaks. The low branches of the old apple tree Jason slept under were fully leafed, leaving him completely shaded. After adding several more of the old apple trees with their twisted trunks, the young man sleeping under a tree was almost invisible. I smiled, wondering how many people would be able to find him asleep in the grass.

When I put down my pencil, Adam whispered, "Most won't even see him. And the ones who do will feel they've discovered a secret. It's wonderful, love."

I turned to face him, delighted with the compliment. "Thanks. That's exactly the reaction I was hoping for." Without thinking, I leaned back and kissed his cheek. He turned toward me, his lips almost touching mine. I gasped as his dark blue eyes looked into mine. I couldn't decipher his expression and he backed away almost immediately, standing abruptly.

He sounded slightly hoarse. "I should get back, Cara. Maybe you should wake up Jason now."

Why had his mood changed so quickly?

"I'm awake, just too comfortable to get up," Jason said.

Adam wasn't smiling when he said, "Enjoy the rest of your afternoon. If I have time, I'll join you and your father for tea later. Thank you again for lunch."

I was still confused as I watched him stride away. Still lying comfortably on the quilt, Jason turned to face me. "I suspect that your favorite bodyguard is in love with you, cousin."

"What? What on earth gave you that idea? Adam's a good friend, that's all."

Jason sat up, laughing quietly. "Well, it's clear to me that his feelings go way beyond friendship. You don't see the way he looks at you, you know." Arlynn had said the same thing.

These were thoughts I'd been trying to ignore, so I packed up my drawing pad and pencils. "I think it's time for us to get back. You're letting your imagination run away with you."

He stood up, still smiling, and helped me fold up the quilt. As we walked out of the old orchard, he said, "It's been a memorable day, cousin, for a lot of reasons. I'm happy I was able to share it with you." He wrapped one long arm around my shoulders as we walked back into the village together. My cousin was a sweetheart, but I couldn't help wishing he was a bit less perceptive.

CHAPTER 8

When I reached my father's cottage, Jason left to run an errand, and I walked in to find my father and Adam waiting for me, tea already made.

My father smiled as I helped myself to a cup and sat down. "This has been an exciting day for you, hasn't it?"

"Exciting is an understatement. I think that sense of urgency I was feeling had everything to do with Rowenna. She needed a friend and your mother has been gone for a long time. I don't know the first thing about dragons, but I'm guessing they're not solitary creatures. She told me she has an egg that hasn't hatched, so I wonder what happened to her mate."

Adam shook his head. "I never thought dragons were real. I've lived in several other villages and I've never heard anyone talk about dragons. Makes me wonder how long they've been here; I can't believe she's the only one."

"You're right. If there are more out there somewhere, do you think they might be dangerous?" I asked.

My father chuckled. "You certainly have a lot to talk to Rowenna about. As far as being dangerous, we should probably be grateful she considers the Blackthornes friends. Legends always talked about dragons breathing fire, so we have to hope she feels friendly toward all of Blackthorne Forest."

I refilled our cups with tea.

"Will you be spending any time at the practice field while you're here?" Adam asked.

"Yes, although to be honest, that was the last thing on my mind this week. I'm more relaxed now, so I'll go over to the field to practice in the morning. I can practice by myself. You probably have work at Garrett's."

"Well, we're almost caught up with our furniture orders, so I can be available if you need me." He stood. "Thank you for the tea, Brian. I'll see you both at dinner."

"Thanks for your company in the orchard today. I'm glad that you and my father were there."

Adam winked at me and left.

My father was quiet for a few minutes. When he spoke, his voice was soft. "You really are growing up too fast."

Briefly, I wondered if that comment had anything to do with Adam.

Jason strode through the front door. "Am I too late for tea?"

We'd had our tea in the sitting room, so I invited Jason to sit down and got another cup from the kitchen. I filled it with tea and handed it to him. Having more time with Jason was a treat. He was easy to be around, probably because he was so sensitive to everyone around him.

We walked over to the dining hall later, and found Conor and Arlynn sitting together. It was one of Arlynn's nights off from cooking. As much as I was enjoying my meals, the waistband of my jeans was letting me know I'd gained weight again. Good thing I'd be going home soon.

As we were leaving after dinner, my father pulled Conor aside. "Stop by later tonight. Cara has something to tell you, but I think it should be kept quiet." Looking curious, Conor said he would, giving my shoulder a squeeze as he left with Arlynn.

I hadn't seen Adam at dinner and assumed he and Garrett were working on a new furniture order. When I saw one of the cooks rushing out the door holding a large tray, I was sure of it.

I made tea when we got home, and my father joined me on the couch. "I thought you might have more questions about your Elven heritage, things we haven't talked about yet. That's one reason I invited Conor to join us. Since he's our wild animal specialist, I thought we should tell him about Rowenna, just in case his help is needed at some point. If he doesn't know about her, seeing a dragon in Blackthorne Forest would be quite a shock."

I was sure Conor would take it in stride, shocked or not. I had yet to see anything Conor couldn't handle.

While we waited for Conor, my father told me about Duncan Brady, Elvenwood's head gardener. He had a gift with plants, especially the vegetables that grew here practically year-round. All he had to do with a dying plant was touch it and speak to it, and it began to thrive. Elvenwood's gardens grew more than enough food for the Elves. My father explained that there was a church in Thornewood

THE DRAGON'S SONG

that regularly provided groceries to needy families. Once a month, they found crates of fruits and vegetables left at their back door by an anonymous donor. They had never figured out who was responsible for the monthly gifts.

"How does Duncan keep everything growing through the winter?"

My father smiled. "Well, you know I have a certain control over the weather." I nodded. "You'll find out this winter when you visit Elvenwood, it won't be as cold here as it is in Thornewood. The orchard will continue to produce apples until January. Duncan has coverings for the hot weather plants, and they'll continue to grow year round. Of course, each group of plants gets a season off, but there's always another group growing."

That was good news. I wasn't a fan of winter, snow and ice, or parkas and snow boots. "You mean when I get sick of winter weather, I can come here and warm up?"

"Well, it won't be like summer here, but I think you'll find it more comfortable."

"Dad, what about the rest of Blackthorne Forest? I've been in the woods by our house during the winter and it's cold; except for the evergreens, most of the trees are bare."

He smiled again. "If you'd walked farther into the forest, you'd find it gets warmer the closer you are to Elvenwood. Some of the trees don't even lose their leaves, and some actually keep their fall colors through most of the winter."

"I'll be looking forward to winter this year, for the first time ever!"

Conor walked in, overhearing my last statement and smiled. "I never saw much of you during the coldest months, but come Spring, you'd be back with your drawing pad. You never knew it, of course, but I always missed seeing you during those cold months."

I smiled as I poured a cup of tea for him. "Well, I never knew that I'd find warmer weather if I just kept on walking."

Conor sat down next to me with his tea. "What did you want to see me about, Brian? I hope there are no new problems."

I could see my father trying to stifle a smile as he asked, "What do you know about dragons?"

Conor said, "I've always thought dragons were only an old legend, probably nothing more than myth. Why?"

"Cara, tell Conor what we've just learned."

"Um, remember how I was having a premonition about something about to happen?" He nodded, frowning slightly.

I explained about the melody that had been stuck in my head, as well as the research I'd done with my grandmother's diary. When I described the dreams I'd had of Rebecca Blackthorne talking about her friend Rowenna, he stopped frowning, nodding at me to go on.

"You know how I hear my father's voice in my mind." He nodded. "Well, I started hearing this strange voice that was asking me to sing. Jason heard her voice too.

"I finally found mention of a dragon song, along with the words to the song, in Rebecca's diary. I felt sure this was what the strange voice wanted me to sing. Jason went out to the old orchard with me. He played, and I sang what Rebecca had written down as 'The Dragon's Song.' Within minutes, Rowenna found us."

Conor sat mesmerized. "Don't tell me. Rowenna is a dragon?"

"Yes," I said. "She's been alone since Rebecca Blackthorne moved away. I think Rowenna has always been a friend to the Blackthorne women, and they kept her a secret. She told me she's always been a friend to the Elves."

Conor asked, "Is she the only one, or are there more of them?"

"I'm guessing that she lost her mate years ago. She said she has an egg that won't hatch, so she must have had a mate at some point. I think she's just been very lonely, feeling that she'd lost her only friend."

Conor said, "I'd love to see her, just once, to know that dragons are real."

"Well, Adam joined us for lunch, and Jason and I played her song again. We saw her fly out of those distant mountains and head for us, but when she saw Adam, she simply circled the orchard and then headed back to the mountains. I'm guessing she's only comfortable with the Blackthornes."

Conor sat there, shaking his head. "This is amazing. I can't believe that dragons are actually real. I hope I'll get at least a glimpse of her some day. How big is she?"

I looked at my father. "Dad?"

"I'd say her wing span is at least forty feet. She's big. Her eyes are a golden color, and her scales are a mixture of green, gray, and some other colors. She's a beautiful creature. While Jason played and Cara sang, Rowenna practically purred. It was a very rough-sounding purr, but a purr nonetheless."

I looked at Conor. "I'll be going out there again tomorrow around lunch time."

THE DRAGON'S SONG

Conor chuckled. "I may find I have some business to take care of near the old orchard tomorrow. I would give anything to see her. By the way, does anyone else know about her?"

My father said, "Just you and Adam. I don't think Rowenna would appreciate a lot of attention, so I think we should keep her existence to ourselves."

After giving me a hug, Conor left, still shaking his head, muttering, "Dragons...."

CHAPTER 9

The next morning my father and I had breakfast at the dining hall. The enticing scent of just-baked muffins drew me through the door, where we spotted Adam digging into a huge plate of scrambled eggs and bacon. We filled our own plates and joined him.

"You're devouring those eggs like a starving man," I kidded him. "Didn't you get dinner last night?"

He nodded, explaining, "Garrett and I did have dinner brought in, but we worked until almost midnight. By that time, we were both hungry again, but the kitchen was closed."

My father asked, "Did you get a new furniture order after we saw you yesterday?"

"Yes. Ryan went into Thornewood to see Mr. Callahan with a few last-minute requests for supplies, and he brought back a new order from that furniture store in Greenville. It's a big order, so we'll probably be kept busy for at least a month."

My father smiled. "Well, at least you had some time off yesterday. By the way, we filled in Conor last night. He's our resident wild animal expert and I thought he should be aware of Cara's new friend."

Adam chuckled. "Good idea. But other than the five of us, I assume you're keeping her existence a secret."

"Yes, for as long as we can. Cara, you might want to caution Rowenna about flying during the daytime; she'll be spotted eventually if she's not careful."

"I was thinking about that this morning. If I get a chance to talk with her today, I'll make sure she knows she might be seen. Of course, if she only flies around those distant mountains, no one will see her. There's nothing out there, is there?"

"Just mountain lions and bears. That's all within the boundaries of Blackthorne Forest. She's safe out there."

After breakfast, Adam left for the wood shop, and my father and I walked over to the practice field. My father said, "I think I'll tag along, just to see the progress you've made. I haven't watched you at practice in weeks."

"Okay. Are you sure you don't have any important business to take care of this morning?"

"No. I told you I want to spend as much time with you this week as possible. I know you won't have much free time once you're back in school." He smiled a bit sadly. "You really are growing up too fast, Cara." He settled his hand on my shoulder as we walked out to the practice field.

The field was empty. My father stood at the edge of the field as I stood about twenty feet from the bear target and shot my arrows as quickly as I could, aiming at the arms and knees. I hit my targets perfectly. I moved the target back another ten feet and started shooting again. Once again, I didn't miss. I pushed the target back ten more feet, which was the greatest distance I'd tried so far. I wasn't as fast at this distance but I was still able to hit the arms and legs every time.

It was time to switch to my knives. After retrieving my arrows and moving the target closer, a distance of only ten feet, I began throwing quickly, hitting arms and legs only. I knew my speed was best with my knives, but when I pulled my knives out of the target, I looked back to where my father was standing and was surprised to see a group of Elves standing there with him, smiling at me and applauding.

Wearing a big smile, my father waved me over to them. "Word has spread about your skill with both bow and knife, and someone must have mentioned that you'd be here practicing this morning. I think these gentlemen had to see it for themselves."

The men were all older than my father and probably harder to convince. The eldest stepped forward to shake my hand. "Miss Blackthorne, I thought my grandson was exaggerating when he talked about your skill. After all, if I'm not mistaken, you started training barely two months ago." I nodded. "To have accomplished so much in so short a time is unheard of, my dear. I was especially interested in your non-lethal approach to training. Your father is very proud of you; frankly, we all are." He smiled, bowed to my father and with one raised eyebrow, said, "Brian, your father would be amazed."

One by one, they walked up and shook my hand. As a group, they turned and left the field, returning to wherever they'd come from.

"Who were those men? It was nice of them to come by to see me, but I don't think I've met any of them before, have I?"

He helped me put the bow and arrows away in the equipment shed. "Those were the Elders of Elvenwood. For them to come to the field to watch your practice is a real honor." He chuckled. "They apparently thought what they'd been hearing about you was grossly exaggerated. They had to see for themselves. And now they have."

Laughing as we walked away from the field, he said, "I don't think anything you do will surprise them now, sweetheart."

CHAPTER 10

It was turning into a typical hot August day. When we got back to the cottage, my father brought the jug of spring water out from the cold cellar and poured a large cup for both of us. We sat down and enjoyed our cold drinks. "There are a few things I want to say while they're still on my mind." I saw his lips twitch slightly. "First, Ryan brought back a note from Harry Callahan to say that there is a car sitting in front of your house with a big red bow on the roof!"

I practically leaped off the couch. "That must be my car! My new-old car! Thank you, Dad! I can't wait to see it. Even more, I can't wait to drive it!" I hugged his neck until he gasped, "Can't breathe, Cara."

I sat back on the couch, almost bouncing up and down. "That's such great news. Thank you." He grinned. "You're very welcome, dear. Just remember to stay away from mailboxes." I stifled a groan.

"I also wanted to tell you how pleased I am that you and Arlynn have resumed your friendship. You might not have realized it, but she was terribly upset about your disagreement, especially when she got to know Adam and realized how wrong she'd been."

I smiled. "I'm glad too. I missed her. Other than Kathleen, Arlynn is really the only female friend I have here in Elvenwood."

"Actually, dear, every woman in Elvenwood considers you a friend."

That was a surprise. A nice one.

Smiling, he put one arm around my shoulders. "Hungry? It's lunchtime. Let's walk over to the dining hall."

When we got there, we again found Conor and Arlynn having lunch together. Their relationship was obviously on solid ground.

"Brian, Cara, there's plenty of room over here. Come and sit with us." Arlynn wore a big smile. I wondered if there was an announcement on the way.

Conor grinned at me. "Cara, I hear your practice this morning attracted quite an audience."

"Cara put on a good show for the Elders," my father said, looking pleased.

We had a vegetarian lunch with several kinds of salads along with just-baked bread and, of course, apple pie. Once again, Elvenwood was doing its best to fatten me up.

Arlynn asked how long I was staying. "I know I promised to model for you. I have a free afternoon, so are you going to be drawing today?"

I grinned at her. "That sounds like a perfect way to spend this afternoon. We can gossip while I draw!"

She laughed, her face a lovely shade of pink. We agreed to meet at my father's cottage in a half hour.

We walked back to the cottage and my dad said, "I'll be gone this afternoon. I have some business to take care of with Harry in Thornewood. If it's all right with you, I thought I'd stop and have dinner with your mother before I come home."

"That's fine. I was afraid Mom would be lonely without me." I raised one eyebrow. "Besides, how often do you get a chance to spend time alone with Mom?"

He smiled, his face turning pink. "That's true, dear. But dinner without you won't be the same." He looked down at me and winked. I shook my head, laughing.

After he left on Smoke, his huge grey horse, I went inside to wait for Arlynn. The day had become even hotter, so I changed into shorts and a tank top. Arlynn walked in just as I returned to the sitting room.

"Would you like some water or a cup of tea before we leave?"

She sank into the couch with a smile. "If you're not in a hurry, tea would be wonderful. I've had a busy morning. I baked bread right up until lunchtime."

While we waited for the water to boil, I said, "You and Conor seem to be spending more time together." I grinned. "Looks like things are going well."

She blushed. "Yes, I think things are going very well. Although Conor seemed distracted this morning, distracted but excited at the same time. He wouldn't tell me why and I'm curious."

"Well, I'm sure you'll find out what's on his mind, sooner or later." If Rowenna showed up this afternoon while Arlynn and I were out drawing, it would definitely be sooner.

When we finished our tea, I asked, "Can you suggest a spot where there are white roses, or some white birches? If you're going to blend into your surroundings, I need a place where there's a lot of white in the background. Any ideas?"

She thought about it for a few seconds. "I think I saw a grove of white rose bushes not far from the old apple orchard. I think you've already been out that way. It's about a quarter of a mile south of the old orchard where roses have been growing wild, many of them white. You can see some of the mountains from there too. It's not the well-groomed look of the gardens and orchards you're accustomed to, but it's quite scenic, although a bit wild."

"That sounds perfect. I've been craving something more dramatic to draw. Let's take some cold water with us; today's a scorcher."

She laughed. "I love so many of your human expressions. But you're right; it is really hot today."

I took a jug of cold water out of the cold pantry and we left the cottage.

I couldn't believe how many old, antique roses grew wild out here, and I wondered who had planted them years ago. They had been left to grow naturally, and the whole area was a riot of pink and white roses. I was guessing whoever had planted them loved those colors.

Fortunately, at this time of day some of the white roses were partially shaded by an old Elm tree so Arlynn wouldn't have to sit in the sun and bake while I drew her. I spread the old quilt out and took my drawing pad and pencils out of my bag. I had Arlynn stand behind two of the larger rose bushes and turn to smell their scent. I thought her silvery hair would blend in with the flowers. Since she was wearing the usual green tunic and slacks, I changed the color of her clothing to white. She wouldn't be as hidden as the Elves in my other drawings. She was only partially camouflaged behind the roses. To her right, the mountains of Blackthorne Forest rose above the trees.

After I sketched in the roses and Arlynn's position behind them, I said, "You can come over here now where it's a little cooler, and I'll fill in the details from here." I was completely covered by shade from the Elm tree I sat under, but Arlynn was red in the face from posing partially in the sun. I handed her the jug of water and she sat down next to me, obviously happy to be out of the sun.

"We probably should have done this earlier in the day before it got so hot. Are you okay?" I asked her.

She took a deep drink and nodded. "I'm fine now."

I continued to draw in the details of the white roses, with dozens of pink and white rose bushes in the background, and the soaring mountains on our right. Arlynn gasped and stared wide-eyed at something above us. When I turned around, Rowenna was circling us, above the grove where we were sitting. There was nowhere she could land so she circled lazily, not far from us, but close enough to be recognized. I must have been humming her song without realizing it.

I said, "Don't be frightened. That's Rowenna. She's a friend." Arlynn gasped again. "You're not telepathic, are you?" She shook her head, her mouth hanging open. "Okay, then I'll speak out loud. Rowenna speaks to me in my mind." Looking slightly calmer, Arlynn nodded, her crystal blue eyes still the size of saucers.

"Hello, Rowenna. This is my friend Arlynn."

The dragon dipped her head to Arlynn, her green and gold scales gleaming. She said, *Beautiful friend.*

I chuckled. "Yes, but she's in shock right now. She didn't know there was a dragon living in Blackthorne Forest." Rowenna's rough laughter filled my head.

Her rusty voice said, *Mate of your beautiful friend hides in the trees nearby.* More rough laughter.

"That's Conor, another friend. He's never seen a dragon before, never thought dragons really existed. He loves animals and takes care of all the wildlife in the forest."

She nodded once more, circling the grove again, and headed back to her mountain. I heard her rough voice once more. *Cara . . . friend,* and then she disappeared.

Arlynn was silent for several long minutes. I asked, "Are you okay?"

She took a deep breath. "How long have you known there's a dragon in our forest? I never believed dragons were real."

I was glad to see color returning to her face. "I only met Rowenna yesterday, but she's been communicating with me for more than a week. I think she was the reason for that premonition I had. Maybe for my anxiety attacks too. I knew something important was coming, but never in a million years did I think I'd be meeting a dragon!"

I told Arlynn about Rebecca Blackthorne's diary and about the melody I couldn't get out of my head.

"Have the anxiety attacks stopped now?"

"Well, I do feel better now. I think there's some kind of connection between Rowenna and me, a connection she only feels with Blackthorne women. She's felt alone and friendless since my grandmother moved away, and that was before I was born. I think she became aware of me when I started visiting with my father."

Arlynn shook her head. "It's amazing. I don't think anyone in Elvenwood today has any idea that dragons exist, or that there's a dragon living close by. Conor knows about this?"

"My father and I told him about her last night. He was hiding somewhere nearby today, and Rowenna spotted him." I chuckled. "She referred to him as your mate."

Arlynn turned pink, but she smiled and said softly, "I wonder how she could tell?"

"Well, dragons are magical creatures, just like Elves." I winked at her. "Now let me finish this drawing and we can get back to the village and cool off."

It took another half hour to add the finishing touches to my drawing. Then I packed up my art supplies and we left for home. As we walked, Arlynn was full of questions about my new friend, most of which I couldn't answer. "I think I'll have to go out to the old orchard again before I leave, so I can have a longer conversation with her. There are a lot of things I want to know too."

When we reached the dining hall, Arlynn had to help with dinner preparations. "Come back for dinner, Cara." She grinned. "I think there's an apple pie with your name on it."

I groaned. "You're not happy unless you send me home with a few extra pounds, are you?"

She laughed. "Don't complain; those pounds are all going to the right places. You look more grown up every time I see you."

"Well, thanks for modeling for me. I'm going home to take a cold shower, and I'll be back later for dinner. Save me some pie."

I hummed Rowenna's song as I walked to the cottage, and I could faintly hear her rusty voice in my head. *Cara . . . my song . . . thank you.*

I never dreamed my new friend would be a beautiful, but lonely, dragon.

CHAPTER 11

Since my father was having dinner with Mom, I was prepared to have dinner alone, but when I got to the dining hall, I found Adam had saved a seat for me.

"Not eating in the wood shop tonight?"

He laughed. "No, I needed to look at a prettier face than Garrett's tonight. I also heard a rumor that our cooks have made something very special for us. Your father was able to talk your mother into sharing her meat loaf recipe, and I think the dining hall will be full."

I had to smile as I sat down next to him. "Sounds good. I know how much you enjoyed it when Mom made it at home."

He turned those piercing dark blue eyes on me. "So what have you been up to since I saw you last? More drawing?"

"Yeah, I finally got Arlynn into one of my drawings. You should stop by later to see it. It's different from my other pictures." I giggled and said softly, "Arlynn also got to meet my new friend; I'm not sure she's recovered from the shock yet."

Adam's eyebrows shot up. "It sounds like Rowenna isn't as shy as we thought, but I'm guessing she feels safer around women."

I nodded. "It seems that way, although she didn't seem nervous when she saw my father. Conor got a peek at her this morning too. He was hiding behind some trees, but she spotted him and actually referred to him as Arlynn's mate."

Adam chuckled. "Another couple headed to the Joining Tree, I'm guessing."

I was feeling reckless. "How about you, Adam? When will you be going to the Joining Tree?"

He leaned down and whispered in my ear. "Not until you grow up, love." He winked and turned that devastating smile on me. My insides promptly melted. Fortunately, that was when the cooks started carrying out platters of thick-sliced meat loaf, potato salad, and green salads loaded with bell peppers and tomatoes. By the time everyone filled their plates, I was able to breathe normally. I wondered if he'd been serious or just joking with me.

THE DRAGON'S SONG

It was definitely time to eat dinner and get my unruly brain under control.

The room was quiet as everyone tried meat loaf for the first time. Apparently, my father's love for Mom's meat loaf was well known. After a few minutes, I saw heads nodding in approval and conversation started up again.

Adam said, "As good as this is, I think your mother's meat loaf was better. But don't tell our cooks I said so." He still managed to eat three helpings before he put his fork down. I couldn't tell the difference. Mom's meat loaf was great, but the Elves' version was equally good.

When the platters of meat loaf were empty, they were promptly removed and replaced by delectable six-inch high apple pies. This time I groaned out loud.

Laughing, Adam said, "Don't worry, love, apple pie looks good on you." I didn't know whether to feel insulted or complimented, so I threw caution to the wind and ate two pieces.

Arlynn waved at us from the kitchen as we left. We waved back.

Adam asked, "Will you show me today's picture now? With Arlynn as your model, it has to be spectacular."

"Sure, come home with me and I'll make tea. I'm not sure when my father will get home, so I'd enjoy some company."

He smiled down at me and held my hand on the walk home. I felt happier than I had in weeks.

When we got to the cottage, I lit a small fire and got the tea ready. "Make yourself comfortable. I'll get my drawings." When I walked back into the sitting room, Adam was standing in front of the fireplace looking at the drawing I'd done of my mother. My father had framed it beautifully and hung it where he could see it from his favorite chair.

Adam turned to me, smiling. "Your father is obviously fond of this drawing. When did you do it?"

"A year ago. Before I met my father, Conor asked me if I would give his 'boss' one of my drawings. Of course, I didn't know he was referring to my father. Conor chose this drawing, telling me he thought his 'boss' would like it." I smiled. "That was before I knew anything about my father." I sighed. "My life really changed after that."

Adam walked over to the couch and sat down as I poured our tea. He picked up my drawing pad and began looking through it. Today's drawing of Arlynn surrounded by white roses was on the top. "This is beautiful. I think there's a little more drama in your latest drawings; this is really wonderful." He continued to look through my drawings, finally closing the folder.

"I've only known you for a few months." Shaking his head, he said, "Although it seems longer. But even in that short time, your artwork has changed; it's more mature, more imaginative." He smiled, handing the folder back to me.

"Thanks. I wish I could stay here indefinitely and do nothing but draw. But I'll be back in school in the human world next week." I laughed. "It's going to be an easier adjustment this time."

"It's usually more difficult?" he asked.

"Yeah. I always dreaded going back to school, but I feel like a different person now. And I have a mythical new friend which feels good, but kind of strange."

I had a sudden idea. "I need to speak to Rowenna tonight. I want to caution her about flying during the day. I'm really afraid someone outside of Elvenwood might see her.

"I also want to ask her how far away she can hear me singing. There was one night I was sitting on the back porch at home and thought I heard wings overhead. I'd been humming her song and I guess she heard me. But that was at least five miles from her mountain."

"You want to make sure you can keep Rowenna happy once you're back in school, right?"

"I won't have as much time to spend in Elvenwood, but I want her to know she has a friend, that I won't forget her."

Adam looked out the window at the darkening sky. It was twilight. "I'll be glad to walk out there with you if you think she'll be willing to come close enough for you to talk with her. I think I made her nervous the last time she saw me."

"I'm sure I can talk her into it. Can we go out there now?"

Smiling, Adam stood and reached for my hand.

It was dusk as we walked through the village. "When are you going home?"

"Day after tomorrow. I'll need a couple of days to get myself ready for school, catch up with Amy and Kevin, compare class schedules." I grinned. "Drive over to the Grille for cheeseburgers in my new car. You know. Important stuff."

He laughed. "Of course. Very important stuff. I'll try to get away on the weekends as much as possible. I'm looking forward to your senior year too, you know."

I looked up at him. "Really? It'll probably be football games, parties, basketball games, more parties. Are you sure you won't get bored?" I teased.

THE DRAGON'S SONG

"Spending time with you is never boring." He turned those dark blue eyes on me and my stomach did a few flips-flops. I would have to work harder on my mental control. Much harder.

A few minutes later we reached the foot of the mountains where I'd spoken to Rowenna before. Adam let go of my hand and stepped back into the grove of old apple trees when I began to sing. In seconds I heard the familiar sound of huge wings heading in our direction. But rather than landing where she had before, she turned away. I heard her rough voice. *Cara, you're not alone?*

"Rowenna, the man is Adam, my friend and bodyguard. He's a good man."

I continued to hum the melody of the dragon's song as she circled overhead, probably deciding whether or not it was safe to land. Gradually she flew lower, finally settling in the same spot she'd landed on before.

Again, she spoke in my mind. *Why do you have a bodyguard, Cara?*

"There's an evil man who has caused a lot of trouble for us this year. He hates my father and has tried to take revenge by hurting me. My father wants me to have a bodyguard whenever I'm outside my house, except when I'm here in Elvenwood."

Her rough voice became louder. *Where is this evil man? I will burn him.*

"The police have been searching for him for months. He probably left the area. We don't know where he is now."

When he comes back, he will burn.

I gulped and took a deep breath. "If and when he comes back, a lot of people will be after him. But there are a couple of other things I wanted to ask you about. I worry you'll be seen when you fly during the day. Flying after dark will be safer."

She tilted her huge head to the side, as though she was considering what I'd said.

Her voice in my mind said, *Yes, Cara. Night is safer. But if you need me, I will fly at any time, day or night.*

"If I need you? Do you mean you want me to call you if I'm in trouble?"

Yes. Always.

"Well, it's nice to know you'll be looking out for me. I have one other question to ask."

She nodded her head once, her golden eyes watching me.

"When I'm at home, outside the forest, and not here in Elvenwood, if I sing for you, will you hear me?"

The rusty sounds I was hearing had to be laughter. *Dragons can hear far, far away. I heard my song from your other home. I flew over to listen.*

I chuckled. "I wondered why I was hearing wings and feeling magic in the air. I'll be in school next week and not in Elvenwood as often. But I'll sing your song from my mother's house and wherever I may be in Thornewood. I want you to know that I'll be thinking of you. I won't forget."

Cara, who protects you outside Elvenwood?

"I always have a bodyguard with me. It's either Adam or my friend Ryan, sometimes Gabriel, or Gavin, or Patrick, or Neal. Sometimes it's my father."

I thought I heard a bit of surprise in her voice. *So many. This is good.* She nodded her big head. *Please sing for me now, Cara.*

As I sang the Dragon's Song, I saw those large golden eyes close. My father had been right. Rowenna was purring. There was no other word to describe the deep rumbling sound coming from her.

When the last note drifted away, she rose to her feet, lifted her enormous dark wings, and flew away. It was almost dark now, but I was sure she was heading toward her mountain. As usual, I felt magic swirling around us, following the dragon as she flew away. Rowenna's magic felt like soft silk brushing against my skin.

I was staring off in her direction when a warm hand closed around mine.

"Ready to go now?" he asked.

"Yes." I laughed. "It seems that Rowenna and I are looking out for each other, doesn't it? You could hear her voice in your mind, couldn't you?"

"Your dragon's voice is very distinct. I would imagine that anyone who's telepathic will hear her. Your father heard her, didn't he?"

"Yes, and so did Jason. And that makes me wonder if anyone else in Elvenwood has been hearing a strange voice in his head. Something I should probably ask my father about."

We walked back to the village, Adam holding my hand. When we reached my father's cottage, the oil lamps in the sitting room were lit, which meant my father was home.

He looked up from some papers and smiled as we walked in. "Where have you two been this evening?"

"Adam walked me out to the foot of the mountains where I spoke to Rowenna the other day. There were a few things I wanted to talk to her about."

"There's hot water. Make yourselves some tea and tell me about it."

I poured a cup for each of us, and I told my dad everything that Rowenna and I had talked about.

"Since you, Jason, Adam, and I are all telepathic, we've all been hearing Rowenna's voice. Do you think there might be other telepaths in the village who have been hearing her, wondering where the voice is coming from?"

My father's eyebrows shot up as he considered my question. "I suppose it's possible. Not all Elves are telepathic." He hesitated, frowning. "I don't really want to announce to everyone that there's a dragon nearby, but I think the Elders should be made aware of her presence. I'll meet with them tomorrow and ask for their counsel. Tomorrow's your last day here, isn't it?"

"Yes. I need to get home and get ready for school. Are you going to ride home with me, Dad?"

"Since I have some things to take care of here, I was thinking Adam could take you home. It will be the weekend, so if Garrett doesn't need him, he can spend the weekend in camp and be there whenever you need him." He chuckled. "I'm guessing you'll be enjoying your new car, won't you?"

I nodded. He grinned and said, "Well, Adam has strong nerves so I'm sure he can handle it." Adam looked amused, a slight smirk curving his lips. I rolled my eyes. Maybe some day everyone would forget about that mailbox.

CHAPTER 12

I woke to the sound of rain hitting the windows the next morning. I'd planned to spend my last day in Elvenwood with Ian and Jason, but it was so dark outside, I didn't think I'd be going anywhere. I still hated rainstorms and the sound of heavy rain was already making me tense.

After I'd washed and dressed, I walked into the sitting room to find a basket of muffins and a bowl of assorted berries sitting on the long table. I was fairly sure I knew where they'd come from. Arlynn was trying to make up for the fight we'd had a few weeks ago. And she'd run over in the rain to make sure I'd have breakfast. She was a very, very good friend. She knew how I felt about storms.

My father must have left early, but there was hot water over the fireplace. As I brought in cups from the kitchen, a tall figure wearing a kind of hooded poncho pushed the door open and ran in, shaking rain all over Roscoe who had been waiting by the door. Roscoe promptly shook water everywhere else.

"Morning, cousin," said a laughing voice from under the poncho. Jason quickly shrugged out of his rain gear and hung it on a peg by the door. "I hope you've made tea," he said.

I had to smile whenever Jason was around. He was such a delight, always upbeat and happy. "Morning, Jason. You're just in time for breakfast. Arlynn must have stopped by before I was even awake."

He winked at me. "It's always a good idea to stay on good terms with the ladies who cook."

"Well, sit down and have breakfast with me. Your company is really welcome today."

As he filled his plate, I said, "I paid our new friend another visit last night. I thought I should warn her about flying during the day. I wouldn't want some trigger-happy idiot taking a shot at her."

He nodded. "Yes, I heard Rowenna myself. Even though I didn't hear what you were saying, it wasn't too hard to figure out what your conversation was about. It sounded like you've gained another protector."

THE DRAGON'S SONG

I shuddered slightly. "Yes, she threatened to burn up Donald Gaynes. Not that he doesn't deserve it. The fairy tales always told of dragons breathing fire. I guess it's true."

Jason smiled grimly. "Well, that's one weapon your bodyguards don't have."

"Yeah, but if I were to get in trouble and call her when I'm outside Blackthorne Forest, there's no telling how many humans would see her. I really can't risk that. I suggested that she do her flying after dark, but she insisted that if she's needed, she'll fly anytime, day or night. That worries me."

"Cara, if you're out in public when you run into trouble, you'll have at least one bodyguard with you." He thought for a few seconds. "I don't think you'll have to call on her, except as a last resort."

Jason and I spent the next few hours talking, which helped distract me from the sound of the storm. He had dozens of questions about the human world, especially high school and the usual teenage activities. I knew that many Elves were happy with their lives in Elvenwood and had no desire to venture into the human world. Jason was an exception. He seemed to crave the opportunity to meet new people and experience new things.

"You'll always be welcome to join me for the weekend school activities; it'll be fun."

His eyes sparkled. "You have no idea how exciting this will be for me. Don't misunderstand; I love Elvenwood. But there's a sameness to our days and seasons that has become boring. There's so much out there that I'm afraid I'll never experience. I've been running errands in Thornewood for your father, but it's not enough."

He smiled sadly. "And now there isn't even Amy's bakery to add some sweetness to my trips to town."

The fire that destroyed Amy's family bakery had been on my mind too.

"I know I never mentioned it, but any time you want to ride over to my house to visit with Mom and me, you'll always be welcome."

We'd been sitting on the couch as we talked. "Thank you, cousin. I'll definitely take you up on that." He was smiling again.

It was getting close to lunchtime when my father rushed in wearing another hooded poncho, and carrying a large covered tray.

He grinned as he shrugged off his poncho. "Hope you two are hungry. I stopped at the dining hall on my way home and commandeered some lunch."

Jason raised one eyebrow. "I've been listening to Cara's stomach for the past half hour. Hope you brought enough." I narrowed my eyes at Jason and he laughed.

My father set the tray down on the long table and waved us over. "Cara, please bring in some large cups while Jason gets a jug of water from the cold cellar. I'm hungry too. Unfortunately, your breakfast arrived just as I was leaving this morning."

I uncovered the tray to find two kinds of fresh bread, condiments, sliced turkey, thick sliced tomatoes that were enormous, a block of crumbly white cheese, and several tarts which I assumed were apple. My stomach really was making some embarrassing sounds.

We made thick sandwiches as I asked, "Where were you all morning, Dad?"

"I went to see the Elders, for the reasons we discussed last night." He looked at Jason. "It occurred to Cara that any of our telepathic Elves might be hearing the dragon's voice too, so I decided it made sense to meet with the Elders and make them aware of Rowenna's presence. I would rather keep her a secret, but some of our Elves are undoubtedly wondering where that voice in their head is coming from."

My father ate twice as much as Jason and I did, so I got up and put water on to boil for tea while we waited for him to finish. I was humming the dragon's song as I got the tea things ready. When I carried the cups to the table, both my father and cousin were looking amused.

Jason said, "I think you just made a certain dragon happy, cousin. I should have brought my flute with me."

As I poured the tea, I shook my head. "You know, half the time, I'm not even aware I'm humming that melody. It must be hard-wired in my brain."

My father finally pushed his plate away and picked up his tea. "To answer your earlier question, the Elders know exactly who the telepaths in Elvenwood are. Once they got past their initial shock, they felt as I do, that letting everyone know about Rowenna would be a mistake.

"Each Elder who is telepathic will visit with each Elf who has that ability—there are only about half a dozen—and explain to them what they've been hearing. Those Elves will be sworn to secrecy. At the same time, the Elders will reassure them they have nothing to fear from Rowenna, that she considers herself a protector of our community."

My father looked at me with a smile. "In case you're wondering, when my mother lived here, hearing Rowenna's voice wouldn't have been a problem. As intuitive as my mother is, she's never been telepathic. Her relationship with Rowenna must have been through that song; it couldn't have been through any kind of conversation. I'm sure Rowenna was delighted to learn that you could hear her."

Just then we heard a sharp crack of thunder and the steady rain turned into a torrent, pounding against everything outside. I cringed, as goose bumps broke out on my arms and I began to feel panicky. I looked at my father. "Can't you control this? Maybe slow it down or something?"

I knew I sounded frightened. Once again, I could hear rain pounding on the tent my kidnappers had held me in, and my heart pounded in sync with the rain.

He reached across the table and grabbed my hand, squeezing it. His voice was soft as he said, "Sweetheart, we've had a fairly dry summer. The rain is needed for our crops. I had to promise our chief gardener I wouldn't interfere with the rain again. I'm sorry it's still bothering you. I thought you'd gotten past your rain phobia."

I thought I had too, but I was becoming more nervous by the minute.

Another figure in a soaked poncho ran through the door, stopping abruptly when he saw my father and Jason.

Adam didn't even take off his dripping poncho before he looked into my eyes and said, "It's bad again, isn't it." It was a statement, not a question.

I nodded. "I can handle rain, but not these awful storms. The sound of the rain pounding on everything . . ."

He dropped the poncho on the floor just inside the door and walked over to me. Crouching in front of me, he turned those incredible dark blue eyes on me and whispered, "You need to talk about it, love. All of it." The look in his eyes told me how concerned he was. He stood and turned to my father.

"Brian, can I have a word." My father nodded, a pained expression on his face, and led Adam into the kitchen.

While they were out of the room, Jason stood and gently pulled me out of the chair at the table and led me to the couch. As soon as

I was curled up in one corner, he put another log on the fire, using a poker to coax the flames higher until I began to feel warmer. He quickly made me a cup of tea, wrapped my cold hands around it, and sat down next to me.

His voice was soft. "I thought you'd recovered from your kidnapping; we all thought so. But you haven't, have you?" Worry filled his eyes.

I shook my head. The tea had warmed up my hands. I hoped it would warm me up on the inside too. I was sipping the hot tea as my father and Adam returned to the sitting room.

Adam sat down at the other end of the couch, watching me. My father pulled his large easy chair over and set it in front of me. He sat down, clenching his hands in his lap, brows wrinkled. There wasn't really anything he could do, and I wanted him to understand that.

"Dad, please don't think my problem is your fault. It's my problem. I'll have to figure it out."

"Sweetheart, Adam pointed out something I should have realized. I blame myself for being so dense." He looked down at his hands, took a deep breath, and looked up at me with those familiar green eyes.

"Your mother and I never asked you to talk to us about your kidnapping and all the painful things you endured. We didn't ask for details. We should have. I realize now that I wasn't just sparing you those memories. I was sparing myself. I didn't want to hear what you'd suffered. That was selfish of me. Adam believes you won't recover completely until you've talked about all of it."

He reached over and took one of my hands. "Whenever you're ready to talk, sweetheart, I'll be ready to listen."

Jason wrapped one arm around my shoulders and whispered in my ear, "Me too, cousin. Whatever you need, I'm here."

I looked over at Adam, sitting quietly at the opposite end of the couch. He smiled slightly, as though encouraging me.

I looked back at my father's grim face and blurted, "I wish Mom was here."

He dropped his head and looked at his hands again. When he raised his head, I could see pain in his eyes. "So do I." He turned to Jason. "I think we all need more tea."

As Jason got up, there was a knock at the door. Jason was closest so he opened the door to find Kathleen, wrapped up in what looked like a blanket.

My father rushed to the door, pulling a very wet Kathleen in with him. "What brought you out in this storm? Are you all right?"

THE DRAGON'S SONG

She nodded. "I'm fine, but I had a feeling Cara might need me. I brought some of my special tea, the kind I made for her after she and the boys were attacked a few weeks ago." She looked at me sympathetically. "The storm is upsetting you, isn't it?"

Her understanding words pushed me over the edge. I closed my eyes, but I could feel the tears running down my cheeks. I hated feeling weak, especially in front of others.

Kathleen pulled a small bag from her waistband and handed it to Jason. "Use this tea just for Cara. It will calm her."

While Jason made our tea, I said, "Kathleen, since my mother can't be here, would you please stay? There are a lot of difficult things I need to talk about. Adam's already heard most of it." I looked up into her light blue eyes. "It's about my kidnapping and why I'm still so frightened of storms like today's. Adam believes that talking about it will help me get over it."

"Of course I'll stay, dear." She kissed my cheek, handing me the cup of tea Jason had just made, and sat down near me, next to the fireplace.

Jason passed around fresh cups of tea to everyone else and sat down close to me. I sipped my tea until I began to feel calmer. As my memory took me back to the day I was kidnapped, I began speaking.

I told them about my panic when I couldn't find either of my two bodyguards at school during the storm, the crowd that pulled me outside of school with them, the mud making it impossible for me to run, and then the kidnapper clubbing me over the head.

My father's head was down, his eyes closed. I had never wanted my parents to hear all the painful details, but maybe keeping them to myself hadn't been such a good idea.

I drank more of my tea and looked over at Adam. His dark eyes encouraged me to go on.

I described waking up lying on the ground in a tent, my mouth, wrists, and ankles taped with duct tape, my head pounding like it was split in two, and the nausea from the pain in my head. I described the sound of the rain beating against the walls of the tent, keeping time with the pounding in my head.

At that point I had to stop and drink more of my tea. I paused for a few long minutes and then went on.

I told them how I squirmed and wiggled, one painful inch at a time, to reach the tent wall, knowing I had to get out of the tent somehow, and how I had to fight the nausea because my mouth was taped shut and I didn't dare vomit.

Finally, I turned to Jason. "Can you tell them the next part?"

He nodded and described how he helped me slide under the side of the tent and escape my kidnappers briefly. Then he proudly told them how I'd fooled the two men and used *Vox* when they tried to recapture me.

The worst of the story was over, so I talked about how Jason had carried me through the woods while we waited for my father to find us, and my first encounter with Smoke, my father's huge horse. Finally, I admitted that while I was only half conscious, I saw Conor and the other Elves without the glamour they usually wore. "I was sure I was hallucinating." That made everyone smile, but there were tears on Kathleen's cheeks. She said, "You've gone through hell the past three months, dear. Please remember that we are all here for you, and we always will be."

My father looked like he'd just endured every painful minute of my kidnapping right along with me. He leaned forward and took both my hands in his. "You should have told us sooner, Cara. You shouldn't have felt you had to carry this burden alone."

I knew he wanted to make everything better for me, but I also knew he couldn't.

"I'm not a child anymore. I'm sure there will be more burdens in the future that I'll have to carry alone. But maybe this particular burden will feel a bit lighter now." I'd finished my tea, and felt exhausted.

I stood up and gave my father a tight hug, kissed Kathleen's cheek and said, "Thank you for being such a good friend." I walked back to the couch and hugged Jason who whispered, "Call on me anytime."

That left Adam. Remembering his no hugging rule, I sat down next to him and kissed his cheek. I whispered, "Thank you for being here." He smiled and whispered back, "Always." Then he closed his eyes briefly, as though he knew he'd said something he shouldn't have.

I stood and faced the wonderful people who only wanted to take away my hurt. "I love you all, but Kathleen's special tea has done its job. I need to sleep. Thank you for listening."

I left the room, feeling a bit lighter than I had an hour ago. My pretty green and yellow bedroom was waiting for me. Kicking off my boots, I crawled under my soft quilt. I don't even remember my head hitting the pillow. The sound of the storm outside had completely faded away.

The Dragon's Song

It was dark outside my windows when I woke up. Without a clock, I couldn't tell whether it was afternoon or night, before dinner or long after.

Memories of my kidnapping were again fresh in my mind. It hadn't been easy to talk about, but if it would help me overcome my fear of storms, maybe it was worth it. Of course, I wouldn't know until the next bad storm rolled in. Ordinary rain I could handle, and even that was an improvement from months ago.

I sighed. I'd come to Elvenwood this week to get rid of the tension I'd been feeling, and I thought it had worked. I'd met a dragon, surreal as that seemed, and I had been feeling better without that feeling of doom hanging over me. Until today's storm, that is. I couldn't expect my father to stop every storm for me. Even though he had a strong affinity with the weather, rain was necessary for everything that grew. I realized now that I had simply put my rainstorm phobia out of my mind during our unusually dry summer, but ignoring it hadn't made it go away.

I finally got up and walked into the sitting room. My father was sitting on the couch in front of the fire. For a change, there were no papers in his hands; he was just staring into the flames.

I sat down next to him, resting my head on his broad shoulder. One arm reached around me and I felt him drop a kiss on my head.

"How are you feeling?" I could hear the worry in his voice.

"Better now. The rain has died down; it's not bothering me now."

"Do you think this will happen every time there's a storm?" he asked.

"I don't know. I guess I'll have to wait and see. But at least normal rain doesn't bother me anymore. Even the sound of raindrops made me nervous for a while." I looked up at him. "That's progress, isn't it?"

He let out a deep sigh. "Sweetheart, I think we should discuss this with your mother."

I cringed slightly. "Mom tends to be overprotective. I don't want her fussing over me every time it rains; that would drive me nuts."

He smiled wryly. "I know, dear, but your mother is a very intelligent woman. She may have some ideas on how to help you with this problem. When I think back over the past three months, you've been through so much, it's a wonder you're not howling at the moon."

That made me smile. "Guess that's something to be thankful for, right?"

He hugged me tightly. "Dinner was served a few hours ago. How about running down to the dining hall with me to see if we can scavenge some leftovers?"

"You didn't eat?"

He shook his head. "I thought I should be here in case you woke up and needed me."

"You must be starved. I think the rain has stopped. Let's go raid the kitchen."

It was a successful raid. We found bread, cheese, and apple tarts, brought it all home and had a light-hearted supper in front of the fireplace. It felt like a picnic, and I think my father and I were both feeling a lot better by the time we went to bed. Tomorrow I'd be home. I fell asleep quickly.

CHAPTER 🍎 13

The sun was bright in the sky when I woke the next morning, and I breathed a huge sigh of relief. Sunshine was my friend; rain was not. And I was going home today.

I was lying in bed comfortably when it occurred to me that although the premonition I'd had was gone, some anxiety was still there, embedded in my subconscious like a low pitched humming I could hear only when it was totally quiet. I didn't think it had anything to do with the storm that had freaked me out the day before. I had no idea what it meant.

I heard my father moving around in the sitting room, so I washed up and packed quickly. When I walked into the sitting room, there was a welcome basket of muffins waiting on the table, and my father had already made tea for us.

"Morning, Dad. Did you save me a few muffins?"

He looked up, smiling. "If you don't get over here quickly, I can't guarantee there will be any left."

I smiled and sat down with him. "Thanks for making tea. How soon will I be leaving?"

"*We'll* be leaving in half an hour, dear," he said. "I decided to take you home myself. Adam will be accompanying us, of course, but I want to talk to your mother today."

That took the smile off my face. "You're going to talk to Mom about my rainstorm problem *today*." I took a noisy deep breath and looked at him.

"I don't think we should put this off any longer. So, yes, today I want to discuss it with your mother. Don't worry. You don't have to sit through our discussion. You can call your friends and go out and enjoy your new car."

As if that would be possible while he gave Mom more reasons to worry about me. We had our tea and muffins silently. I had nothing more to say. The sunshine had already gone out of my day.

When I'd finished eating, I ran across the road to say goodbye to Ian. He nodded sadly as I explained that the heavy rain had kept me at home the day before. I knew he was disappointed, and I knew it was mostly my fault. Things like dragons and rainstorms had gotten in our way.

"Maybe sometime soon, I can take you back to my Mom's with me for a visit and you can see where I live. Would you like that?"

His eyes were suddenly bigger and his freckled face lit up. "Can we really do that?"

"If your mother approves, I think we can. I'm sure my mother would love to meet you, so let's plan on it in the near future."

His face was clearly confused. "When's the near future?"

I couldn't help smiling. "The next time I come to visit overnight, you can come with me when I leave the next morning. I'm just guessing, but it will probably be at least a month from now. I'll be back in school in a few days, and I won't have all my weekends free. But I'll be back as soon as I can, I promise."

Ian finally smiled. "All right, but I hope it will be soon. I miss you when you're not here. I miss Uncle Brian too. He's not here as much anymore."

I hugged Ian, kissing his cheek, which turned his face red, and said goodbye. My father had the horses ready to go, and I saw Adam waiting.

After seeing Ian, I was slightly more cheerful, but it was still a very quiet ride home. Adam smiled and winked at me when I mounted Pigeon, but I had a feeling he already knew why my father was riding with us.

When we reached my father's camp, Adam left us, reminding me to let him know if I was going out after I got home.

"I will be going out, probably very soon." I glanced at my father. Adam nodded, his eyes understanding as he led his horse to the camp's makeshift stable.

A few minutes later, Smoke and Pigeon walked up to my mother's back porch as Mom rushed out the back door to greet us. I got down from Pigeon and walked into Mom's arms. I threw my arms around her and whispered, "I missed you." She looked up at Dad, probably surprised to see he wasn't smiling.

She looked at me closely and said softly, "I can see something's wrong, dear. What is it?"

My father put his arm around her shoulders. "Let's go inside. We need to talk."

When I walked into my mother's sunny, welcoming kitchen, I smelled cinnamon and vanilla, two of my favorite scents. "Did you bake?" My mother loved to cook, but baking was not something that occurred in the Connelly home often. She always joked she didn't need the calories.

She smiled at me. "I was home today, so it was a choice between housework and baking. Easy choice." On the breakfast bar was a cinnamon-colored Bundt cake covered with sugar sprinkles. It looked, and smelled, delicious. She added, "I thought it might be good after lunch."

If a cinnamon cake could get rid of a bad mood, I was ready for some now.

My father said, "Your mother and I can talk while you go out to see your new car. After all, there's nothing we'll be talking about that you haven't already heard, dear."

Mom was looking back and forth between us, clearly puzzled. The next second, I was sure he was sending her a mental message because she nodded and tossed a set of car keys to me.

"Go take a look, honey. Kevin was sure you'd love it."

I left by the front door, completely wrapped up in my own thoughts, but when I reached the sidewalk I stopped short and stared.

In front of my house, wearing a big, red bow, sat a large, sleek, shiny black car. Even sitting there, it looked fast. It also looked twice the size of Mom's economy car. I approached it slowly, finally running my hands over the satiny black paint. I had no idea what it was, but it was a lot more car than I'd expected.

Walking around the extensive length of the gleaming black car, I unlocked the driver's door and slid behind the wheel. The seat was a bench-style that would seat at least three people, and the width of the windshield seemed huge to me. Nervously, I put the key in the ignition and turned it. The sound of the engine wasn't too loud, more like a strong purr. Then I stepped on the gas a little harder, and was thrilled to hear the engine actually roar. Wow! The black car even sounded powerful, powerful and fast.

Why on earth would my mother get me a fast, powerful car? So I could get away from bad guys faster? I couldn't help grinning. There was no limit to the mailbox damage I could inflict now.

I lowered the window, reached out and pulled the red bow off the roof. This car was definitely too masculine to be wearing a bow. I tossed it in the back seat. That was when I noticed a white envelope sitting on the back seat. I reached back to grab it and was surprised to see my name written on it in what was obviously a man's handwriting.

I opened it. "Dear Cara, I have enjoyed driving this car for the past five years and believe it will be the perfect car for a young lady who has worked hard learning how to defend herself. This car will protect you in many ways. Take good care of it and it will take care of you. Congratulations on your first car, and drive safely. Sincerely, Thomas O'Donnell, Chief of Police, Thornewood, NY."

I was speechless. This big, beautiful car had belonged to the Chief of Police. And now it was mine. I began checking out where all the controls were, which buttons did what, and was happy to see a CD player as well as a radio. I had another thought that made me laugh. Chief O'Donnell had been kind enough to remove the light bar from the top of my car. Too bad. I would have had fun with that.

I heard a knock on the passenger window and looked over to see Adam standing there, eyebrows raised. I lowered the window with a grin. "Was there something you wanted, Adam?"

"Going somewhere, Miss Connelly?"

I giggled. "Get in, and we can go together."

He slid in beside me. "Where are we going?"

"Hmm. I haven't decided yet. Could you stand an early lunch?"

He chuckled. "If it consists of a cheeseburger and fries, no problem. By the way, have you actually driven this car yet?"

"Nope. This will be its maiden voyage with me behind the wheel."

He grinned. "Should I be afraid?"

Laughing, I said, "I don't think so. This used to be the police chief's car, so I'm pretty sure other drivers will simply get out of my way when they see me coming. By the way, are my parents still sitting in the kitchen talking about me?"

"I'm afraid so, love. When I heard you start the car's engine, I went to your mother's back door and your father pointed in this direction."

"Adam, this car is making me feel powerful, so who cares about a little rainstorm phobia? We're going down to the Grille." I put my new car in Drive and drove away from the house. I had to be careful not to press too hard on the gas; it was extremely responsive.

"You know, I still don't know what kind of car this is, but I love it. It looks dangerous, doesn't it?"

He chuckled. "Cara, any car with you behind the wheel would look dangerous."

I couldn't help laughing. "You may not agree, but I feel totally safe in this car. It has a protective vibe, don't you think?"

"I hope so. You're going fifty miles per hour right now."

Shocked, I glanced at the speedometer. He was right. This car rode so smoothly, it didn't feel that fast. "Sorry. I'll slow down."

When we reached The Grille, there was a nice big parking space in front. They obviously knew I was coming. Parallel parking wasn't one of my best skills.

"I can smell the burgers. Let's go eat."

It was Saturday, but it was a little early for lunch so it wasn't crowded. I knew it would be packed in about an hour. We took a booth and placed our order.

"How do you like riding in my new car?" I asked.

"It was fine, love. You were right; people did stay out of your way. And so did every mailbox we passed. I'd say that car was a good choice." He looked at me with a grin as I rolled my eyes.

Nope. I would never live down that miserable mailbox. Not ever.

The football team crowded through the door, laughing and bad-mouthing each other, the way all teenage boys seem compelled to do. Sean spotted us and came over while the rest of the team filled up two of the largest booths.

"You're back! When did you get home?"

"This morning. You guys must have had practice this morning."

He rolled his eyes. "Yeah, Coach is an early riser. No time for breakfast, so I'm starved now. Can I join you?"

"Sure, have a seat. You know Adam."

"Hey, Adam." Sean flagged the waitress and placed his order. "By the way, how did you get down here? I didn't see your Mom's car outside."

Adam and I smiled. "Did you miss that big, black car out front?" I asked.

"THAT car? That's yours? Holy crap, do you know what that is?"

I laughed. "Well, other than it's mine and I love it, no, I really don't know what it is. Do you?"

"That's a Crown Vic Police Interceptor, big V-8, and it looks like the one the Chief was driving. It's yours? Are you serious?" What was it about boys and fast cars?

"It was the Chief's car. My parents bought it for me. Chief O'Donnell thinks that car is perfect for me. He said it will protect me in many ways, quote, unquote."

"Well, yeah. I see his point. If anybody hits you, your car probably won't get a scratch." He looked at Adam. "How do you like it?"

Adam smiled easily. "It's very comfortable, so comfortable, Cara was doing fifty and didn't realize it."

Sean nodded. "Yeah, those cars are fast. Gotta watch your speed. Well, congratulations on an awesome car. I hope you'll take me for a ride in it sometime."

The waitress brought our burgers, fries and milkshakes, and we all dug in. There was no conversation for several minutes. Sean must have inhaled his first burger. He picked up the second one. "How was your week with your father? Are you all chilled out now? You look great."

I glanced at Adam. "Actually, I was feeling a lot better until yesterday."

"What happened yesterday? Oh, yeah, it rained. We had some thunder. Storms still bother you?" He sounded surprised.

I nodded. "I can handle normal rain, but the heavy storms bring back too many bad memories. Adam thinks it's still bothering me because I never talked about it much. So yesterday, I talked about it, all of it."

"And do you feel better now?" Sean asked softly.

I shrugged. "I guess I won't really know until the next big storm."

"I'm sorry. I had no idea it was still bothering you. If there's anything I can do, let me know." He looked guilty, as though he'd let me down in some way. He hadn't.

We finished eating. Talking about my rain problem had pretty much wiped out the good mood I'd enjoyed driving my new car.

Sean walked out with us. "Please call if you need anything at all. Friends, right?"

"Sure. See you in school next week."

Adam and I got into my new car, and I pulled away from the curb slowly, Sean watched from the sidewalk. He waved and walked back into The Grille.

Adam and I didn't talk on the way home. When he walked me to the back door, he squeezed my hand. "They're only trying to help because they love you. They'll respect your wishes. Just give them a chance, all right?"

I nodded. "Okay. Thanks for your company." I looked up into those intense dark blue eyes. "Sometimes it feels like you're my anchor, you know? All of this would be a lot harder without you."

ᴛʜᴇ DRAGON'S SONG

I stood on my toes, kissed his cheek, and walked into the kitchen where my parents waited for me.

CHAPTER 14

My parents sat at the table, cups of coffee in front of them. They both gave me reassuring smiles when I walked in.

"Can I make you some lunch, dear?" Mom asked.

"Adam and I ate downtown, but a cup of coffee and a piece of that cake would be good." I filled a cup, cut a piece of cake and sat down with them. My somber mood was obvious, I'm sure.

My father asked, "How do you like your new car?"

So far, the car was the one bright spot in my day. "The car's great. I really love it. Thank you both for buying it for me. It's the perfect car for me; those mailboxes don't stand a chance now." I couldn't resist.

Mom gave me a narrow-eyed look, but Dad couldn't hold back a laugh.

"Chief O'Donnell left me a note. It's really nice knowing who the previous owner was, especially when he's the Chief of Police. Did Kevin really pick it out for me?"

My mother nodded with a smile. "When I called Harry Callahan, he told me that the Police Dept. was retiring several of their police cars so Kevin and I went down to Chief O'Donnell's office and he showed us the cars he was replacing. The others were all white; only the Chief's car was black. Harry also told me that Tommy has always been conscientious about maintaining the department's cars, so he thought any one of them would be a good buy. Mileage on the Chief's car isn't as high as the other vehicles either. Tommy let Kevin take it for a ride, and Kevin thought you'd love it. Tommy had it cleaned and detailed before he brought it over to us."

"I'll have to thank Kevin too. It's a powerful car. I really have to watch the speed so it doesn't run away with me. Kevin was right. I love it."

I knew we couldn't put off the conversation I'd been dreading any longer, so I looked at my mother to let her know I was ready to hear whatever she had to say about my problem with storms.

She nodded. "This is actually good timing. I watched a special news program on Post Traumatic Stress a few days ago. You've heard of PTSD, haven't you?"

"Isn't that mainly something that happens to people in the military? You know, the ones coming home from Iraq and Afghanistan?"

"For the most part, yes, although PTSD is also being diagnosed for others who have been through terrible experiences. I think what you've been calling a 'phobia' is really a form of PTSD."

"Well, how do I get rid of it?"

"The TV show I watched mentioned treatments like biofeedback training, meditation, yoga, psychiatric therapy, and medication, depending on how severe the condition is. Cara, we don't think your condition is severe. The only time you have any symptoms at all is during heavy storms. The rest of the time, you seem fine. You sleep well, eat well, and you don't seem depressed. I think Adam and your father had the right idea. Talking about it with people you trust is probably all the therapy you need."

"So you don't think I'm a basket case?"

"Of course not, dear." She glanced at my father. "Considering everything you've gone through since last spring, I think you're remarkably well balanced. We're both very proud of you. I have some books and DVD's at the store on relaxation techniques and meditation, which might help you handle storms in the future. I'll bring some home and we can both try them. Meditation might be good for both of us."

That was a relief. I could handle meditation.

"I was afraid you'd want me to see a shrink, Mom, and that's not something I'd do willingly." The thought of spilling my guts to some stranger horrified me. I could always talk to my close friends, but other than them, I had a definite thing about my privacy.

My mother actually snorted. "I'm sure there are some therapists who actually do some good for people seriously in need of help, but I'm not a fan. I've always felt that common sense goes a long way towards solving most problems." She stood up and poured more coffee for us.

When she sat down again, she said, "Your fear of storms may go away eventually, or it may not. If it's something you have to live with, you just need to learn some techniques that will allow you to handle storms more easily."

Dad was right. My mother was a very intelligent woman.

"Thanks, Mom. That really helps. I'm willing to try meditation."

She leaned over and dropped a kiss on my cheek. "I'll bring a DVD home and we can learn together. One very basic technique is just to concentrate on your breathing for a few minutes."

I got up and put my coffee cup in the dishwasher. "Dad, are you staying for dinner, or do you have to get back?"

He looked at Mom.

She chuckled. "Please stay for dinner, it's spaghetti night."

My father grinned, and Mom added, "Better call Kevin."

Spaghetti night with three of my favorite people was just what I needed. "I'll be upstairs. I have a few calls to make. I dropped a kiss on my father's cheek on my way out of the kitchen, and he squeezed my hand, winking at me.

I was so relieved, I flopped down on my bed as soon as I reached my room. I was okay. I wasn't a nut case. I just had a little trouble with heavy rain. Not a big deal. I would meditate it away. Ralph curled up right next to me. Cuddling with my dog was also an excellent form of therapy.

The first person I had to call was Kevin.

"Hey, short stuff, welcome back! How do you like your new car?"

"I love it. Thanks for picking it out for me. Why did you think it would be perfect for me?"

He laughed. "I had visions of you racing through Thornewood, a whole flock of white police cars trying to catch you. Good thing you don't have a lead foot, babe, because that car is fast."

"Yeah. I drove it to The Grille this morning and didn't even realize I was doing fifty.

By the way, tonight's spaghetti night. You interested?"

"Absolutely. Around six?"

"Yep. See you then. If you're really good, I'll take you for a ride after dinner."

He gave an evil laugh. "I'm always good, babe. See you later."

My next call was, of course, Amy.

"When did you get back? I've missed you." She hesitated. "It's been a rough week around here."

"I just got home this morning. I've had a few problems too. But what's going on at your house? Any news about the fire at the bakery?"

There was silence for about thirty seconds. "The police still consider it an arson case, but they haven't found the arsonist yet. My parents are still talking about retirement rather than rebuilding the bakery." She sighed. "They're still nervous wrecks, so I've been staying close to home. I'm wondering how they'll handle it when I go back to school next week." She sounded kind of strange.

"I'm so sorry. Your family doesn't deserve this."

"No, they don't. I was planning on calling you tonight. I was wondering if your father will be there." She sighed again. "I have something to show him, something he'll want to see."

Something was definitely wrong. "Sure. My father and Kevin are both having dinner with us tonight. Why don't you join us? We eat around six."

She didn't answer right away. "Actually, I think it would be better if I come over after you've had dinner. Would that be all right?"

"Of course. Whatever time is good for you. We'll be here."

She said she'd come by around seven and hung up. She didn't sound like her usual upbeat self. Why did she want to see my father?

I put it out of my mind and ran downstairs to make a salad.

As always, spaghetti night was fun and we all ate too much. Kevin, of course, was making jokes about my driving, the universal threat to mailboxes, and the future safety of the citizens of Thornewood now that I was on the road. Mom kept shaking her head, rolling her eyes occasionally, while my father frequently choked on his spaghetti. I was sure Kevin now had enough new material to see him through senior year.

We finished off spaghetti night with bowls of chocolate ice cream topped with whipped cream and nuts. After that, we all admitted we'd eaten too much and would need help getting out of our chairs. Naturally, that's when there was a knock on the front door.

I felt like I was rolling as I walked to the door. When I opened it, I found my other best friend standing there looking like her world was coming to an end. Since the bakery had burned down, that probably wasn't far from the truth.

I reached out to her and we hugged, Amy holding on to me longer than usual.

I whispered, "I'm here for you. We're all here for you, whatever you need. Come on in. We just finished dinner and I think Mom's making a fresh pot of coffee."

She looked down at me and said, "Good. We'll need it."

I took her hand and led her into the kitchen. Mom put the pot of coffee on the table and hugged Amy. She looked surprised to see the expression on Amy's usually cheerful face.

My father stood, came around the table and put one arm around my friend. He said, "You have good friends here, Amy. Don't forget that."

She nodded. "I know, Mr. Blackthorne. Neal's been telling me the same thing all week."

Kevin stood up, clearly disturbed by what he was seeing on Amy's face. As soon as my father sat down, Kevin wrapped both arms around her. "Hey, Red. It can't be that bad, can it?" She just closed her eyes for a few seconds.

She sat down next to Kevin, her hand in his. She looked around the table at all of us. "I know I have the best friends in the world. But I'm learning that there are times when that might not be a good thing."

She reached into her pocket and pulled out the new tablet she'd bought for our senior year. "Cara, have you checked your Facebook page since you got back?"

"No. Why?"

She opened Facebook on her tablet and handed it to me. Under private messages, there was this:

> "You and your family may have escaped the fire at your bakery recently. But there will be other fires. Your home could burst into flames some night when everyone is asleep. It's doubtful you would escape that one. Of course, homes and businesses aren't the only things that can go up in flames. Cars have been known to explode, killing everyone inside.
>
> You made poor choices when you chose your friends. For instance, your tall, thin friend, the one driving around in a new Jeep, might have survived being shot by an arrow. A gunshot won't be as easy to survive. And, of course, there's that Jeep he's so proud of. I'd enjoy hearing it go "Boom," especially if he's inside it.
>
> Last but not least, your little friend Cara survived one kidnapping. She won't survive the next. It might be fun to kidnap her mother as well. And there's that

lovely, old house her mother owns, just at the border of that forest I wanted to buy. Houses and forests are easy to burn, you know, but especially when their owners are inside with no way out.

Mr. Blackthorne will learn how foolish he was to refuse my offer to buy a piece of Blackthorne Forest. And when I'm done punishing everyone who matters to him, he won't have his precious forest either. I won't leave a single tree, blade of grass, or weed standing.

People who interfere with my plans will always pay a high price."

Amy added, "The name on the account is Gaynes Land Development.

My stomach had quickly tied itself up in knots while she read the message. Kevin's face tightened as he was reading the awful words over Amy's shoulder. Her usually cheerful face was white, making her freckles stand out even more than usual.

My father held out his hand and she handed the tablet to him. He read the message and said to Mom, "Alicia, please call Chief O'Donnell and ask him to come over here."

My father's face was completely white while his green eyes looked like lasers. He looked as though he was ready to inflict some serious damage on Donald Gaynes.

Amy and Kevin still held hands, dread evident in their faces. Mom stared at my father, not exactly angry, but frowning and wearing a "here we go again" expression. She called the Chief and he said he'd be right over. My stomach was tied up in tight, painful knots. I was on the verge of losing my dinner.

Mom poured the Chief a cup of coffee when he arrived, and Amy gave him her tablet. His frown got deeper as he read. Finally, he handed it back to her asking, "Are you on Facebook a lot, Amy?"

She said she was. He nodded, explaining, "We've been monitoring Gaynes online activity since he left town, hoping to locate him, but there's been no activity until now. When did you see this message?"

"Last night. I guess he picked me because Cara and Kevin are hardly ever on Facebook."

Kevin snorted. "Yeah, I can only take so many cat videos."

The Chief looked at my father. "Brian, I'll have patrol cars parked in front of this house, the Strauss home, and the Sinclair home tonight and every night until Gaynes is in jail. I know you'll have your men out there too. Let's meet in the morning and coordinate our efforts." He turned to my friend. "Don't worry, Amy; we'll be covering this town like a blanket."

No one looked relieved. My father's face looked like it had been carved out of stone. Chief O'Donnell told us once again not to worry, and I walked him to the door.

When I got back in the kitchen, my father stood and headed for the back door. "I have to contact my men. I'll be back in a few minutes." Even his voice sounded strange. Watching him walk out the door brought back that horrible unsafe feeling I'd had right after the kidnapping. For weeks I never felt safe unless my father was with me. This time, I wasn't even sure that his presence would be enough. I felt cold, deep inside.

Mom said softly, "I have a feeling we'll be surrounded by Elves from now on. Your father is probably calling out every able-bodied man he has. Gaynes has pushed him too far."

CHAPTER 15

Before Amy and Kevin left, Mom invited them over for Sunday brunch. "Since Cara's father will be meeting with the Chief early tomorrow morning, I think he'll want to meet with all of us afterward. We'll need to know exactly what their plans are." She attempted a smile. "So we might as well start our day with a good breakfast."

Amy and Kevin both said they'd be here in the morning. After we exchanged tighter than usual hugs, Amy left with Neal, and Kevin left with Patrick. When I opened the front door, there was already a patrol car parked in front of our house, and I was sure the police were parked in front of Amy's house and Kevin's house as well. Chief O'Donnell hadn't wasted any time.

By the time I got back into the kitchen, my father had returned, and Mom was pouring two glasses of wine. I decided to make a pot of Kathleen's tea. I'd probably need a gallon of it. Mom glanced at me, looking worried. My father still hadn't said much.

Finally, he looked up at us. "Alicia, I hope you won't mind, but I'll be spending my nights here for the time being."

Mom nodded. "I think Cara and I will both feel safer if you're here." He picked up his wine glass and downed it in one gulp. Mom poured him another glass.

I poured myself a cup of the calming herbal tea and another one for my mother. I'd just thought of someone else who might be at risk.

"Dad, do you think Sean's safe? Gaynes had him beat up last spring. Even though Sean's not my boyfriend now, he's still a friend."

My father nodded slowly. "You're right. We can't ignore the possible threat to Sean and his family. Please call him and ask him to join us in the morning. Don't tell him too much tonight. Just say we've had news of Gaynes and you think he should be here." He squeezed my hand.

"Okay. I'll go call him now."

Sean sounded surprised when he answered his phone. "Hey, Cara. Is everything okay?"

"Uh, not really. Can you come over for brunch in the morning?"

"Well, sure. I'm always available for your Mom's Sunday brunch. What's really going on?"

"It's not exactly a social occasion. We have news about Gaynes and thought you should hear it too since you were involved with the attacks last spring. My Dad wants us all together because we have some plans to make."

"Sounds serious. Are you all right?"

"Yeah, I'm fine." A total lie. "We're all fine." Another lie. "My Dad is meeting with Chief O'Donnell early tomorrow morning. He'll come back in time for brunch and fill us in. Come over around ten, okay?"

"Sure. I'll be there."

We said good night and hung up. Hearing his familiar warm voice had been comforting for the few minutes we were on the phone. But the knots in my stomach were becoming painful cramps.

Mom looked at my father. "Brian, are you going to be all right?" She looked worried.

He started running his hands through his long hair, the way he always did when he was frustrated. Finally, his voice low, he practically growled, "I will see Donald Gaynes wiped off the face of the earth if it's the last thing I ever do."

Mom put her hand over my father's clenched fist. "Brian, between your men and the police force, I'm confident that Gaynes and any of the criminals working for him will be arrested very quickly. You and Tommy O'Donnell work well together. I have faith in both of you and I'm sure his men and yours will keep all of us well protected." She patted his hand and he looked at her with so much love in his eyes, I almost felt I should leave the room.

He turned to me and spoke softly. "I love you and your mother more than you will ever know. I will do everything in my power to see that neither of you suffer any further harm. You have my word."

He stood. "I need to speak to the men I've called to my camp, but I hesitate to leave you for even a short time."

"Dad, there's a police car parked in front of our house already, and there are two officers inside it. We'll be fine." For his sake, I knew it was important to appear confident.

My father closed his eyes for a few seconds, and nodded. "Ryan and Gabriel are on their way to the house now. If all my men were telepathic, I wouldn't have to leave."

Five minutes later, there was a knock at the back door. My father opened the door to Ryan and Gabe. "Ryan, I want you inside the house with Cara and her mother. Gabe, I want you guarding the area behind the house. I'll return as quickly as possible."

Ryan came in and Mom handed him a cup of coffee. He smiled his thanks. I watched Gabe through the window as he ran through the yard with my father, stopping in Mom's garden, where he had a good view of both the yard and back of the house. It was too dark to see my father as he disappeared into the trees.

Standing just inside the back door, Ryan asked, "What was it that set off the alarm this time?"

I told him about the threatening message Amy received. It was the first time I'd ever seen Ryan truly shocked. He muttered, "The man's a lunatic."

Mom poured more tea for the two of us. "Cara, when your father returns, I think we should turn in for the night. We'll be up early in the morning. I think my brain needs to shut down for a while." She'd been so calm until now, but the tension was beginning to show.

"We're on the same page, Mom. I think my brain has already shut down." But then my brain reminded me that I hadn't sung to Rowenna today. "Actually, some fresh air would be good. When Dad gets back, I'd like to spend a few minutes out on the porch."

"Now?"

"Yeah, I need to breathe in the forest for a few minutes. It always calms me." It would also make a certain dragon happy.

"If your father approves. But just for a few minutes, dear. It's late."

Dad returned about ten minutes later, looking calmer and more in control. "There are currently fifty men in camp, all skilled in weapons and all aware what we're up against."

"Brian, you look much better now. I'm going up to bed so I'll say good night, but Cara wants a few minutes out on the porch, if you think it's safe."

"I'll be up in a little while, Alicia. I'll sit outside with Cara. Ryan, there are chairs on the front porch. I'd like you stationed in one tonight. I think your night vision is better than that of the police out there. I'll station Gabriel on the back porch when we come in. If anything stirs, use your whistle."

When Ryan left for the front porch, my father and I went out to sit on the back porch.

Once we were seated outside, my father asked, "Was there something you needed to speak to me about, dear?"

"Not really. I just need to let Rowenna know I haven't forgotten about her."

Finally a smile. He chuckled. "Sing her song. I'll enjoy hearing it too."

So I did, but very softly. And once again, I heard the sound of large wings overhead, felt the shimmer of magic, and knew Rowenna had heard her song. But instead of flying back to her mountain, her rough voice in my mind asked, *Cara, why are so many Elves in the woods near your mother's house?*

I gave her a brief summary of the threats Amy had received, and explained that the Thornewood police would be working with us. I could hear her wings as she circled overhead.

I will protect you, your friends, and the Elves. I will burn evil humans when I find them. This Dragon will be in the sky over Thornewood every night.

I wasn't sure the police would understand, but what could I say?

"Thank you, Rowenna. Please be careful."

Always careful, Cara. Good night.

My father had heard everything Rowenna had said, and as she flew away, he actually started to chuckle.

"Well, I guess we should consider Rowenna our secret weapon. But I think I'd better tell Chief O'Donnell about her. After all, he's a Halfling. He understands the Elven world, but I'm afraid Rowenna may come as quite a shock." His soft laughter continued until we went into the house.

CHAPTER 16

Getting some sleep that night was a lost cause. I could hear my father prowling around the house for hours, until I finally heard my mother's soft voice. "Brian, get some rest now. It's only a few hours until dawn." After that, I heard no more footsteps.

The next time I opened my eyes, the sky was light so I got up and took a long shower. I closed my eyes under the warm water and just concentrated on breathing. By the time I dried off, I felt calmer. If that's what meditation involved, I was all for it.

It was September, but the weather was still hot so I threw on shorts, a t-shirt and tennis shoes. It was too hot for boots, but I'd had a lightweight leather holster made while I was in Elvenwood. It fit comfortably around my waist and held two of my knives, one at each hip. Wherever I went, my knives were going too.

When I got downstairs, Mom was already in the kitchen getting breakfast ready. Dad was sitting at the table drinking coffee and watching Mom.

"Good morning." I bent down to hug my father and moved to the breakfast bar to hug Mom. She was beating eggs with cheese, onions and milk, ready to pour into two already baked piecrusts. "Mom, you must have started cooking before the sun was up."

She smiled. "No, I haven't been in the kitchen that long, dear. But I think we'll have a full house this morning, and I want to have enough for everyone to eat. I'll grill sausages too and there's already a pan of cornbread in the oven." No wonder the kitchen smelled so good.

My father shook his head, looking guilty. "I'm afraid I kept both of you awake last night. Forgive me."

He was unusually quiet this morning. I hoped a lot of the things he was worrying about would be resolved in this morning's meeting.

He looked at the clock, finished his coffee, and stood. "It's time for me to meet Chief O'Donnell. Harry will be here to pick me up any minute. I'll wait on the front porch. I think the police left at dawn, but my men are stationed all around this house, so no one who doesn't belong here will get anywhere near the house. I'll be back as soon as I can." He kissed Mom on the cheek, gave me a quick hug, and left through the front door.

Mom watched him stride through the door with a worried look. "I think your father will feel more like himself after he and the Chief make their plans, and your father can speak to your friends and his men with some definite ideas for dealing with all those threats. I think he's found the extent of these new threats overwhelming."

I could relate. "You don't seem overwhelmed. How come?"

"Well, the police are on board and the entire police force will be working with your father and his men, although I don't think anyone but Tommy O'Donnell knows who your father and his men really are. Nevertheless, that's a very large number of people who will be taking care of Amy and her family, Kevin and his mother, and us, probably Sean and his family as well. I don't know how many people Gaynes has on his payroll, but they're badly outnumbered and probably don't realize it."

Pushing away from the table, her coffee cup slipped out of her hands and shattered on the hardwood floor. My mother was more nervous than she wanted me to know. Naturally, she wouldn't admit it.

"Sit down, Mom. I'll sweep this up." She wouldn't meet my eyes as she sat down again. I got the broom out and swept up the broken china.

I decided that a large pot of Kathleen's calming tea was what we needed. My only plan for the day was to remain calm. Maybe that would reassure my friends.

Mom sat down and had a cup of tea with me. At nine o'clock she put both quiches in the oven and took out the cornbread. The sausages were on the griddle, ready to cook. She went to the pantry and brought out a large bag of oranges, dropping it in my lap.

"Here, honey, make yourself useful." I set up the juicer on the bar and started making orange juice. That kept me occupied until I heard Kevin's familiar knock on the door.

Kevin came in the door, still looking almost as nervous as he had last night. Patrick was right behind him. "I'm going back to keep an eye on your house, Kev. Your mother's home, isn't she?" Kevin nodded. "I'll come back here when she leaves the house." He slapped Kevin on the shoulder and ran back down the steps.

As soon as Kevin was inside and the door was closed, he put his arms around me, resting his face on top of my head.

"You didn't get much sleep last night either, did you?"

He let go of me and snorted. "Did the bags under my eyes give me away?"

I grimaced. "We have matching bags this morning." I led him into the kitchen where he went straight to Mom and hugged her.

"How are you feeling today, Mrs. C?"

"I'm fine, Kevin. I think by the time you leave here, you'll be feeling a lot better too. The Thornewood police force and Brian's men will have this situation under control quickly. They won't let any one of us get hurt. Try to relax, dear. Have some of Cara's tea."

"I think I'm going to need some strong coffee just to stay awake, Mrs. C." Mom poured him a cup and Kevin joined me at the breakfast bar while I continued squeezing oranges.

"There was a police car around the corner last night, keeping an eye on our house," Kevin said. "Naturally, my mother went straight to the officers and demanded to know what they were doing there." He sighed. "Fortunately, they told her they'd had a report of a prowler in the neighborhood. We'll all be better off if we can keep her out of this."

He was right. Betty Sinclair would only make matters worse if she knew about the threats.

Next to arrive were Amy and Sean. He smiled but looked curious. I brought them into the kitchen where Amy got another comforting hug from Mom, and Sean got a nervous smile.

"Amy, want to try this calming tea for a change?"

"No, thanks. I really need coffee this morning. You probably didn't get much sleep either, did you?"

"No, but I did some meditation in the shower this morning, and I feel a little calmer now."

Amy looked surprised. "Meditation?"

"Yeah. I want to learn more about it, but it's something that would help all of us relax."

Sean wore a blank expression. "Will you please tell me what's going on?"

I handed him a cup of tea and said to Amy, "You'd better show him the message. Sean was involved in the last round of attacks, so we decided we couldn't leave him in the dark."

Amy nodded, took her tablet out of her bag, logged on to her Facebook page and handed the tablet to Sean. "Read this."

His face changed as he read the frightening threats from Gaynes. Finally, he handed the tablet back to Amy and looked at us. "This is worse than last spring. He's the one who set the fire in the bakery, isn't he?"

Amy said, "Well, either him or someone who's working for him. The Chief doesn't think Gaynes is back; he believes he's still somewhere in Canada."

"Chief O'Donnell posted patrol cars in front of our houses last night. I'm sure my Dad will ask that one be posted at your house too. He already has fifty Elves stationed at his camp. I think there will be cops and Elves everywhere, starting today."

Sean raised one eyebrow. "And Tuesday we'll be back in school."

Mom reminded him, "You all got accustomed to having bodyguards in school last spring. This shouldn't be any more difficult than that was. I seem to remember your bodyguards enjoyed themselves tremendously. And so did all of you."

I thought, yeah, until the storm.

CHAPTER 🍎 17

When my father returned an hour later, he held his shoulders straighter and his head higher. Mom handed him a cup of coffee and he sat down with us.

Mom said, "I'm sure everyone is hungry, Brian, so we can talk after we eat." She smiled. "You look a lot better than you did when you left."

My father nodded. "Chief O'Donnell and I have made plans that will ensure everyone's safety. I'll explain everything after we've eaten."

Mom cut slices of quiche for everyone, put a basket of corn muffins on the table, and began grilling sausages. "Help yourselves."

After everyone had eaten and coffee and tea had been placed on the table, my father began. "Chief O'Donnell is throwing the entire weight of the Thornewood Police Dept. into our plans. He's also sending copies of that threat Amy received to every police department, nationwide, as well as Canada. But he said he wished he had a picture of Gaynes. Apparently, the man has always been careful not to be photographed. His drivers license picture must have been taken when he was sixteen, and it's not very good."

Kevin looked at me. "Gavin said the picture of Gaynes you painted on your target was accurate. You could take a picture of your target for the Chief."

My father added, "We'll walk over to your practice area later and you can take a picture. I know the Chief will be delighted to have any kind of picture of Gaynes the way he looks today.

"There will be a police car parked in front of each house every night. That includes your house, Sean. You weren't mentioned specifically in these latest threats, but we're not taking any chances. In addition, there will be more police cars patrolling Thornewood than usual. The police will be patrolling on foot as well. Special attention will be paid to any unfamiliar faces and cars seen in town, and Chief O'Donnell has cancelled all vacations until further notice.

"That brings us to the threat to your vehicles. The Chief has a list of your cars and license plate numbers. They'll be subject to frequent checks for explosives, wherever they're parked, at home, at school, downtown, anywhere. Anyone who wants to plant a bomb will need to be invisible because there will be eyes on our homes and vehicles 24/7. Of course, the police will be keeping eyes on all of you as well. They won't interfere unless they suspect something is wrong. If any one of you is stopped by a policeman, don't be alarmed. He will simply be making sure that you're all right.

"As for my men, other than your bodyguards, most of my Elves will be working undercover, guarding your homes day and night. You probably won't see them, but they'll be there. And they'll be armed. They won't step in unless they think you need help. Since you all have those little phones, Chief O'Donnell asked that you all put him on something called 'speed dial.' He wants you to call any time you see or hear anything suspicious, no matter how small." I needed to give my father a crash course in cell phones.

I asked, "Will we have the same bodyguards we had before? And will they be with us outside school as well?"

"Your bodyguards will stay close to you whenever you're out of your homes. Of course, they'll be with you in school too. Ryan will be with you, Cara; Neal with Amy; Patrick with Kevin, and Gabriel has volunteered to act as Sean's bodyguard. Sean, you probably remember Gabe; he was one of Cara's bodyguards last spring." Sean nodded.

"I don't want any one of you, and this includes you, Alicia, to leave your home without a bodyguard for any reason. That would be the only time you'd actually be vulnerable. Conor and Arlynn volunteered to work at the bookstore with you. They'll take turns. Since they've both worked with you before, I thought you'd be comfortable with them."

She raised one eyebrow. "I will be. And traffic in the store will probably pick up while they're there." My father rolled his eyes and everyone smiled. The mood in the kitchen got lighter and more relaxed as my father outlined all the steps that were being taken to protect us.

I asked, "What about the school activities we've been looking forward to? Like football games, and other events held outside school."

"Chief O'Donnell suggested you attend those kinds of events as a group whenever possible. After all, the larger the group, the more protection each of you will have."

Amy and Kevin looked at each other. "No problem," Kevin said.

Sean looked at me, both eyebrows raised. "That'll be fine with me if it's okay with Cara."

I nodded. "Sounds good. Hanging with these three will be fun." Everyone nodded, a few smiles beginning to emerge from the tense faces of my friends.

"If any of you have questions any time, don't hesitate to ask. I'll be staying here with Cara and her mother." My father looked at each of my friends. "I'll be available to all of you, day or night." He turned to me. "Let's go over to your practice area now so you can take that picture for the Chief."

Mom told my friends, "You're all welcome to stay for coffee or tea. No one has to rush out. Frankly, I'd enjoy the company."

"We'll be back in a few minutes," I said. "I'll email the photo to the Chief. Will you guys wait for me?"

Sean smiled and nodded. Amy and Kevin said they'd stay. Dad and I walked next door to my practice area. I took the cover off my target and used my phone to take a picture of my painting of Gaynes. As soon as I'd sent it to the Chief, we walked back to the house.

My father frowned. "Is there some way you can make a copy of that picture you just took? My men also need to know what he looks like."

"Sure. I'll print it and make copies for you."

"And you can do all that with that little phone?"

I couldn't help giggling. "Yep. Twenty-first century, Dad."

He smiled, shaking his head.

When we walked back into the kitchen, the atmosphere was a lot more relaxed. My friends were comparing their class schedules for senior year. Amy was complaining about the science class she was required to take in order to graduate. She hated Science. Sean was complaining about the English teacher he'd have this year because the man was known for insisting his classes share his love of Shakespeare. Kevin was laughing because he had already accumulated enough points to graduate and, except for a couple of required courses, he could take any fun class he chose to round out his senior year.

"Do you have your schedule, Cara?" Sean asked. We're all trying to see if we'll be sharing any classes this year. It doesn't look like Amy, Kevin, and I have any classes together."

"Wait a sec, I'll run upstairs and print mine out." I was back a minute later and spread my class schedule out on the kitchen table. My father helped himself to coffee and sat down next to Mom.

Sean set his phone on the table next to my printed schedule. My eyes were going back and forth between my schedule and his until I sat back, sort of in shock. "You're in all but two of my classes, P.E. and Art. How did you manage that?"

He laughed, shrugging. "I didn't manage it. Got lucky, I guess." He wore a satisfied smile.

"Let me see that," Kevin said, looking surprised. I handed him my schedule and aimed Sean's phone at him. Kevin finally snorted. "Who'd you have to bribe, McKay?"

Sean just shook his head, looking smug, and winked at me.

I looked over at my mother, who was trying, unsuccessfully, to look serious. Finally, she started chuckling as she stood up. "More coffee, anyone?"

Amy stood. "As good as that sounds, I'd better get back. My folks are nervous when I'm not there. Maybe they'll calm down when I tell them how much the Thornewood police are doing to protect us." Then she smiled. "Besides, my mother was getting bored without the bakery to go to, so she started making apple strudel before I left."

"Ooh. Save me a piece," I said. "Can we get together at your house tomorrow?"

"You know, I think it would be good for my parents if you all come over. My mother will start baking again, my father will try to boss her around—which never works—and it'll cheer them up." She looked at Sean and Kevin. "Are you two in?"

"I'm definitely in," Kevin said. "Your mom's baking kills."

Sean added, "I'll be there too. Just give me a time. After all, it's our last day before school starts. Let's have some fun with it! We'll be so well guarded, there won't be anything to worry about."

We were all smiling by that time. I walked Amy to the door, gave her a hug and sent her out to Neal, who waited on the porch. I was pleased to see his eyes light up when Amy walked out.

There was a knock on the back door as I returned to the kitchen. I went to the door to find Kevin's father, Kelly O'Rourke, standing on the back porch with Adam. Kelly asked if he could see Kevin, and Adam said he just wanted to make sure I was all right.

"Come on in. My father's here too so he can fill you in on anything you don't already know."

Mom invited Kelly and Adam to sit down and proceeded to make a fresh pot of coffee.

My father described all the steps being taken by the police force as well as the part the Elves would play in protecting our homes.

Adam looked at me, obviously worried. Turning to my father, he said, "I know Ryan and I will both protect Cara with our lives. But since she seems to be Gaynes' number one target, I think she needs more than just the two of us."

My father nodded. "Every one of our Elves is aware of that and will be keeping Cara in his sights as much as possible. No one will be able to get near her."

Kevin and Sean were watching and listening closely, their eyes moving back and forth between Adam and my father. Adam did seem more intense than usual.

"I think we can stick to the same plan we had before. Ryan will be with Cara in and out of school during the week, and you'll take over on the weekends, Adam. If Cara feels she needs you during the week, she can always let you know." Adam nodded but he didn't seem completely satisfied. Mom patted his shoulder and handed him a cup of coffee. Even she could see how worried Adam was.

My father turned to Kevin and Kelly. "Kelly, I want you to stay close to Kevin's house, day and night. We're trying to catch an arsonist."

Kelly said, "That's what I wanted to speak to you and Kevin about. I want to help in any way I can." He looked at Kevin sitting beside him. "Will it cause you any problems with your mother if I'm around every day, son?"

Kevin nodded. "It would probably be a good idea if Mom doesn't see you. She doesn't know about these threats, and we'd all prefer to keep her out of it if we can."

Kevin's mother, Betty Sinclair, didn't know about the Elves. She also didn't know that Kevin's Elven father, with whom she'd had a one-week fling eighteen years ago, was back and spending time with his son. Kelly had never even known he had a son. Betty Sinclair had always been totally wrapped up in her career rather than in Kevin. At this point, Kevin preferred keeping it that way.

My father kissed Mom on the cheek and stood. "I need to meet with the Elves who are in camp to go over the Chief's plans with them. I want them to be undercover, but at the same time, aware of where the police are. Adam, you and Kelly should come with me. We need everyone well coordinated." Looking at Mom, he said, "I'll be back soon."

Adam walked over to me and whispered, "Let me know if you need me. I'll be listening for you." He gave my shoulder a quick squeeze and left with my father and Kelly.

Sean and Kevin looked at each other. Sean said, "I've never seen Adam like this. He's usually so laid back. I wouldn't want to get in his way when he's in bodyguard mode."

I shrugged. "Yeah, he worries about me. But he's saved my life twice so I'm not complaining."

Mom got up from the table and said, "You boys are welcome to stay as long as you like. I'm going upstairs to take a nap."

"Thanks for brunch, Mrs. Connelly," Sean said with a smile.

Kevin added, "Fantastic as always, Mrs. C."

Mom said, "I'm glad you're both here. Cara needs her friends, especially now." She turned to me. "If anything happens, wake me." I nodded and hugged her. I could feel the tension in her body, but I knew she wouldn't talk to me about it.

Once we heard the door to her room close, Kevin said, "This is a lot different from last spring when we were all being threatened. We didn't know who was behind it, and you hadn't met your father yet. The police weren't involved either. I don't know about you two, but this feels like a whole new can of worms."

Sean nodded. "There were so many things then that we didn't understand. Plus, you two now have skills to protect yourselves. Maybe I should start carrying a big stick." The sarcasm was obvious, but I knew he felt vulnerable.

Kevin shook his head. "That won't be necessary. You've got Gabriel for a bodyguard. He's even bigger than you. Besides, Cara already found out just how good he is in a fight."

"Yeah," I said. "When Gabe, Ryan and I were ambushed on our way to Elvenwood a few months ago, Gabe was awesome. He stayed on a galloping grey while shooting arrows at our attackers. And he didn't miss, despite being injured."

Sean said, "You both talk about those greys so much. Will I ever get a chance to see one?"

Kevin looked over at me. "Do you think your father will let Sean visit Elvenwood?"

"Well, we know Sean has some Elven blood, so I think the gateway would open for him. I'll ask my father. Since Conor is Sean's cousin, I don't see why not."

I could see Sean's mood lighten when he began to smile. "I've been fascinated with Elvenwood ever since Cara told me about it. I would really love to see it for myself."

I had been wondering about more immediate problems. "I've been thinking about the kind of attacks I went through in the past. All, but one, were carried out when I was with a bodyguard; that didn't stop them. Adam was with me when one of Gaynes' friends tried to run me down in the street. Ryan and Gabriel were both with me when we were ambushed in the woods. Ryan was with me when that man tried to kidnap me at the lake. I actually had two bodyguards just before I was kidnapped during that storm; but neither one was able to help me." My memories brought that anxiety back even stronger than before.

I sighed. "I don't know what kind of thugs Gaynes has hired this time, but even with bodyguards, they always find a way to get to me. I think the Chief's advice that we stick together as much as possible is a good idea."

Kevin added, "From the way that message Amy received was worded, it sounded to me like Gaynes doesn't care who gets hurt this time. He's out for revenge. I think we all run the same risk this time around."

Sean nodded. "Sounded that way to me too."

They were right. I'd been thinking of myself, but we were all in danger.

CHAPTER 18

I must have tossed and turned all night because when I got up and staggered into my bathroom, my hair looked like I'd had one finger plugged into a light socket. I climbed into the shower to repair the damage. While the hot water ran over me, I closed my eyes and tried to calm my mind for a few minutes, concentrating on my breathing, and nothing else. Once again, it relaxed me. While I dried off, I felt better.

Amy called first, letting me know her parents were delighted that we were all coming over. Mrs. Strauss was making apple tarts and muffins this morning in honor of our visit. I knew Kevin would be thrilled. She asked if I'd call the boys and arrange to drive over in one car. I counted heads in my mind and decided that my new car could hold six, so I told her I'd do the driving.

Kevin was the first one I called. "Hey, short stuff. Feeling any better this morning?"

"Yeah, a little meditating in the shower and I feel more like myself now. Are you okay?"

"Not too bad. I'm more worried about keeping my mom out of it than anything else. I don't even want to think about what she'll do if she spots my dad outside."

"I'm sure he'll stay out of sight. He doesn't want to complicate things any more than you do. The reason I'm calling is to coordinate getting over to Amy's this morning. I have the biggest car so I'll pick up you and Sean and our bodyguards. Sound okay to you?"

I could hear his smile over the phone. "Sure. Can I drive?"

"No way. It's my car and I'm doing the driving. Don't you trust me?" If he said one word about mailboxes, he'd be walking to Amy's.

He laughed. "No, babe, I'm not worried about your driving. I just want to drive that big black machine again. It's such a cool car."

"Amy said we could come over any time after ten, so what time's good for you?"

"Mrs. Strauss is baking, isn't she?"

I giggled. "You know she is. Apple tarts and muffins."

"Well, I can be ready in two minutes. What time is it now?"

"Kevin, it's not even nine yet. Cool your jets. I'll come by at ten to pick you up."

My friend, the walking stomach, reluctantly agreed.

"I'll see you in an hour, Kev. I have to call Sean now."

When Sean picked up the phone, he said, "Good morning, beautiful." I hadn't heard that greeting since we broke up. My stomach did a small backflip. I told it to calm down.

"Amy called to say her folks are really happy we're all coming over today. Her mom's baking up a storm, of course. She said any time after ten would be good. How's that work for you?"

"Sounds good. My dad needs the car, so can you or Kevin give me a lift?"

"I'm picking up both of you, and our bodyguards. Have you seen Gabriel yet?"

"Yeah, he came in last night to meet my dad. I had to explain the situation to my father. Mom's visiting one of her sisters in Boston, so I'm hoping she'll never know what's going on. Gabe thought he should meet my dad so that he wouldn't be mistaken for a prowler. He knows Conor and my dad are cousins, which seemed to make both of them more comfortable."

"How's your dad handling all of this?"

"Well, I had to tell him about everything that happened last spring, including your kidnapping. He didn't know about that, but he's on board now and understands what we're all up against. He did say that he'd like to speak with your father, so maybe you could let your dad know."

"I will. I know my dad feels terrible that my friends are involved. Anyway, I'll pick up you and Gabe a few minutes after ten. I'm really hoping we'll have fun today so we can forget about all this crap for a little while."

"Ditto. See you later, beautiful." His deep voice was getting to me.

I hung up and scolded my stomach for doing another backflip. After all, Sean and I were just friends now. He wasn't my boyfriend anymore. Just friends. Right.

An hour later Ryan and I picked up Kevin and Patrick and headed to Sean's house. We saw more police cars on the roads than usual, and uniformed police were all over the downtown area. One of them waved at us when I stopped at the light at the corner of Elm and Main where there was a shiny new mailbox on the corner. I could hear snickers from the backseat.

"One word, Kevin, and you'll be walking." I looked at Ryan sitting next to me. He looked sympathetic even though he was smiling. When we pulled up in front of Sean's house, his father came out with him and walked over to my side of the car, bending down to talk to me.

"Cara. It's good to see you again," Mr. McKay said. "I think we both missed you." He smiled and winked at me. I'd always liked Sean's father. He was tall like his son, his hair still blond but graying, and he had the same warm brown eyes. I hadn't seen him since last spring.

He said softly, "I never knew what you'd gone through months ago, and I'm sorry Sean wasn't more understanding. Growing pains, I guess." He smiled. "I'm glad you're friends again. I hope I'll get a chance to speak to your father soon. I'd like to help, if I can."

"Thanks, Mr. McKay. I'll let my dad know and he'll be in touch."

Sean and Gabriel climbed into the back seat with Kevin and Patrick and we left for Amy's house.

Gabe chuckled. "Your new car looks really powerful. I'll bet we could outrun the bad guys, if we had to."

I shivered slightly. I hoped that would never be necessary.

When we reached Amy's house, everyone piled out of my car with Gabe and Patrick heading for the backyard, and Ryan joining Neal on the front porch. I rang the doorbell and Amy invited us in. Wonderful baking smells hit us as soon as we walked through the door. I was sure Kevin was already salivating.

After hugging all of us, Amy led us into the large kitchen where her parents were working. Her dad was punching down dough for bread, and Mrs. Strauss was just taking apple tarts out of the oven.

Mrs. Strauss put the tarts on the counter and came over to greet us. "Cara, liebchen, it's so good to see you, and Kevin, my always hungry boy, and Sean, you've gotten so tall. Welcome!" I'd always loved Mrs. Strauss' Austrian accent; she'd been in this country since before Amy was born, but still sounded as though she'd just arrived from her native Vienna. It had been quite a few years since Kevin and I had had play dates at Amy's house. Amy's mom always made the best goodies for us when we visited. She was a short, round woman with Amy's curly red hair, the color still as bright as it had ever been.

"Hi, Mrs. Strauss. It's so nice of you to invite us here today. Your house smells amazing!" I kissed her rosy cheek.

She laughed. "I love baking for people, and Amy's friends have always been my favorite people. With the bakery closed, I have too much time on my hands. So you're all doing me a favor. Now go on into the den, and Amy will bring in the tarts and a pot of fresh coffee. I know you're all coffee drinkers, even though I think you should all be drinking milk. You're still growing, you know." Amy smiled, rolling her eyes.

Mrs. Strauss bustled back to the stove and Amy led us into their den, a large room at the back of the house where we'd played when we were children. Windows on three sides provided a beautiful view of their backyard. I spotted Patrick and Gabe out there, partially hidden in the large grove of apple trees. I'd forgotten how large Amy's backyard was. It had to cover at least an acre, maybe more. There had always been fruit trees in their yard, apple, pear, lemon, and cherry, but the trees had grown a great deal since I'd played there.

It occurred to me that there were too many places for someone to hide in that yard.

The four of us talked about school and our senior year while we gobbled apple tarts and drank the best coffee I'd ever tasted. Amy confided that her mother always added a little cinnamon to the ground coffee. And for those of us who didn't drink black coffee, there was heavy cream, rather than milk.

Kevin chuckled. "You're going to have to invite us over more often. This is a real treat."

Amy smiled. "All of this is mainly because the bakery is closed. Normally, my parents are working there, not here. I think they really miss the bakery. I'm hoping they change their mind about rebuilding and reopening. We'd all be happier if they could just get past their fear. But these latest threats aren't helping."

We talked about sports; both Sean and Amy were exceptionally athletic. Sean had already started football practice, and Amy was looking forward to soccer season. Kevin was one of Thornewood High's mathletes and head of what Amy jokingly called "Nerd Central." When we were freshmen, Kevin might have been considered a nerd, but he'd turned into a tall, slender, good looking young man who had begun attracting some female attention around the end of our junior year. And since he was under contract to a video game manufacturer, he was also a successful entrepreneur with money in the bank. Kevin's new black Jeep was a symbol of his success.

I asked him, "Have you finished "Zombie Revenge" yet? I'm waiting for my complimentary copy."

He grinned. "Yeah, I sent it off last week. Don't worry; I made copies for you guys, although Sean's the only gamer in the group. What do you and Amy do with your copies anyway?"

Amy laughed. "You won't believe it, but my dad is a serious gamer. While Mom watches her TV shows at night, my father is glued to his game console. Your first game is still his favorite."

Kevin looked surprised. "I'll definitely add your dad to my short list of beta players; the others are a few guys in my math classes who give me feedback."

He turned to me. "I see you brought your messenger bag with you, short stuff. Got anything new to show us?"

I'd never shown my Elf drawings to anyone but Sean, so I pulled the entire folder out of my bag and spread them out on a game table that sat in a corner. Amy turned on the lamp that hung over the table. I wondered how long it would take them to spot the Elves hidden in each picture.

"You did these while you were in Elvenwood, didn't you?" Amy asked.

"This is a special series of drawings that I did over the summer," I said.

Kevin took a closer look. "Special?" Then he chuckled. "These are really great. You have to look closely before you see what's hiding there."

Amy bent over the table. "Well, your drawings are always wonderful... oh, am I seeing what I think I'm seeing?" she asked me. I nodded, smiling.

Sean said, "You showed me this one, but you've done so many and they're all fantastic. Didn't you say that Francis Sullivan encouraged you to do this series?"

Naturally, Amy's shriek was the next thing we heard. "Francis Sullivan? Not the famous artist who paints kids playing?"

"The same one. He liked my drawings the first time he saw them and thought I should do more of what I've been calling my Elf drawings."

Amy gasped. "You don't mean that Francis Sullivan is an . . ."

"He lives in Elvenwood. It's a well-kept secret, of course, so don't say anything to anybody, okay?"

She looked insulted. "I can keep a secret, you know." Kevin and I just looked at each other and tried not to laugh. Amy was an incurable gossip, but to be fair, she had kept our secret. So far.

Pointing to the picture I'd done of Arlynn hiding in the grove of white roses, she asked, "This gorgeous creature isn't real, is she? I mean, I know the Elves are all unusually good looking, but this one had to come straight out of your imagination, right?"

Kevin laughed. "She's as real as any of us. She gave me my first knife-throwing lessons, and to be honest, it was really hard remembering to look at the target instead of at her."

Amy's mouth hung open. "Are you serious? She's real? I hope she's married, Cara, because no girl would stand a chance if she's actually available."

"Relax, Amy. She and Conor are in a relationship. I think they're both off the market."

She started fanning herself, as though we'd just saved her from a fate worse than death. "Well, I hope I never have to stand next to Arlynn. It would destroy what little confidence I have."

Kevin was laughing as he got up to pour more coffee for us. From the front of the house, we heard a loud crash, like breaking glass, and we all ran through the kitchen and out to the front porch, Mr. Strauss right behind us.

Ryan and Neal were standing out in the street in front of a raging fire that seemed to be burning nothing. Ryan called out, "Call the Chief. Tell him to look for a black van with no markings that's heading toward Main Street." Amy pulled out her cell phone.

Mr. Strauss had gone back in the house to grab a fire extinguisher and ran into the street to put out the gasoline that was blazing in the middle of the road. The smell of the gasoline made my nose hurt. Neal stayed there with him as Ryan walked to the porch to talk to me.

"Where'd that fire come from?" I asked him.

"This black van drove by very slowly. Neal and I were watching it carefully, but I don't think the driver saw us. When they were right in front of this house, the driver threw a bottle with a flaming rag at the house. It would have gone through one of the windows if I hadn't caught it. I threw it back at the van but the driver took off fast and it shattered in the street." He looked down at his hands that were slightly red. I hoped they wouldn't blister.

Kevin and Sean were standing behind me, listening. Sean said, "That was what's called a Molotov cocktail, Ryan. It could have done a lot of damage if you hadn't caught it."

Amy had called Chief O'Donnell while Ryan was describing what had happened. It wasn't more than two minutes before we heard sirens. Three police cars sped down the street, screeching to a stop in front of Amy's house. Chief O'Donnell jumped out of one, rushing to where we were standing.

"Is everyone okay?" he asked.

"We're fine," Amy said. "But if Ryan hadn't caught the bottle thrown at our window, the house would be on fire." She pointed at the burn marks and broken glass on the street.

The Chief shook his head. "When I got your call, I sent two patrol cars out to look for that black van, but it was gone, probably made it to the highway. Did anyone get the license plate?"

Ryan said, "It was covered with something so it couldn't be read. Probably mud."

The Chief didn't say anything right away. Frowning, he said, "You must have been followed when you came over here. Whoever's working for Gaynes must have thought with all of you here, they could do a lot of damage with just one Molotov cocktail. If we'd been able to catch that van, we might have gotten some answers. I don't think they'll try anything else while you're here, so will you all be here for a while?"

I looked at Amy. "Should we stay? If your parents are too upset, we can go home."

Mr. Strauss said, "We're not going to chase you away. You all wanted to spend a good day together before school starts tomorrow, so let's go back in the house. We were making lunch when all this happened. Come in, please." He sounded worried.

Chief O'Donnell said, "Call me if anything changes. My men will keep their eyes open for that black van." He got back into one of the police cars and we went back in the house with Mr. Strauss. That was when I realized that Mrs. Strauss hadn't come outside with us.

I found her in the den, sitting at the game table with my Elf drawings in front of her. Hadn't she heard the commotion in front of the house? Maybe she was hard of hearing.

Everyone else was in the kitchen, talking while Amy made fresh coffee.

I sat down with Mrs. Strauss. She seemed fixated on one of my Elf drawings. "What do you think of them?" I asked.

"Cara, liebchen, these people you've hidden in your drawings, you know them, don't you?"

That was a surprise. I didn't think Amy had told her parents about the Elves.

Hesitating, I asked, "Did Amy tell you about my father . . . or something?"

She laughed softly. "No. I knew people like these back home, in Austria. They lived in the forest near my village."

"Why do you think I know the imaginary people in my drawings?"

She smiled and shrugged. "There's always been something about you, liebchen, that's a little fey, I think." She turned back to my drawings, picking up the one I'd drawn of Adam, leaning against a tree at the pond.

"Now, I have to look hard to see this young man, but he reminds me of the young men from the forest where I grew up. So very handsome, but different from the men in my village."

She put the drawing down and turned to me. "I've always believed that Blackthorne Forest is home to the same kind of people I knew back home. And this town is richer for them. Your bodyguards are from the forest, aren't they?"

What could I say? She knew and understood, and I felt sure she would keep our secret.

"Yes, the boys are all from the forest. They work for my father, Brian Blackthorne."

She gave me a warm smile. "Thank you for trusting me, Cara. Your secret is safe with me. You've told Amy about the people from the forest, haven't you?"

"Of course. I only met my father a few months ago. I knew nothing about him until I turned sixteen. It . . . changed my life. It was a little difficult to absorb, and having the support of friends like Amy, Kevin, and Sean was a huge help."

She leaned over and kissed my cheek. "Let's go into the kitchen and get some of that coffee they were supposed to be making. I'm sure you're all hungry after all that commotion outside." Aha, she wasn't deaf. She had simply chosen to ignore it.

Mr. Strauss had been busy making sandwiches, thick roast beef sandwiches on his homemade bread. The kitchen was filled with the wonderful smell of fresh-baked bread. Amy carried a tray of sandwiches into the den, followed by Kevin with a pot of coffee. Amy's parents joined us.

When we'd all finished eating, Mr. Strauss said, "It's good that you're all here today because what happened earlier makes me think that the Chief was wrong when he said you'd all be safer if you stick together when you're outside your homes. It seems to me that keeping you together just gives these attackers an advantage. They can kill many birds with one stone." He frowned, looking embarrassed. "Well, not kill exactly, but you know what I mean."

I thought he made a good point. Kevin added, "Actually, if there hadn't been so many of our bodyguards present, it could have been worse. When we're not all together, it's one person and one bodyguard, which I think is more of a risk."

Mr. Strauss shook his head, frowning. "You may be right, but how can we be sure?"

The doorbell rang and Amy's father got up to answer the door. We heard him say, "Hello, Mr. Blackthorne. Please come in. We're all fine. There was no damage."

My father walked into the den and all conversation stopped. Even in jeans and a button-down shirt, he had a commanding presence. His eyes found mine immediately. I smiled to let him know I was fine.

He looked around the room at all of us and seemed to breathe a sigh of relief. "The Chief contacted me to let me know what happened here this morning." He shook his head. "I am relieved that no one was hurt and no damage was done. Both the police and my men did exactly what they were supposed to do to avert a disaster."

Mr. Strauss pointed to another chair. "Please have a seat, Mr. Blackthorne."

"Thank you, Mr. Strauss. I'm glad I have the chance this afternoon to speak to all of you, especially you, Mr. and Mrs. Strauss, because you have suffered the most from this madman's rampage against me and those dear to me."

Mrs. Strauss' accented voice came from the doorway to the den. "We do not blame you, Mr. Blackthorne. We have never blamed you."

My father looked over at the small, middle-aged redhead in the doorway. "You're very gracious, but I do feel responsible, responsible for the closing of your bakery, responsible for the impact to your income and your way of life. These are not small things. If and when you decide to rebuild your bakery and reopen your business, I am pledging my help, in every possible way. I know that the people of Thornewood would be extremely happy to see the doors of the Strauss Bakery open again.

"But right now, we must focus on the safety of our children and our homes. You all know that our Police Chief has dedicated his entire force to protecting you, your homes, and your vehicles. His men are working around the clock, seven days a week, to keep us safe. My men are doing the same. You've all seen the bodyguards who are accompanying our children, but there are dozens more, who you won't see, guarding your homes and keeping an eye on all of you. Starting tomorrow, there will be plainclothes police inside Thornewood High as well. It won't be possible for any strangers to enter the school.

"I'm sorry that today didn't turn out the way you planned," he said, looking at Amy, Sean, and Kevin. But I still think you're all safer when you're together, you and your bodyguards."

Mrs. Strauss bustled into the den with the coffee pot, refilling cups and handing a cup to my father, who smiled his thanks. Then she placed a tray of muffins on the table and invited us to help ourselves. Naturally, the muffins were fantastic, just as good as the muffins Arlynn baked.

We talked among ourselves as we ate. Amy and I talked about our back to school clothes, while Sean and Kevin talked sports and gaming. My father and Amy's parents were smiling. I could hear my father asking them questions about the bakery. Mr. and Mrs. Strauss appeared to be considering the necessary repairs, which was a good sign.

We all passed a relaxed hour eating, drinking coffee, and chatting. When I looked at the clock, it was four o'clock, getting close to dinnertime, and I thought we'd taken up space in the Strauss' home long enough.

"I think it's about time we cleared out so Amy and her family can think about dinner. Dad, would you like to ride with us? I'll be taking Sean, Kevin, and their bodyguards home."

I wondered if he'd be nervous about my driving.

He stood, dwarfing everyone else in the room, and thanked Amy's parents for their hospitality. He murmured to Mr. Strauss, "Please let me know if I can be of help at any time."

My father turned to me with a grin. "I've been looking forward to riding around town with you, and I promise I won't even nag you about your speed." Kevin snickered.

Amy hugged each of us at the front door, even my father who seemed pleased. When we walked out on the front porch, Ryan pulled a silver whistle out of his pocket and blew it. Naturally, we couldn't hear anything, but Gabriel and Patrick came running around the house from the backyard.

My father asked, "Are there others back there now?" Gabriel nodded, so I knew more Elves had arrived to keep an eye on Amy's house.

Kevin and my dad climbed into the front seat of my car, while Sean, Gabe, Patrick and Ryan piled into the back seat. My father was sitting next to me, so I mentioned that Sean's father wanted to see him.

"Since your mother is still at the bookstore, this is probably a good time," he said. He asked Sean, "Is your father home now?" Sean said he was, and my dad said, "Let's take Kevin and Patrick home first, then we can come back to see Sean's father."

"Okay, Dad." I started the car, racing the engine a bit just to see my father's reaction. I was surprised when he laughed, saying, "I really must learn to drive a car. I think it would be fun."

He sounded so enthusiastic, kind of like a boy with a new toy, and I couldn't help laughing. "You should learn. You could take lessons like I did. I don't know if you could actually get a license, but at least you'd know how to drive." He nodded, smiling.

By this time I was doing forty on Mill Road, just about to turn the corner to our street, and my father hadn't said a word about my driving. He actually seemed to be enjoying the ride. When I reached Kevin's house, there was already a patrol car parked on his cul-de-sac. I pulled up in front of his house, and he and Patrick climbed out.

Kevin leaned in. "Thanks for playing chauffeur today, short stuff. Which one of us is driving to school tomorrow?"

"I'll have to let you know. Sean and Amy might need a ride. I'll call you tonight."

He said goodbye and walked into his house, while Patrick ran around to the side of the house. I knew Kevin's dad was probably in the woods behind the house. They'd be well protected tonight.

I headed for Sean's house and my father said, "You drive very well, dear. But I am glad we got you a car that will give you some extra protection." He patted the dashboard and said, "It seems very sturdy."

From the back seat, Sean was chuckling. "Mr. Blackthorne, this car could probably out run most other cars on the road; it's really fast."

It only took about five minutes to reach Sean's house. We saw police cars on every street.

When I pulled up in front, Ryan and Gabe climbed out first and moved to the front and back of the house. Sean got out and opened my door to help me out. My father got out, closing the door carefully and ran his hand over the car's roof, nodding in approval.

Sean opened the front door and ushered us in. His father was sitting on the couch with a science fiction novel in his hand. He stood to shake my father's hand with a smile.

"Thanks for coming by, Mr. Blackthorne."

He led my father to the table in the dining room, and they sat down. My father said, "Please call me Brian. Since our children are friends, I'm happy to meet you. I understand Gabriel explained the present situation to you already."

Sean took my hand and we went into the kitchen. "Let's let them speak privately. We've already heard it all, more than once. Would you like some tea? I told my mom about the tea I had at your house, so she picked up some Chamomile tea at the store. It's not as relaxing as Kathleen's tea, but it's not bad."

"Thanks, tea sounds good. I've had so much coffee today, I may not be able to sleep tonight."

He smiled. "Yeah, I know what you mean." He boiled some water, poured it over the tea in two cups and handed one to me. He pulled out a kitchen chair for me and we sat down at the small table in the corner of the kitchen. It wasn't big and sunny like Mom's kitchen, but it had a kind of comfortable intimacy that I liked.

"Going back to school tomorrow seems kind of anti-climactic after the last few days," he said. "And I know our bodyguards are great, and there will be plainclothes cops in school, but I'm relieved we'll be in the same classes." He chuckled. "We can protect each other," he said with one raised eyebrow. "You'll be wearing your knives, won't you?"

"Absolutely. I probably shouldn't mention it, but I had a waist holster made for me in Elvenwood. I can carry two more knives, one at each hip. And, of course, I have two more in my boots."

I couldn't miss the shocked expression on Sean's face. "Cara, don't you think that's overkill?"

"Nope. I refuse to feel defenseless, especially in school."

He nodded, obviously remembering that I'd been kidnapped right outside school last spring. Finally he smiled. "Well, now I'm doubly glad we're in the same classes. You can protect me!"

A little while later, Mr. McKay and my father walked into the kitchen, looking as though they'd reached some kind of agreement.

My dad said, "I think we should get home, Cara. Your mother will be getting home any minute. Conor is with her today, but she'll worry if we're not there."

Mr. McKay said, "Say hello to my cousin Conor for me, Brian. And please let him know he can call on me for help too."

Sean and I stood up, and when I said goodbye, Sean surprised me by kissing my cheek. "See you tomorrow in class," he said with a grin. His father and mine glanced at each other, both trying not to smile. The threats from Gaynes probably weren't the only things they'd been talking about.

CHAPTER 19

I woke up earlier than usual Tuesday morning. The alarm hadn't gone off, but some part of my brain must have known it was back to school day and the beginning of my senior year at Thornewood High. I pushed the anxiety into the back of my mind.

While I was in the shower, I realized I felt completely different than I had every other year on the first day of school. And not because of the Donald Gaynes/bodyguard situation either. I'd always dreaded the first day of school, wishing I had a cloak of invisibility so no one would notice me, or stare at me, or heaven forbid actually talk to me. I'd always felt so out of place, but I'd come a long way in just a few months.

I actually looked forward to getting back in school, seeing the new friends I'd made a few months ago, as well as getting ready for either college or art school. That decision still had to be made. I refused to allow the black cloud that was Donald Gaynes ruin my mood or my senior year.

After blowing my long hair dry and pulling it up into its usual ponytail, I dressed in a new pair of jeans and a green t-shirt that matched my eyes. Boots were next, fitted with two of my knives. Until the weather got colder, and I could wear heavier clothing, my waist holster, which held two more knives, would have to remain at home. Sean thought that wearing a waist holster was overkill, but after yesterday's near-disaster, I wasn't so sure.

Mom was waiting for me in the kitchen, ready with the traditional plate of pancakes that were customary every year on the first day of school. Pancakes were Mom's way of comforting me on back to school day because I'd always dreaded it. But this year, pancakes were just a yummy way to start the day.

Before I even sat down, there was a knock on the front door. I looked at my mother with a smile. "You called Kevin, didn't you?" She laughed. "I thought you might need some help eating all these pancakes. Your father already ate a few before he left for his camp."

I had to smile when I opened the door. Kevin had a big smile on his face. "Morning, short stuff. Do I smell pancakes?" He followed me into the kitchen, stopping only to hug Mom before sitting down and helping himself to a stack. "Definitely the way to start the day," he muttered as he poured syrup on his pancakes. I had to agree as I dug into the stack on my plate. "Thanks, Mom. This is perfect."

She sat down and had a few pancakes with us, then poured each of us a cup of coffee. We polished off breakfast quickly and were ready to go.

"Great breakfast, Mrs. C. Thanks for calling me; we only had a few corn flakes left at my house."

Mom rolled her eyes. Kevin's mom didn't make it to the grocery store very often. I heard her mutter, "I'm going to draw her a map."

After Mom's usual hugs and wishes for a good day in school, we left, meeting up with Patrick and Ryan on the front porch. Over the phone last night, we'd organized our carpooling plans. Kevin and I would take weekly turns driving to school. Sean's father would take Amy and Sean and their bodyguards to school every morning. Since Mr. McKay was out making business calls during the day, he would only be able to pick up Sean from football, or basketball, or baseball practice late in the afternoon; Sean played every sport offered at Thornewood High. Kevin and I would take Amy and her bodyguard home from school every day. My father and Sean's both thought we were safer in groups. It didn't look as though I'd ever be alone again.

The four of us climbed into my big car and left for our first day of school. Everyone was in a good mood, Patrick and Ryan clearly looking forward to seeing the parade of teenage girls Thornewood High provided. My cousin Jason had confided that our bodyguards had talked of nothing else last spring when they accompanied us to school every day. I was glad there was some compensation for having to play bodyguard, giving up their normal lives, for what might be months.

When we got to school, finding a parking space for my big car was a challenge. Kevin said, "We may have to get here earlier than usual to get a spot close to school." He was right, but today we had to walk a block to school. I was glad there were four of us.

We found Amy, Sean, Gabriel and Neal standing in front of school waiting for us. "No problems for any of you this morning?" Kevin asked.

"Nope, everything has been calm," Amy said. "Let's hope it stays that way."

The first bell rang and we all trooped into the school's main entrance. After agreeing to meet for lunch, everyone went their separate ways, except for Sean and me, of course.

Our day started off with Environmental Science, a class being offered for the first time this year. It sounded interesting, but I knew that would depend largely on the teacher.

My father's influence with the school board was evident again. Sean and I had been assigned to seats next to each other, with Gabe and Ryan right behind us.

An hour later, I knew this would be an interesting class. It was being taught by a new teacher, a young man who obviously loved the subject. Our bodyguards had been smiling and nodding throughout the class. I was confused until I realized this was a subject they had probably been born understanding. Elves, after all, were connected to the earth, the weather, and all growing things. They might be as expert on environmental science as our teacher.

When we walked to our next class, History, we noticed the undercover cops in the halls as well as uniformed police at the entrances. Sean whispered, "I'm feeling extremely well protected this morning."

Ryan said softly, "It is nice to know we have so much back-up."

Sean and I glanced at each other, both of us smiling. I was sure the police considered our bodyguards as back-up, rather than the other way around.

As we changed classes, we saw friends in the halls, everyone waving and smiling. I wondered what they made of the police presence in school today. Then I wondered if they even noticed.

I enjoyed History class too. We'd be studying World War II and the Holocaust this term, and I knew it would be interesting. I'd been fascinated by that war ever since I'd read The Diary of Anne Frank in ninth grade.

Once again, Sean and I were seated next to each other, with our bodyguards behind us.

I was actually in a good mood that lasted right through our Economics class where we were about to learn all about Credit and Investments.

When Sean and I, and our bodyguards, reached the lunchroom, Amy had already laid claim to the largest table. She and Neal were trading jokes as Kevin and Patrick came through the lunchroom door. I couldn't help noticing how many heads turned at the two of them.

Kevin had definitely come into his own with his longer curly hair that was finally in style, jeans that fit him like a glove, and a newly acquired air of confidence. He was as tall as Patrick, whose curly red hair and blue eyes made him what Amy called a chick magnet. He smiled back at every girl who smiled at him, while Kevin seemed oblivious to the female attention he received.

Our bodyguards, Ryan and Gabriel, were attracting plenty of attention too. I'd almost forgotten about Gabe's natural charisma. He was doing exactly what Patrick was doing, smiling at every girl in the room. I could almost hear the feminine sighs as he sat down at our table. Ryan, who was already committed to Lora back in Elvenwood, just rolled his eyes at Gabe's behavior.

We talked about our new classes over lunch. Amy was threatening to drop out of school; she had Advanced Science this year, a fate worse than death as far as she was concerned. Kevin calmed her down by promising to tutor her. The few classes Kevin was required to take this year left him time to take some fun classes of his choosing. Of course, being Kevin, his idea of a fun class was Government, covering criminal law, civil law, and human rights. And since he still had a free period, he had signed up for Art and Art History, which meant we'd share that class. He said, "I didn't know I'd have to choose another class until this morning. The Guidance department emailed me, so I decided to get into your class, just for fun." I wondered if Kevin actually had some artistic talent. It wouldn't surprise me.

After lunch we left for our fourth period classes, Sean and I headed for English Literature, Ryan and Gabe right behind us.

I'd always loved English, and it was the same teacher I'd had last year, so I knew I'd enjoy the class.

In each of our classes, I was surprised at how seriously Sean was taking each subject, asking good questions and taking notes. When I mentioned this during one of our walks between classes, he said, "I have to get an athletic scholarship to a good college, so my grades are really important this year." I was impressed.

We parted ways after English, as Sean had Trig and I had Art.

Before he left, Sean said, "Cara, I have football practice after school so I won't see you until tomorrow. Can I call you tonight?"

I couldn't help teasing him. "You mean, we haven't spent enough time together today?"

"Yeah, but we can't really talk freely between classes, or in class."

"Okay. I'll talk to you tonight. Good luck in Trig." He grimaced.

THE DRAGON'S SONG

Kevin and Gabe arrived at Art class right after Ryan and I did. Before we walked into class, I noticed two plainclothes policemen walk by. They both nodded to us. I smiled at them and we went into class. Miss Burrows gave me a friendly wave and directed everyone to an easel.

"This year some of you are going to use watercolors, some will try oils, and a few of you may want to use pen and ink. But today, use whatever tools you find at your easels to draw a picture that represents your summer. You don't have to finish it today; you can take the rest of this week, so make it good!"

Elvenwood had dominated my summer. Drawing a dragon probably wouldn't be believed, but finally I knew what I wanted to draw. The tools at my easel were pen and ink, which I was comfortable with. I got started and emptied my mind of everything but my sketch of beautiful grey horses running through the forest.

When I reached a good stopping point, I looked over at Kevin and decided to take a peek at his drawing. I walked up behind him and stopped short. He had sketched an outline of a girl aiming a bow and arrow at a target. It was just an outline with no details filled in, but it reminded me of a type of folk art I'd seen. I couldn't wait to see where he'd go with his drawing.

"This looks really interesting, Kev. Anyone I know?" I teased. He whirled around, clearly surprised to find me looking over his shoulder.

He smiled. "Well, you might be the inspiration for my drawing, but it won't look like you, I promise."

The bell rang so we put our artwork away. Miss Burrows motioned to me from the front of the room. It had to be about watercolors.

"I'll have watercolors for you to work with next week. I'm looking forward to seeing one of your beautiful landscapes done in watercolor. I just have one suggestion. Get yourself some watercolor supplies to use at home. It's a technique that takes some real skill, and I'd like you to get used to mixing and applying the colors. Just don't get discouraged if your colors run down the page at first; everyone has that problem when they start."

I thanked her and promised to get some supplies to use at home. Ryan was waiting for me at the door. Kevin and Patrick had already left. Kevin and I both had P.E. for our last class and Ryan and I headed for the girl's gym. He'd have to wait outside the gym, of course, but he'd have an excellent view of the other senior class girls as compensation.

P.E. was a surprise. Miss Lincoln decided that physical fitness was the perfect starting point for senior girls. We spent forty-five minutes doing push-ups, sit-ups, squats, and sprints around the gym. There was a lot of moaning and groaning from my classmates, but I had no problem. My summer had left me in good shape.

After quick showers, we threw our clothes on and left the gym, most of the girls complaining about the push-ups and sit-ups. I just smiled. Sandy joined me in the hallway, laughing. "You put most of the girls to shame. Didn't you used to have a t-shirt that said, Small but Mighty?"

I had to laugh. "Yeah, but I outgrew it. I may have to get another one and just wear it for P.E."

Smiling, she pulled me aside. "I don't mean to be nosy, but I saw you and Sean together everywhere today. Are you two finally back together?"

I knew someone would ask that question sooner or later. "Sean and I are just friends for now. We'll see how it goes. He's still a great guy, but I don't think I want a steady boyfriend again."

She nodded, a thoughtful look on her face. "Once burned, twice shy?"

"Yeah, I guess it's something like that." I shrugged.

"Well, I'm glad you and Sean are friends again." She chuckled. "You really taught him a lesson. Sean and I have been friends all our lives, but I always thought things came a bit too easily for him. I think you're good for him."

She gave me a smile and a quick hug. "See you tomorrow, Cara."

I continued down the hall with Ryan, who had stepped aside when Sandy stopped me. It was really thoughtful of him to give me some privacy to speak to a friend, and I told him so. "I don't want to crowd you too much, lass. But I hate letting you out of my sight; waiting for you outside the gym made me a bit nervous."

When we got outside, Kevin, Patrick, Amy and Neal were waiting for us. Everyone was comparing notes about our first day as seniors. But there was a sudden tension in my neck that made me frown. No one noticed. I was getting a bad feeling in my gut.

There were some laughs and a few complaints, mainly from Amy, as we stood there. We were standing in a kind of semi-circle, Ryan, me, Kevin, Patrick, Neal, and Amy on the end. We all turned when we heard a loud engine and saw a black van speeding around the corner, practically on two wheels. When it was almost even with us, a hand holding a gun appeared in the open window and it was aimed at Amy.

My knife was in my hand before I could think about it. I threw it at the van, where it pierced the hand holding the gun. The gun hit the street and the van sped up even faster and disappeared around the next corner. No one said a word. Kevin was the first one to regain his senses, pulling out his phone and calling Chief O'Donnell.

When I turned to look at my friends, I saw knives in Ryan's and Patrick's hands, disappearing quickly as the uniformed cop who'd been at the front entrance ran toward us.

After being assured that we were all okay, he said he'd already called in the speeding black van. He was sure one of their patrol cars would spot it. He jogged to the street to pick up the gun lying there.

I realized I was breathing hard and I took a minute to try to slow my breathing until I felt calmer.

When I looked at my friends, Patrick had stepped in front of Kevin, Ryan was standing in front of me, and Neal had Amy wrapped up in his arms, his back to the street. I felt as though I had just awakened from a bad dream, even though I was aware that it was my knife that had hit the man holding the gun. Ryan put one arm around me and said softly, "I've never seen anything like that, lass. You're incredibly fast."

I looked at him and nodded. It was almost like I'd been watching a scene from a movie, not something that was actually happening. I thought I might throw up.

Kevin's voice was strained. "The Chief is on his way."

Patrick looked at me and said, "Good job."

I thought I heard sobs coming from Amy. I walked over to her and placed my hand on her shoulder. She raised her head from Neal's shoulder and whispered, "Thanks." I could see tears on her face. I heard Neal whispering soothing words in her ear.

The uniformed cop whose name badge said "M. Rankin," told me he'd seen the whole thing. "It took me a minute to figure out where that knife came from, Miss Connelly." He shook his head. "You have amazing reflexes. The Chief will need statements from all of you." Kevin and I both groaned.

That was when the Chief's car pulled up. He came straight to me. "There's a good chance we'll stop that van this time. There's a roadblock at each entrance into Thornewood. But I'd like to get all of you inside so you can tell me what happened. Let's go find a quiet place where we can all sit down."

Chief O'Donnell led us to an empty classroom. I hadn't realized that my legs were shaking until I sat. Kevin slid into the chair next to me and reached over to grab my hand. We exchanged a look. He finally smiled and whispered, "Wonder Woman." I couldn't help groaning.

The Chief pulled out a notepad. "Officer Rankin says when the passenger in the van put a gun out the window, a knife was thrown instantaneously, hitting the man's hand and forcing him to drop the gun. He looked straight at me. "Is that correct, Cara?"

I nodded. "I think so. I just remember seeing the knife hit that hand and watching the gun drop."

The Chief shook his head. "It must have been an automatic reaction when you thought your friend was threatened. Your father did mention that you and Kevin are both highly skilled in knife throwing."

I nodded. "Nothing like that has ever happened to me before. It all seemed like a bad dream, not real, you know?"

He said, "I understand." Looking at Kevin and Amy, he asked, "Is that what you saw? Is there anything else you can remember?"

Kevin squeezed my hand. "I remember seeing that gun pointed at Amy, but the knife flew through the air before I could move."

Ryan and Patrick nodded. Ryan said, "None of us had time to react; it happened that fast."

The Chief shook his head, closed his notebook and stood. "I'm sorry you had to deal with this today, but glad you have more protection than I realized." He looked at me, one eyebrow raised. "I'm going to follow you home today. I saw where you parked about a block from here. Officer Rankin and I will walk you to your car, where you'll wait until you see my car pull out."

"Chief, I have to take Amy and Neal home, then Kevin and Patrick."

"Fine. I'll be right behind you," he said.

When we reached Amy's house, I said, "Please call me tonight if you want to talk."

"I will. You saved my life today." Then she snickered, sounding more like herself. "My parents will probably put you in their will."

I shook my head.

"We'll talk later, okay?"

"Absolutely," I said as she and Neal got out of the car. I waited while they walked up the stairs. Neal took a seat on the front porch after giving Amy a hug, and Amy went into the house.

Kevin said, "I wonder how her parents will take this. They might want to lock her in her room until those guys are all in jail."

I drove to Kevin's house next, the Chief's car right behind me. When I pulled up in front of his house, Kevin leaned over and wrapped both arms around me. "I'm sure glad you're my friend," he joked. "But seriously, you were great today." He kissed my cheek and climbed out of the car with Patrick, who grinned and said, "I never should have bet against you, Cara. Ryan was right."

I stuck my tongue out at him and he laughed as he followed Kevin. When I'd asked my father for self-defense training, the Elves took bets on how well I'd do. I'd been determined to show them they'd been wrong to doubt me.

A minute later, I pulled in front of my house. My father stood on the front porch with his arms crossed. He wasn't smiling.

I'd been hoping I could tell my parents myself, maybe after dinner when they'd both had a glass or two of wine. But no such luck. I turned off the ignition and got out of the car, Ryan by my side. The Chief had parked behind me and was already heading for my father. I hoped he would stay calm and not overreact. Amy wasn't the only person who could end up locked in her room for the duration.

CHAPTER 20

My father held the front door open for the Chief and me, while Ryan winked at me and took a seat on the porch. As soon as we were inside and the door was shut, my father wrapped his arms around me and kissed the top of my head. He whispered, "Are you all right, sweetheart?"

I rested my head on his broad chest. "I'm fine, Dad. Amy's fine, Kevin's fine, we're all fine." Well, at least physically we were all fine.

With one arm around me, he walked me into the kitchen, the Chief right behind us. He looked down at me and finally smiled. "Would you please make coffee for us? I'm afraid I'm helpless without a fireplace and a pot of water."

"Sure, but I'll have to teach you how to use the coffee maker one day soon."

As soon as the coffee maker beeped, I poured coffee for everyone, taking a cup out to the front porch to a grateful Ryan.

The Chief asked, "When will Alicia be home? I know she'll want to hear everything and Cara won't want to go through all of it twice."

I looked at the clock on the wall. "Who's with Mom in the bookstore today?"

"Conor's with your mother. I know he'll insist she lock up promptly at five, so they'll be here shortly."

He asked, "How's Amy? I'm worried about her and her family. I don't understand why they've been targeted."

"Amy's okay. She was pretty shook up when it happened, but Neal was able to calm her down. She seemed to be feeling more like herself by the time I drove her home."

The Chief said, "I was wondering the same thing. I think the main reason is that they're friends of yours. And I guess they've been easier to attack. But today, I think it was mainly because Amy's a tall, attractive redhead wearing colorful clothing. She simply stood out from the rest of the group."

I was curious too, but the Chief was right. Amy was so tall, she usually stood out, and today she'd been wearing a vivid red-orange shirt, almost the same color as her hair.

Just as I was pouring everyone another cup of coffee, I heard Mom's car pull up in the driveway. I had no idea how she was going to react.

Mom must have seen the Chief's car parked out front and rushed in with a worried looking Conor right behind her. When she saw my father and me sitting at the kitchen table, alive and well, she let out a deep sigh of relief.

She looked at Chief O'Donnell, shook her head, and said, "Tommy, you'll never know what the sight of your car in front of my house does to my blood pressure." She and Conor sat down with us as I got up to pour more coffee.

The Chief nodded. "Sorry, Alicia. I should probably have a large sign made up and plastered across my windshield saying, "EVERYONE IS OK."

Mom gave him a brief smile. "Good idea." She looked at my father and me again. "So I gather something bad happened today, but you two weren't harmed, right?"

Dad said, "Right. I'll keep it brief. There was another attempted attack today, and Cara saved Amy's life. The only one who got hurt was the attacker."

I knew that would be a bit too brief for Mom.

Mom's eyebrows were up around her hairline. She looked at me and said, "A few more details would be good."

I told her about the attempted attack and assured her that Amy wasn't hurt, just shocked. "Mom, the Chief doesn't think Amy was the planned target, it's just that she stood out because she always stands out."

Looking at my father, I whispered, "I'll need to replace that knife."

I thought he looked kind of sad. "I'll take care of it, dear."

I sensed a certain tension in the air between my mother and father.

The Chief broke the silence. "One of the kids called us right away and so did the patrolman stationed at the school's entrance. Two police cars went after the speeding black van, and four more formed a blockade at both ends of town. That van can't get out of town, and we'll be combing the entire town looking for it and the men driving it. They won't get away this time."

Mom said, "Tommy, please let us know the minute those men are caught. None of us should have to live with this feeling of impending doom." She sighed deeply. "Of course, Gaynes will probably just send more of these criminal types. I don't understand why no one's been able to find him."

"Well, now that we finally have a picture of Gaynes, it won't be as easy for him to hide, wherever he is. Where did you find that picture, Cara?" the Chief asked.

"From our practice area next door. I painted it on my target. A friend of ours, who has seen Gaynes, said it was accurate."

The Chief frowned. "Cara, how were you able to paint an accurate picture of a man you've never seen?"

"I saw him in a nightmare right after my kidnapping."

My father added, "We've learned recently that Cara's dreams seem to be somewhat prophetic."

The Chief nodded slowly and looked at me. "Do me a favor, please. Next time you have a dream that seems prophetic, if it has anything at all to do with these present threats, please call me. Sometimes a little advance warning is helpful." Maybe that bad feeling I'd had *was* a little advance warning.

The Chief looked curious as he asked, "Do any of your friends have abilities like yours?"

"Well, Kevin and I both trained in archery and knife throwing over the summer. He's very good at both. But I don't know whether he's carrying a knife with him. I'll ask."

He gave me a hard look. "I didn't know that you were going to school armed with knives. I understand why you need to feel you can protect yourself. I'm glad you were able to protect your friend today. The officer who was at school today is the only one, other than myself, who knows that you were armed. Gossip being what it is, the entire force probably knows by now that you're an expert with a knife." He sighed. "There will probably be some fallout. School administration will not be pleased."

I couldn't help feeling a little nervous. They couldn't throw me out of school, could they?

The Chief stood. "Thanks for the coffee. I'll be in touch if there's any change. Call me any time." Mom walked him to the door. A minute later I heard his car's big engine start up.

Mom came back into the kitchen looking worried. "We really have to discuss Cara's insistence on carrying her knives everywhere she goes. Cara, you could be suspended from school. Every school in the country forbids weapons on campus. I don't think Thornewood

High has a policy like that at present, but I'm sure that will change before this week is out."

"Mom, I was outside school when I used my knife, not inside. Won't that make a difference?"

She looked unsure. "Maybe. But the issue will be that you were carrying your knives while you were in school. That will have to change. We'll wait to hear from your principal, which I'm sure will be very soon." She sighed. My father sighed. I sighed. Thankfully, Conor smiled and winked at me.

Mom said, "Well, I'm in no mood to make dinner tonight. Why don't I call for pizza? Brian, Conor, do you like pizza?"

I could have predicted what my father would say. "What's pizza?"

Mom looked at me and said, "You can do the honors."

I explained. "Pizza is a thin layer of dough that's baked with tomato sauce, cheese, and a variety of other toppings. You'll love it."

My Dad and Conor looked at each other and shrugged. "We'll try it," my father said. I just wished that the Pizza Palace delivered, but we'd have to settle for pizza from the delivery shop downtown. I called and ordered two large pizzas with sausage, pepperoni, onions and mushrooms. "They'll deliver in about thirty minutes. Mom, do you want me to make a salad to go with?" She did, so I got busy pulling veggies out of the fridge and began chopping.

While Mom and Dad talked about the knife problem, and the unexpected attack on Amy today, Conor came over to the breakfast bar where I was chopping peppers and sat down. I may have been chopping harder than usual.

"Considering what happened this afternoon, you seem surprisingly calm."

I looked up into Conor's silvery eyes. I'd always been able to talk to Conor. He'd always seemed like the big brother I never had.

"To tell you the truth, my stomach has been in knots since I saw that black van speeding in front of school this afternoon. I know Mom is a nervous wreck now, and my father is feeling a lot of anger he's keeping inside. I'm trying not to make them feel worse.

"I used to feel safe, that nothing bad could possibly happen to me. That's what I thought up until last spring. It seems so naïve, so stupid, now."

He placed a hand on my shoulder. "You shouldn't have to live this way. Your friends shouldn't have to live this way. This is why your father doesn't sleep at night. He feels responsible for all of it.

Fortunately, you've been strong enough to handle it, even if you're doing a fair amount of acting."

He ran a hand through his thick hair. "I'm confident Gaynes will be stopped eventually. And then your life will be normal again. But you'll never be that naïve young girl again, will you? Perhaps that will give you a head start in your adult life." He smiled, those silvery eyes sparkling. "You're already a force to be reckoned with. The human world will have to be on their toes."

As usual, Conor said exactly what I needed to hear.

I looked up into those wise eyes. "Thanks, Conor. I'm really glad you're here."

He gave my shoulder a squeeze. "Always have been, always will be."

The doorbell rang and I rushed to the door. The pizzas were here. When I opened the door, it was Ryan's back I saw first. The poor deliveryman was standing in front of Ryan, looking confused.

"It's okay, Ryan. We ordered pizza to be delivered. If you'll let the deliveryman in, I might even give you a slice!"

Looking a little embarrassed, Ryan moved away from the door, saying "sorry" to the young man holding the pizzas. I paid the man, and minutes later, we were eating. I was curious to see the Elves' reaction to their first taste of pizza. When I saw their eyebrows pop up, I knew it was a hit.

I took two slices out to Ryan and waited to see his reaction. He sniffed it cautiously and then took a bite. A big grin followed a few seconds later. "This pizza is right up there with your ice cream sundaes, lass." During the summer, I had introduced our bodyguards to the joys of ice cream sundaes, which they all loved.

When I got back into the kitchen, the first pizza was gone, and my father and Conor were starting on the second. Mom was laughing at them. "Cara, better grab a slice now; it's not going to last long."

The pizza was gone ten minutes later and they started on the salad I'd made. It was fun watching a simple dinner of pizza and salad being enjoyed so thoroughly.

When I'd cleaned up the kitchen, and my father had been sure to tell us we could order pizza any time, I went upstairs to call Amy.

She picked up her phone, saying, "I'm glad you called. My folks haven't stopped frowning and wringing their hands since I told them what happened. I should have kept it to myself. My father's been pacing for hours." She sounded worn out.

"I'm sorry. Chief O'Donnell thinks the only reason that guy aimed at you was that you stood out from our little crowd with your red hair and that tomato red shirt you were wearing. He doesn't think that you were personally targeted."

"I will never wear anything but black again. You may have to come over and explain the Chief's theory to my parents; I'm not sure they'll believe me. They have elevated you to sainthood, by the way."

I groaned. "You know, Neal looked like more than just a bodyguard after those hit men took off. It looks like your relationship has heated up."

I could hear her smile in her voice. "Yeah, he's been extremely protective ever since the fire at the bakery. I'm not complaining."

"That's good news. Tell your folks everything is under control. The Chief said those guys can't get out of town. He'll catch them soon. By the way, let's meet inside the doors at school from now on. No sense taking chances."

"Absolutely. See you in the morning."

I called Kevin next, just to make sure he wasn't feeling he had a target on his back.

"Hey, Kev. How are you doing tonight? Is everything cool at your house?"

"Yeah, short stuff, it's quiet here. Mom's still out selling houses or something. I spent some time out in the backyard with my dad, and being with him helped me calm down. It's getting dark so he's watching the house from the woods, and I'm back inside." He chuckled. "I learned that Elves love pizza."

"We had pizza tonight too. My father is also a fan. We've introduced the Elves to meat loaf, ice cream sundaes, and now pizza. They've loved everything."

He added, "Tacos and Burritos are next. Do you think they'll like hot peppers?"

"Probably. By the way, we'll meet Amy and Sean inside the front door at school tomorrow. That was an order from the Chief. Standing outside just makes us targets."

After Kevin and I said good night, I was getting ready for a nice, long soak in the tub when my phone rang. It was Sean, sounding upset. I wondered who had called him.

"Hey, beautiful. Are you okay?"

"I'm fine. Who told you about our little problem outside school?"

"I wouldn't call an attempted shooting a little problem. Sandy spoke to Amy, then called me and filled me in. It sounds like we're all targets, doesn't it? Unfortunately, you and your knives can't be with all of us all of the time!"

I snorted. "Well, I can try as long as I don't get kicked out of school for carrying weapons to school."

"Does anyone at school know you carry knives with you?"

"Not until now. The Chief said the one patrolman who saw what happened at school will probably be spreading the word as we speak." I sighed. "He thinks the entire police force will soon be aware of my skill in knife-throwing. From there, everyone in town will probably know by tomorrow."

"Oh. I guess that won't go down well with school authorities, will it?"

"Nope. Mom says all we can do is wait to hear from them. I just hope they won't suspend me. The thing is, I didn't use my knife inside school. We were outside when those creeps drove by and pulled a gun."

"I don't think they should penalize you for saving someone's life. That would be ridiculous."

"I know, but I can understand why weapons shouldn't be allowed on any school campus. Think about all the school shootings that have been happening all over the country. Mom thinks Thornewood will have a no weapons policy by the end of this week."

"Yeah, I can see that happening, and I understand the reasoning for it. At least I think we're all safe when we're inside school. Between the police and our bodyguards, I can't see any of Gaynes' goons getting inside the building, can you?"

"No, I feel safe inside school. But we still have to get to and from school. That's when I feel vulnerable."

"Well, I think the Chief is right about keeping our group together as much as possible. By the way, Kevin learned knife-throwing with you over the summer, didn't he?"

"Yeah. But I don't think he carries his knives with him like I do. After today, he might. And I think he should. He can throw a knife as well as I can. And I know our bodyguards have their knives on them. I saw proof this afternoon."

After a few seconds of silence, his voice was soft as he said, "I know we're all at risk, but you're the one I worry about. You're that lunatic's primary target. I remember that you were practicing non-lethal methods of archery and knife throwing. But if Gaynes comes after you himself, I hope you'll be able to stop him permanently."

"Sean, if I ever come face to face with Donald Gaynes, he won't walk away."

"Okay. I just wanted to make sure you weren't having some kind of delayed reaction to what almost happened this afternoon. I keep forgetting how strong you are. You know how I feel about you, but I want you to know how much I admire you." I was at a loss for words. A few quiet seconds passed. Then he said, "See you at school in the morning."

"Night, Sean."

As I soaked in a tub full of herbal-scented bubbles a little while later, I thought about Sean. I knew he wanted to be more than my friend. And then a pair of cobalt blue eyes popped into my mind.

I wondered who would be starring in my dreams tonight.

CHAPTER 21

When I climbed out of the tub, I realized I hadn't sung for Rowenna in a day or two. I could hear Mom and Dad talking in the kitchen. It sounded like the subject of their discussion was my knives. This was probably a good time to stay out of the kitchen.

Instead, I opened one of my bedroom windows and hoped Rowenna would hear me. With my elbows on the window sill, I leaned out and started humming her song. It was only a few minutes before I felt magic in the air and the sound of heavy wings beating their way toward me. I began softly singing the words to the dragon's song, the melody drifting from my window into the forest and the sky. As she came closer, her magic wrapped around me like a blanket of silk.

When I sang the last few lines, I looked down and was shocked to see the gleam of Rowenna's scales on the ground. There was a Dragon. Sitting. In my backyard. My mother would have a stroke. I no longer heard voices coming from the kitchen. What I did hear was that familiar, rusty voice in my head. *Beautiful, Cara. Thank you. When I hear you sing, my heart sings.*

What should I say? Honesty was usually the best policy. I had nothing else.

"Rowenna, my mother is human. She doesn't know anything about dragons, or about you. My father and I were afraid it would upset her, and we really don't like to upset her."

Cara, I am sorry. I'll leave now.

I sighed. "I'm afraid it's too late. You're about to meet my mother."

I put on my bathrobe and ran down the stairs to the kitchen. I wasn't surprised to find my mother at the kitchen window, hands on her hips. My father was still sitting at the table. Judging by the tight expression on his handsome face, he was braced for trouble. I stopped by his chair and he whispered, "I think she'll probably accept an explanation better from you, dear."

I walked to the window, reached for Mom's hand. "Let's go out on the porch. There's someone out there I want you to meet." Mom turned to me, her eyes huge, and asked, "Is it safe out there?"

THE DRAGON'S SONG

I nodded and she took my hand. I led her out on the porch, faced Rowenna, and said, "Rowenna, this is my mother, Alicia. I love her very much." Then I turned to Mom. "I'd like you to meet my friend Rowenna. She was my grandmother's friend too."

It was full dark outside now, so the dragon wasn't completely visible. The light from the house and from the almost-full moon shone on her scales, creating a strange, glittery creature of some kind sitting in the grass. The only things that were clear were her bright, golden eyes.

Mom said softly, "Hello, Rowenna. I'm always happy to meet Cara's friends. Although I have to admit, you are quite a surprise."

I could hear the dragon's rough chuckles. *I am happy to meet Cara's mother. Alicia. A beautiful name. Please know that I will protect Cara just as you always have. She is a special child. You are lucky.*

I had heard Rowenna's words in my mind, but I was amazed to hear Mom say, "My daughter is the light of my life. I'm happy to know she has yet another protector to keep her safe. Thank you, Rowenna. By the way, I like your song too. It's lovely."

Chuckling again, the huge dragon spread her wings and gracefully rose into the sky. I looked at Mom. "You can hear her words too, can't you?"

"Yes. Your father once told me I was a surprisingly good receiver, although I can't send a message the way he can."

"So, you're not upset about the dragon?" I was still surprised at how calm she'd been.

Shaking her head, she took my hand and led me back inside where my father waited for us, looking far more relaxed than he had when I came downstairs.

We sat down at the table and she said, "With all the fantastic changes in your life during the past three or four months, I guess I shouldn't have been surprised to learn that as unbelievable as it seems, you have a friend who happens to be a dragon."

She turned to my father. "I think I've reached my limit, Brian. I love you both, but I need a break." She sounded exhausted. Then she simply closed her eyes and put her head down on her arms.

My father looked at me, clearly worried. He got up and moved to the chair next to hers. At first he hesitated, but then he simply reached around her and pulled her over against his broad chest. Wrapping his arms around her, he started whispering things I couldn't hear.

It was time for me to go to my room.

Unfortunately, there were no pleasant dreams that night. I kept seeing a hand holding a gun pointed at me.

CHAPTER 22

The next morning I drove around the corner with Ryan and picked up Kevin and Patrick. It was early enough that we found a parking space almost in front of school. Sean's father drove up right after we did, dropping off Sean, Amy, Gabe, and Neal just as we reached the main doors.

Inside the main entrance, Amy reached out and grabbed me, hugging me tightly. "Cara, you will always be my very best friend no matter how old we are. You saved my life yesterday! I think it took all night for the whole thing to sink in."

Once I could breathe, I hugged her back. "What are friends for?" That broke the tension and got everyone smiling.

Kevin put his arm around Amy and said, "So you're wearing nothing but black now?" Amy was dressed completely in black from head to toe. She'd even painted her nails black.

She looked at me. "I don't want to stand out. Ever. Again." Kevin surprised me by bending down and kissing Amy's cheek. His voice was husky as he added, "You'd stand out in a burlap bag, Red."

Of course, when he realized what he'd done, he turned bright red. With a grin, Amy kissed him back. "Thanks, Kev. I needed that."

I must have been a little slow that morning, but I finally realized there was an arm around my shoulders. I looked up at Sean, who was gazing at me with so much affection in his eyes, I could feel my face turning pink. I was about to remind him that we were just friends when the first bell rang and the principal stepped out of his office and motioned to me.

"Miss Connelly, may I have a word?" Mr. Weiss was an easygoing man and a favorite of the student body, so I wasn't too nervous. But I knew the word he wanted would be about the knives I carried.

Sean gave my shoulder a squeeze and whispered, "good luck." Amy and Kevin left for their classes, both giving me the thumbs up sign. I followed Mr. Weiss into his office.

"Please sit down." He sat down behind a big desk that was piled high with papers and file folders. "I think you know what we have to discuss. Chief O'Donnell stopped at my house last night to explain exactly what happened after school yesterday."

His dark eyes were sympathetic. "He also filled me in on some things that I wasn't aware of. I didn't know about your kidnapping last spring, or about the threats you received just recently. I have to admit that I was rather curious about the group of new students who showed up last spring, and then again when school began yesterday. But the head of the School Board insisted that they had to be admitted right away, and they do seem like nice young men."

He smiled and I knew he understood more than he was saying. "I now know that these boys are bodyguards for you and your friends. I completely support the need to protect our students. And I understand that you did exactly that yesterday when you threw a knife at a gunman who was aiming at Amy Strauss.

"I understand why you feel you have to protect yourself. But with the police presence in school now, and the fact that you and your friends have bodyguards with you at all times, I don't believe that you need your weapons when you're here, attending classes. You've always been a good student, a well-behaved young lady; you've never been in trouble of any kind. I know that none of our students are in any danger from you. Nevertheless, I can't allow you, or any student, to be inside this school armed with weapons." My heart dropped a little.

"So here's what I propose we do. Come to my office every morning when you arrive at school, and turn your knives over to me for safekeeping. When you leave at the end of the school day, I will return them to you. Is this a solution you can live with?"

"I think so, Mr. Weiss. You're being more than fair. To be honest, I expected to be suspended."

He smiled and stood. "I'm glad we've been able to settle this without bloodshed." He nodded. "You can feel safe here at Thornewood High. I wish I could say the same for the world outside our doors. Now hand me your knives and then you can get to class."

I pulled my knives out of my boots and he put them in the top drawer of his desk. "I'll see you at three o'clock. Have a good day."

I left his office feeling a great sense of relief, as Ryan and I rushed to my Science class. When I slid into my seat next to Sean, he mouthed, "Is everything okay?" I nodded and smiled, and he reached for my hand and squeezed it.

There was so much stuff swirling around in my head, I don't

remember much about that class, but I promised myself I'd read a few chapters in my textbook that night.

On our way to History, Sean said, "Weiss didn't suspend you, did he?"

"No, Mr. Weiss was really cool about it. I just have to hand over my knives when I get to school, and he'll return them to me when I leave."

"Well, that's a great solution. Weiss obviously understands the situation."

"Yep. Chief O'Donnell paid him a visit last night. Mr. Weiss was really great."

We'd reached the door to History class before I realized my hand was wrapped up in Sean's. I guess it felt so natural, I never noticed when he took my hand. I looked up at him, slightly confused.

He dropped my hand, sighed and pulled me away from the door. "I know that to you, I'm just your friend. But to me, you're a lot more than a friend." He looked down, turning slightly away from me. "If you don't want me to touch you, or even hold your hand, just tell me."

I could almost hear his heart pounding, and I heard his voice in my mind. *"I can't stay away from her. She needs me even if she doesn't realize it."*

My heartbeat picked up a little too. I couldn't hold back a smile, so I took his hand and muttered, "Shut up, Sean," and pulled him into class. The relieved smile on his face showed me he was happy.

During class, I found myself thinking of Adam sporadically. I felt slightly disloyal but didn't understand why.

At lunch everyone was relieved I hadn't been suspended. Our bodyguards glanced at each other and Ryan said very softly, "It's a good thing we're not being searched." It was only then that I remembered that our bodyguards were well armed too. I looked around to make sure no one would hear us. "How many knives are all of you carrying?"

Ryan said four, Gabriel three, Patrick two, and Neal two. I was grateful.

When we were leaving the lunchroom, Sean again put his arm around my shoulder and said he'd call me that night. I wouldn't see him after school because of football practice. He smiled and told me that Coach was trying, unsuccessfully, to recruit Gabriel for football. He gave my shoulder a squeeze and left us with Gabe on his heels.

After my last class, Ryan and I stopped at Mr. Weiss' office where he returned my knives and told Ryan, "Take good care of her."

We met Kevin, Amy, Patrick and Neal at the front entrance and walked out together. When we were all safely inside my big car, I breathed a sigh of relief.

Kevin said, "Nobody seemed very hungry at lunch today. If any of you have recovered your appetite, we have three things to celebrate today. First, Cara's not being suspended from school. Second, no one tried to kill us today. And third, I just received a big check for 'Zombie Revenge.' The video game producer I work with loved it and added a nice bonus to my check. Burgers and milkshakes at The Grille are on me."

Amy and I both congratulated him. She said, "You're probably Thornewood High's most successful entrepreneur, Kev. I think we'll all be happy to help you spend some of that big money."

I grinned at Kevin and muttered, "Last of the big time spenders, huh?"

He laughed. "Well, girls and boys, what good's money if you don't spend it? I've got my eye on some new computer gear too. And," he chuckled, "as a gift for my mother, I'm going grocery shopping after school tomorrow. I plan to fill up that huge, empty refrigerator-freezer sitting in the kitchen. I'm beginning to feel guilty about mooching meals from Cara's mom all the time."

"Well, that kinda hurts, Kev," I said. "We love having you come over for meals. If you stop coming over, Mom will be disappointed."

From the back seat, I heard laughter. Patrick said, "I'll be happy to take his place."

We all laughed, and for a while, I wasn't thinking about threats or men with guns.

CHAPTER 23

When the doorbell rang after dinner, my father opened it to find Chief O'Donnell on the front porch. He'd stopped by to let us know his men had found the two men in the black van. They'd been hiding in Gaynes' empty office building at the edge of town. They admitted they'd been hired by an unnamed third party to come to Thornewood and cause trouble for a certain list of people. The kind of trouble specified included shootings, arson, kidnappings, and anything else the men could come up with. They'd been given our names, addresses, and even pictures taken from our Facebook pages.

Even though both men were now in jail, I felt terribly vulnerable, realizing how much information about us was available to the criminal world. Just thinking about it made me feel slightly nauseated.

The Chief sat down at the table with us and warned us not to feel over-confident about our safety. He felt sure Gaynes would just hire more men to come after us. I was sure he was right.

Mom had recently developed dark circles under her eyes. She handed the Chief a cup of coffee. "So we just wait for the other shoe to drop. Do you know who the third party is?"

"All we have is a phone number, but every law enforcement agency is working on it. Gaynes can't stay hidden forever. For the time being, nothing will change here in town. The police will continue to be everywhere, plainclothes police will continue to be present inside school, and I'm sure we can count on your men, Brian, to keep an eye on everyone."

My father said, "Of course. And we appreciate everything the police force is doing."

When Chief O'Donnell got up to leave, my father walked him to the door. I heard them speaking in low tones out on the front porch.

Mom stood to put the empty coffee cups in the sink. "Cara, you should call your friends, just to let them know they're safe, at least for tonight."

"Good idea. We can all get one good night's sleep. I don't know about the others, but I seem to wake up every hour, thinking I'm hearing a noise outside."

Mom smiled sadly. "Me too, dear."

I ran upstairs and curled up on my bed with Ralph in his usual spot at the foot of the bed. I called Amy first since she was the one who'd been the most recent target.

"Hey, Cara, any news?"

"The two men in the black van have been arrested. They couldn't identify Gaynes, though. They never met him. The Chief is fairly certain that Gaynes will be sending more men, but at least for now, we can feel safer."

"Well, my folks will be a lot happier just knowing that those two guys are in jail. Is the police presence going to change now? I really hope they'll continue to be visible everywhere in town until Gaynes is in jail. I don't know about you, but I won't feel completely safe until that happens." She sighed. "This has sure put a damper on our senior year plans." I felt the same way.

"The Chief isn't changing anything. The police will be fully present for the duration." I chuckled. "Petty crime in Thornewood will probably be non-existent for a while. I'm looking forward to a good night's sleep. I've been awake a lot every night this week."

She snorted. "I've been doing push-ups and sit-ups every night until I was exhausted. If nothing else, I'll be in superb physical shape when all of this is over."

"Sleep well tonight. See you tomorrow."

I called Kevin next and gave him the news.

"I wonder how long this break will last, babe. I imagine more bad guys will be on their way. I thought we were going to enjoy senior year."

"Yeah, I was looking forward to that too. But since we have to be on guard for the time being, I was wondering about something. Do you have your knives on you?"

He hesitated. "We haven't talked about it, and to be honest, I wasn't planning on it. But after the Molotov cocktail was thrown at Amy's house on Monday, I decided to have a few knives on me, so I can reach one in a hurry."

"Are you going to turn yours in to Mr. Weiss every morning like I'm doing?"

"Uh, no. Not until I have to. You have to remember, because of your kidnapping, you have a perfect reason to carry a weapon. I'm sure Mr. Weiss took that into account. I don't have that excuse, so rather than risk being suspended, I'll just carry my knives quietly. So please don't even tell Amy, okay?"

"It'll be our secret. I just hope you won't need them, Kev."

"You and me both, babe."

I figured Sean would call a little later, so I took a quick shower and blew my hair dry so I wouldn't have to get up as early in the morning. I was in my pajamas and ready for bed when the phone rang.

"Hi beautiful." Hearing that greeting each time he called was making me nostalgic. No one but Sean had ever called me beautiful. When we were first dating, that greeting in Sean's warm, deep voice had always given me chills. The good kind. I took a deep breath and reminded myself to rein it in. Sean was only a friend.

I had learned recently, however, that there were different degrees of friendship, and blue-eyed Adam was a different kind of friend. If "friend" was the right word.

"Hi, Sean. There's finally some good news." I told him about the arrest of the two men who had been plaguing us, but explained that the Chief thought there would probably be more on the way.

"I wonder how long it will be before the next crew arrives."

"No idea. It could be days or weeks. Who knows how many felons Gaynes has on his rolodex."

"Well, we might have a few days to relax. That at least covers our first football game Friday night. You guys are all coming, aren't you?"

"You bet. We wouldn't miss it." I was too embarrassed to tell him I'd never been to one of Thornewood's football games. "I'm sure our bodyguards will love it. Gabe's not playing, is he?"

He laughed. "No, as much as he'd like to. Coach will have Gabe on the bench, which is about as close to the action as he can get. It's really too bad he can't play. He's big, fast, smart and totally fearless. I know Coach would love to put him on the team."

We said good night, and I went to my bedroom window. The woods were full of lights. My father's camp must be fully occupied tonight. I thought of Rowenna, alone on her mountain, and began humming her song. When I felt magic stirring in the air, I sang the words softly, knowing she'd hear them. When I'd finished, I heard her rough voice in my mind. *Thank you, child. I'll be watching your house. Sleep well.*

Feeling reassured for several reasons, I said good night to Mom and Dad and got into bed. I was almost ready to close my eyes when I heard another voice in my mind, a soft voice I hadn't heard in a week.

Cara, I've been thinking of you all week. Your father has kept me informed so I know you're unharmed, but I've been worried about how you're handling the stress. How are you feeling?

I whispered, "Adam. I'm holding it together, just trying to take it one day at a time. As long as we don't have another bad storm, I should be okay."

Will you be needing me this weekend? Is there anything you want to do outside school?

"Yes! Thornewood's first football game is Friday night. We're all going. Will you be joining us?"

Absolutely. I'm looking forward to it. When you're not around, Cara, my life is much too quiet. He chuckled.

"See you Friday, Adam."

Good night, love.

For the first time that week, I relaxed. I closed my eyes and drifted off, knowing that my father was in the next room, Adam was thinking of me, and a protective dragon was flying overhead. It was a good night.

CHAPTER 24

The rest of the week was actually what we used to call "normal." No more Molotov cocktails, no new threats on Facebook, and no men pointing guns at us. I was afraid we were being lulled into a false sense of security, but I tried to enjoy it while it lasted.

The atmosphere in and out of class on Friday was positively electric. With our first football game of the season scheduled that night, Sean and the other football players were high-fiving and fist bumping all day. It was hard not to share Sean's good mood.

But then I remembered that it was Adam who would be taking me to the game tonight, and my fickle heart started beating a little faster.

Since Kevin hadn't had a chance to drive his new Jeep all week, he would be our designated driver tonight. The game would start at six thirty, so we had sandwiches for dinner. I wrapped up a few for Kevin and our bodyguards, and when I walked out the front door, I found Adam waiting for us on the porch. He greeted me with that devastating smile, and it was all I could do not to throw myself at him and force one of those forbidden hugs on him.

We stood on the porch grinning at each other until Kevin's Jeep pulled up at the curb. I got the feeling Adam had really missed me this week, and my stomach was full of butterflies. I told them sternly to quiet down.

He took my hand and we ran out to Kevin's car and climbed into the back seat. Patrick was in the front with Kevin. I was quite pleased with the seating arrangement. When I looked over at Adam, he looked pleased too. For this brief moment in time, all was right with my world, even though I knew it couldn't last.

The parking lot behind the football field was already packed. As Kevin drove around the lot slowly, he finally said, "I'll have to get creative." He created a parking spot right behind the refreshment stand, muttering, "Hope I don't get towed."

When we walked around the refreshment area, we found one of the plainclothes cops keeping an eye on the crowd. Kevin walked up to him to let him know where he'd parked his Jeep, and the cop said he'd keep an eye on it.

Amy would be riding to the game with Sean's father. We'd arranged to meet at a certain spot in the stands where we wouldn't stand out, just in case we were being watched.

No sense making it easy for our enemies, wherever they were.

Amy's red hair made her easy to find, despite the fact she was dressed completely in black: black jeans and tennis shoes, black sweatshirt, and, of course, black nail polish. No one would ever accuse Amy Strauss of being less than perfectly coordinated.

She and Mr. McKay waved to us from the middle row of stands, and we climbed the stairs until we reached their row. There wasn't much room on either side of them so we were really pressed close together, something no one seemed to mind. Kevin and Patrick maneuvered around Mr. McKay, and sat down close to Amy and Neal, while Adam and I sat on their other side.

I'd always disliked crowds, but being in the midst of enthusiastic teens and their families was kind of fun, especially with Adam close at my side. The excitement surrounding Thornewood's first football game felt amazing. The cheerleaders were down at the edge of the field jumping, doing cartwheels, and chanting some version of "Go Team Go." They looked fantastic in their red skirts and white sweaters, tossing red pompoms in the air as they yelled the name of each player. We couldn't miss the applause when Sean's name was heard. He seemed to be everyone's favorite quarterback. I only knew which position he played because Mr. McKay explained it to me. He'd have to explain a lot more to me once the game started. I knew almost nothing about the game of football. Maybe it was time for me to learn.

Adam was about as close to me as he'd ever been, thanks to the crowd, and he leaned down and said, "I hope you're going to explain this game to me. It's not one I'm familiar with."

Mr. McKay was going to have his work cut out for him tonight. He'd already told us about the opposing team, wearing black and gold, called the Cougars. They were from another small town named Miller's Creek, about thirty miles away. He said the two teams were well matched, both from small schools. We'd be playing Greenville in a few weeks, a much larger school, and a much greater challenge for little Thornewood.

The teams took their places on the field and the game began. Mr. McKay was tossing out terms like "first down, second down, fumble, field goal," and so on. I was trying to understand the action on the field, but it was a struggle. Adam, on the other hand, seemed to follow it more easily. At the end of the first half, the score was 0 to 6, in favor of the visiting team. Mr. McKay explained that Sean had made three good passes but the player receiving the ball had immediately been buried under the other team's defense. He muttered, "They've got to try another tactic. Maybe Sean should just run the ball. He's fast enough."

During half time, the cheerleaders were doing their rah-rah thing out on the field, trying to stir up the Thornewood crowd. It seemed to be working. People around us in the stands were cheering. Many were clapping.

When the second half began, the players were running back on the field, taking their positions when one of Thornewood's players suddenly dropped to the ground. I couldn't tell who it was, but Mr. McKay was already pushing his way over to the stairs and was running out of the stands to the field. I was right behind him, and Adam was close at my back. Had it been Sean? My heart was in my throat.

When we got to the edge of the field, we couldn't see the player who had fallen. He was surrounded by coaches, referees, and the rest of the team. Gabriel ran over to us. "It's not Sean. It's another player Sean's size. I thought I heard a sharp crack just as he fell. It sounded like a shot, maybe a rifle."

Adam turned around looking at the hills surrounding the field. He pointed to the closest hill. "I can see someone running down that hill, heading for the street." It was too far away for any of us to reach in time.

I pulled out my cell phone and called the Chief. When I told him a player might have been shot and where we'd seen a possible shooter, he said, "I've got a patrol car in that area. I'm on my way."

Mr. McKay was still with the crowd surrounding the injured player when the ambulance pulled on the field. The downed player was loaded on the vehicle, and it pulled away immediately, sirens blaring.

When the crowd cleared away from where the boy had collapsed, I saw Sean. He was looking right at me. I mouthed, "Are you okay?"

He nodded, then mouthed, "It should have been me," as he hit himself in the chest. I was afraid he was right. I nodded. With his hands on his hips, he turned his head away and I could almost hear a certain four-letter word that I'd never heard him use before. He looked at me again and I mouthed, "I'm sorry." He nodded, pulled his helmet back on and walked away to rejoin the team clustered at the side of the field with their coaches.

Mr. McKay walked back to us. "The game is being stopped. The police are already evacuating the stadium. We have to leave now."

Police were now in the stands, directing people to the exit, doing their best to keep everyone calm.

Something was making me jumpy. I realized I was picking up Sean's emotions and he was angry. Really, seriously angry.

My hand was wrapped up in Adam's as we pushed our way through the crowds leaving the field. I wondered if the police had caught the man we'd seen running from the hill beyond the football field. I began to shiver and Adam's hand tightened around mine.

Mr. McKay was going to wait for Sean, so Amy and Neal would ride home with the rest of us. Kevin's Jeep would be packed. It was still parked behind the refreshment stand, but when we walked up to it, I thought my heart was going to explode out of my chest.

"Don't touch the Jeep," I shouted.

Kevin looked up at me just as his hand was about to open the door.

"Something's wrong, Kev. We have to find one of the police and have your car checked."

He backed off, still staring at me. Everyone backed away from the Jeep, looking at me like I'd just sprouted a second head. Adam tucked me under his arm securely.

Kevin moved closer to me and said softly, "Are you sure, Cara?" I nodded and he walked back to the field to find a cop.

Amy leaned down and whispered, "What's happening with you, sweetie?"

I shook my head. "I'm not cracking up. I think something's been done to the Jeep. They could kill a bunch of us at the same time, right? The air around the Jeep doesn't feel right. I don't know if it's possible to feel evil, but I could feel it more strongly the closer I got to the Jeep."

Adam leaned down to ask, "A premonition?"

"No, not exactly. I just know the Jeep isn't safe."

I saw Neal and Patrick exchanging glances, eyebrows raised. They probably thought my brain had sprung a leak, but I didn't care.

Kevin and a uniformed officer jogged around the refreshment stand a few minutes later. The officer came up to me and asked

THE DRAGON'S SONG

quietly, "Are you sensing something, Cara?" The Chief must have told his men about my premonitions.

"Officer, please check the Jeep for something explosive. Or maybe cut brakes or something. I'm sure it's been tampered with." He nodded and said, "Okay, I'll radio for our bomb expert. But I want you kids to back off now. Go stand on the field until we're done."

The field was a good distance away from the refreshment stand, so we trooped over there, Adam holding my hand, Kevin holding Amy's, Patrick and Neal right behind us.

Two police cars arrived, lights blinking, headed for the area we'd just left. Adam said, "There are benches on the other side of the field. Let's go wait over there." I was sure he was trying to get us even farther away from Kevin's Jeep. We saw another police car pull up and a man wearing a helmet and wrapped in a quilted suit of some kind emerged, heading for the refreshment stand.

Kevin said, "He must be the bomb expert."

Turning to me, Amy asked, "Cara, what exactly did you feel?"

I shrugged. Now that I was this far away from the Jeep, I wasn't feeling the evil vibes I'd felt before. "It's hard to describe. My heart suddenly started pounding and the air around the Jeep felt sick, like someone had died there."

Kevin chuckled. "Of course, if they don't find anything, you're going to feel like an idiot, babe." He was sitting next to me so I kicked him. Hard. Kevin needed to learn when teasing me was not acceptable.

While we waited for the police to do their job, we started talking about the boy who'd been shot. Even Amy didn't know him. Kevin said, "His name is David Somers. He only moved to Thornewood last year, so this is his first year playing football. He's a quiet kid, never says much. I don't think he's made many friends yet. He's Sean's size and moves well, which is why Coach grabbed him for the team. Now that I think about it, he and Sean are even built alike. In their uniforms, from a distance, you really wouldn't be able to tell them apart."

Amy gasped. "Do you think Sean was the target, and the wrong kid got shot?"

I nodded. "Sean thinks so too. He was upset and really angry. We had a little non-verbal communication while David was being taken away in the ambulance.

"We still don't know how badly David's been hurt. Sean must feel awful. He thinks David got shot because of him."

There was no more conversation after that.

It must have been a half hour later before we saw the police cars pulling away from the refreshment stand. One car drove around the field and stopped right behind us. The first officer we'd talked to got out and walked over to me.

"Your ESP was right on the money. There was a bomb mounted under the rear bumper. It would have been set off remotely, probably by a cell phone. The Chief will tell you more later. You kids can drive home safely now. I'll give you a lift back to your car. Hop in."

We squeezed into the police car and Officer Browning drove us back to Kevin's Jeep.

We got out at Kevin's Jeep and just stood there, looking at it for a few seconds. Everyone looked at me. I walked around the car, waiting for my antenna to go up, but when that didn't happen, I said, "It feels okay now."

Kevin's car wasn't really designed to hold six, so I sat on Adam's lap. Even then, it was a tight squeeze. I felt a little guilty because I was perfectly comfortable although Adam didn't seem to be. He barely looked at me on the ride home.

We'd just pulled up in front of Amy's house when my cell phone rang. It was Chief O'Donnell.

"Are you still with your friends?" I said I was. "It might be a good idea for you to stick together for a few hours. I'll need to talk to all of you. Can you all stay in one place for a while?"

I asked him to hold on while I relayed what he'd said and asked Kevin and Amy if they'd like to come to my house.

They agreed; Amy just wanted to run into her house and let her parents know where she'd be. She wanted Neal to stay there with her parents. I told the Chief we'd all be at my house, and he said he'd see us in about an hour.

As soon as Amy returned, Kevin headed to my house. I said, "The Chief may have information about the shooter and about David's condition. It'll probably be easier for him to talk to all of us together."

Amy added, "I hope it's not bad news." I didn't say anything; I had a sick feeling in the pit of my stomach.

We reached my house just as a police car pulled up in front. It must have been one of the cars called to the football field earlier. The driver waved to us as we got out of the Jeep. Patrick ran around the corner to keep an eye on Kevin's house, and Adam sat down in a chair on the front porch, after giving my shoulder a gentle squeeze.

My parents were sitting in the kitchen enjoying Mom's favorite red wine. My father stood up when we walked into the kitchen. "How was the game?" he asked, smiling.

Amy and Kevin both looked at me. "There was a serious problem. The game was cancelled." My mother put her glass down, closing her eyes for a few seconds.

She forced herself back to normal hostess mode quickly. "Amy, Kevin, please sit down. Would you all like coffee?"

"Don't get up, Mom. I'll make coffee and a pot of tea. We'll need it. Chief O'Donnell is coming over. He said he has news for us."

As I made a fresh pot of coffee and boiled water for tea, I began telling them about the shooting at the game. Kevin told them what he knew about David, and that he'd been shot when he ran in front of Sean, which suggested that Sean was the real target.

My parents looked shocked, then sick. My father's eyes again turned into green lasers, and his face looked like it had been chiseled out of stone.

I put the coffee pot and cups on the table. "I'm afraid there's more."

Mom just put her head in her hands, and Dad stood up and began to pace.

When I didn't say anything, Mom lifted her head and said, "Talk to us, Cara. We'd better hear it all."

Amy was sitting next to Mom and she put her hand over Mom's. Kevin had been next to my father. I wasn't sure how to explain my extrasensory experience with Kevin's car.

Kevin began, "Cara saved us from being blown up in my car. During the game, a bomb had been placed under the rear bumper." He gave me a strange look. "I don't know how she did it, but she knew there was something wrong with the car. She wouldn't even let me unlock the door. I brought a cop back to where I'd parked and he called for their bomb specialist. We waited on the field until they'd gone over my car thoroughly, found the bomb and disabled it."

I sat down on Mom's other side and she grabbed my hand. I could see she was trying to hold back tears. "Mom, it's okay. I think we're all kind of shaky, but thankfully none of us was hurt. We're still waiting to find out how David is. Maybe the Chief will have news when he gets here."

Meanwhile, my father paced from one end of the kitchen to the other, his hands clenched at his side. I sent him a mental message: *Dad, please calm down. You're making me nervous.*

He turned around, looked at me, let out a deep breath and seemed to relax a little. He nodded, said, "Sorry," and sat down.

I refilled coffee cups, poured myself a cup of Kathleen's calming tea and sat down just as we heard a car door slam out front. Every muscle in my body tensed.

The Chief was here.

CHAPTER 25

My father went to the door and let in Chief O'Donnell. His expression was grim. The tension in my stomach had turned to nausea, but I did my best to appear calm.

I heard my father ask Adam to come in too. The Chief sat down at the table and Adam took a seat at the breakfast bar. Mom quickly poured the Chief a cup of coffee. He thanked her without saying anything else.

I took a cup of tea over to Adam and sat down at the bar with him. Being close to Adam's warmth seemed to relax my stomach a little.

The Chief was still silent. I think we all knew the news wasn't going to be good. Kevin and Amy exchanged worried glances.

Mom finally broke the silence by saying, "Tommy, we're all on edge. Please tell us why you're here."

Finally, he looked up at us and said, "We've got the man who took a shot from the hill. We found his rifle too." He picked up his cup for another sip of coffee, as though he was reluctant to continue.

My father said, "Who is he? Who sent him?"

The Chief said, "It hurts to admit this, but he was one of my men. He only joined the force a year ago. He'd been a Chicago cop before moving to Thornewood. While Gaynes was here trying to purchase land for his planned development, they became friends. That friendship didn't end when Gaynes started threatening you and Cara and making trouble for your friends." He looked disgusted. "We've had a snake in our midst all this time, feeding information to Gaynes."

My father asked, "So he's in jail now? Will you be able to keep him there? Does he know where Gaynes is?"

"He'll be in jail for the rest of his life. He refused to tell me where Gaynes is, but I'm not finished with him yet."

Kevin asked, "What about David Somers? Is he going to be okay?"

The Chief closed his eyes for a second. I knew the worst had happened.

He looked up at us and just shook his head. "I'm sorry to tell you this. David Somers died at the hospital shortly after he arrived there. The bullet pierced his helmet."

No one said a word. Suddenly Amy ran upstairs, looking green. I heard her throwing up in the bathroom. Mom got up and followed her upstairs.

I think my heart stopped briefly. If it hadn't been for Adam's warm hand holding mine, it might not have started beating again.

After a few minutes of silence, the Chief said, "I thought the McKays would be here too. I haven't spoken to them yet." He sighed deeply.

Kevin still looked dazed. "Was the shooter the same person who placed the bomb under my car?"

"I think so. I believe you actually told him where you'd parked your Jeep."

Kevin groaned. "That must have been the cop standing by the refreshment stand." He snorted. "I was afraid I'd get towed." He slapped himself in the head.

I was wondering if Sean and I had been right about who the intended target was. "Chief, Sean and David looked a lot alike in their uniforms. They were the same size, same height, same build. We think David might have been shot by mistake. The shooter might have aimed at Sean and David simply got in the way. What do you think?"

The Chief nodded, looking even sadder. "That thought crossed my mind too." He stood slowly. "Thanks for the coffee. I have to go talk to the McKays now." We heard his deep sigh.

My father stood and walked out with the Chief. I could hear their voices from the front porch.

Mom and Amy came back downstairs. Amy was paler than usual.

I saw tears running down her face. Kevin wrapped his arm around her shoulders, his head close to hers.

Mom had tears in her eyes when she said, "That innocent young boy, his life cut down for no reason. It's tragic. And it could happen to any one of you. That man has to be stopped!"

She sprang out of her chair and rushed to the front door. When the door closed, I could hear her voice. She was actually shouting at the Chief. I could barely hear my father's voice or the Chief's. Mom was really on a rant.

Adam leaned over and whispered, "I always knew that getting on your mother's bad side would be a very bad idea."

"She's afraid for all of us," I said. "So am I. I dream of guns and fires almost every night, and I wake up sweating. It's just that I don't know what else the police and Dad's men can do that they're not already doing."

Adam added, "They'll come up with something. I have a great deal of faith in your father and in Chief O'Donnell."

Amy muttered, "It's gonna take more than faith, Adam."

With David's death, the situation had become unbearable. I think we were all wondering who would be next.

CHAPTER 26

When Mom and Dad came back inside, they seemed surprised to find us sitting quietly. After one shock too many, I was kind of numb. Amy and Kevin weren't talking at all.

My father looked at us. "The Chief knows more has to be done to protect all of you." Glancing at my mother, he said, "Alicia has made that point quite clearly."

Kevin said, "Mr. Blackthorne, the entire police force is already working 'round the clock. Your men are all over town, staying out of sight, but watching everyone. What more can be done? The Chief can't call out the National Guard."

My dad shook his head. "I wish I had an answer. We're going to meet again in the morning. The Chief mentioned getting additional help from the Highway Patrol, but I don't know what additional steps can be taken." Turning to me, he asked, "Sean thinks that David was shot by mistake, doesn't he?"

"We all do. Sean was terribly angry, and I'm sure he's feeling guilty. He's going to be devastated when he learns that David didn't make it."

Mom was still standing in the doorway, her arms crossed over her chest. Finally, she walked over to each of us and hugged us tightly. Amy started crying again. Kevin said, "Please don't worry, Mrs. C. We're all going to be okay."

After she hugged me, my father put his arms around her. "We'll figure this out, Alicia. We won't let any more of our children get hurt."

Mom just shook her head, wiping the tears from her eyes. "I'm going upstairs to try to calm down. I'm sorry. I didn't mean to upset any of you. It's late. I think we all need to get some rest." She tried to smile. "Maybe things will look a little brighter tomorrow. I'll say good night now." She turned and climbed the stairs slowly.

Adam stood. "Kevin, I'll ride with you while you take Amy home. I believe Patrick is still at your house."

I walked Amy and Kevin to the door and promised to call them as soon as there was any more news. It was a sad end to what had started as a fun night at a football game.

My father still sat at the kitchen table, looking like his world had just imploded.

I poured him a cup of tea and sat down with him. "Dad, this isn't your fault, you know."

He shook his head, running his fingers through his hair. "It all started with me, Cara. Simply because I refused to sell a piece of the forest." He sounded sick at heart.

"No, Dad. It started because Donald Gaynes thinks he should get everything he wants. The man is clearly insane. He's responsible for two deaths now. You're not responsible for any of the things he's done."

He took my hand and held it. "In my mind I know you're right. But my heart feels otherwise. And I'm afraid your mother feels I'm at least partially to blame." He closed his eyes and squeezed my hand.

"Gaynes is a psychopath. No way are you responsible for him."

"Thank you, sweetheart." He gave me a smile that didn't reach his eyes. "It's late. You should go up to bed. I'll be down here for a while. I need to send a few messages to my men."

He kissed my cheek and I went up to my room. I stood in the shower until the water began to run cold.

Meditating in the shower helped a little. By the time I got into my pajamas, the knots in my stomach were almost gone, but the sadness over David Somers' death remained. By now, Sean had been told, and was probably in a great deal of emotional pain. It was late, but I had to call him.

When he picked up his phone, all he said was, "Cara." I could hear the pain in his deep voice.

"Sean, is Chief O'Donnell still there?"

"No, he left a little while ago. My father's still downstairs, but I needed some space so I'm in my room."

"Yeah, me too. I know it's late, but I had to call you. I think I know what you're feeling. I just wanted to let you know that I'm here if you want to talk. Amy and Kevin went home a little while ago. We're all sick about David. And my father feels like everything that's happened is his fault."

I heard a deep sigh. "I know how he feels. An innocent kid is dead because he ran too close to me. I can't help feeling responsible."

"It wasn't your fault. I wish I could convince you and my father of that. Every bad thing that's happened is because a psychopath didn't get what he wanted and now wants to hurt as many people in Thornewood as he can. Sean, do you think it would be better if *you'd* been killed?"

He didn't say anything for several seconds. "No. I don't have a death wish. I understand the logic in everything you're saying. It just hurts so bad, knowing that a kid I barely knew is dead. And shouldn't be. And *wouldn't* be if he didn't look like me in the uniform." I heard his voice break.

A few seconds of silence, then he whispered, "I'm sorry, but all my walls are down tonight. You know what I need right now? I wish I could be with you, holding you in my arms, kissing your sweet face. You're what I need, Cara. You're the only one who can heal my heart."

My heart was pounding. I felt so much for this boy, even though I couldn't tell him exactly what he wanted to hear. And I was feeling some guilt too.

"Sean, I feel sort of responsible for what you're going through."

"Why?" He sounded bewildered.

"If you'd never met me, never met my father, never gotten involved in our problems, you wouldn't be going through all of this now." I took a deep breath. "You don't deserve any of this."

His voice was soft. "The walls are still down tonight so I can tell you this. Knowing you has been worth anything I had to go through. I feel as though my whole life has been about loving you. Nothing else has been as important."

His words brought tears to my eyes, and a need deep inside of me that I didn't know what to do with.

"I'm here for you, whenever you need me.

His voice sounded better. "Thanks, beautiful. Just talking to you tonight has helped. But I'd better let you get to bed. Maybe we'll both be able to sleep now."

"I hope so. Listen, I don't know what will be going on here tomorrow, but if you don't have other plans, why don't you grab Gabe and come on over here. Plan to spend the day with me."

"That sounds really good. There's no one I'd rather be with. I'll call you in the morning, okay?"

"Okay. Try to get some sleep."

We said good night and I realized I felt a lot better than I had before I called him.

My sleep was full of dreams that night. I kept hearing a gun shot and seeing a boy in a red and white football uniform fall to the ground. I saw Sean standing over the boy's body, his helmet in one hand and tears running down his face.

That scene repeated, over and over, until I finally said, "Enough."

I got up just as the sky grew light and the forest birds began to sing their cheerful morning songs. They reminded me that life goes on, despite the grief, pain, and evil that at times seemed to be all around us.

CHAPTER ♥ 27

I was up earlier than usual, so I didn't expect to find anyone in the kitchen when I went downstairs. I was surprised to find my father standing in front of the coffee maker, just staring at it. I couldn't help smiling. "You have to do more than look at it to make coffee." He turned around, with a frustrated look on his face.

I hugged him. "Today I'll teach you how to make coffee." I handed him the coffee pot and had him fill it with water. He put in a fresh filter, scooped coffee out of the can, and within seconds, fresh coffee started dripping into the pot and there was a satisfied smile on my father's face.

"I still think it's easier to boil water in my fireplace. But making coffee isn't really that difficult." He dropped a kiss on my head. "Thank you, dear."

Mom came down the stairs and seemed surprised to find us both smiling. Dad said, "Can I pour you some coffee, Alicia? With a little help from Cara, I made it myself."

That put a smile on Mom's face. "It's really nice to come downstairs and find coffee waiting for me." She had a cup of Dad's first pot of coffee and still smiling, went upstairs to get dressed for work.

"Are you meeting with the Chief this morning, Dad?"

He nodded. "I'm waiting to hear from him. I'm not sure where we're meeting; it might be here. Are you feeling better this morning?"

"A little. I called Sean last night. He was really upset but I think talking about it helped both of us. I invited him to spend the day here. Maybe that will help too."

"Good idea. You and your friends can help each other recover from this tragedy."

There was a knock on the back door and I opened it to find Conor and Arlynn on the back porch.

I invited them in and was immediately wrapped up in Conor's arms.

"I was so sorry to hear about the shooting last night. Was the boy who was shot a friend?"

"He was new to Thornewood. I'm afraid no one knew him very well. Even the other football players didn't know much about him except that he was quiet. Sean feels terrible." I explained why Sean thought David had been shot by mistake.

Shaking his head, Conor said, "I only rode in this morning to accompany Arlynn. She's working at the store with your mother today. But I'd like to see Sean too."

"Well, you're in luck," I told him. "Sean's going to spend the day with me, so if you stick around for a while, he'll be here."

My phone rang. I looked at the display and smiled. "Synchronicity," I said.

"Hi, Sean. How are you feeling this morning?"

"Hi, beautiful. Talking to you last night really helped. I even got some sleep. I'm not calling too early, am I?"

"Actually, your timing is perfect. Conor's here. How soon can you come over?"

"Well, that's what I need to talk to you about. My dad needs his car today, so I'll need a ride."

"If either Conor or my Dad will ride shotgun, I can come over to pick you up now."

Conor said, "I'll go with you. Just to make sure Thornewood's mailboxes are safe, of course." He chuckled. I just shook my head.

My father was trying not to smile and not doing a very good job. "That may be a sore point. It's best to avoid mentioning mailboxes in Cara's presence."

Arlynn gave me a sympathetic look. "Don't pay any attention to them. Your mother told me you drive very well."

My father said, "Why don't you and Conor go pick up Sean now. I'd like to see him too."

Arlynn added, "So would I. I've heard so much about him, Cara."

Conor looked at me. "Shall we?"

"Sure. Just let me give Sean a quick call."

Sean was delighted, so Conor and I left by the front door. I was surprised to see Adam sitting on the porch.

"Adam, have you been here all night?" He must have; he looked tired.

He smiled. "The policeman out front fell asleep. I thought one of us should stay awake. Where are you going so early?"

Conor said, "We're going to pick up Sean and bring him over here for the day. Brian's inside. Why don't you go in now and get a cup of coffee."

Adam nodded and stood up to go inside. Conor walked me to my car and stood at the curb, looking my car over for a few minutes.

"What's the matter?" I asked him. "You're not nervous, are you? I can assure you I haven't hit anything in weeks," I grinned.

He smiled, his silvery eyes sparkling. "I hate to admit this, Cara, but I'm a lot more comfortable on a horse."

I started the car, racing the engine for a few seconds just to see his reaction. His eyes got big for that few seconds.

"You did that on purpose, didn't you?" he said.

I chuckled. "Don't worry. I really am a safe driver."

As we drove through town, we saw police cars on almost every block, and cops in uniform patrolling the downtown area. The police presence in Thornewood was impressive.

"Your police chief is doing everything he can to keep you and your friends safe. It's hard to believe that the man who shot that boy was one of his men."

"I'm sure the Chief is sick about it. That man had been in touch with Gaynes since last spring, feeding him any information he had. I guess the moral of that story is that even people you trust can fool you."

Conor looked over at me. "I hate hearing that kind of disillusionment from someone so young."

I shrugged. I didn't like it either.

We pulled up in front of Sean's house just as Sean and his father walked out. Conor got out to talk to Mr. McKay and gave Sean a hug before he walked around to my side of the car.

Sean leaned into my window and kissed my cheek. "Hi, beautiful." I was glad to see he was able to smile today.

"Hop in. Conor said he was hoping to see you, and there's someone else at the house who wants to meet you." I chuckled. "Prepare yourself."

He climbed into the back set and leaned forward, resting his arms on the back of my seat. "Who is it? Why the mystery?"

"You remember my mentioning Arlynn, don't you?"

"Yeah. I think you said she was too beautiful to be human, right?"

"Yep. Well, she's heard me mention you and since you and Conor are cousins, she wants to meet you. She and Conor are kind of attached." I couldn't help smiling. "They're perfect for each other."

"I'm looking forward to it." He sat back, smiling, as Conor got back in the car.

ᵗʰᵉDRAGON'S SONG

We waved goodbye to Mr. McKay and drove back to my house. As we drove through the downtown area, Sean muttered, "Cops everywhere. Thornewood's practically on lockdown. This is what Gaynes has done to us."

Conor said, "It's temporary. The man will be caught and thrown in jail."

I thought I heard Sean mumble, "Not soon enough."

When we got back to my house, we found my parents and Arlynn waiting in the kitchen. My mother got up and put her arms around Sean, which surprised him.

"I'm so sorry, Sean. I know you feel awful, but you must understand that what happened wasn't your fault. That horrible man is to blame."

"Thanks, Ms. Connelly. Cara's been telling me the same thing."

When Mom moved aside to let Sean walk into the kitchen, Arlynn stood up and came around the table to meet him. As I expected, Sean's mouth dropped open.

"Hello, Sean. I've been looking forward to meeting you." Just the sound of Arlynn's musical voice was enough to render Sean speechless. She put her hand out to him, and naturally, Sean just stood there. I elbowed him and he came back to life and shook her hand.

"Hi Arlynn. It's, uh, great to meet you."

Conor sat there, apparently unaware of Arlynn's effect on Sean. Of course, he saw Arlynn every day and had probably forgotten how amazingly beautiful she was.

My father put one arm around Sean. "I'm glad you're here today, son."

Everyone sat back down at the table and I made a pot of Kathleen's tea. Mom and Arlynn had just enough time to enjoy their tea before they had to leave for Mom's bookstore. When they left, Mom asked my father to keep her posted after he met with Chief O'Donnell, and Dad walked them outside to the car.

Conor turned to me and asked what we were planning to do all day. I suddenly had an inspiration.

"I'd like to take Sean to Dad's camp and introduce him to the greys. He's been fascinated ever since I told him about them. Do you think that would be okay?"

My father walked back into the kitchen and said, "Sounds good to me. And while you're at it, why not take Sean into Elvenwood and show him around." Sean's mouth dropped open.

If there was any way to take Sean's mind off what had happened the day before, my father had found it. I knew Sean would love it.

There was a big smile on Sean's face. "Mr. Blackthorne, are you sure it will be okay? I mean, I'm not a Halfling like Cara."

"You have Elven blood. Your grandfather is a Halfling, and your great-grandfather is an Elf. I think they'd both be delighted to see you."

Sean looked like his head was about to explode. "They're both in Elvenwood? Seriously?"

My father nodded with a smile. "Sean, we live so much longer than humans, at a certain point, we have to disappear from view so as not to raise questions. That's why your grandfathers now live in Elvenwood."

Sean looked dazed. He whispered, "I thought they had both passed away."

Conor asked, "Can you ride, Sean?"

"My father took us to a dude ranch for vacation two years ago. I rode every day while we were there. Ever since Cara told me about your greys, I've wanted to see them. Can I really ride one today?"

Seeing Sean's excitement put a genuine smile on my face.

My father nodded. "Absolutely. We have quite a few of our greys stabled at my camp. Conor will find one for you to ride. After breakfast, that is. Cara, would you be so kind as to make breakfast for us?"

Uh-oh. I hoped we had enough bagels for Sunrise Specials. I got up and went hunting for the ingredients and found bacon, tomatoes and cream cheese, everything I needed.

"I'll make Sunrise Specials for us. Good thing we have bagels 'cause it's the only thing I know how to make."

"You made one for me last spring. This is a treat," Sean said.

When they were ready, I took one out to the front porch to Adam, who thanked me with the usual gorgeous smile. "You're an angel. You must have known I was starving."

The Sunrise Specials were a hit. I'd made one for my father a few months ago, but it was a first for Conor.

Once we'd finished breakfast and Sean helped me clean up the kitchen, Conor walked us through the backyard and into the forest. My father stayed at the house, waiting to hear from Chief O'Donnell.

THE DRAGON'S SONG

As we walked past the stream where Sean and I had spent time together last spring, he looked at me and said softly, "Good memories, Cara. I hope we can come here again sometime."

They were lovely memories. We had sat under the trees. I drew pictures of the landscape while Sean read his dad's old science fiction novels. Those were the peaceful days, the wonderful days, before all the bad stuff started. I couldn't help sighing. He heard me and took my hand.

He whispered, "We'll come back one day and it'll be wonderful again."

I couldn't fool myself thinking about something that might never happen. But I wasn't going to spoil his dream. Not today.

CHAPTER 28

When we entered my father's camp, I was surprised to see Gabriel waving at us as he ran over. "I figured I should be where Sean is. Don't worry. There are two more men watching your house, Sean."

Conor said, "We'll need to find a grey for Sean to ride. Gabe, if you'll accompany them to Elvenwood, I can stay here. Brian wants Adam and me with him when he meets with Chief O'Donnell."

Gabe was all smiles. "I haven't been home in a week, so I'll be happy to ride with you. I need clean clothes, and I want to stop in to see my parents. They worry."

I smiled. "Like all parents."

He nodded. "Okay, let's go visit the greys and see if one will volunteer for Sean."

Sean looked surprised. "One of them has to volunteer to let me ride him?"

"The greys aren't like any horses you find in the human world. They can communicate with us," I said. "And they have very definite likes and dislikes." I grinned at him. "I have a feeling one of the female greys will volunteer."

Sean's face got pink and he gave me a look.

"Oh, come on, Sean. All the girls like you; you know that," I teased.

Gabe laughed. "Yeah, he's almost as irresistible as I am."

By this time, Sean's face was red, but he had to laugh. Gabe was even bigger than Sean, and just as good looking. The girls at school had eyes for both of them.

I greeted Dusty, Gabe's horse, one of the greys I was especially fond of, and got nuzzled in return. "Sorry, Dusty, no apples today. But I'm happy to see you." He snorted and it sounded like laughter.

I said hello to all the greys. "Would one of you like to bring Sean to Elvenwood for his first visit? He's a good friend of mine and I want to show him a part of his heritage he's never known about."

One of the greys started nodding her head vigorously and stomping her hooves. I took that as a "yes." Gabe led her over to us so she could meet Sean.

"Her name is Cloud. She's very fast." Gabe chuckled. "She may try to run off with you, so you'll have to let her know who's boss." The grey snorted and tossed her head at him.

Sean approached her slowly, giving her a chance to look him over closely, something all the greys do the first time they meet someone. She looked him up and down, sniffing at him delicately. After a few minutes, she lowered her head to his and blew into his hair. Sean laughed and Cloud made a laughing sound, nuzzling the top of his head.

Gabe grinned. "I think she likes you. Of course, you seem to have that effect on all the girls." Sean groaned. "Knock it off."

By that time, we were all laughing. Conor watched us with a smile on his face.

I found Pigeon and one of the boys saddled her for me. When I walked back to Sean and Gabe, Sean took one look at Pigeon and gasped.

"Wow, Cara. She's beautiful. Her coloring is so unusual." Pigeon really was a beauty. Her hair was a mixture of light and dark gray and her mane and tail were snow white. "She's the perfect size for you." Pigeon lapped up the compliments and started doing her little dance.

"Okay, young lady, settle down. You do want to run, don't you?" She nodded her head up and down and stood still while I got my foot in the stirrup and lifted myself on her back. I whispered, "I've missed you." I hadn't ridden her in at least a week. In my mind, I heard, *I've missed you too, Cara*. It was the first time she'd actually spoken to me. I guessed she and I had finally bonded, just like my father and Smoke.

A few feet away, Sean turned to Cloud and asked, "Are you ready?" She whinnied, nodding her big head up and down. He got his foot in the stirrup and lifted himself up.

Gabe was already on Dusty's back and we were ready to go.

Conor said, "Sean, I've already sent a few messages ahead, so your arrival won't be too big a shock to a few people." I could see affection in his silver eyes as he patted Cloud's neck and told Sean, "I wish I could go with you to introduce you around, but I'm sure Cara can handle that part of your visit. Enjoy yourself."

We rode out of camp slowly, Sean and I riding behind Gabe who asked, "If we let the greys run, Sean, do you think you can stay on her?"

Sean just grinned. Gabe grinned back, whispered in Dusty's ear, and the boys took off. Behind them, I whispered to Pigeon, "We can't let them beat us, can we?" She immediately picked up the pace and ran. There were a few spots on the path where it was better to ride single file, so I made sure I got in the lead. Bending down over her neck, I told Pigeon to fly! And she did. She might be smaller than the other greys, but she was also faster.

We pulled up at Elvenwood's gateway, that impenetrable looking barrier of trees and boulders, with Sean and Gabe right behind me. Sean looked at me. "What is this?"

Gabe winked at me and softly uttered the Gaelic words. A slight mist appeared, and the barrier was no longer there. Instead, we were looking at the wider path into Elvenwood. Sean turned to me, obviously amazed.

"Welcome to Elvenwood," I said. As we rode on, I could feel the magic in the air and wondered if Sean could feel it too.

Gabe said, "I'll leave you two here. I'm heading for home, but I'll see you both in the dining hall for lunch." He grinned at us and Dusty took off at a trot.

Sean and I rode slowly and I waited for Sean's reaction.

He was looking all around him, at the thatch-roofed cottages, each with its own garden full of flowers and fruit trees. "Cara, why does the air feel different here? This may sound crazy, but it feels like the village just said, 'Welcome.'"

"Elvenwood recognized your Elven blood and welcomes you as one of their own. What you're feeling in the air is magic."

He looked over at me, amazement written on his face, and began smiling as we rode on. I pointed to my father's cottage as we rode past it. "We'll walk back here after we take the greys to the stable. I want you to meet Will. By the way, prepare yourself to see Elves without the human glamour they adopt when they're outside Elvenwood."

I saw one eyebrow shoot up as he thought about it. He shook his head again and continued to smile. "This is surreal. I feel like I've been dropped into Oz!"

"Yeah, I know. I felt the same way the first time I visited. Elvenwood has always seemed a bit like a fairy tale to me." He nodded, grinning.

We rode our greys into the stable and dismounted. Before I knew it, I was being lifted off my feet and hugged by Will. "Welcome back, Cara. The greys and I have all missed you, lass." He put me down and turned to Sean. "And you brought us another McKay. What's your name, boy?"

Sean smiled and held out his hand. "Sean McKay, sir." Will's huge hand dwarfed Sean's. "Well, it's good to meet you, Sean McKay.

"Are you just visiting us for the day, lass?"

"Yes. Thornewood has been really difficult lately, and I thought Sean and I deserved a break. Sean didn't know Elvenwood existed until I started visiting a few months ago."

Will grinned. "Welcome to Elvenwood, lad."

We thanked Will and left the stable. "Kathleen's cottage is just down the road. I always like to stop in to see her when I'm here. I'm sure she'll remember you. She did a great job on your face."

"I remember thinking she had to be a magician."

I laughed. "She definitely is. There's magic all around us here. More than you know." I couldn't help thinking about Rowenna. I wondered if Sean could handle that much magic.

We visited Kathleen and she was happy to see Sean again, with his face unmarked this time. Looking Sean up and down, she grinned and said, "I can't get over how much you look like Conor when he was your age. Such bonny boys."

As we walked back to my father's cottage, Sean looked as though he was trying to absorb everything he was seeing. Elves peeked out of every cottage we passed. Some waved at us. Some just stared at Sean, which wasn't surprising. He was worth staring at.

"Why are they staring at me?" he asked.

"Mmm, well, round ears for one thing. And, of course, you're a younger human version of Conor, something they don't see every day."

"Yeah, but you have round ears. You're obviously human."

"They're used to me. And some of them think I'm more Elf than human anyway."

He looked at me and smiled. "I can understand that."

We'd reached my father's cottage and found young Ian fidgeting on the front step.

"Cara, you're back! How long are you staying? Who's this?"

I couldn't help laughing at my freckle-faced young friend. "Ian, I'd like you to meet my friend, Sean McKay. He's Conor's cousin. We're only here for the day, I'm afraid. We'll be going back to Thornewood this afternoon."

His face dropped. "I was hoping you'd be staying overnight and taking me back with you in the morning. You promised, remember?"

"I'm sorry. This would be a very bad time for you to leave Elvenwood. Thornewood's not safe right now."

His eyes got wide. "I heard my father say that a boy had been killed. Was he a friend of yours?"

Sean said, "We played ball together, but I didn't know him very well. His family only moved to Thornewood a few months ago."

Ian nodded, his brow creased. "Is that why you're here, Sean? So you won't get killed?"

"Not exactly," I said. "My father's men, along with the police, are keeping our town as safe as possible. Several of the bad men have been caught and put in jail. I just thought bringing Sean to see Elvenwood for the first time would be good for him. Kind of like a short vacation."

"Well, that's good, but I hope next time you'll stay longer." The little boy hesitated. "And I hope no one else gets killed."

I ruffled his fair hair. "Thanks, Ian. We'll see you later."

He ran back to his cottage and Sean and I walked into my father's home as a blur of brown fur raced to the door to greet us. Sean laughed. "This has to be a relative of Ralph's, right?"

I bent down to rub the dog's velvety ears. "Yep. This is Roscoe, Ralph's father. He's just like Ralph; he loves everybody." Sean sat down on the floor to play with the overjoyed dog.

"Thirsty?"

He smiled. "Yes. More tea?"

"Not this time. You're in for a treat." I went to the cold cellar and took out a large jug of water, pouring a large cup for each of us.

"Take a taste of this. You won't find water like this outside Blackthorne Forest."

"I remember this. Kathleen gave me a drink of water the day she healed my face. I thought it was the herbs she'd given me that made it taste so good."

While he drank his water, he walked around my father's sitting room, stopping at the fireplace. "You drew this, didn't you?" He pointed to the framed drawing hanging over the mantle.

"When Conor asked me for one of my drawings to give to his 'boss,' he picked this one out of all the drawings I had with me that day." I smiled. "I didn't know who his 'boss' was, of course. He chose this one because my mother is in it. He knew my dad would love it."

Sean nodded and smiled. "How are your parents getting along now? He spends a lot of time at your house, doesn't he?"

"He does, and I think it makes Mom happy, although she'll never say so."

"That must be where you get your stubbornness." He winked at me.

I snorted. "My father thinks so too."

There was a soft knock at the door and I opened it. Two older men stood there. They both had the same warm brown eyes and friendly smiles.

"You must be here to see Sean. Please come in."

Sean had turned from the fireplace, wide-eyed.

One of the two men I remembered from the day the Elders had visited me at the practice field.

They both bowed to me and the older man said, "It's very nice to see you again, Princess." Although they both must be elderly, at least by human standards, they stood tall, moving with the grace of much younger men. They were both blond but graying, much as Sean's father was, and their resemblance to each other was unmistakable. I wondered what their real ages were.

They turned to Sean, who still stood by the fireplace. With a warm smile, the older of the pair said, "I'm Mallory McKay, your great-grandfather, and I am very pleased to meet you, Sean. I never thought I would have this opportunity." He reached out to shake Sean's hand as Sean approached him with an wide-eyed expression. Sean took his hand, saying, "Great-grandfather. Wow!" Both men chuckled.

The younger of the pair put one arm around Sean's shoulders. "You were named after me. I remember you when you were just a baby. You liked to sit on my feet." He chuckled. He added more seriously, "I left for Elvenwood permanently when you were only four or five. I've always been sorry I couldn't watch you grow up."

I invited them to stay for tea and it was like a family reunion for the next hour. Before they left, they both expressed the hope they would see Sean again.

"Well, that's up to Cara," he told them.

"Of course you'll see each other again," I said. "You're family. Sean can visit as often as he likes." That put a big grin on Sean's face, and both grandfathers looked pleased. They both thanked me for my hospitality and left.

Sean practically collapsed on the couch, looking as though he'd just learned that Santa Claus is real. I poured him another cup of tea and sat down on the couch next to him.

"I really like your grandfathers. They have that same warmth that you and your dad have. Conor has it too; must be a family trait."

He simply nodded. He seemed temporarily speechless.

When we left for the dining hall, he said, "My father's going to be shocked. I'd better be sure he's sitting down before I tell him who I met today."

As we walked, he reached for my hand automatically. I didn't mind. "Why do you think your father never talked about this part of your family? Wasn't he close to his father?"

He shrugged. "I have no idea. Until I met you and Conor, I knew nothing at all about my grandfathers, just that they'd both 'passed away.' Which, of course, was a lie. I need to have a long talk with my dad when I get home."

We saw Gabriel as soon as we walked into the dining hall and he waved us over to his table. He was sitting with a few young men I only knew by sight, so he introduced both Sean and me to them. Of course, they all knew who I was, but seemed surprised to meet Sean, although they all said the same thing: "You look just like Conor McKay!" When Gabe told them that Sean and Conor were cousins, they began treating him like an old friend.

Within minutes, platters of fried chicken and bowls of salads were placed on the table, along with just-baked bread and honey butter. Sean's mouth hung open. He leaned over and whispered, "Do the Elves eat like this every day?"

"Yep." I couldn't help laughing. "This is where the five pounds I gained over the summer came from."

He filled his plate to overflowing and there was no conversation after that. All I heard were a few happy grunts. Gabe grinned at me, nodding at Sean.

When we'd all finished eating, Gabe asked, "Cara, have you been training?"

"No, not recently. I'm afraid my practice area at home isn't considered safe right now. I'm probably a little rusty."

"Why don't you and Sean come down to the field with me? You can practice and I can give Sean an archery lesson. The children won't be on the field for another few hours, so it's all ours."

Sean grinned. "I've been wanting to learn some of Cara's new skills ever since I watched her practicing."

As we walked out of the village toward the practice field, it was obvious that word had spread. More Elves looked out as we walked by, some waving at us, a few nodding at Sean.

A smile seemed to be permanently plastered to Sean's face. "I feel like I'm being welcomed by everyone in the village."

Gabe chuckled. "Sean, you look so much like Conor, it's obvious to everyone that you're one of us." He chuckled. "Besides, we Elves are a friendly lot."

Sean wrapped his hand around mine again. Looking down at me, he said, "Bringing me here today was a wonderful idea. Thank you."

Gabe laughed. "Save your thanks until you find out how hard it is to hit a target with an arrow, something Cara excels at."

Sean turned to me. "Gabe's been dying to find a sport I suck at. This may be his big chance."

"Nah. I think you'll pick it up quickly."

When we reached the field, Gabe opened the equipment shed and took out two bows and two pouches of arrows. He handed the smaller bow to me. Seeing that, Sean couldn't hide a smile. Gabe said, "You won't be laughing when you see what she can do with that small bow."

He removed the cover from the grizzly bear target and walked back to us. Sean chuckled. "That's your artwork, isn't it?"

I nodded. "There's a mountain lion on the other target. Gabe asked me to paint something to motivate the kids."

Gabe walked back to us and showed Sean how to hold the bow, corrected his stance, and said, "Pull that arm back and see if you can hit the target. Keep that elbow up and keep your eyes on the target. Now shoot."

As expected, Sean was a natural. He hit the target on his first try. Not in the center, but close enough. He looked at me and grinned.

Gabe just shook his head. "Is there anything you're not good at, McKay? Take a few more shots while we're here. It takes practice to develop speed, but if you shoot for too long, you won't be able to use that arm tomorrow."

Sean shot off the rest of his arrows slowly, hitting the target every time, once in the exact center. The satisfied smile never left his face.

Gabe said, "Why don't you get some practice, Cara. That'll take some of the wind out of his sails."

"I'd like to improve my distance skills." Gabe ran up and pushed the target back another ten feet.

I started to shoot, slowly at first, and as I got used to the longer distance, I sped up and went through the bag of arrows quickly. I was pleased to find I wasn't rusty at all. I retrieved my arrows and as I returned to where the boys stood, Gabe was grinning and Sean looked awed. My self-confidence went up a notch.

"You're even faster than you were the last time I watched you practice." Sean turned to Gabe. "You know, it's too bad our bodyguards can't bring their bows with them when they're in Thornewood. I wish Archery was offered at school; I think a lot of guys would sign up for it." He chuckled. "Cara could be one of our instructors."

Gabe smiled, raising an eyebrow. "Every guy in school would sign up if Cara was the instructor."

Sean looked at Gabe, obviously thinking about that last statement, and nodded. "Right. Not such a good idea. Cara has enough fans as it is."

"Hey, guys. I'm standing right here!" I said.

Gabe laughed. "We should be heading back in another hour. I have to go pick up my laundry. I'll meet you at your father's cottage." He took off in a different direction as Sean and I walked off the field.

Again, he took my hand, the same way Adam always did. I realized I'd hardly thought about Adam today and felt a twinge. Why would I feel like that? I was free to hold any hand I liked. But I wondered how Adam would feel about it.

"Let's take a walk through the apple orchard where I've done most of my drawings. If we can pick up some apples for the greys, they'll be your friends forever."

I was still mulling over the idea of taking him into the old orchard, where he might get a glimpse of Rowenna. I wondered if he could handle one more shock.

I was wearing a tank top under my t-shirt, so I pulled off the t-shirt to hold all the apples we were picking up off the ground. Sean looked slightly alarmed for a few seconds, until he saw my tank top.

"Whew, don't scare me like that."

He looked down at me and lifted a skeptical brow. "You're more than a little unpredictable, you know." He shook his head. "Nothing you do surprises me anymore."

I grinned at him. "Good."

My t-shirt was full of as many apples as it could hold, so I tied the sleeves together and handed the sack I'd just created to Sean. "We'll have to save a few to give Cloud and Pigeon when we get back to camp."

We'd reached the edge of the orchard, where we could see the ancient, gnarled apple trees ahead.

It was a warm day so we took a break under one of the largest of the old trees. Sean's voice was soft as he leaned back against the trunk of the tree. "I don't know how to thank you for today. I was about as low as I've ever been." He looked around. "This place, the magic in the air, the smiles from all the people who don't even know me, has kind of restored my outlook on life. I'll hate to see this day end."

I smiled. "It's not over yet." I began humming Rowenna's song. Sean asked, "Did you ever figure out where that melody came from?"

"I did, but it took a few days of research to find it." I continued humming, watching the sky for a familiar figure. When I glanced at Sean, his eyes were closed. I looked back at the sky and spotted Rowenna just leaving her mountain home.

"Um, Sean, there's someone else I'd like you to meet, but please don't be frightened."

Opening his eyes, he looked over at me. "Frightened? Why would I be frightened?"

"Well, my friend Rowenna is a little unusual. I doubt you've ever met anyone like her before."

"Oh. Okay. When will I be meeting her?"

"In less than a minute. Look up at the sky."

"The sky?" I knew when he caught sight of her because his mouth dropped open. He whispered, "You've got to be kidding."

I heard her voice in my mind. *Who have you brought to meet me today?*

I decided to answer her mentally. *Rowenna, this is Sean, a close friend who suffered a terrible shock yesterday when one of his teammates was killed. Sean was actually the target. That evil man I told you about is still sending other men to attack us. I brought Sean to Elvenwood today to help him recover.*

She answered, I understand. I am glad you brought him to meet me. She circled the old orchard and landed where she had before. Her golden eyes looked sympathetic.

"This is my friend Rowenna. We communicate mentally, like I do with my father. I've told her what's been going on in Thornewood. She said she's glad I brought you here to meet her."

His mouth was still open.

I nudged him. "Sean, say hello."

He continued to stare at the huge, golden-eyed dragon sitting twenty feet in front of him.

I decided to speak to her out loud. "I'm afraid he's in shock. We'll have to give him a few minutes."

She huffed a little, her version of laughter.

Finally, he found his voice, although it shook a little. "Uh, hello, Rowenna. It's very nice to meet you."

She nodded slightly, bending her long neck and dipping her large head a few inches.

Cara, please tell him I'll be watching for him when I fly over Thornewood at night. And let him know that if he feels threatened, he can call my name in his mind. I'll hear him and I'll come.

I repeated her words to Sean. His eyes widened. "She'd do that for me?"

Tell Sean that there is no room for evil in our world, and that I will burn it to ash wherever I find it.

I told him what she'd said.

He answered her. "Thank you, Rowenna. I think I'll feel safer now, knowing you're flying over Thornewood at night."

She nodded again. In my mind, I heard, *Take care of your friend, Cara. He has a brave heart, and he loves you.*

She spread her gleaming wings and rose slowly into the sky, turning toward her mountain home. We watched her until she disappeared behind the purple mountains.

A few minutes passed quietly before he said anything. "Um, Cara, will there be any more surprises today? I just want to be prepared."

I wrapped my hand around his and smiled. "No, not today. Are you ready to go home?"

He looked at me with a tired smile. "I'm ready." He chuckled. "I don't think I can handle anything else today."

I leaned over and dropped a kiss on his cheek. "I'm glad I could share all of this with you. Elvenwood is such a big part of my life, I wanted you to experience it."

He whispered, "Thank you." Then he kissed me. Not on the cheek. My stomach did that old familiar backflip and I remembered why I'd been so attracted to him when I met him last spring.

We stood and walked through the orchard, hand in hand. Occasionally we glanced over at each other and smiled.

I was reminded of our first weeks together last spring. It was déjà vu, all over again.

CHAPTER 29

We walked out of the orchard and headed for the stable, where I hoped I'd find Gabe.

He smiled when we walked in. "You weren't at your father's cottage, so I thought I'd find you here. The sun's going down and we need to get back to camp while it's still light."

He grinned at Sean. "How did you like your first visit to Elvenwood?"

"I'm still trying to absorb it all, to be honest. It's another world here in Elvenwood. I hadn't expected everyone to be so welcoming." He smiled at me. "It's been a really great day."

Will had saddled our greys, so we were ready to go. After thanking Will, leaving the apples for the greys, and saying goodbye, we rode out of the stable. When we passed my father's cottage, Ian came running from his yard to say goodbye.

"When are you coming back?"

"I'm not sure. I'm hoping it will be soon, but it all depends on the problems we're dealing with at home."

Frowning, he nodded. He walked over to Sean. "I hope you don't get hurt. Come back and see us again."

Sean reached down and tousled Ian's hair, smiling. "I'd love to come back. I'll see you then."

We rode toward Elvenwood's gateway slowly. I think we were all sorry to leave.

Twenty minutes later we rode into my father's camp. I looked around, surprised to see only a few of my father's men. When we left, there were at least twenty men in camp. Gabe looked around, calling out a few names until one of the younger boys ran out of one of the tents.

"Evan, where is everybody?"

"Just a few minutes ago, we got a message from Brian, and most of the men left for Cara's home. A few of them took their greys. There are only a few of us left here. No one explained why they had to leave."

Gabe and I looked at each other. "Something must be very wrong." My heart started pounding.

Gabe urged Dusty forward, and we followed. We usually walked back from camp, but Gabe was in a hurry. Sean looked over at me, his face worried.

We rode right into my backyard, stopping at the back porch. The grass was trampled, so the Elves riding greys had been here, but they were gone.

I dismounted and ran into the house, Sean right behind me. Gabe got as far as the porch and said, "I'll be out here. I want to leave water for the greys. No one's guarding your house right now. Just let me know what's going on when you find out." I nodded to him and opened the back door.

The kitchen was dark. I walked through the house to the front door. I could feel that the house was empty. When I opened the front door, the only car in front of the house was mine. There was no one on the front porch either.

Sean's cell phone rang. It was his father, asking when he'd be coming home. Sean turned to me. "Should I stay?"

I didn't know what to tell him. Just then I heard my father's voice in my head.

Are you at home, Cara?

"We just got here. Where is everybody?"

I want you to stay there. Adam is on his way back to the house. He'll explain.

"Sean and Gabe are here. Sean wants to know if he should stay."

Please tell Sean to call his father. We may need him.

"Okay. Are we in danger again?"

You're not in danger right now, sweetheart, so stay put.

"All right. Please stay in touch. I love you."

I love you too, Cara. Even in my mind, his voice sounded strange.

Sean was still holding his cell phone, waiting for an answer.

"My father wants you to ask your father to come over. He said he might need him. That's all I know. He said Adam's on his way here and that he'll explain what's going on." I felt more panicky by the minute. My heart was already pounding.

He passed the message along to his dad, who said he'd be over as soon as he could get here.

Sean looked at me, his expression worried. "Your dad didn't tell you what's going on?"

I shook my head. We were standing at the front window. I put my elbows on the windowsill and leaned my head against the glass. "It must be something really bad. He wouldn't tell me anything, except that I'm not in danger right now and he wants me to stay here."

Sean wrapped his arms around me and pulled me close. His warmth felt so good, I suddenly realized I was cold, from the inside out. Every part of me felt chilled.

"You're freezing." He pulled me even closer, one hand cradling my head until I placed my head against his neck, between his chin and shoulder, the way I used to whenever we danced together. It was comforting and my heartbeat started to slow down. I closed my eyes, taking deep, slow breaths until I felt calmer.

Minutes later, he placed one hand under my chin to lift my face and bent down to kiss me. And I needed that kiss, just like I needed his warmth and his strong arms around me. Without even thinking about it, I was kissing him back. His arms tightened around me.

We heard a car pull up in front of the house. He whispered, "That's my dad." I kissed him one last time and pushed him away. We looked out the window and saw his father walking up to the front porch.

I turned away from the window and got a sudden shock. Adam stood in the doorway to the kitchen, his dark blue eyes pinned on me. *Crap.*

Judging by the disapproving look on his serious face, he'd been standing there for a while. He must have come in the back door.

"Bring everyone into the kitchen, Cara. I'll explain what's happened this afternoon." Adam turned away and walked into the kitchen, leaving me staring at his back.

I opened the door for Mr. McKay and led Sean and his dad into the still-dark kitchen, switching on the lights quickly. Adam had brought Gabe in with him. I invited everyone to sit down and made a quick pot of coffee. Adam was silent as I made coffee and put cups on the table.

When I sat down, Adam looked at me and said, "Your mother has been abducted."

I must have gasped because Sean immediately reached for me.

"Arlynn witnessed it, but it happened so fast, there was nothing she could do. It was almost closing time, and your mother ran to the mailbox on the corner to mail something. An SUV with blacked out windows stopped and grabbed your mother off the sidewalk in seconds. They were gone before Arlynn could even get out of the store."

He turned to Sean's father. "Mr. McKay, Brian asked if you would join him downtown. The police and all the volunteer firemen who aren't on duty are doing a door-to-door search all over town in an effort to find Miss Connelly. One good thing came out of the Chief's meeting this morning with the State Police. The Highway Patrol has each exit out of Thornewood blocked. Every vehicle is being stopped and inspected. The men who took Cara's mother cannot get out of town, so they must still be here. There are only two ways in and out of town, and the Highway Patrol has had them blocked since noon today."

Sean's father stood. "Where do they need me?"

"Teams of searchers are meeting at The Crescent Moon. Brian and Chief O'Donnell were still there when I left."

"Sean can help with the search. Can I bring him with me?"

Adam looked over at Sean. "At the moment, we don't think Cara's friends are in any danger. They're trying to round up as many bodies as they can for the door-to-door search. Sean can help with that."

Sean whispered, "Sorry. I'll call as soon as I can." He squeezed my shoulder and got up to leave with his father.

I walked them to the door. Mr. McKay said, "Don't worry, Cara. We'll find her." Sean gave me a quick kiss and they left. I stood there at the door, suddenly aware that it wasn't kisses from Sean I needed most.

I walked back into the kitchen. "There must be something I can do. How can you and my father expect me to just sit here and do nothing? And why are you here and not out there searching? Both of you!"

Gabe and Adam looked at each other. I could see the unspoken message passing between them: *Calm her down, whatever it takes.*

Gabe shifted in his seat and stood. "I'm going outside. I'll watch both sides of the house. Cara, I'm sure that's why your father wants me to be here. There's no police car in front of your house tonight." He looked at Adam and then back at me. "They'll find her. Call me if there's any news." He left by the back door, leaving Adam and me alone.

I looked at Adam. "You didn't answer my question, Adam. Why aren't you out there searching for Mom?" I knew my voice didn't sound normal. "She's going through what I went through last spring. She's probably tied up, possibly hurt, and definitely terrified. And we're just sitting here!" I realized I was yelling and suddenly there were tears running down my face.

He came around the table and lifted me out of my chair. Adam's arms were around me before I knew it. I sobbed, tears soaking his tunic as I leaned against his chest.

His voice was soft. "I'm here because your father thought you might need me. Maybe I should have asked Sean to stay. Then I'd be out searching too. Would that have been better, Cara?"

I shook my head, still sobbing. "No, Adam. I need you." I was torn. Sean wanted to be here with me. Adam was here because my father wished it. And my mother was missing. Emotionally, I was a mess.

"I keep thinking there's something I should be doing to help, you know?"

He led me into the living room and we sat down on the couch. Pulling a linen handkerchief out of his tunic, he gently wiped my tears. "There are at least a hundred people out there, searching for your mother. I don't see what else you could do."

I leaned against his shoulder, trying to get myself under control. I cried until I got the hiccups, and then I stopped, sniffling. Adam handed me his handkerchief. I needed to blow my nose, but how could I blow my nose into Adam's linen handkerchief? He must have been reading my mind because he whispered, "That's what it's for, love."

After I'd blown my nose and calmed down, Adam asked, "Do you think you could find something for us to eat?"

Food, my mother's favorite remedy for everything from a concussion to a broken heart.

"I'm no cook, but I can make sandwiches."

Getting busy in the kitchen helped. At least I was doing something useful. I put water on the stove to boil and got down the teapot and some of Kathleen's herbal tea. Mom must have gone shopping the day before because the fridge was packed. I found a pound of sliced roast beef and there was a new loaf of sourdough bread in the bread box. After the sandwiches were made, I took two outside to Gabe along with a cup of tea, and Adam and I sat down to eat in the kitchen.

"Thank you, love. I haven't eaten since breakfast. Some food will be good for you too." He smiled, raising one eyebrow. "I expect you to finish at least one of these sandwiches."

I had been sipping my tea, thinking about Mom, but I picked up a sandwich and tried to eat. As soon as I took a bite, I realized how hungry I was, and my sandwich disappeared quickly. I poured more tea for both of us, and then sat back, still thinking about my mother.

I heard my father's voice in my head as I looked at the clock on the wall. It was nine o'clock. Mom had been missing for more than four hours.

Cara, the police have searched every vacant house and building inside Thornewood, but we haven't found your mother yet. We'll search all night, if necessary. Are you all right?

"I'm okay, Dad, just worried about Mom. Adam and I just finished some sandwiches. Have you eaten anything?"

Don't worry about me, dear. Everyone knows we're searching for your mother, and many of the people we've spoken to have brought food out to us. Sean and his father are searching their neighborhood. I have a feeling we should be searching in the forest, but we'll have to wait until dawn to be able to see anything in the woods. He sounded frustrated.

Then I remembered our secret weapon. "No, we don't have to wait until dawn! Rowenna has been flying over Thornewood every night. I have a feeling her night vision is a lot better than ours."

I've been sending your mother mental messages all night. I think she's been hearing me. She knows everyone is searching for her, and she knows I won't rest until I find her. If Rowenna can search the forest, we may find her sooner.

"Okay. I'm going to contact her right now. I'll be in touch."

"Come on, Adam. Bring your tea, we're going out on the back porch so I can call Rowenna."

I stood at the porch railing and called Rowenna. It was only a few minutes before I heard the giant wings overhead and felt her magic surround me.

You sound so sad tonight, I heard her rough voice say.

"We need your help. My mother was abducted this afternoon. We're sure the men who took her were hired by that evil man I've told you about. The police and Elves have been searching, but she hasn't been found yet. Police have been stationed at both entrances to Thornewood since noon today, so the kidnappers haven't been able to leave town. My mother has to be nearby. I have a feeling she's being held in the forest, but the men can't start searching until dawn. Can you see what's below you in the woods while it's dark?"

Yes, Cara, I see clearly at night. I'll start searching for Alicia now. If she is in the forest, I will find her, and the evil men who took her.

We felt her wings moving the night air powerfully as she flew away. She was definitely in a hurry.

After I let my father know that Rowenna was already searching the woods, we sat down to wait.

Gabriel came running around the side of the house. "What was that? Something huge flew over the house, and I know there aren't any birds that big!"

I looked at Adam. He whispered, "Gabe's not telepathic. He wasn't told."

"Uh, Gabe, come up here and sit down with us. I have something kind of unbelievable to tell you."

A little later, after a calming cup of tea, Gabe got up and returned to the front porch. As he went down the stairs, I heard him mumbling what sounded like, "Dragon?

Where did she come from? Next they'll be telling me that leprechauns are real . . ."

Adam looked over at me and winked.

That was the only light moment in this whole awful night.

CHAPTER 30

Normally, Gabriel's grumbling would have made me laugh, but not tonight. I was going to sit on my back porch until Rowenna found my mother, no matter how long it took.

"How are you doing?" Adam asked. "You're too quiet."

"Just thinking. Even if Rowenna finds Mom, how will she be able to get Mom out of a car, or away from them? If Mom's hurt, Rowenna may try to kill them."

He looked over at me. "I hope those men survive long enough to be questioned. They might know how to contact Gaynes."

"You're right. I'd better let Rowenna know that we want to capture those men alive."

I sent her a mental message, but without a response, I couldn't be sure she'd heard me.

I heard my father's voice in my head. *Have you heard anything from Rowenna yet?*

"No, Dad. I'm trying to be patient."

That's the hardest thing, sweetheart.

I whispered, "I know."

Adam reached over and wrapped his warm hand around my cold one.

An hour later, there was still no word from Rowenna and it was getting colder on the porch. I went inside, grabbed an old, heavy sweater of Mom's along with a warm afghan from the couch. I wrapped myself up in the sweater and put the afghan around Adam's shoulders.

"Thanks, love. Your lips were beginning to turn blue."

"Well, the later it gets, the colder it will be out here."

"Are you planning to stay out here all night?"

"I'm staying out here until Rowenna has searched the entire forest, if that's what it takes. I just know Mom's out there somewhere."

"Premonition?"

"Gut feeling, Adam. You can't ignore those."

It was quiet for a few minutes.

"Cara, can we talk while we wait?"

I was pretty sure I knew what he wanted to talk about. "Okay. You have questions, don't you?"

He gave me an almost-smile. "Yes, I do. In the interests of keeping your social life straight in my mind, are you and Sean together again the way you were last spring?"

I wasn't sure how to answer. "Well, he's not my boyfriend anymore. I don't think I want a boyfriend."

"Well, he's obviously more than a friend, Cara. You don't kiss all your friends that way, do you?"

I sighed. "No, of course not." I thought about how best to explain what he'd witnessed.

"When we got home and found the house empty, I knew something was very wrong. I think Sean just wanted to comfort me."

He took a deep breath and looked away. "I'd say you were doing a bit of comforting yourself."

And, of course, he was right.

"Are you in love with Sean?"

I turned and looked him in the eye. "No, Adam. I don't think I know what being in love feels like. But I like Sean a lot, and I am attracted to him." *What girl wouldn't be?* I wanted to be honest with myself.

He gave me a sharp look. "So you do know the difference between being in love and simply being attracted to someone."

"Adam, my mother explained these things to me a few years ago. I'm not an idiot."

He shook his head. "It's been my experience that most young girls don't know the difference. If they're attracted to someone, they think they're in love. I hope you won't make that mistake."

I was starting to feel annoyed. "Why do you care? It's my life."

Dropping my hand, he stood. "I care. Never doubt it. I'm going inside to make coffee. If we're staying up all night, we're going to need it."

"You know how to make coffee?"

He gave me an arrogant look as he opened the door. "I've seen you make it often enough. It doesn't appear too difficult."

I followed him into the kitchen, just to make sure he didn't set the coffeepot on fire. I stood behind him and watched him fill the coffee pot with water, take coffee out of the cupboard, put a new filter into the basket and spoon the coffee in. He poured the water into the coffeemaker, put the lid on, placed the coffeepot on the warmer, and pressed the "On" button.

"Very good. I think I'll let you make the coffee from now on."

He turned and gave me that devastating blue-eyed smile that would make any girl swoon. Except me, of course. *Who was I kidding?*

When the coffee was ready, he took the entire pot out on the porch. I followed with cups, cream and sugar. We were set for the night.

I heard from my father approximately every thirty minutes, but had no news for him.

"Adam, how long do you think it will take Rowenna to fly over every part of Blackthorne Forest?"

"You have to remember how huge this forest is. If Rowenna is flying low, searching carefully, it will take a long time to cover four thousand acres. She may not be able to search the entire forest tonight."

I sighed and poured another cup of coffee.

Suddenly I heard someone walking around the side of the house, and not quietly.

"Hey, guys. I was in my backyard talking to my dad and I thought I smelled coffee. What are you doing out here so late? It's after midnight."

"Come on up, Kev. Didn't your father tell you what's going on?"

"No. I only saw him for a few seconds before he had to leave. Something about a search in the forest." He sat down next to me. "Who are they looking for?"

"Kev, you'd better sit down. Mom was snatched off the street this afternoon, right in front of her store. The police and Elves have been searching door to door in town, and a friend of ours is searching the woods now." I felt tears forming again. "We've heard nothing yet."

Kevin's mouth was hanging open. "Oh, no, babe. Not your mom." He was sitting on the edge of the deck chair and reached over to grab my hand.

"Do you think she was grabbed by men hired by Gaynes? Oh, stupid question. Who else could it be?" After a minute he asked,

"Who's searching the forest? You can't see anything out there at night."

"Yes, I'm sure it was Gaynes' men. The Highway Patrol has had both exits from Thornewood blocked all day, so they couldn't have left town. Every vacant house and building has been searched, so where else could they have gone? They have to be in the forest."

He shook his head. "I doubt they'll find anything until daylight. We don't even have a full moon tonight."

Adam leaned over and whispered, "You haven't told him about Rowenna?"

I shook my head. I hadn't seen Kevin since the game Friday night.

"What are you two whispering about? What aren't you telling me, Cara?"

"Uh, Kev, I'm not really keeping anything from you. I just haven't had a chance to talk to you privately in a while."

"Okay, what don't I know?"

"The last time I spent a few days in Elvenwood, I made a new friend. Her name is Rowenna. Last spring, she's what we would have considered, um, a mythical creature."

Just then I heard her rough voice in my head. I held up one hand to Kevin.

Cara, I don't see any people, but I see a shiny black box in the south side of the forest, not far from the wide road.

I spoke out loud, excitedly. "That's probably the automobile they were driving when they grabbed Mom. If there's no one outside the black box, they're probably still inside it."

Kevin whispered to Adam, "Who's she talking to?"

"She's talking to Rowenna."

Can you send your father and his men here? I'll circle this area until they arrive.

"Keep circling. My father and the police will get there as soon as possible. I'll call him now. Thank you, Rowenna. I'm so grateful."

Out loud I said, "Dad, Rowenna has found them. At least she's found their SUV. She didn't see anyone outside the car, so maybe they're still inside it. It's on the south side of the forest, not far from the road. Rowenna is in the air, circling the area. She'll keep circling until you get there."

We're on our way, Cara. I could kiss that dragon.

I couldn't help smiling.

I took a deep, deep breath and leaned back in my deck chair. I had to concentrate on breathing slowly, until I felt my heart slow down.

Adam reached for my hand. "I'm guessing Rowenna found them. Fill us in."

"She doesn't see anyone on the ground, but she saw what she described as a shiny black box parked on the south side of the forest. She'll circle that area from the air until my father and the police get there."

I had a sudden thought, a very bad thought. "I hope they haven't hurt Mom. If there's even one scratch on her, my father will kill them before the police can ask a single question."

Adam said, "I thought you were worried about what Rowenna would do to them."

I looked at him. "Rowenna can burn them; but my dad might use his knives. And he will, if they've hurt Mom in any way."

Kevin grabbed my arm. "You know I love your mom as much as you do. Please tell me who Rowenna is. A super-hero who can fly and burn people?" His eyes were almost bugging out of his head.

Adam and I looked at each other and nodded. "That's exactly who she is, Kev. She's a dragon, a very large, beautiful, fire-breathing dragon. My father thought they were extinct. They're not, at least not in Blackthorne Forest."

For once, Kevin was speechless, his mouth hanging open again as he shook his head slowly. Finally, he said, "A dragon. Who would ever believe it?" He snorted. "I'll probably wake up in the morning and find this was all a dream."

CHAPTER 31

We could hear police sirens just as Rowenna glided down, landing in our backyard. I stood and ran to the railing. The dragon's magic wrapped itself around me like a soft quilt.

"Rowenna, did you see my mother? Is she all right?"

Your father lifted her out of the black box and set her on her feet. He wrapped a blanket around her and carried her to the white vehicle with the flashing lights, so I believe she is all right. I would like to wait here until she arrives home.

"Did the police catch the two men who took her?"

She didn't answer right away. *Those men did not run away, Cara. Don't worry.*

I breathed a deep sigh of relief. Mom was okay. "We're so grateful to you, Rowenna. You're welcome to stay as long as you like."

She bent her long neck and nodded, her golden eyes half closed.

"You must be tired. You were searching the forest for so many hours. Is there anything I can do for you?" I asked her.

She made that huffing sound that always seemed like laughter. *No, Cara. I'll just rest here on the soft grass until your mother gets home. Dragons can fly long distances without rest. I'm fine.*

It suddenly occurred to me that Kevin hadn't made any sound other than a gasp when she landed in the yard. I turned to see him totally wide-eyed, mouth hanging open, hands clutching the arms of his chair.

"Kevin, are you all right? Would you like me to introduce you to Rowenna?"

He stood slowly, clearly trying to pull himself together. His eyes still fixed on the huge creature in the backyard. "Yes, please."

I turned to Rowenna. "This is my best friend, Kevin. I'm afraid he's in shock at the moment."

She lifted her huge head, opened those golden eyes, looked straight at Kevin, and said, *Hello, Halfling. I will always protect the Elves and their friends. You have nothing to fear from me.*

I told him what she'd said.

Kevin let out a noisy breath he must have been holding.

"I'm pleased to meet you, Rowenna, and I want to thank you for finding Cara's mom tonight. She means a lot to me."

Rowenna nodded to him and half closed her eyes again. She wouldn't admit it, but she looked tired.

I heard the police car's sirens getting closer and then they pulled up in front of our house. Rowenna's head went up, her golden eyes wide open.

Cara, should I stay here?

Adam said, "It's so dark tonight, if she closes her eyes, she'll be hard to see out there."

Rowenna promptly closed her eyes. *I'm only waiting until I see Alicia.*

When I heard a car door slam, I ran into the house, Kevin at my heels, and opened the front door as my father brought my mother up the porch steps. She was wrapped in a blanket, her hair a mess, and her pretty face had no color at all, but she looked up and smiled at me.

As soon as they came through the door, I threw my arms around her and squeezed her. Kevin leaned over me and bent down to drop a kiss on her head.

She hugged me back and whispered, "I love you too, but please let me go upstairs and clean up. Then I'll come back and hug everybody."

"Do you want some help, Mom?"

She shook her head. "I'm all right, dear." She walked upstairs to her room slowly, trying not to trip over the blanket wrapped around her.

I looked at my father and got a shock. His normally handsome face was haggard, as though he'd aged fifty years in one night.

I grabbed his arm. "Dad, are you all right? Can I get you anything? Tea? Coffee? I think we have some brandy in the pantry."

He took a deep breath and put one hand on my shoulder. "I think the brandy will do me the most good right now, sweetheart. Your mother should have some too. She refused to go to the hospital, or even let the paramedics check her out. She insisted we bring her home."

That sounded like my mother. I went to the pantry and brought out the bottle of brandy. It had been in there so long, I had to dust it off. I poured a small glass for my father and he and Kevin sat down at the kitchen table while we waited for Mom.

THE DRAGON'S SONG

It was only a few minutes before Mom came downstairs, dressed in her comfy old sweats. She'd washed her face and combed her hair, but she was still far too pale.

My father refilled his glass with brandy and handed it to Mom. "Please, Alicia, drink this." He smiled weakly. "For medicinal purposes, of course."

She drank it down quickly. "Is Rowenna here? I need to see her."

"She's been waiting for you, Mom. She's out in the backyard."

"I think she saved my life." She rushed out the back door.

We followed her outside to see her rush down the steps and walk straight to the huge dragon resting in the grass. Rowenna's eyes opened wide when she saw Mom heading for her. She bent her long neck so that she and my mother were at eye level. Mom placed her hand on the dragon's face and began speaking to her. She spoke softly so I couldn't hear what she was saying, but I could hear Rowenna's words.

Alicia, I told you I would find you. You will recover from this experience. You're a strong woman and Cara needs you. I will never be far if you need me. The Elf Prince loves you, and he is in more pain now than you are. You must take care of each other.

Mom patted the dragon's scales one more time and walked back to the porch. We all watched as Rowenna's large wings lifted her into the air. I hummed her song as she turned toward the mountains, and I heard her rusty voice in my mind say, *Cara. . . friend.*

When I could no longer feel the dragon's magic, we went inside. The clock on the wall showed it was after two a.m.

Kevin put his arms around Mom. "Time for me to go home and let you get some rest, Mrs. C. I'm glad you're safe. I think tonight aged me at least ten years."

Mom smiled and hugged him back, whispering, "I love you, Kevin. Get some sleep now."

I walked him to the front door where we simply held on to each other for a few minutes. Kevin whispered, "You and your mom are my family. I don't know what I'd do if anything happened to either one of you." When he finally let go of me, he said, "I'm bringing brunch in the morning. Don't let your mom do anything, short stuff."

"Where are you going to get brunch, Kev? You can't cook!"

"I'll raid the deli downtown and I'll be here around eleven. Sound good?"

"Sounds great. See you in the morning."

Despite everything that had happened tonight, there was a patrol car parked in front of our house again. Mom was home, but I knew we weren't safe. My mother didn't really look like herself. Not around the eyes.

When I walked back into the kitchen, Mom and Dad were standing at the breakfast bar, each with a glass in their hand. The brandy bottle wasn't as full as it had been.

Mom looked at me. "I know you have questions, but they'll have to wait. I'm going upstairs now, dear. Your father's going to run me a bath and then maybe I'll be able to sleep. I'll see you in the morning, sweetheart." She put one hand under my chin. "Don't look so worried. I'm all right." I wasn't sure I believed her.

As she turned to go upstairs, I looked at my father. His voice was soft. "Tonight I'll take care of her, Cara. Tomorrow we can all take care of her."

I had one urgent question. "Did the police get the two men?"

He nodded.

"Okay, Dad. Kevin's bringing brunch in the morning so Mom doesn't have to do a thing."

He finally smiled, but he still looked like he'd gone through hell tonight. I kissed him good night and he followed Mom upstairs.

When I stepped back into the kitchen, I found Adam standing at the stove, actually boiling water in Mom's hot water kettle.

"You seem very comfortable in our modern kitchen."

He turned to me and winked as the kettle whistled. Lifting the kettle off the stove, he poured boiling water into the teapot, added the tea, and smiled at me. "I thought you might need some of this relaxing tea of Kathleen's. You still look tense."

I snorted. "You're supposed to be my bodyguard, Adam, not my nursemaid."

He turned those deep blue eyes on me. "Sometimes you need both. This is one of those times. You've been like a coiled spring all night."

He had me there. Those eyes of his could convince me of anything.

After two cups of tea, I was still too tense to go to bed, so Adam and I sat in the kitchen quietly, occasionally mentioning Mom's abduction and Rowenna's assistance in rescuing her.

"Adam, I don't think they hurt her. I didn't see any marks on her, did you?"

His eyes were sympathetic as he reached for my hand. "Cara, she may just have been tied up, extremely uncomfortable, and scared. I'm sure she'll talk about it when she's ready. Other than being grabbed off the street and thrown into a vehicle, it's possible that nothing else happened. Actually, your mother seemed better than I expected when she got home."

I thought about what he'd said and had to admit he might be right. I nodded. "Yeah, it didn't look as though she'd been slapped around or anything. I couldn't bear the idea of anyone hurting Mom."

"Your father is with her now, which is probably what she needs most." He smiled and squeezed my hand. "Why don't you go do some of that meditation you've been talking about and then go to bed. The sun will be up in about three hours."

As usual, he was right. I'd meditate in the shower and then try to get some sleep.

"Okay. Let me get a pillow for you and I'll say good night. If you're tired, stretch out on the couch in the living room. You've been up all night too."

I could have used one of his rare hugs, but he didn't offer one so I gave him a gentle punch on the arm and ran upstairs, tossing a pillow down to him.

The shower really did relax me as I stood there with my eyes closed, just concentrating on my breathing, the warm water beating down on me. I managed to turn the water off before I turned into a prune. After I dried off, I slipped into my favorite soft t-shirt and tried to get comfy in bed, but when I heard voices from Mom's room, I got tense all over again.

This was the worst. Mom was crying softly, probably so I wouldn't hear her. But the walls in our old house weren't very thick. I'd only heard my mother cry once before, and that was when she found out that I'd met my father. At least he was with her now. I could hear his deep voice comforting her. She kept crying as though her heart was broken, and I cried with her.

I couldn't stay in my room and listen to Mom crying, so I pulled on a pair of sweat pants and padded downstairs. I debated turning on the stove to make more tea, but I'd had enough tea tonight to float a small boat. My eye was drawn to Mom's old rocking chair in the corner of the kitchen. I often sat there when I needed to think. I curled up in the old chair and put my head back, closing my eyes. I was rocking a little, when I heard his soft voice from the doorway.

"What's wrong?"

I opened my eyes. "I can hear Mom crying. I can't bear it."

"Come into the living room and sit with me. I don't think either of us is going to sleep tonight."

I stood. "I'm sorry. I didn't mean to wake you."

Adam held his hand out to me. "It's all right. Elves don't need much sleep."

I took his hand and he led me to the couch, where he'd obviously been sleeping. I could see the imprint of his head on the pillow, and the afghan had been pushed aside.

"You were sleeping. I'm sorry."

"It doesn't matter. Maybe we can relax together. It will be dawn soon."

He made himself comfortable in the corner of the couch and I sat down next to him, close, but not too close. He looked comfortable, resting his head on the back of the couch and I tried to do the same thing, but I was too short so I simply leaned against his arm. I must have dozed off. The next time I opened my eyes, Adam's arm was around me and my head was against his chest. I closed my eyes and went back to sleep.

CHAPTER 32

I woke up when I felt Adam move his arm from around me. I sat up and stretched. Dawn had come and gone. I turned to him. "Adam, if you'd like to wash up, you can use my bathroom. There are clean towels on the shelf over the tub."

He stood abruptly, heading for the stairs. "Much appreciated. I won't be long. Do you think you could make coffee while I'm washing up?"

"Sure." I followed him, heading into the kitchen as he went upstairs to my bathroom.

I made coffee and then decided to keep busy by making fresh orange juice. I was sitting at the breakfast bar using the juicer when Adam came downstairs.

"Thanks for the use of your bathroom. Is the coffee ready?"

"Help yourself. You know where we keep the cups. Pour a cup for me, would you?"

A minute later, he put two cups of coffee on the breakfast bar and sat down next to me. He had even added cream to my coffee. I looked up and smiled. "Thanks. Would you take over for me with the juicer while I run upstairs? I'll only be a minute."

I ran upstairs, threw cold water on my face and brushed my teeth. I cringed when I looked in the mirror. There were gray circles under my eyes. Half my hair had come out of my ponytail during the night and I looked like I'd been mugged. Impatiently, I pulled the rest of my hair down, ran the brush through it, and went back to the kitchen.

There were no sounds coming from Mom's room. I hoped they were getting some sleep.

When I sat down at the breakfast bar, Adam handed me my coffee. "Drink up, love, you look like you need coffee this morning. I'll finish making the juice." I sighed and drank my coffee.

I looked at the clock on the wall and was surprised to find it was only a little after eight. I yawned. "I never get up this early on Sunday."

Adam smiled. "I'm usually up before the sun rises, so I feel like I overslept this morning."

"I just hope Mom and Dad sleep as long as possible. They both looked wrecked last night, especially my father. He looked twenty years older."

He nodded. "Yesterday aged him."

We sat there together until all the oranges had been squeezed, and we had two quarts of juice ready. I took the juicer to the sink, took it apart and washed it while Adam poured himself another cup of coffee.

"Let's take our coffee out on the porch. Your parents will sleep longer if the house is quiet."

Outside the air was cool and crisp. It was beginning to feel like autumn, a time of year I loved. The landscape was so colorful as the leaves began to fall. It was a wonderful time for an artist. Sadly, I wondered if I'd have any opportunity for drawing and painting in the forest before winter set in.

Adam's voice was soft. "You wish you were out there drawing those trees you love, don't you?"

I smiled at him. "Yeah, some trees and maybe an Elf or two."

It wasn't long before my phone began to ring.

"Hi, beautiful, how's your mom?"

"She's still asleep, but she seemed all right when the Chief brought her home last night. A little shaky, but all right."

"Ah, that's a relief. The Chief called us when she'd been located. We were still knocking on doors at our end of town. How are you feeling? It must have been an awful night for you."

"I'm okay, just tired. We didn't get much sleep."

There was a slight hesitation before Sean said, "We?"

"Adam stayed here with me. Everyone else was out searching."

"I wanted to stay with you, but your father and mine both thought I'd be more use outside, knocking on doors." I heard a deep sigh. "I'm glad you weren't alone, even if it wasn't with me."

"Well, I'm glad you were here earlier."

I'd been speaking very softly, but Adam looked over at me with a wry smile. I would have to speak to him about minding his own business when it came to my relationship with Sean.

Once I was off the phone, I turned around and faced him. "Remember, you're the one who encouraged me to accept Sean's apology last summer. As far as my relationship with him is concerned, you can butt out now."

He had that amused look on his face, the one that had always irritated me. "Does that mean you'll be kissing Sean whenever you think you need 'comforting?'"

Now he was pissing me off. "Yes. I like kissing Sean. And it's none of your business."

Still looking amused, he said, "Have you ever kissed anyone else? So that you'd have some basis for comparison, I mean."

It was time for me to be somewhere else, somewhere I wouldn't be tempted to dump my coffee over his head. I got up and went into the kitchen and began taking down plates, cups and silverware. Kevin wouldn't be here with brunch for another hour and a half, but I needed to keep my hands busy and my mouth shut.

I heard him say, "I think I just got my answer to that question."

A few minutes later there was a soft knock on the back door. I swung it open, prepared to tell Adam what he could do with his questions, but Arlynn was standing there, an unsure smile on her beautiful face. On her arm was a big basket of muffins. I looked over her shoulder and saw Adam striding through the yard into the woods. He waved a muffin at me.

Arlynn said, "Did I come at a bad time? I'm sorry. I just wanted to find out how your mother is feeling. Uh, I can leave if this isn't a good time."

I pulled her into the kitchen. "I'm sorry. It's not a bad time. I was just irritated with Adam. Come on in. I know Mom will be glad to see you. She and my father aren't up yet. They got home very late last night."

She handed me the basket of muffins she'd probably just made this morning.

"I brought your favorites, apple cinnamon. I hope Alicia likes them."

"I'm sure she'll love them. They might even inspire her to start baking. Mom loves to cook, but baking isn't one of her favorite things."

We heard Mom's voice from the top of the stairs. "I love baked goods. But I knew if I started baking my own, I'd just end up wearing them around my hips." She walked into the kitchen, smiling when she saw Arlynn. She looked a lot better this morning, which was a relief. In faded jeans and a pink t-shirt, she didn't look much older than I did.

She gave us both hugs and sat down at the table. "Cara, please pour me a cup of coffee to go with these beautiful muffins. Arlynn, it was sweet of you to bring them. I don't think I have the energy to make our usual Sunday brunch, so your muffins are a welcome treat."

I handed her the coffee, poured another cup for Arlynn, and sat down next to her. "Kevin's bringing brunch today. He told me not to let you do anything."

She actually laughed. "I didn't know Kevin could cook."

"He can't. He's raiding the deli downtown. He'll be here around eleven."

She was smiling. "I can't wait to see what he brings us. The deli has the best bagels and lox, and the most delicious homemade dill pickles." It was such a relief to see her smiling. My dad must have worked his magic last night.

"Is Dad still sleeping?" I asked.

"No, he's enjoying a hot shower, a real treat since he tells me they only have cold showers in Elvenwood."

"Yeah. It was fine when the weather was hot, but cold showers in the winter aren't something I'd want to live with."

Arlynn smiled. "Believe it or not, you get used to it. By the way, Cara, what kind of tea is this? It's, uh, quite strong."

I felt like an idiot. "Oh, I'm sorry! That's not tea. I gave you coffee. If you add cream and sugar, you might like it better. But I can make tea, if you'd like."

She added the cream and sugar, took a sip, and smiled. "This is really good." Another coffee convert.

I heard my father's footsteps on the stairs and looked up to see him wearing what Mom called his "street clothes," gray slacks and a button-down shirt.

He looked embarrassed, putting his hands in the pockets of his slacks. "I don't have any other clean clothes here."

I thought he looked fantastic. And a hundred percent better than he'd looked the night before. Maybe Mom was the one with the magic.

Mom looked up, obviously pleased. "You look fine, Brian."

I grinned at him. "Better than fine, Dad. You look very handsome. I like your street clothes."

His face was slightly pink. "Thank you, dear."

Looking thoughtful, Mom said, "You should probably bring a few changes of clothes to keep here."

Eyebrows raised, he said, "You wouldn't mind?"

"Of course not." The look on her face said a lot more.

Arlynn looked at me and we both smiled. She knew how much I wanted my parents together.

We nibbled on muffins and drank coffee until we heard the doorbell ring. I opened the door. Kevin held three large deli bags and wore a big smile. Right behind him was a grinning Amy who was carrying a huge bouquet of Chrysanthemums, gold, white, and bronze, all the autumn colors I loved.

"Hope you don't mind me tagging along. I just want to give your mom a big hug and these flowers." She whispered, "I didn't know what had happened until Sean and his dad rang our bell last night. Is she okay?"

"I think she's all right, but we haven't really had a chance to talk about it. Kevin, bring all that food in. Amy, you have to stay for brunch. And say hello to Arlynn."

They followed me into the kitchen, where Amy practically tackled Mom, hugging her and half-crushing the flowers she carried.

"These are for you, Mrs. C. I hope you don't mind me crashing your Sunday brunch. Kevin brought enough food for an army."

Mom gave Amy an equally warm hug, thanked her for the flowers, and stood to take a look into Kevin's bags from the deli while I put the colorful mums in water.

Amy's eyes were riveted on Arlynn, who smiled. "Hi, Amy, it's lovely to meet you."

Kevin pulled out a big bag of fresh bagels, a tub of cream cheese, a package of lox, and a plastic bag full of their homemade dill pickles. That was just the first bag he was carrying. The second bag contained a fresh loaf of rye bread, a package of rare roast beef, a block of Colby cheddar, and a jar of spicy mustard. The third and final bag held an entire sour cream cheesecake. Kevin folded up his bags with a happy smile. "Let's eat!"

"Kevin, you've really outdone yourself." Mom dropped a kiss on his cheek. "You didn't have to do all this, dear."

Kevin looked down at her, affection clear on his face. "After all the meals I'm bummed from you, it's the least I could do. I'm just glad you're home and in one piece, Mrs. C."

He looked down, his face pink.

Mom squeezed his arm and whispered, "I love you too, Kevin."

I couldn't help noticing that Amy kept staring at Arlynn, as though she wasn't quite sure the beautiful Elf was real.

I put all the food Kevin had brought on plates, put the fresh orange juice on the table and invited everyone to help themselves. And they did; the bagels and lox disappeared first. Next, Kevin and my father made themselves thick roast beef sandwiches and I made another pot of coffee.

Amy seemed surprised to see Arlynn eating a bagel and obviously enjoying it. She said, "Arlynn, you eat bagels like we do?"

Arlynn laughed. "What did you think I ate?"

In a dreamy voice, Amy said, "I don't know. Moonbeams maybe?"

I saw Mom struggling to keep a straight face as Arlynn blushed a deep pink.

Mom turned to Kevin. "Thank you so much, Kevin. Everything was delicious."

Kevin grinned, his eyes going to the cheesecake that was still sitting on the breakfast bar. "There's more, Mrs. C."

We decided to save the cheesecake for later, and Amy helped me clean up the kitchen and load the dishwasher.

Amy kissed Mom on the cheek. "I've got to run. My mother had an urge for Apple Cobbler this morning. I promised to give her a hand."

Kevin said, "Apple Cobbler . . . hey, Amy, can I come over later?"

Amy looked at Arlynn. "I'm sorry if I embarrassed you. I've really enjoyed meeting you. It's just that you kind of take people by surprise."

Arlynn smiled and blushed again. I was used to her, but I understood why her silvery hair and crystal blue eyes had taken Amy by surprise. She could have been one of those gorgeous Elves in "Lord of the Rings."

I walked Amy to the door. "So where's your studly bodyguard this morning?" she asked with a grin.

I just shook my head. "He was here earlier, but I got annoyed with him, and he left."

Amy looked amazed. "Cara, how can you get annoyed with a guy who looks like Adam and who's totally devoted to you?"

"Adam needs to butt out of my relationship with Sean. Who I kiss is totally my business, not Adam's!"

"Ooh, we have to talk. Call me later?"

I said I would, hugged her and she went out the door where Neal was waiting for her on the porch.

When I got back in the kitchen, Kevin was eyeing the cheesecake.

Mom said, "It was so nice of Amy to bring my favorite fall flowers, wasn't it? I'm going to keep them right here in the kitchen and enjoy them. Having your friends here this morning was good for all of us, I think."

Kevin asked, "Does anyone else have room for cheesecake?"

I rolled my eyes. Arlynn nodded with a smile.

I was surprised when Mom said she'd have a small piece. Dad smiled his approval and said he'd like a piece too.

Half an hour later, there was only half a cheesecake left.

Mom said, "Kevin, you really should take the rest of the cake home, along with the rest of the roast beef. I know how hungry you are all the time. I enjoyed it all immensely."

"My pleasure, Mrs. C." He chuckled. "After all, you've been feeding me since I was five."

Mom stood. "I think it's time for a nap. All that good food made me drowsy. Thanks again, Kevin. I'll see you later. Arlynn, dear, thank you for bringing those wonderful muffins. Please stay as long as you like." After hugging each of us, she left to go upstairs. My father got up, whispering, "I don't want her to be alone." He followed Mom upstairs.

When we heard her bedroom door close, Kevin said, "I couldn't help noticing that your dad was very quiet today. He hardly took his eyes off her."

I nodded. "I noticed too. He's worried about her. I am too."

"Has she said anything about what she went through?"

"Not yet. Mom has always kept the big things to herself. I don't know whether she'll want to talk about it or not. But I heard her crying last night."

Looking troubled, Kevin shook his head. "The Chief captured both men, didn't he?"

I shrugged. "I think so, but I don't know any more than you do. I haven't spoken to the Chief. He just dropped off Mom and Dad last night and left. I think he knew that Mom wanted to be home with her family."

Kevin nodded. "I think that's what she needed to feel safe again. To be home and to be with your dad."

I nodded. "One good thing that's come out of all these threats and stress, my parents have gotten a lot closer. My independent mother finally realizes she needs my father, which, in my opinion, is a very good thing."

Arlynn added, "The love between your parents is obvious, just in the way they look at each other. But I do hope what she experienced won't have any lasting effects. She does seem a little shaky, not quite herself."

Kevin and I looked at each other. We knew Arlynn was right.

She said, "It's time for me to be going. I have to meet Conor at your father's camp. He'll be riding back to Elvenwood with me. He's also kind of running things while your father is taking care of your mother."

After promising to give Conor a hug for me, she dropped a kiss on my cheek and left through the backyard.

After another piece of cheesecake, Kevin said, "We're back to school in the morning, short stuff. It seems like this weekend has been a month long. It's hard to remember that David Somers was killed Friday night, not even forty-eight hours ago."

I'd almost forgotten how this awful weekend started. I sighed. "I wonder how everyone else in school is handling it."

"I won't be surprised if there are counselors at school this week to help any of the kids who are still shell-shocked by David's death." Kevin shook his head. "I really regret that I never had a chance to get to know him."

After we talked a while longer, I helped Kevin pack up the leftovers so he could take them home. "I think I can see what you'll be having for dinner, Kev."

He grinned. "Yeah. Roast beef sandwiches and cheesecake. But for now, I've got to work on my newest game. I think I'm going to call it *Dragon Wars*."

I snorted. "Gee, I wonder where you got that idea."

"Don't forget, babe, you have to tell me more about your newest friend. Springing her on me like that last night was a major shock. I'm surprised my hair didn't turn gray!"

"Well, you're driving to school next week, so we can talk in the car. By now, I'm sure all of the Elves know about her. My father wanted to keep her existence a secret, but that idea's shot now. I'm sure the Elves who were in the woods last night got a good look at my amazing new friend."

Kevin still looked a little awed. "She's magnificent. I'm still waiting to find out how she managed to find your mom last night, and I'm dying to know what she did to those kidnappers."

"I'm really curious myself." I could have asked Rowenna, but at the time, I was more concerned about my mother.

After Kevin went home with his leftovers, I made myself a pot of tea and ran upstairs to get my English books. I'd already fallen behind with homework. With the house so quiet, this was a good time to catch up.

I was deep into Macbeth when there was a soft knock on the back door. Pushing my books aside, I got up to answer the door and was surprised to find Adam on the porch.

"What do you want?" I wasn't feeling polite.

"You're still mad at me."

Crossing my arms over my chest, I said, "Yep."

He sighed. "The weekend is almost over, so I won't see you again until next weekend. I didn't want to wait that long to apologize. You were right. Your relationship with your friends is none of my business." One eyebrow shot up. "As long as none of them are hurting you, that is."

"None of my friends are going to hurt me, Adam."

"One already did, not long before I met you."

Of course he was referring to Sean and the painful break-up we'd had in June.

"I think I can safely say that won't happen again. Sean doesn't want to lose me again."

"So you *are* his 'girlfriend' again."

"No, Adam, I'm no one's girlfriend. I don't want another boyfriend. I don't think I want to depend on anyone that much again."

He nodded, but he wasn't smiling. "Well then, I guess you're free to kiss anyone you like. I won't interfere."

"Does that include you, Adam?" *Why on earth did I say that?*

He laughed softly, pinning me with those dark blue eyes. "That would be playing with fire, love."

Still chuckling, he walked down the steps and headed for the woods. I watched until he disappeared in the trees.

CHAPTER 33

I was just putting away my English homework when Mom and Dad came downstairs around suppertime. They helped themselves to coffee and sat down with me.

"Got all your homework done?" Mom asked.

I rolled my eyes. "Yeah, but I'm not a fan of Macbeth." I waved my book in the air. "Wish my teacher had chosen one of Shakespeare's more lighthearted plays."

She nodded. "I think we've had enough tragedy." My father put his arm around her. He was still watching her closely.

When I admitted I was a little hungry, Mom heated up soup and we made sandwiches for supper.

After we'd eaten, there were things I wanted to ask Mom, but something told me to wait. Maybe it was the careful way my father was watching her, the way you'd watch a bomb you thought might go off. She had said all the right things today when Kevin, Amy, and Arlynn visited. But she seemed brittle, not at all like the self-confident Alicia Connelly I'd always known.

"Mom, are you really okay?"

She looked at me, and then shook her head. "Not really, but I'm just glad to be home with you and your father. I've decided to stay home from the bookstore this week. I called Christina and she agreed to work at the store until I'm ready to return." She frowned. "I just don't want to see people or answer questions right now. Chief O'Donnell wants to come over to talk to me, and I can't put him off indefinitely. Cara, I'd like you and your father to be here when I speak to the Chief. That may make it easier."

"Sure, Mom. Is there anything I can do for you now?"

She smiled. "Just keep singing for Rowenna. I owe her more than I can tell you." She got up, saying, "I'm tired again, dear. I think I'll go to bed early."

My father didn't say anything, just put his arm around Mom and followed her upstairs.

I was sure there were Elves near the house keeping an eye on us, so I went out on the back porch by myself, turning all the lights off first. The nights were getting cooler now so I grabbed Mom's sweater on my way out.

There was only a crescent moon in the sky, leaving the backyard and the forest almost completely dark. Ralph had followed me outside but instead of curling up the way he usually did, he got up on his back legs, putting his front paws on the railing, his ears at attention. I wondered what he was hearing, but then the familiar wave of magic surrounded me and I knew Rowenna was above us. I began singing her song softly.

I heard her rough voice. *Cara. Is Alicia all right?*

"Not exactly. She doesn't want to talk about it. She only said that you'd saved her life."

When she came outside to see me, I wished I could give her some of my strength. Her body is strong but it will take time before she feels safe again. Please tell her I'll be nearby every night if she needs me.

"I'll let her know, Rowenna. I know she's very grateful to you."

I began singing her song again as I felt her great wings stirring the air above me, her magic gradually leaving me.

Ralph whined, sitting in front of me and putting his front paws in my lap. I felt that he just needed reassurance that everything was okay. I stroked his head and explained that the creature he'd heard and smelled was a friend and wouldn't hurt us. He whined again, licking my hand. He also sensed that something was not quite right with Mom. Ralph had always been a sensitive animal.

I whispered, "She'll be all right, Ralphie. She needs some time to recover; she's not feeling very good right now. She'll be home this week so you can give her lots of love. That may help."

I leaned down and dropped a kiss on his velvety head. I heard him sigh. I knew he had understood every word I'd said.

We sat outside together until it got uncomfortably cool. It was still too early to go to bed, but I didn't know what else to do with myself, so I went up to my room with Ralph at my heels. Still tense, I thought it might be a good night for a relaxing bubble bath. I started running the bath water and threw in a handful of herbal bath salts. In minutes my bathroom smelled like a leafy glade in the forest, which was exactly what I needed. I hadn't had enough time in the forest since school started, and I missed it.

If leaning back in the tub, closing my eyes, and visualizing the forest around me could be considered meditating, then I meditated for at least a half hour. When the water cooled off, I got out, dried off and pulled my soft, oversized t-shirt over my head. My phone started ringing just as I walked out of the bathroom.

It had to be Sean.

"Hi, beautiful." His deep voice was just what I needed.

"Hey, Sean. Did you catch up on your sleep today?"

"Yeah. How about you? You were tired when I spoke to you earlier."

"I'm not really tired now. Just kind of at loose ends. Finished the Macbeth homework and didn't know what to do with myself. Mom went to bed early and Dad went with her. He hasn't taken his eyes off her all day. She's not herself right now."

"I'm sorry, Cara. It's good your dad is there."

"Yeah, it is. Hey, did you ever tell your dad about meeting your grandfathers?"

He chuckled. "You should have seen the shock on his face when I described meeting both my grandfather and great-grandfather. He didn't even know my great-grandfather was still alive. His father, my grandfather, didn't leave Thornewood until my grandmother passed away and my father was an adult. That left my dad with no other family, as far as he knew. With my grandfather living in Elvenwood, and the story given out that he had died too, my dad's memories of his father began to fade, I guess.

"When Dad met my mother, he never told her about the Elven part of his family. His mother and grandmother were both human. My mom had never heard the old stories about Blackthorne Forest. She grew up in Boston."

"Do you think he was afraid to tell her he was descended from a long line of mythical creatures?" I couldn't help giggling. "I guess I can see where that might have been a problem."

He chuckled. "Yeah. I seem to remember you were afraid of the same thing when we started talking about Blackthorne Forest and the old legends."

"Yeah, I was afraid you'd head for the hills."

"Ah. And you wanted me to stick around?"

THE DRAGON'S SONG

He had me. "Yep. Do you think your father will get back in touch with his dad and grandfather now that he's been reminded that they're still alive and well?"

"He's thinking about it. But I still think he's afraid to tell my mom. That's something he'll have to figure out. I don't really think Mom would freak out."

"I remember once wondering if you and your dad had ever considered that your outstanding athletic ability might be part of your Elven heritage. Have you ever thought about it?"

"Huh. Athletics has always been such a big part of my life, I just considered myself lucky. But I guess it's possible."

"Well, now that I've given you some food for thought, I'd better say good night." I chuckled. "Hope it won't be keeping you awake tonight!"

Sean had a great smile, and I could almost hear him smiling.

"If your voice is the last thing I hear every night, I'm happy. Well, as long as you're not telling me to get lost!"

I was smiling too. "I'll see you at school in the morning. Pleasant dreams."

"All of you," he added softly.

Once I was off the phone, I knew I should find a way to tell Sean not to expect more from me, but this was probably not the best time. I wanted to be honest with him, but I didn't want to hurt him.

I walked to my bedroom window. Leaning on the windowsill, I looked out at the lights shining through the trees. My father's camp was probably full tonight. I wondered who was taking care of things in camp while my dad was staying with us.

I didn't even have to wonder. Two seconds later, I heard a familiar soft voice in my head.

Everything's under control here. Conor and I are taking turns filling in for your father. Everyone here is aware that his place is with your mother right now. You can call on me if there's anything you need.

"Adam, were you reading my mind?"

I could hear him laughing. *No. I was watching your house and saw you come to your window.*

"Oh. Okay. I'm going to bed now. Will I see you during the week?"

If you need me. Ryan will be with you for school. He hesitated. *Cara, I hope you know that you can call on me anytime. If there's a storm, if you're frightened or just uneasy, you can call me and I'll come to you.*

"Okay. Thanks, Adam. Good night."

Good night, love.

I turned out the light and got into bed, thinking of Adam, of course. As annoyed as I'd been with him earlier, that's how grateful I was feeling now.

Ralph was already snoring at the foot of my bed. I was picturing Adam's dark blue eyes in my mind as I drifted off to sleep.

CHAPTER 34

When I ran downstairs in the morning, I was surprised to find my father standing by the stove, looking rather helpless.

It was a comical sight. I couldn't help smiling. "What's wrong, Dad? You look kind of lost."

"Well, your mother always makes breakfast before sending you off to school, so I thought I should do the same. She's still asleep and I didn't want to wake her. She had a restless night."

"I'm sorry to hear that, but you don't have to make breakfast. Really." I pulled a box of cereal out of one of the cabinets, got milk out of the fridge, and got down bowls, spoons and glasses.

"This is a non-cooked breakfast. All you have to do is pour the milk into the bowl. There's also orange juice in the fridge. We can have an easy breakfast together."

Looking relieved, he got the juice out of the fridge, poured a glass for each of us and sat down with me. "I thought I should at least try to fill in for your mother, but you seem to have everything under control."

"Dad, if Mom doesn't feel like cooking, that's fine. She deserves a break. After all, I can make salads and sandwiches. We won't go hungry."

"And I can make coffee by myself now," he said with a smile.

"Will you be here with Mom until she's feeling better?"

He nodded. "She gets nervous if I'm out of the room for even a few minutes." He looked frustrated. "It's as though her bedroom is a cave she's crawled into to lick her wounds. She'd rather avoid the rest of the world. Except for you, of course. She's not trying to avoid you, dear."

"I think I know how she feels. After my kidnapping, just leaving the house was scary. This house, with you and Mom, was my cave. And I was always nervous when you weren't here. It took weeks before I began to feel more like myself."

My father nodded. "I remember. We'll just have to be patient with your mother. I'll put off Chief O'Donnell as long as possible."

"Time for me to leave for school. Kevin's driving this week." I stood up and dropped a kiss on his cheek. "Please give Mom my love. I'll see you after school."

Ryan was waiting for me on the porch, looking serious. "How's your mother, lass? We're all worried about her."

Kevin had just pulled up at the curb, so I said, "Wait 'til we get in the car. I know Kevin and Patrick will want to know too." Ryan took my hand and we ran to the curb where Kevin's Jeep was parked.

"Hey, short stuff, hi, Ryan. How's Mom today?"

Ryan and I climbed into the back seat. "I think it's going to take her some time to recover. She's still not willing to talk about what happened. She'll be staying home from work this week."

"Gee, she looked good when I saw her yesterday. What happened?"

"I think she just put on a good face for you and Amy. She doesn't want to worry anyone. But I know she's having trouble sleeping, like I did after my kidnapping. My dad hasn't left her side."

"Your mom's always been so strong, I guess I took it for granted that she could handle this. I'd like to stop by to see her again if she's up to it. Give her my love, would you?" Kevin was quiet until we reached school.

It had started to rain so we dashed into school where Amy, Sean, Neal and Gabriel were waiting for us outside the principal's office. Mr. Weiss motioned to me from his doorway and I walked over and handed my knives to him.

"Everyone knows what happened to your mother on Saturday. How is she?"

I gave him an abbreviated version of what I'd told Kevin and the boys. He shook his head sadly. "I'm very sorry, Cara. Please give your mother my regards." As he walked back inside his office, he muttered, "I'm beginning to understand the knives."

When I returned to my friends, Amy grabbed my arm. "How's your mom today?"

I explained that Mom seemed okay physically, but that she was a little shaky emotionally. "She loved your flowers and put them in the middle of the kitchen table because they're so cheerful. She needs a lot of cheerful around her right now."

Looking sad, Amy said, "I'm so sorry, Cara. I thought she looked a little too good yesterday. She doesn't want us to know how she's really feeling, does she?"

I shook my head.

Sean put his arm around me. "We'd better get to class. See you all at lunch." He led me down the hall, where I was stopped every few seconds by someone saying how sorry they were about what had happened to Mom. A few students asked how she was feeling, surprising me by saying they knew her from The Crescent Moon. One girl said, "I always love going into your mom's store. I love the incense she burns and she's always so warm and friendly. I got my favorite silver necklace there. Please tell her Paige said hi."

I said I would, again amazed that so many people actually knew my mother.

If Sean hadn't pulled me into class, I probably would have been out in the hall receiving good wishes for Mom for an hour. Even our Science teacher took me aside to say, "Please give your mother my regards. The entire faculty was shocked to hear what happened to her. I hope she'll be well soon." I thanked him and went to my seat.

Sean held my hand all through the class I barely heard. I'd have a lot of catch-up reading to do if I couldn't get my mind back on my classes. I mentioned this to Sean on the way to our next class. "Don't worry. I take a lot of notes. You can borrow them."

I'd been so lost in my own memories, I hadn't noticed all the writing he had been doing.

At lunch the message we'd been expecting came over the loudspeaker. A counselor would be available in the guidance counselor's office after school for any students who needed help dealing with David Somers' death. The counselor would be there until 9:00 p.m. All students were encouraged to stop by.

I looked at Sean. I whispered, "I hope you're planning to go."

He looked down at me, his face sad, and nodded.

Amy asked, "Are you going, Cara?"

"No, I want to get home to my mother. Kevin, I can take the bus if you want to stay for the counselor."

"That's okay, short stuff, I'll be going home with you. I mean, I feel terrible about David's death, but I didn't really know him. He was in my PE class, but we never even spoke."

Kevin looked at Sean, "David was on the football team. Did you get to know him at all?"

Sean shook his head. "He was really quiet. All I knew about him was that he'd just moved to Thornewood and never played football before. But he had potential; he was big and moved well. Coach was thrilled to have him."

Shaking his head again, he muttered, "I keep thinking it should have been me."

I grabbed his arm. "No, Sean, it shouldn't have been you. You've got to stop feeling guilty about something that you couldn't have prevented. I'm glad you're seeing the counselor after school."

He leaned over, brushed his face against my hair and said softly, "I'll call you tonight."

I knew I had to find a way to tell Sean how I felt, but this wasn't the right time.

We said goodbye and Kevin and I headed for Art class, with Ryan and Patrick right behind us. Ryan said, "He still thinks it was his fault the other boy was killed?"

"Yeah. Sean's carrying a heavy load of guilt. I hope the counselor can help him."

Kevin added, "I think the counselor will have to deal with more than David's death. A lot of students are frightened because they never thought anything like this could happen here. It's like their sense of security has been badly damaged." He looked at me with one eyebrow arched. "Of course, our sense of security disappeared months ago."

Our bodyguards exchanged serious glances. Thanks to Donald Gaynes, we were all aware that our safety in the small town of Thornewood had been merely an illusion.

I wasn't even able to focus in Art class. PE only required me to exercise and do a little tumbling, something I could do without thinking. After the final bell, I met Kevin, Patrick and Ryan in the hall, and we headed for the principal's office so I could collect my knives.

It had stopped raining, which was a relief. As the four of us walked to Kevin's Jeep, a big kid I'd seen around school stepped in front of me abruptly, almost knocking me off my feet. He was tall but looked soft, reminding me of the Pillsbury Dough Boy.

He frowned at me, his mouth turned down in a sneer as he spit out, "David's death is all your fault. My father told me all about you. If you and your family weren't around, the bakery wouldn't have burned down, there wouldn't be guys riding around aiming guns at us, and David Somers would still be alive. You and your father are to blame for every rotten thing that's been happening in this town." I just stood there, shocked.

THE DRAGON'S SONG

He thrust his arm out as if to push me to the ground, but Ryan and Patrick were suddenly standing in front of me, their hands on his chest, pushing the big kid back at least a foot. He almost lost his balance, yelling, "You've caused so much trouble, you had to bring professional bodyguards into our school. You're a menace, Cara Connelly!"

The police officer on duty outside the main entrance was coming toward us just as the big kid's friends started advancing on the four of us. There were at least six boys, obviously looking for trouble, one carrying a baseball bat.

The cop must have radioed for backup at the first sign of trouble because before a fight could break out, we heard sirens heading our way. Kevin looked at me, as we both breathed a sigh of relief.

I looked toward the school's entrance just as Principal Weiss came through the door fast, clearly angry. He must have caught some of the interaction through his window. He met the police car that had just pulled up next to us. Chief O'Donnell climbed out slowly with a frown on his face. Mr. Weiss and the Chief had a quick conversation as the officer who'd called for help stood in front of the big kid's group with his arms crossed over his chest.

"Kev, who is that big kid who was yelling at me? Do you know him?"

"Ed Wilson. He's always complaining about something, and he's a bully. I've never seen him pick on anyone his own size. He's 17, a junior. I don't think anybody likes him."

"What about the guys with him?"

"Only two of those guys go to school here, and they've been troublemakers since the fifth grade. I've never seen the other guys before; they must be from out of town."

Principal Weiss went over to Wilson and his group and began reading them the riot act. It was the first time I'd ever heard him raise his voice. Unfortunately, Wilson started yelling back and I heard the same kind of complaints that he'd yelled at me. The big kid stood there with his hands on his hips, as though he was the victim.

I could hear Mr. Weiss' angry voice. He suspended Wilson on the spot, threatened to do the same to the other kids who were students at Thornewood High, and told the unfamiliar kids that the police wanted to speak to each of them. The Thornewood students all looked shocked to see our normally easy-going principal so angry. The out-of-towners began looking nervous as two police officers descended on them and led them into two separate police cars.

After Chief O'Donnell sent the two police cars to the station, he walked over to Kevin and me. He had a few questions about what had happened, which I answered, but I had a few questions for him.

"Chief, Ed Wilson seemed to know a lot more than most of the students do. He knew that the fire at Amy's bakery was linked to us. He said his father told him about me. He blamed me for the men who tried to shoot Amy. He also blames me for David's death. I know the police force understands how I'm connected to all of these things. But how does his father know about my family and me?"

Chief O'Donnell looked at me and sighed. He actually looked embarrassed. "Cara, I'm afraid that Ed Wilson's father is a cop, and I guess he's been taking his work home with him."

He looked down and shoved his hands into his pockets. "The accusations Ed was throwing at you had to come from his dad, who hasn't learned to keep his mouth shut about cases we're currently working on." He shook his head. "I'll be speaking to Officer Wilson tonight. I'm really sorry about this, Cara. I know you have enough to deal with right now."

He turned to leave but stopped. "Please give my regards to your mother. She doesn't have to talk to me today, but I will need her statement as soon as possible."

"I will, Chief. We appreciate your patience."

He nodded. "I'll be following you home today, just to make sure no one else bothers you." He got into his new cruiser, starting the car and letting it idle while he waited for us to climb into Kevin's Jeep. Once we pulled away from the curb, the Chief pulled behind us, following us to my house.

As Ryan and I got out of the Jeep, Kevin said, "Let's talk later, short stuff."

"Okay, Kev. After dinner."

He nodded and drove around the corner to his house. Ryan walked me to the front door. "See you in the morning, lass. I'll be out here tonight if you need me."

"Thanks for protecting me earlier. You and Patrick moved so fast, I thought you had wings. I'm grateful."

He nodded, completely serious. "We would never let anyone hurt you, lass."

He sat down on the front porch as I opened the door and walked inside. The house was quiet but I could smell coffee, so at least something was normal.

My parents were sitting in the kitchen quietly. Mom was drinking Kathleen's tea, but Dad was drinking coffee. They both looked worn out.

I dropped my backpack on the floor. "What's going on? You both look awful." This didn't seem to be the time for tact.

Mom was running her fingers through her curly hair, and it looked like she'd been doing it a lot all day. "If I could just get a decent night's sleep, I think I'd be better able to cope, dear."

My father was holding her hand. "Alicia, Kathleen makes another tea that she's given Cara a few times when she was really upset, and it helped Cara fall asleep. Would you like to try it? If I ask, I'm sure Kathleen will be glad to bring some over. Besides, I'd like you to meet her, and I know she'd like to meet you. I think you'd like her."

"Yeah, Mom, Kathleen's great. She's been a really good friend."

Mom looked thoughtful. "Well, I do like this other tea Kathleen makes. Normally, it relaxes me. But right now, I need something stronger." She nodded decisively. "Brian, please invite her over here. I'd like to meet her."

Looking relieved, Dad said, "I'll go outside and send her a message. I'm sure she'll come as soon as she's able to." Smiling, he went out on the back porch.

There were times when telepathy was more efficient than a cell phone.

"Mom, there's one other thing we haven't had a chance to tell you. I spoke to Rowenna last night. She wanted to know how you were feeling. She wanted me to tell you that she'll be nearby whenever you need her."

Her eyes were wide as she looked at me. "If she hadn't found me when she did, it would have been so much worse." She looked down at her hands, frowning.

She was almost whispering as she said, "They were supposed to kill me, Cara. I wasn't supposed to survive." My father came in as she said those words.

"The police have those men, don't they?" I asked him.

"I haven't heard differently," he told me.

She pressed her face into my father's broad chest. I could see tears on her face.

I could barely hear my father's deep, velvety voice, but I think he said something like, "This will never happen again, Alicia. I'll protect you myself."

Mom nodded and dried her eyes. "I'd like to thank Rowenna again, Cara. Would you call her please?"

I went out on the porch and began singing the dragon's song. Rowenna must have been close because the air was full of magic within seconds and the huge dragon lowered herself into the grass in the backyard.

Mom joined me on the porch, my father right behind her. "I want to speak to her privately, dear." She walked down the steps and kept going until she was just a few feet in front of the dragon.

Apparently, Rowenna could send her message to just one person when she chose to. I couldn't hear what she was saying to Mom, and Mom's words were too soft to hear. They were speaking for a while, Mom nodding every so often.

Finally, Mom placed one hand on the dragon's face. "Thank you."

Rowenna nodded her huge head and looked up at me. *Good bye, Cara.*

Spreading her great wings, she rose into the darkening sky and was lost to view within seconds, leaving a fine trail of magic behind her.

My mother was smiling as she walked back to the porch. She looked as though a weight had been lifted off of her. When she walked up the steps she threw her arms around me. "I love you, Cara. We are so lucky to have you in our lives."

"I love you too, Mom." Her mood had changed so much, I wondered what Rowenna had said to her.

She let go of me and walked to my father, wrapping her arms around his waist.

"I love you, Brian. I always have."

He put his hands on either side of her face, bent down and kissed her. It was a lengthy kiss. Finally he raised his head. "I've loved you since the first day I saw you, Alicia."

I was thrilled. I felt warm and happy on the inside. I couldn't take my eyes off of my petite, redheaded mother and my tall, dark and handsome father. Together, the way they were always meant to be.

A few minutes later, my parents realized they had an audience and turned to me, looking slightly embarrassed.

I couldn't get the smile off my face.

CHAPTER 🍎 35

When I looked at the kitchen clock, it was only seven. "Is anyone else hungry?"

Mom looked at Dad and asked, "Pizza?"

The enthusiastic grin on his face was answer enough. I called and ordered two pizzas. Ryan was on the front porch. I was sure he'd be hungry too.

My father still had his arms around Mom and seemed reluctant to let go, but sitting down at the table required it, and he contented himself by just holding her hand. When I looked at Mom, she was actually glowing. I was now convinced that love was the greatest remedy for any kind of pain. Apparently, Rowenna had been able to successfully communicate that fact to my mother.

When both pizzas had been demolished and I'd cleaned up the kitchen, I told them I had to call Kevin and went upstairs. I had a feeling they would need some privacy. Before I left the room, Mom said, "Cara, I'm going to ask Tommy O'Donnell to come over tomorrow afternoon when you get home from school. He has questions I need to answer and I'd like you and your father to both be here." She pushed her curly hair out of her eyes. "I don't want this miserable thing hanging over us any longer. I know we have other problems to deal with."

"Sounds good to me, Mom. I don't know what Rowenna actually did to you, but she's obviously a miracle worker." I dropped a kiss on her head and on Dad's and ran upstairs.

I curled up on my bed with Ralph and phoned Kevin.

He picked up his phone with "Hey, short stuff. How's your mom tonight?"

"Kev, you're going to find this hard to believe, but I think she's fine now. Better than ever, in fact."

"Really? What happened?"

"Rowenna happened. She seems to care about Mom. They spent about a half hour together this evening and Mom's much better now.

She even agreed to see Chief O'Donnell tomorrow and answer his questions. She wants to get over this whole thing and just move on. I'm so proud of her."

"Wow! I'm really happy for your mom. Are she and Rowenna bff's now?"

"Seems that way. Rowenna took to Mom immediately. Mom hasn't said anything about it, but I think Rowenna was speaking to her while she was still tied up in the kidnapper's SUV."

"Cara, I'm wondering what Rowenna did to those kidnappers. I was speaking to one of the cops parked out in front of my house a while ago. He said there's only one of those two men in jail now. When I asked about the second one, he said, 'he's dead.'"

That was a surprise. "I wonder if Rowenna will tell me what happened."

"It'd be interesting to find out, babe. If Rowenna is as fond of your mom as she seems to be, I'm kind of surprised both of those men weren't found dead.

"By the way, did you tell your parents about that business with Ed Wilson this afternoon?"

"No. When I got home from school, there was no way I was going to say anything that would upset them. Of course, the Chief may mention it when he's here interviewing Mom tomorrow, but I hope he doesn't."

"Actually, it would be to his advantage not to say anything. Think about this, Cara. One of his trusted officers killed David Somers, and another one tells his family confidential information about open criminal cases. I'm wondering about the integrity of the rest of the police force, and I'm thinking a lot of people will be wondering the same thing if it gets out."

I sighed. He was right. "Well, with Wilson suspended, maybe the rest of this week will go smoothly." I tried not to think of what Gaynes might try next.

"Don't count on it. We have no idea how many other people Wilson has been shooting his mouth off to. He has a big mouth and no sense at all. He has what I call a persecution complex. He thinks every problem he's ever had was caused by someone else. You know the type."

"Kev, do you really think he's stirred up other kids who will blame us for David's death and all the other problems Gaynes is responsible for?"

"I think we'll find out tomorrow."

On that uncomfortable note, we said good night. I realized that if there was going to be trouble, it was better to be prepared.

CHAPTER 36

The next morning I was in the shower, trying to meditate for a few minutes, when I realized I hadn't heard from Sean the night before. Before he left to see the counselor at school, he had said he'd call. My mind had been so full of other things, I'd forgotten.

Worried, I barely noticed what I was wearing as I got dressed. But I made sure my knives were tucked securely into my boots.

Laughter was coming from the kitchen as I ran down the stairs. That was a surprise.

I walked in to find Mom and Kathleen sitting at the table, smiling and chatting.

When Kathleen saw me, she got up to give me a hug. "Cara, dear, it's good to see you. It was such a treat to be invited to come and meet your mother." She grinned. "I now know why you've grown up to be such a sweet girl. Your mother is lovely."

She sat back down with Mom as I leaned down to drop a kiss on Mom's cheek. Seeing my mother with Kathleen was amazing. Why had I never noticed it before? With their auburn hair, blue eyes, and peaches and cream complexions, Kathleen and Mom could be sisters. They were both smiling at me, probably wondering why I was still standing in the doorway staring at them.

"What is it, Cara?" Mom asked. "Did you forget that your father invited Kathleen to visit?"

I shook my head. Ducking back into the hallway, I took down a small mirror from the wall and set it in front of Mom and Kathleen. "Can you two see what I'm seeing?"

They looked at each other, looked into the mirror, and then looked at each other again and burst out laughing.

Mom looked at me with a big smile. "Sweetheart, I guess I understand why you talk about Kathleen so much. When you've been in Elvenwood, she's looked after you the way I would. Am I right?"

"Mmm, sort of. Kathleen's been a wonderful friend whenever I needed help. But you have to admit, you two look like sisters."

Kathleen laughed. "Alicia, do you think we might be related?"

Mom shook her head. "It's not likely. I don't have a drop of Elven blood. We found that out when Brian tried to bring me to Elvenwood. The gateway wouldn't open."

"Well, Cara's right. We do look a great deal alike. It makes me wonder."

There was a basket of familiar-looking muffins on the table, so I took one and put a little butter on it. It was delicious. "Did these come from Arlynn?"

"Of course, dear. When Arlynn heard I was coming here this morning, she ran over to my cottage with these muffins before I left.

"Alicia, Arlynn wanted me to tell you she's planning on coming by to see you in a day or two." Lowering her voice, she said, "She feels terribly guilty about you being abducted right in front of her when she was assigned as your bodyguard. I don't know that she'll ever forgive herself."

Mom shook her head. "There was absolutely nothing she could have done. It happened too fast. If it was anyone's fault, it was mine. Brian specifically told me never to go outside without a bodyguard, and without thinking, I ran out of the store to mail some things at the corner, something I do almost daily. Those men must have been watching the store. I played right into their hands. It certainly wasn't Arlynn's fault."

She turned to me. "I already called Tommy O'Donnell. He'll be here after you get home from school." She sighed. "Then I'm hoping we can put this whole awful thing behind us."

I wouldn't bring it up, but I knew Gaynes wasn't through with us yet.

As I munched on another muffin, I asked, "Mom, how well do you know the Chief? He treats you like an old friend."

She chuckled. "Tommy and I went to high school together. I think he had a little crush on me, but we never dated. We've been friends for years."

I stood and slung my backpack over my shoulder. "Where's Dad?"

"When Kathleen got here, he walked out to his camp to see his men. He'll be back soon."

I hugged them both and left to meet Kevin and the boys. I was thrilled seeing Mom looking and acting like her old self. Inviting Kathleen over to see Mom had been a stroke of brilliance. A female friend her own age, someone she could be open with, was exactly what she needed.

Ryan was waiting for me on the porch, and I told him that Mom was feeling like herself again. That put a smile on his face. "Wonderful news, lass. I'm happy for all of you."

When we climbed into Kevin's back seat, we were both smiling. Kevin knew the news was good. "Your mother has to be feeling better. I haven't seen that smile in days."

"Yeah, Kev, she's so much better, I'm having trouble believing what I'm seeing. Kathleen came to visit this morning, which helped a lot. There was a lot of laughter in the kitchen this morning."

Kevin grinned as he glanced over his shoulder at me. "That's very good news."

I remembered Sean. "Kev, have you heard anything from or about Sean since we left school yesterday? He said he'd call me last night, but he didn't. I'm kind of concerned. He was going to see the counselor after school."

"No, I only spoke to one of our classmates last night. Brandon Wong has been in all of my math classes since Ninth grade. He called to say he'd heard some talk from a few kids at school yesterday afternoon that all the threats the Thornewood police have been dealing with are directly linked to you and your family. He knows you and I are friends and asked if what he'd heard was true."

"What did you tell him?"

"I told him who Donald Gaynes is and why he's out for revenge. He didn't know you'd been kidnapped last spring, but he knew your mom had been grabbed. He was shocked when he heard the true story. He thinks Gaynes is a psychopath. He said if he hears any more rumors, he'll set them straight."

"Well, you did say we'd find out today if Wilson's been talking trash about us."

We got to school and ran into the building, looking for Amy and Sean near the principal's office, but they weren't there. Kevin and I looked at each other. We both had the same bad feeling.

Mr. Weiss waved at me from his office and I walked over and handed him my knives.

"Mr. Weiss, do you have a few minutes?" I asked.

He said he did so I waved Kevin over.

"Kev, tell Mr. Weiss about the rumor that reached you last night."

Kevin told him what Brandon had heard, and the principal just shook his head.

"Apparently, Ed Wilson has managed to do more damage despite being suspended. Chief O'Donnell told me he was going to speak to Officer Wilson, but perhaps I should call the Wilsons in for a conference. I'm sorry, Cara, I know you've been having a tough time. If there are any more problems, please come to me right away."

I thanked him and we left his office doorway just as Amy ran in the main door. As soon as she got close enough, we could see she was upset. Neal was right behind her and he was frowning too.

"Where's Sean? What's happened?" I asked her.

"Cara, Sean's in the hospital. When his dad didn't show up to pick me up this morning, I called his house. I don't know the details, but his mom told me he got into a fight with three guys after he left school yesterday. It was kind of late because of the counseling session, so Sean and Gabe walked home. I don't know what the fight was about, but Sean and Gabe both got clobbered with a baseball bat one of the kids was carrying."

Kevin looked at me. We knew what the fight was about, and we knew who started it.

"Amy, I think Kevin and I know what they were fighting about. We'll explain later. But how badly were Sean and Gabe hurt?"

"According to Sean's mom, Sean has a lump on his head, a lot of bruises, and his nose was broken again. She wasn't sure about Gabe because he wouldn't go to the hospital, but she thinks he's in better shape than Sean."

The bell rang and we all had to scurry to get to our first class. All I could do was get on my cell phone between classes and see what I could find out.

By lunchtime, all I'd learned was that Sean was being kept in the hospital because of the head injury. They also wanted a plastic surgeon to take a look at his nose, which had been broken quite badly. His mom didn't know when he'd be released, but she'd seen him and said he'd call me as soon as he was allowed to use his phone.

When I tried to apologize, she stopped me. "Cara, I know who the responsible party is. My husband filled me in. It certainly isn't you or your father who's caused all this trouble. Sean's more worried about you than he is about himself."

I met Amy, Kevin, and our bodyguards in the lunchroom and told them what Sean's mom had said. "I'm going to tell Mr. Weiss about this. He saw what happened outside school yesterday with that kid carrying a baseball bat. He needs to talk to Sean to verify who Sean and Gabe fought with, although there's no question in my mind." Kevin looked at me and nodded. "Yeah. No question at all."

Then we had to fill in Amy and Neal about Ed Wilson and what he and his buddies had done yesterday. Amy said, "You think Wilson and his crew attacked Sean and Gabe, right?"

"Had to be them," Kevin said. "I don't believe in coincidence. Wilson would have knocked Cara down yesterday if Ryan and Patrick hadn't stepped in. Mr. Weiss saw the whole thing and suspended Wilson, which must have really pissed him off. The attack on Sean happened later." Then he told Amy about the rumor Wilson was spreading and where he was getting his information.

Amy frowned, shaking her head in disbelief. "When Weiss finds out about Sean, Wilson will be expelled. Suspension isn't nearly enough for what he's done. And another cop problem? Where did the Chief get these guys?"

Kevin said, "The Chief has only been the Chief for the past four years, when the old Chief retired. He inherited most of the men on the force. At least he can hire two good men now. Of course, I'm assuming that Officer Wilson will soon be history."

The bell rang, and as we were leaving the lunchroom, I said, "I'll see the Chief this afternoon. He's coming over to talk to Mom and get her statement. I'll let him know about Sean."

Amy said, "Call me tonight." I said I would and Kevin and I left for Art class with Ryan and Patrick. For the next hour, I didn't think I'd be able to concentrate on Art.

When the last bell rang after PE, Ryan and I walked to the Principal's office to retrieve my knives, but also to let him know what had happened to Sean.

I knocked on his door and he called, "Come in, Cara." He took my knives out of his desk drawer and handed them to me. I thanked him and said, "I thought you should know that Sean McKay is in the hospital. I spoke to his mother and she said he got into a fight with three boys on his way home from the counseling session yesterday. One of the boys had a baseball bat."

He nodded, his face troubled. "Mrs. McKay called me this morning to tell me Sean's in the hospital. She doesn't know when he'll be coming back to school. And, Cara, I know what you're thinking, but we don't know for sure who Sean fought with, so I'd appreciate it if you'd keep this to yourself."

I said I would. I tucked my knives into my boots and Ryan and I left. Kevin and Patrick were waiting for us in the entryway.

It was one of those beautiful Indian Summer days, very cool in the morning, but heating to the high seventies by lunch time. At three o'clock, it had cooled off a little but the air felt great and the familiar smell of falling autumn leaves surrounded us. It was one of my favorite times of the year.

I would have enjoyed the beautiful autumn day more as we walked to Kevin's Jeep, but it was parked at the end of the block so we were hurrying. We didn't manage to get to school early this morning so we didn't get one of the coveted parking spaces right in front of the school's entrance.

The Eastern edge of Blackthorne Forest lay directly across the street from the school. As we reached Kevin's Jeep, I turned to say something to Kevin and felt something hard and sharp hit my face. When I put my hand up to my face, it was bloody.

Ryan was at my side and quickly turned me to face him. "You're bleeding, lass. Quite a bit, actually." Patrick pulled a towel out of his backpack and handed it to me. "Use this to put pressure on your forehead, Cara." He dropped his backpack and said, "I'll catch him," and sprinted into the woods across the street.

Kevin unlocked the Jeep and herded me into the backseat. "Don't worry about the blood. The seats are vinyl; it'll come off." My ever-practical best friend.

I realized that the small towel was now full of blood and it was running down my face and neck. The bleeding hadn't slowed down at all. I looked at Kevin who was making a call on his phone. My head was swimming a bit and I couldn't make out what he was saying. I think Ryan took the towel out of my hand and replaced it with something he pulled out of his backpack. Another towel which was quickly bloody. Ryan took over, putting more pressure on my face. Suddenly dizzy, I put my head back on the seat and closed my eyes.

It couldn't have been more than a few minutes before I heard sirens. An ambulance pulled up next to us, and two EMT's jumped out with first aid equipment. They got into the backseat on either side of me after Ryan got out to make room for them.

The older of the pair asked, "What happened, Cara? Can you remember?"

"I'm not sure. Something hard hit me in the face and then I realized I was bleeding."

"Are you feeling dizzy, sick to your stomach?"

"Just a little dizzy."

The younger man had been cleaning off my forehead and the side of my head, finally spraying something medicinal on it and strapping something tight over the spot that had been bleeding so much.

He smiled. "You have a long cut just above your eye, but it's not deep and won't need stitches. Head wounds always bleed a lot; that's normal. You should see your doctor to have the dressing changed. If it starts bleeding again, please have someone take you to the emergency room in Greenville. The good news is it missed your eye."

I thanked the two men and they climbed out of the Jeep, quickly replaced by Chief O'Donnell. I saw Mr. Weiss standing outside the car talking to Patrick.

The Chief asked, "How do you feel?"

"Like I got hit in the face with a rock."

"You did. But it missed your eye, and the paramedic said it won't leave much of a scar. Did you see where the rock came from?"

"No. But Patrick must have because he took off into the woods chasing somebody."

"I'll be speaking to Patrick next. I was on my way to your house to see your mother. Maybe I should wait a day or two. Seeing you bandaged up like this will upset her, and I really don't want to make things worse."

I nodded. A delay was probably a good idea. When I looked up, Mr. Weiss was looking in the window at me as though he wanted to talk to me.

The Chief got out of the Jeep, telling me to call him immediately if I needed anything.

Mr. Weiss leaned in the window, asking how I felt. I assured him I would survive and tried to give him a smile. He looked worried.

"I was just speaking with Patrick, one of your bodyguards. He saw the rock fly out of the woods and tried to run down the person who threw it. He didn't manage to catch the boy; he jumped into a car a block from here and took off. But Patrick saw him clearly." He sighed. "You can probably guess who it was."

I nodded, wishing I hadn't when my head began to ache. "It had to be Ed Wilson. He hates me. I don't understand why. He doesn't even know me."

"Don't worry about Ed Wilson, Cara. I'll take care of him. He won't be coming back to school, and I'm recommending his parents get professional help for the boy."

"Okay. Thanks, Mr. Weiss."

Kevin got behind the steering wheel and looked back at me. "Ready to go home?"

"Yeah. I need some aspirin and a nap."

Patrick got into the front seat with Kevin, and Ryan climbed into the backseat next to me. "Feeling any better, lass?"

"I think better means there's no blood running down my face, but my head hurts and I'm tired. If no one else needs to talk to me, I want to go home."

Kevin started the car and pulled away from the curb. "We have a police escort again. The Chief is right behind us."

That was reassuring. I closed my eyes and tried to tune out the world.

CHAPTER 37

Someone must have contacted my father because he was standing on the front porch when we pulled up, his arms crossed over his chest, his face like stone. I sighed.

Ryan sprang out of the Jeep and reached in to help me out. I had a feeling he was the one who'd sent my dad a message, which had obviously upset my father more than I thought a cut over the eye warranted.

My father ran down the steps to me and wrapped me up in his arms for a few seconds. I didn't smell the forest on him as strongly as usual, the price of spending most of his time in the human world, I guessed.

"Cara, are you all right? How does your head feel? Was it one of Gaynes' hired men who did this?"

I was really tired so I only made it to the porch steps before I had to sit down, Chief O'Donnell not far behind me. My father sat down next to me, wrapping my hand up in one of his.

"Dad, you can relax. I'll be okay. It's not a deep cut and doesn't even need stitches. I just have a nasty headache."

"We know who threw the rock, Brian," the Chief said. "It wasn't one of Gaynes' thugs. It was the same boy who beat Sean with a baseball bat last night and put him in the hospital. Apparently, he thinks that you and your family are solely responsible for all the tragedies that have taken place in Thornewood for the past few weeks. Your bodyguards protected Cara from him yesterday, but he had two more boys with him when he went after Sean. Don't worry; we'll pick them up today. Gabe put two of them on the ground before he was knocked out."

My father helped me stand. "Come on inside, sweetheart. Kathleen is still here and she can take a look at your wound." He turned to the Chief. "Thank you for following them home. It might be a good idea to wait a day or two to talk to Alicia."

The Chief nodded. "That was my thinking too. Cara, I hope you'll feel better tomorrow. You won't have to worry about Ed Wilson anymore."

He walked back to his car and drove off. Kevin and Patrick still stood by the Jeep.

"You guys should go on home. I'll probably see you tomorrow."

Kevin came over to me and gave me a gentle hug. "Call me in the morning if you decide to stay home. But I hope you'll be feeling a lot better tomorrow." He dropped a kiss on my head and got back in his Jeep. Patrick waved as they drove around the corner.

My father took my hand and led me into the house where Mom waited just inside the door, a frown on her face.

She put one arm around me and led me into the kitchen where Kathleen was waiting. "Looks like I picked the right day to visit, Cara dear. I brought my bag with me. Let me take a look at the cut on your head."

"Mom, could I have some aspirin."

"Of course, dear." She got up and went to the pantry, bringing a bottle of aspirin back with her. She put a glass of water and two aspirin in front of me, and I swallowed the pills down quickly. My head really hurt.

Kathleen lifted the bandage gently and took a look at my cut. "Thankfully, it's not deep, dear. I know the paramedics cleaned it thoroughly, so I'll just put an herbal mixture on it and fasten the bandage down again. These herbs will prevent you from scarring. In a month, there won't even be a mark on your pretty face. The herbs should prevent any further bleeding too."

She rummaged in her large bag for the supplies she needed and mixed up several herbs and some kind of oil into a paste. She spread the paste over my cut and taped the bandage down. "Leave it alone for at least twenty-four hours, dear. I'll come back to check it tomorrow afternoon." She smiled. "It will heal beautifully. And these herbs may help you sleep too."

She was right. The pleasant smelling herbs were making me drowsy. "Thank you. I'm glad you were here today."

I stood up, wobbling a little, and my father scooped me up, which was totally unnecessary, and carried me upstairs, setting me on my bed. He pulled off my boots, looking a little startled when my knives fell on the floor. He shook his head. "You have no idea how much I wish they weren't necessary, sweetheart."

"I know. It's okay." The pillow felt good against my throbbing head and my eyes closed.

It was dark outside when I woke up. My headache wasn't completely gone, but it wasn't as bad. I put my hand on the bandage covering my forehead. I wondered if the throbbing was a sign of healing. I'd ask Kathleen when I saw her.

I got out of bed and changed into sweatpants and an old t-shirt. My stomach was growling. I went downstairs, hoping to find leftovers from dinner. Instead, I found my parents sitting at the table with Adam.

"What's going on? I came down to look for leftovers."

"We just had soup and sandwiches, dear," Mom said. "Can I make you a sandwich?"

"That sounds good. Did you make tea?"

She smiled. "That's what we all needed tonight. The teapot's full. Help yourself while I make you a grilled cheese."

Dad asked, "Feeling better after your nap?"

"The headache isn't as bad now." I poured myself a cup of tea and looked up into Adam's dark blue eyes. He'd been watching me carefully since I came downstairs. "Did you come over to check on me, Adam?"

He nodded. "Of course. I heard you had another head injury. I was worried."

I tried to smile, but even that hurt my head. "I'm okay. Guess I have a hard head."

My father arched one eyebrow and said, "I told him you would be fine, but he had to see for himself." Adam's face reddened slightly, but he winked at me, his eyes warm.

"Well, I'm glad you're here. I need to complain to someone. This week has really sucked."

He chuckled as I ate my sandwich and drank some tea. "I owe Rowenna a song, so is it okay if I go out on the porch?" My father nodded, smiling.

Adam stood. "I'll keep you company."

We took our tea outside and sat down. "I can feel rain coming. It'll probably start later tonight." Adam looked over at me. "I think I'll stay in camp tonight, just in case it turns into a heavy storm."

I reached over and put my hand on his. "Thanks, Adam." He nodded.

Leaning back comfortably in my deck chair, I began to sing the dragon's song.

Soon we felt Rowenna's magic envelop us and I heard her wings overhead.

Her eyesight must have been phenomenal because her rusty voice asked, *What's wrong with your head? What is that white patch?*

"I got hit in the face with a rock today, but it's not bad. Please don't worry."

Her voice got even deeper as she asked, *Who hit your face with a rock?*

"It was a troubled boy from school. He's being taken out of school and I don't think he'll be causing any more trouble."

I can stop him for you.

She'd probably like to turn him into a torch. "Uh, no, that won't be necessary. The police will see that he gets the help he needs. He has some serious problems. I have no desire to hurt him."

If that's what you want, Cara. How is Alicia? Where is she?

I heard my mother's voice from the doorway. "I'm fine, Rowenna. You helped me a great deal last night. I'll always be grateful. I feel well now. I can't thank you enough, my friend."

I will always help when you or Cara need me, Alicia.

I could hear the air move as her huge wings lifted her higher into the night sky, and the magic surrounding us slowly dissipated. I hummed her song again.

Thank you, Cara.

When we finished our tea, Adam stood. "I'll go back to camp now, but if the rain turns into a bad storm, I'll come back. Sleep well."

He walked down the steps and jogged through the yard. He disappeared into the darkness. I couldn't even see him as far as the tree line. Knowing he was close gave me a warm, protected feeling.

I said good night to my parents and went back to my room. It was earlier than I normally went to bed, but I was hoping I could go to school in the morning. Before I turned out the light, I called Sean's house and his dad answered the phone.

"Hello, Cara. Sean will be in the hospital for a few more days. He'll be having surgery on his nose in the morning. Right now he's having trouble breathing. He doesn't have his phone with him, but you can call me any time. I'll let Sean know you've been asking about him. By the way, Chief O'Donnell was here earlier. Ed Wilson is in police custody. He won't be doing any more damage. The Chief told me you'd been injured too. How are you feeling?"

"I'm okay. I got hit in the head with a rock, but I didn't even need stitches. I'll be fine. Please tell Sean I wish him good luck with his surgery and that I'll see him soon."

He said he would.

I put my phone down and tried to find a comfortable place for my head on the pillow.

Life in Thornewood had been truly awful for weeks now. I didn't even want to think about all the crimes Donald Gaynes had paid others to commit. Amy and I had been determined to enjoy our senior year. Instead, we were merely enduring it.

When I thought about Sean in the hospital facing surgery, I wanted to cry. I couldn't help feeling responsible. It was just like last spring. If Sean hadn't met me, he wouldn't be dealing with all this pain. And there didn't seem to be anything I could do about it. No one had been able to find Gaynes and lock him up.

I finally fell asleep, feeling totally depressed.

CHAPTER 38

I woke up before my alarm went off, moved my head, and was relieved to find it wasn't throbbing. The headache was gone, and the pain above my eye had dulled. It looked like I was definitely going to school today.

I made a conscious effort to dress in cheerful colors, pulling my one red shirt out of the closet and digging in a drawer for a red ribbon to tie around my ponytail. I had to smile when I was dressed. At least the red contrasted nicely with the white bandage over my eye. Don't tell me I can't coordinate.

When I walked into the kitchen, Mom smiled at me from the stove where she was making—you guessed it—pancakes, her favorite cure-all. Dad was sitting at the table, watching Mom with a smile on his face. Things felt almost normal.

My father looked at me with a tentative smile. "How's the head this morning, sweetheart?"

"It's not bad today. I think I'll live. Pancakes! What's the occasion?"

Mom just shrugged. "I guess we can celebrate the fact that we're both feeling better. I may be crazy, but I have a strong feeling that everything will be better from now on. Like the worst is over, you know?"

I hoped she was right, but I thought it was just wishful thinking. Gaynes was still out there somewhere.

The three of us managed to polish off a dozen pancakes, and then I had to leave for school. "Thanks for the pancakes, Mom. You're the best." I hugged her and dropped a kiss on Dad's cheek. "I'm hoping for a normal day at school today. See you two later."

Ryan was waiting for me on the porch, and Kevin was already parked at the curb.

When Ryan and I climbed into the Jeep, Kevin grinned. "Glad to see your head's still in one piece, short stuff. Feeling better?"

"I'm okay, Kev. Mom's ESP thinks everything will be fine now. I don't know about you, but I'm still waiting for that "fun" senior year to begin."

"Me too, babe." He shook his head, clearly as optimistic as I was.

We were a little early, so Kevin found a parking space in front of the school, actually in front of Mr. Weiss' office window. When we got inside, we found Amy and Neal waiting for us in front of the principal's office.

She grabbed me for a hug that almost lifted me off my feet. "I didn't hear about your rock problem until this morning. Mr. McKay called early to let me know he and his wife were on their way to the hospital for Sean's surgery. I've got Mom's station wagon today. Sean's dad said Wilson—that miserable excuse for a human—threw a rock at you. That's a big bandage. How bad is it?"

"Not so big it'll leave a scar, according to Kathleen. I was lucky she was visiting Mom when I got home. She put some of her magic herbs on the cut and promised me it would heal perfectly."

She chuckled. "One of these days, I want to meet Kathleen. She must be some kind of wizard."

I heard my name and turned to see Mr. Weiss in his doorway. After assuring him that I felt much better today, I handed over my knives.

"I was hoping you'd be early today, Cara. I have to leave for court. Wilson is being arraigned today and I promised his father I'd be there." He shook his head, looking a little helpless. "I don't know what they expect me to do. The boy will probably be locked up until he's eighteen."

Kevin asked, "Is Mr. Wilson still on the police force?"

"As far as I know, Kevin. I hope today will go smoothly for all of you, and for Sean as well. I'll be speaking to his father sometime today."

As I walked between classes, I got a variety of looks from kids I didn't know. Some looked sympathetic, some resentful. Apparently, Wilson's trash talk had been partially successful. In each class, several classmates sympathized about Wilson's attacks on Sean and me. Everyone was angry about what had happened to Sean. After all, he wouldn't be playing any football for a while, and everyone knew how valuable he was to the team.

I heard that five of Sean's friends, all on the football team, had cornered Wilson's two friends outside school this morning. Those two wouldn't be threatening anyone else if they wanted to remain healthy.

Apparently, the out-of-town troublemakers had been convinced to stay out of Thornewood by the police department. I heard that two of them looked a little worse for wear, thanks to Gabriel. Maybe all would be well if the negative talk stopped.

One of the bigger football players, Billy Herron, was in my English class. He leaned down and drawled, "I don't know why anyone would want to throw a rock at a little thing like you, Cara. Sean would tear him apart." Billy had spent his childhood in Alabama and it showed.

I said, "I don't think Sean will get a chance. Wilson will probably be in jail."

He nodded. "Good. We're just hopin' Sean makes a fast recovery. There's some talk that Coach wants to recruit Gabe, that big friend of Sean's. I hope he does. That guy can really move."

That was an interesting thought, and I had to smile. An Elf with magical abilities on Thornewood's football team! That would definitely be against the rules. If they knew about it.

When Kevin, Amy, and I met at lunch with our bodyguards, I shared Billy's comment about Gabe filling in for Sean on the football team. Kevin and Amy were enthusiastic about the idea, but Ryan, Patrick, and Neal just looked at each other, obviously trying not to laugh.

I looked at our bodyguards. "Okay, guys, give. What do you know that we don't?"

Ryan was trying to restrain a grin. "Well, lass, to say that Gabe would have an unfair advantage would be puttin' it mildly."

Patrick laughed. "First of all, Gabe is a bit older than the rest of the boys on the team. Secondly, his reflexes and eyesight are far better than humans consider normal. That's why he's the best archer in Elvenwood."

Neal added, "Compared to the rest of the team, Gabe is like 'Superboy.' He's bigger, faster, stronger, and thinks ahead like a champion chess player. He could probably win the game single-handedly. What I'm afraid of is people recognizing that Gabe's not exactly a normal teenager."

Kevin nodded. "It really wouldn't be a good idea for Gabe to play in Sean's place,
 would it?"

All three bodyguards shook their heads.

"If Coach insists, how can Gabe refuse?"

They all shrugged.

The bell rang, and we left the lunchroom for our afternoon classes.

The resentful looks began to diminish as the facts about the real instigator of these attacks began to spread. More people were learning about Donald Gaynes and his attempted revenge against my father. People were talking, and for a change, that was a good thing.

When Kevin dropped me off after school, the Chief's new black cruiser was in front of my house. Kevin groaned. "What's happened now?"

"Maybe the Chief came by to talk to Mom about her kidnapping. I'd better get inside. She wants me there when the Chief questions her."

"Hope it goes well, short stuff. Give your mom a hug for me."

Ryan stationed himself on the front porch while I went inside. I found Mom, Dad, and the Chief sitting at the kitchen table over coffee. Dad looked a bit tense, but Mom and the Chief seemed fairly relaxed.

Mom smiled as I walked in. "Hi, sweetheart. We've been waiting for you. I want to get this over with today. Pour yourself some coffee and sit down with us."

Chief O'Donnell pulled out a small recorder. "Alicia, I have to record this, but, for obvious reasons I don't want your dragon on this recording. I do want to know everything, including the dragon, but please say you need a drink of water when the dragon's part in this comes up, and I can turn off the recorder."

He turned the recorder on and nodded to Mom. "All right, let's start with what happened Friday around five p.m. in front of The Crescent Moon."

Taking a deep breath, Mom described how she ran to the mailbox.

"Most days there's a police car on that block, but it was five o'clock and they must have left for change of shift. I think the men who grabbed me knew my schedule. They timed it perfectly. When I ran outside by myself, they had their chance. They drove their SUV up next to me, opened the back door and one of them grabbed my arm and pulled me in. It must have taken about three seconds. For a split second, I saw Arlynn's shocked face through my store's window. The man who'd grabbed me put plastic ties around my wrists and ankles, threw me on the floor, and moved up to the front seat with the driver. I tried to loosen the ties but when they cut into my skin and I could feel blood, I stopped struggling.

"They must have driven to the highway entrance first. I heard them swearing and I felt the car turn around abruptly. I guess the road was already blocked. Then they drove to the other road out of town, but they had to turn around again. They were yelling at each other. I guess it hadn't occurred to them that they wouldn't be able to get out of town after they grabbed me."

She described how they spent a long time just driving from one back road to another, staying out of the populated areas, finally taking the road that ran along the south side of Blackthorne Forest.

"From the swearing I heard, I think they saw a police car with its lights on in the distance, so they pulled into the forest as far as the SUV would go until they ran into a group of trees too close together to drive through.

"They finally stopped yelling at each other and began talking in a normal tone of voice. I heard the driver say, 'What are we supposed to do with her if we can't leave town? And there were witnesses when we snatched her, so they know our car.'

"The other man said, 'I'm going to call the boss and see what he wants us to do.' I guess he didn't get an answer because he said he'd try the number again in fifteen minutes."

The Chief asked, "What were you doing while you were lying in the back of the car?"

"I was trying to stay calm, trying not to think about being killed." She looked at me and my dad. "I was trying to focus on the people I love, trying not to panic."

"Alicia, how long do you think you were parked in the woods?"

"I can't be sure. I couldn't see my watch, but it seemed like hours. They kept calling the person they called the boss, but I think it was several hours before they reached him. The driver put his phone on speaker and I could hear it clearly. The voice on the other end told them to wait until dark, kill me and bury me in the woods. Then he told them to drive the SUV to another location, as far as possible from where I was buried, and leave it, after wiping it down thoroughly. He told them they'd have to leave town on foot, through the forest, if necessary, but to stay clear of the main roads where the cops were parked. Then he wished them luck." Her voice shook. I reached over and took her hand, squeezing it gently.

"The man in the passenger seat climbed into the backseat. He was horrible. He smelled bad. He kept smiling at me. His teeth were rotten, and I couldn't stand to look at him. After telling me what he'd really like to do to me, he started waving a knife at me, running it up my arms and legs, putting it against my throat and laughing. He'd lean down and rub his face against mine, laughing and calling me names. Then he began telling me exactly how he was going to cut me up, which parts of me he'd cut off first." She took a deep breath. "You don't need to hear the rest." I looked at my father. There was no color at all in his face.

"Tommy, I'd like a glass of water please."

He turned off the recorder.

"That was when I heard Rowenna's voice in my head. She told me she was flying above us and that my mate would see her and he would rescue me. She told me not to be afraid." She nodded and the Chief turned the recorder back on.

"The driver, I think his name was Frank, said he'd only signed on for a kidnapping, and that he was no murderer. The other man said it didn't make any difference to him, one way or the other. He just laughed and said he'd enjoy cutting me into small pieces."

I looked over at my father. His face was white with anger, and his green eyes glittered dangerously.

The Chief glanced at my father and closed his eyes briefly. "Alicia, would you like to take a break?"

When she looked up at him, I could see anger in her blue eyes. I was relieved I didn't see tears. I was trying hard to keep mine in, and my stomach hurt.

"No, let's continue. I want this over with."

He nodded.

"The two men argued. The driver was against killing me, but the other man said he could find something to strangle me with, that I was so small, it would be easy. He said the boss would have to pay him a lot more, so he didn't mind. He laughed as he said he was looking forward to cutting me up in small pieces after I was dead, and burying the pieces all over the forest. He said they would never find all of me."

"A glass of water please."

The Chief turned the recorder off again, and Mom said, "Brian, you don't have to sit here and listen to any more of this. Please go outside until we're finished."

My father looked like a corpse, an angry corpse. There was no color in his face at all.

"Dad, why don't you go outside for a few minutes, get some fresh air and try to calm down. I know this is hard to listen to, but you're freaking me out."

He looked at me, frowned, and whispered, "I'm sorry, Cara. I'll go out on the porch for a while." He got up from the table and walked out the back door.

The Chief looked at me and said softly, "Thanks."

"That was when I heard Rowenna's voice again. She said, 'Alicia, you are stronger than either of these men. You are a worthwhile human; they are not. Therefore, they cannot hurt you. Your mate is on his way. He'll be with you in a few minutes. I won't leave until he gets here.'

"That's when I heard the police sirens, even though they sounded miles away. The two men heard them too. The driver said, 'We're getting out of here.' He drove through the woods to the main road and I knew he'd try to outrun the police cars. Their sirens were louder and I knew they were closer. The SUV picked up speed and suddenly stopped short, the brakes screeched, and I got tossed against the front seats. The man in the passenger seat cried, "What the hell is that? Frank, Frank, what's wrong with you? Oh, hell."

"I heard Rowenna's rough voice; it sounded like laughter. Then I heard her wings as she flew away. I've always wondered what the other man was thinking when he saw her land on the road."

"You can turn the recorder back on now, Tommy."

"When did you hear the police sirens, Alicia?"

"It was only a few minutes later. The driver drove out of the woods as fast as he could and tried to speed up once he hit the road, but you were right there. Brian opened the SUV's back door and found me on the floor. You gave him a blanket for me because I was cold and he wrapped me up and lifted me out. You cut the ties off of me and drove us home. I didn't want to talk about any of this for a few days, Tommy. I appreciate your patience. That's all I can tell you."

The Chief turned off the recorder and sat back in the chair. "Alicia, I don't suppose you've got anything stronger than tea?"

"Cara, you know where the brandy is. I think we can all use a drink. And you should take one out to your father."

I filled three glasses and took one out to the back porch where my father stood at the railing, gazing out at the forest. It was early evening and the sun had sunk behind the tall pines. It was twilight. I could see a few stars in the dark blue sky.

"Mom's finished making her statement." I handed him a glass of brandy. "She wants you to drink this. She and the Chief are having a drink too."

He tossed down the brandy immediately and put the glass on the railing. Turning to me, he asked, "And what about you, dear? Is there no brandy for my brave daughter?" He wrapped both arms around me and rested his cheek on my head.

"I'm too young to drink." I sighed. Knowing that one man had been willing to murder and dismember my mother had just sunk in and I was cold on the inside.

"Sweetheart, your mother is the strongest person I know. I think she's stronger than I am." His voice sounded choked.

They needed to be together now. I had an idea.

"Dad, why don't you take Mom into the woods to that area by the stream where I like to draw. You can sit on the flat rock and just be together. It's a special place, peaceful and beautiful. Sean once said it was good for his soul."

My father looked at me and I was relieved to see some color had returned to his face. "That's an excellent idea, dear. The forest has its own healing energy. I think that's what your mother and I both need."

We went back into the kitchen where Mom and the Chief were having another glass of brandy. They both looked relieved to see my father looking more like himself.

The Chief stood and said, "Thank you, both of you, for helping Alicia get through this." He looked at my mother. "You're lucky to have each other. I'll leave you in peace now. No need to see me to the door. Good night."

The sooner I could put my mother's chilling words out of my mind, the better.

The Chief left and my father took Mom's hand and brought her to her feet. "Alicia, there's a special place in the forest I'd like to take you. It's a place Cara loves. She thinks it would be a good place for us right now."

She gave him a tired smile. "It sounds perfect. But I don't want to leave Cara alone right now."

My father smiled at me and said, "You won't be alone. Come outside."

We went out on the back porch and I saw Adam walking toward us from the woods. My father had evidently sent him a message that I needed him.

Mom looked at me. "You don't mind if we leave you for a while?"

"I think you need some quiet time together. Adam will keep me company."

She reached out and hugged me, whispering, "Thank you, sweetheart."

They met him halfway through the yard, and my father said, "Take care of her. She's had to listen to too much today."

He climbed the porch steps and turned those cobalt blue eyes on me. "Are you all right?"

I nodded. But then I realized the need to hold it all in was gone. The outrage I had been holding back, over what had been done to my mother, broke loose. The tears started to flow and I gasped, having trouble breathing. And then I heard his soft voice, "Come here, love." And his warm arms were around me, but it wasn't a hug. He was literally holding me together so that I wouldn't fly apart. I kept gasping, unable to get a deep breath.

"You're going to be all right, Cara. Your father sent me a message so I knew what was happening today. It must have been hard to listen to, but you're a strong girl. You'll get all of this sadness out of your system tonight, and then it will be over. Do you understand?"

I nodded, still gasping. He held me, rubbing my back, while I leaked tears all over his chest.

His voice was soft. "You held it together in front of your parents, didn't you?"

I nodded again.

"Hmm. But you can let it all out with me. I wonder why that is."

I sniffled. "Because you're my anchor, Adam."

He chuckled, still rubbing my back. "You mean that *jackass* you used *Vox* on a few months ago?"

I choked on a reluctant laugh. "Yeah, that guy."

He tilted my chin up with one finger, and I could see we were both laughing, sort of.

"How about making some tea for us?"

"Okay. Come inside with me while I boil the water. I don't really want to be alone."

He opened the door and followed me in. "I know. That's why your father called me. By the way, red's your color." Oh. He was talking about my shirt, not my eyes.

I looked into his understanding eyes. "Thank you."

I was finally able to smile as I boiled water and made a pot of Kathleen's tea for us. When it was ready, we carried the teapot and cups out on the back porch, along with a sweater for me, and sat down to drink tea and watch the moon rise over my beautiful, peaceful forest.

After a while, I began humming the dragon's song and soon felt her magic wrap around us. She was flying high above the house and the woods so I could barely hear the sound of her huge wings.

Good evening, Cara.

"Good evening, Rowenna."

Peace had been restored. I wondered how long it would last.

CHAPTER 39

It was late when my parents walked out of the woods, hand in hand. It was almost full dark. I could barely see them. When they climbed the stairs to the porch, I asked them how they were feeling.

They were both smiling. My dad said, "Excellent suggestion. Spending some time in the forest was soothing for both of us."

Mom added, "Very therapeutic, dear. I think I understand why I had such a hard time getting you out of the woods when you were little. It's like another world in there, isn't it?"

"The forest was always my refuge."

She asked, "When did you ever need a refuge, dear?"

"Only when we'd argue."

"Oh," she said, "that's right. All the times you asked about your father, and I wouldn't tell you." She shook her head. "That was unfair of me, Cara. I know that now."

My father's arm tightened around her shoulders. He chuckled. "I didn't think she'd ever turn sixteen."

"I thought I was being extremely fair, making him promise to stay out of your life until you were sixteen. But it was wrong to keep the two of you apart all those years. I'm so sorry, Brian."

My father looked down at her, understanding on his face. He whispered, "Alicia, I'm sorry we couldn't be married the way you wanted. There was nothing I could do." He leaned down and kissed her, obviously forgetting that Adam and I were there, taking it all in.

But Mom knew we were there. She looked at me, slightly embarrassed, and said, "Brian, we have company. Let's talk about this later."

My father straightened up, clearly startled, and grinned. "Sorry. I'd forgotten we weren't alone." He looked at me with a smile. "But I think Cara has one question she wants to ask us."

"What is it, honey?" Mom asked. My telepathic father knew exactly what I wanted to know.

"Mom, I've never understood why my parents never got married, and why you were so angry for so many years."

She and my father sat down with us. My father kept her hand wrapped in his.

He said, "I can explain, sweetheart. I tried to take your mother to Elvenwood so that we could have a traditional Elven wedding ceremony there, but the gateway wouldn't open. That was when we realized she has no Elven blood. We had thought she might because so many long-time Thornewood residents do, but we were disappointed.

"Then we thought we could get married in Thornewood, like humans do. This was before Harry Callahan retired from the FBI and came back to Thornewood to live and help us with these details. Alicia and I went to City Hall to get a marriage license, something I'd never heard of, of course." He shook his head sadly. "That's when we learned you need I.D., like a birth certificate, or a Social Security card, a credit card, a driver's license with your picture on it. I had none of those things. As far as the human world was concerned, I didn't exist. We couldn't get married anywhere."

"And that's why you were so angry, Mom? I mean, it wasn't Dad's fault."

She sighed, looking embarrassed. "There was a lot more to it than that, dear. I was only eighteen, a year out of high school, and I'd just learned I was pregnant with you. My parents were still here then, but they weren't much help. They owned the bookstore but hadn't been taking care of it and the store was failing. I'd worked in the store since I was a child, but I knew it would have to close its doors. My parents wanted to retire. My mother wanted nothing to do with a pregnant, unwed teenage daughter. I think my dad was more sympathetic to my situation, but my mother ran things and Dad wouldn't fight with her.

"They stayed here until you were born. The day I brought you home from the hospital, they left for Florida. I haven't heard from them since. I've sent pictures of you to my dad so he could see his beautiful granddaughter, and he has sent a card to say 'thank you' each time."

"I always wondered about my grandparents, Mom. I'm sorry they've never given you any support. But I still don't know why you got so angry at Dad."

She took a deep breath. "When I told your father that my parents were leaving, and that the store would be closing, and I wasn't sure how I would be able to take care of you, he offered to take you to Elvenwood and raise you there. I realize now he only wanted to help, but I felt as though he wanted to take my baby away from me, as though he had no confidence in me as a mother.

"Cara, you have to remember how young I was, and, frankly, I was immature. I felt betrayed on all sides. Brian wouldn't marry me; my parents wouldn't help me; and then Brian wanted to take you away from me. At least, that's how it felt. Pregnant women are often over-emotional, and I over-reacted in a big way. I stayed mad because it seemed preferable to a total emotional meltdown. I wasn't in a good place, mentally or emotionally.

"Nevertheless, your father bought the bookstore for me, paid for the renovations, and has always supported you. I see now that he wanted to help me, not hurt me, but at the time, I just thought he did those things out of guilt."

She leaned her head on my father's shoulder, whispering, "I'm so sorry."

Very gently, he pulled away from her, got out of the deck chair and knelt on the porch floor in front of her. He took her hand and I realized I was holding my breath.

He said, "Alicia, will you marry me now?"

Mom's mouth fell open. She closed it and I could see tears in her eyes. She squeezed his hand and nodded. "Of course I will, Brian. I've never loved anyone but you."

From the porch floor, my father put his arms around Mom, holding her tightly. "You are my one true love, my mate, Alicia."

I had both hands pressed against my mouth to keep myself quiet, but I felt like cheering! Sitting next to me, Adam squeezed my hand. I looked over at him to see he was grinning. He looked at me and whispered, "This is what you've always wanted, isn't it?"

I just nodded. Words were beyond me.

Mom turned and smiled at me. "I'm so glad we were all together tonight. Cara, you certainly deserve to share in our happiness. If it wasn't for you, I'm not sure it ever would have happened."

"Dad, nothing's really changed. How can you and Mom get married now? You still don't have a birth certificate or a social security card."

My father grinned. "Harry Callahan has taken care of that for me. I have a birth certificate that says I was born in Vermont, in a tiny town no one ever heard of. I have a social security card too, although I'll never use it. So as far as the human world is concerned, Brian Blackthorne exists."

"We'll have two weddings, Alicia. Since we can't have an Elven ceremony in Elvenwood, the Elves can come here. We can have the ceremony right here in your big, beautiful back yard. There's plenty of room for any Elves who are willing to leave our village for a few hours. Some of my people have never been outside Elvenwood, you know."

I was so excited. "Mom, we can have both weddings and one party right here. We'll have it catered. You won't have to do a thing."

Mom couldn't stop smiling. "Cara, I think there's an old bottle of champagne in the pantry. Put it in the freezer now and we'll break it open later.

Turning to my father, she leaned against his shoulder. "Today has really run the gamut, from misery to joy, but it's been a day to remember. We should celebrate!"

I said, "How about Pizza for dinner?" I knew my father would be delighted.

We all enjoyed Pizza and garlic bread for dinner, and we washed it down with Champagne someone had given Mom for Christmas last year. Mom said that she and Dad would celebrate this date every year with Pizza and Champagne, their first tradition.

I thought it was a wonderful idea.

CHAPTER 40

Later that evening, Adam left for camp after congratulating my parents again, and I went to my room to call Sean. I didn't think he'd be answering his phone. After all, he'd had surgery that morning. So I was amazed when I heard his hoarse voice, "Hi, beautiful."

"Hi, I thought I'd be talking to your dad again. How are you feeling?"

"Pretty sore, but the pain pills are great. I'm kinda floatin' right now." He giggled. "All I need is a certain green-eyed angel to float up here with me. Ah, sorry, Cara. I'm really out of it."

I couldn't help laughing. "Well, at least you're not in a lot of pain. Is it just your nose that's painful? I heard you had a big lump on your head too."

"Well, that baseball bat got me in a lotta places, but it's mostly just bruising. Real colorful right now." He giggled again.

He sounded so silly, I had to laugh with him. This was a side of Sean I'd never seen before. And probably never would again once he returned to the land of the sober.

"When do you think you'll be coming home?"

"Whatsa matter, beautiful? Miss me?" More giggling.

"Of course I do. There are a lot of things I want to talk to you about, but they'll have to wait until you're back to normal."

"Aw, come on, Cara. What's been happenin'? It's mean, keepin' me in suspense."

"Most of it will have to wait, my drugged-out friend. But one happy thing I can tell you. My parents are getting married!"

"Ah, that's wonnerful. What you've always wanted, right?"

"Yep. I'm really happy for them. My father proposed to Mom tonight out on the back porch. We celebrated with pizza and champagne."

"Aw, wish I coulda been there, beautiful. Hey, I just had an idea. Will you marry me, Cara? We could have a double wedding." Giggling again.

Laughing, I said, "I'm not sure our parents would approve, Sean."

His voice was suddenly faint. "Well, I love you, Cara, and I think it's a very cool idea, tha's all."

"Are you falling asleep, Sean?"

"Yah, but I'll see you in my dreams . . ." There was silence on the phone. A minute later I heard him snoring.

I hung up, smiling. Sean was responsible for another first in my life, my first marriage proposal! I couldn't help giggling. He'd be mortified when I told him about tonight's conversation. But I wondered if somewhere in his drug-induced state, he actually thought I was his girlfriend again. As soon as he'd recovered, I had to level with him.

I called Amy next. I knew she'd be thrilled when she heard the news about Mom and Dad. The usual shriek came from the phone and I had to hold the phone away from my ear for a few seconds. I laughed. Amy's responses were so predictable.

"Have you talked to Sean yet?" she asked.

Still laughing, I said, "Yeah, but he was really high on pain killers. He was actually giggling. When I tell him about the conversation we had tonight, he may want to leave town."

"What on earth was he saying?"

"Well, I told him about Mom and Dad, and he asked me to marry him; he suggested a double wedding." I was laughing again; Amy was hysterical.

"Even sober, I doubt he'll take it back. We both know how Sean feels about you."

"Well, I certainly won't bring it up again."

We were both laughing when we hung up.

The phone was ringing as I was getting into bed. It had to be my other best friend.

"Hey, Kev. Everything okay at your house?"

"Oh, sure, babe. I wanted to find out if the Chief was actually at your house this afternoon to take your mom's statement, and not because of some new disaster."

"Yeah, Mom was ready to talk about the whole miserable experience. The Chief got the info he needed and Mom got the whole thing off her chest." I sighed. "It was really rough, Kev. Dad couldn't listen to all of it. But I think Mom feels better now that she's talked about it."

"Things like that should never happen to your mom, or my mom, or anybody's mom." He sounded angry.

"Kev, Mom had Rowenna flying overhead, talking to her, reminding her how strong she is, and telling her that my father was on his way to rescue her. Mom assumed that Rowenna landed in the road in front of the SUV so they'd have to stop."

"I'll give that dragon a big kiss if I ever get the chance," he said.

"That'll make two of us," I said. "But I have some good news to share with you too."

"Good. I could use some."

"My parents are getting married! Dad proposed to her while we were out on the back porch tonight."

"Wow! That's fantastic. I'm really happy for them, and for you. I know that's been a dream of yours."

"They both admitted, right in front of me, how much they've always loved each other. I can't even tell you how thrilled I am. They're both so happy."

"You just made my night, short stuff." I could hear him smiling. "See you in the morning."

I put my phone away and climbed under my covers. I thought I was too excited to sleep, but I must have nodded off while I was planning their wedding. I was deliberately pushing all the threatening stuff out of my mind.

When I walked into the kitchen the next morning, everyone was smiling, and I could actually feel the happiness in the air. Mom had gone beyond pancakes this morning. There was my favorite quiche sitting on the table, looking like it had just come out of the oven.

I grinned at them. "I guess we're celebrating this morning, aren't we?"

His arm around Mom, my father said, "It's nice to have something to celebrate, sweetheart. The quiche was your mother's idea, and she's had to physically restrain me from cutting myself a piece." He laughed. "Please sit down so we can eat it now."

Breakfast with my two happy parents was a dream come true for me, but it was over too quickly. I heard Kevin's horn from outside and hugged both of them before I rushed out the door.

"Have a great day, you two. See you this afternoon."

Ryan was wearing a bigger than usual smile when I came through the door. I had to assume he'd heard the news too. I smiled and grabbed his arm as we ran down the steps and jogged to Kevin's Jeep. He whispered, "Happiness is contagious, isn't it?"

"Yes, it is. Did my father speak to you last night?"

He chuckled. "No, lass. But I'm telepathic and there was no way he could keep his happiness and good mood to himself. I'm sure every telepath in Elvenwood is now aware that your father and mother will be wed soon."

Kevin and Patrick heard Ryan's last words as we climbed into the Jeep. Kevin, of course, already knew, but Patrick, who wasn't telepathic, was just now hearing the good news. He leaned over the seat with a big grin. "This is wonderful news, Cara. I'm happy for your parents, and for you too."

I thanked him, hoping the rest of the day would go as well as this morning had.

We met Amy and Neal inside the main entrance when we got to school. For a change, everyone was in a good mood. I didn't even mind handing over my knives to Mr. Weiss.

I was able to concentrate on my classes, which was a good sign, but I missed having Sean next to me in each class. At the same time, the prospect of having to tell Sean the truth about my feelings nagged at me.

At lunch our table seemed a little empty, with only six of us instead of the usual eight. Sean's buddy Danny and his girlfriend Sandy came over to eat lunch with us and fill the empty spots. Danny asked if I'd spoken to Sean yet.

"Yeah, I actually got him on the phone last night, but he wasn't totally coherent. He must be in a lot of pain because they've got him on some serious pain killers." I laughed. "He was actually giggling, something I've never heard him do before!"

Sandy smiled. "No, giggling isn't something I've ever heard from Sean, but I did see his father this morning as he was leaving their house. He said Sean will be there for a few more days. Apparently, the surgery on his nose was extensive. Wilson's baseball bat did a lot of damage."

Danny muttered, "I'd like to take a bat to Wilson's head, that miserable cry baby. He's never happy unless he can complain about someone. And I'll bet his father put a lot of that crap in his head."

Kevin asked, "Is Wilson's dad still on the police force? I thought the Chief would have canned him by now."

I shrugged. "I haven't heard anything more about Wilson or his father. I was concentrating on Mom."

"How's your mom?" Sandy asked. "We were so worried about her. I know she's home now, but is she doing okay?"

Finally a subject I could smile about. "She's fine now. And some more good news: My parents have decided to get married. I'm so happy for them."

Sandy was wearing a big grin. "That's great. Your mom and dad are such cool people."

The bell rang and we were all off to our last classes of the day.

For a change, the rest of the week was uneventful. There were no kidnappings or shootings, no buildings were set on fire, and no one else was injured. It seemed like a minor miracle.

The constant tension in my neck and back told me it wouldn't last.

CHAPTER 41

By the end of that week, Sean was home from the hospital, sporting a dressing that seemed to cover half his face as well as his nose.

"Hey, this is a new look for you," I said with a smile. "'Man Without a Face.' It might catch on."

He rolled his eyes. "At least I'm off pain meds now. I'm feeling better." Sadly, there would be no more giggling. And I decided not to mention his marriage proposal.

He wouldn't be playing football for a while, but at Friday's game, he sat on the bench cheering on the rest of the team, while Gabriel sat beside him wearing what looked like a football uniform under his gray hoodie.

Sean had confided that Coach considered Gabe the team's "secret weapon," but would only put him in the game if, late in the game, Thornewood was losing. That week's game was against another small town that wasn't considered a threat, so Gabe kept the bench warm with Sean while our team won, 21 to 14.

As we had the first week, we attended the game as a group with our bodyguards. There were police stationed all around the field, including that hill that overlooked the field. We tried to enjoy ourselves, but I think each one of us was a little tense, waiting for some new disaster. Our bodyguards wrapped themselves around us as if shots might be fired at any moment. Nevertheless, we yelled until we were hoarse as our team made their final touchdown.

The following week we'd play Greenville, a city five times the size of Thornewood. I suspected Coach's "secret weapon" would be needed for that game.

Mom went back to work at The Crescent Moon, and Conor went with her. He confided that Arlynn didn't feel equal to any more bodyguard duties. Mom had never blamed Arlynn for not being able to stop her abductors, but I think we all understood Arlynn's feelings. Nevertheless, when I looked at Adam, sitting quietly next to me Saturday afternoon, I knew that he would never have let me leave the bookstore unless he was at my side.

My father had wanted to go to the bookstore with Mom, but she insisted his being there would draw in every woman in Thornewood, and they probably wouldn't be shopping. He just rolled his eyes, and agreed that Conor could guard Mom as well as he could.

In my opinion, silver-eyed Conor would attract as many women to the bookstore as Dad would. But for a change, I kept my mouth shut.

Dad left Adam with me, taking the opportunity to spend a few hours at his camp, talking to the men who were still there. I knew there were Elves posted all around Thornewood, especially at Amy's house, Sean's house, and Kevin's, around the corner. They stayed undercover for the most part, but I think my friends all felt safer knowing their homes were being watched.

And that left Adam and me, sitting in the kitchen with nowhere we had to be.

"Cara, it's a nice day. Let's take a pot of tea out on the porch. We should enjoy what you've been calling Indian summer while we can. After all, winter's not far away."

"Ugh. I'd rather not think about winter. It's my least favorite time of the year."

He laughed. "Why? Everything in nature needs time to rest, you know."

"Except for the evergreens, the trees lose all their beautiful leaves, leaving them looking dead. The flowers disappear until spring. It snows, the roads get icy, and I have to bundle up in puffy parkas, wool scarves, hats, and gloves, two pairs of socks and snow boots. Ugh."

With a grin, he said, "And I'm sure you look beautiful, even wearing ten pounds of clothes. Most humans enjoy ice skating, skiing, and many other winter sports, or so I've heard."

I shook my head. "Not me. I tried skating once. Spent more time on my knees and my butt than I did on my feet. As for skiing, my mother's not a fan so we never tried it. She always said she preferred keeping her bones unbroken.

"Do the Elves enjoy any winter sports?"

"I imagine those who live in the mountains probably ski, but I never did. However, we do enjoy ice skating. Even Elvenwood has a pond that freezes hard enough for skating. I'll take you there this winter and maybe you'll be willing to try it again. I skate very well. I'll help you."

I snorted. "Of course you skate well. You do everything well, Adam."

He smiled, amusement clear on his handsome face.

"Do you have any plans for Sunday? I ask so I'll know where I'll need to be tomorrow."

"Amy's coming over for brunch. After that, we have a wedding to plan!"

"Have your parents picked a day for their wedding?"

"No. I'm hoping to pin them down tonight. We talked about having a party in our backyard, so we'll have to do it while the weather's still warm enough. We'll be having two weddings and one party, well guarded, of course."

"Ah. They'll have a human wedding as well as an Elven ceremony." He grinned. "I know everyone in Elvenwood will be ready to celebrate. Some may be brave enough to come here for the party."

"Well, they'll have to because Mom can't go to Elvenwood, although I know she'd love to."

He nodded. "That's a shame. She'd be more than welcome."

We sat and talked, slowly drinking the entire pot of tea, until my father emerged from the woods.

Adam stood. "That may be my cue to return to camp." He looked into my eyes. "Don't forget. You can always call on me if you need me." His dark blue eyes were making strange things happen in the vicinity of my heart. I groaned internally. Those eyes of his were lethal weapons.

My father walked up the porch stairs with an amused smile on his face. "For a change, you two actually look relaxed, which is nice to see after this past week."

"I love this time of year. The leaves are turning into rainbows before they start to fall, and the air has a pleasant snap. It's been really nice just being out here today." I glanced at Adam. "And the company's not bad either." I grinned at them and was pleased to see Adam's face turn slightly pink.

Laughing, my father said, "You don't have to leave, Adam. Stay and have tea with us."

Adam shook his head. "I've already had about a gallon of tea today, and I think Cara has some things to discuss with you. I'm heading for camp. Just call me if you need me." He grinned as he ran down the steps.

Looking confused, my father asked, "We have things to discuss?"

He sat down next to me and I said, "Yes, a wedding. Actually, two weddings!"

He smiled. "Ah, yes. Two weddings. Your mother warned me you were going to make what she called 'a big production' out of this. What exactly are you planning, sweetheart?"

"Well, first of all, you and Mom have to pick a date, and it has to be soon so we can have the party out here in the yard. This warm weather won't last too much longer. Mom may have other ideas, but what I was thinking was that we have your human wedding at City Hall first. You'll probably want Conor to be your best man. I'm pretty sure Mom wants me to be her maid of honor. A few of our friends will want to be there, but it will be very simple."

"What is a best man and a maid of honor? What do the two have to do?"

"It's just tradition, Dad. We're like witnesses to your wedding vows. I think Conor and I will just be there to lend moral support. You know, in case one of you gets cold feet. We'll hunt you down and haul you back to complete your vows."

Grinning, he rolled his eyes. "I trust that won't be necessary, dear."

"I know, just kidding. After that brief ceremony at the courthouse, we'll come back here and have your Elven ceremony. You'll have to tell me what that involves."

"It's very simple, Cara. The eldest of the Elders, if he chooses to leave Elvenwood, that is, will say a few words about the Elven tradition of mating for life, and then read the Elven blessing. Our wedding ceremonies are always held under the Joining Tree, so this wedding will be unlike any wedding my people have seen before. Because Elves don't have anything like divorce, our weddings are sacred ceremonies, followed by great rejoicing. I imagine that's very much like what follows your human weddings."

"Will most of your Elves come here for your wedding?"

He nodded. I expect that a few will remain at home. But I have a feeling your mother's big backyard will be quite full for our wedding." His green eyes twinkled.

"I hope you're right. And tonight I want you and Mom to choose a date. Amy and I have to plan a party and we can't do it overnight!"

"We can discuss this over dinner, dear. I'm leaving most of the decisions up to your mother. Anything she wants is fine with me. I just want her happy."

My cell phone rang. "Hi, Mom.... Okay, will do."

"Is your mother all right?"

"Yep. She just asked me to take the lasagna out of the freezer and make a salad for dinner."

My father's eyes lit up. He'd had Mom's lasagna once before.

Kevin and his father joined us for dinner and it was definitely a party atmosphere. I finally managed to pin down my parents on a date for their wedding: October 10th, which was only three weeks away. Thankfully, Amy had catering experience.

Kevin and Kelly congratulated Mom and Dad. Kelly quoted a humorous poem about marriage that he'd found, and that got us all laughing.

After Kevin and I cleaned up the kitchen, he and his father left. Kevin wanted to get home to work on his new video game, "Dragon Wars," and Kelly would be stationed in the woods behind Kevin's house, as he'd been every night since the "reign of terror" had begun.

I went upstairs to call Amy and left my parents in the kitchen making their own plans. They both looked so happy, I wouldn't allow anything, or anyone, to mess up their plans. We'd all waited too long to be together permanently.

Naturally, when I told Amy the wedding date Mom had chosen, I had to hold the phone away from my ear while she screeched.

"Cara, we have an awful lot to do in the next three weeks. That's really not much time."

"With you to guide me, I know we can get it all done. After all, how long does it take to make a wedding cake?" I was teasing her, of course.

"A menu has to be planned, food has to be ordered, we'll need tables and chairs for your backyard. We have to have flowers and linens for the tables. Maybe hurricane lamps for the tables. . . " Amy was full of ideas, and I was beginning to understand why three weeks was really not much time. I was counting on Amy to help me pull it off in style.

I wanted their wedding to be one we'd remember forever because my mother and father had waited so very long to be together.

CHAPTER 42

Although we'd all grown accustomed to seeing Thornewood's police everywhere, including the hallways at school, for me it was a constant reminder that Donald Gaynes and his goon squad were still out there, probably cooking up more threats to our health and welfare. I was trying to pretend our lives were normal. Occasionally, I succeeded.

At school, classes were going well with Sean beside me, again taking copious notes, which he promised I could borrow.

In Art class, I was finally getting the hang of painting with watercolors. The colors I created were much more saturated than the colors I'd been able to get with my drawing pencils and pens. If I could find a way to get out in the woods to paint, the autumn colors would be wonderfully vivid in watercolor. I could see the colors in my head, and I longed to be out in my beautiful forest.

Miss Burrows, my art teacher, stopped me one day and asked if I would have time to make some drawings for our senior yearbook. She wanted a drawing of the main entrance of the school, along with sketches of the football field during a game. I was happy to agree.

To be safe, I would just have to make sure I had plenty of company when I was outside drawing. Which reminded me again that my life was anything but normal.

On a happier note, Amy was busy lining up vendors for the wedding party. When she asked me what our budget was, I drew a complete blank. But when I asked my father about a budget, he just smiled.

"The sky's the limit, sweetheart. Just have all the bills sent to Harry Callahan's office." His voice got soft as he said, "I want your mother to have the wedding she dreamed of seventeen years ago."

When I told Amy what my father said, she grinned. "No budget? This is going to be fun!"

Instead of going to Art class Thursday afternoon, I had permission to be outside school to draw Thornewood High's main entrance, a really handsome entry featuring a columned portico. The school had been built in the 1930's and featured the kind of classic architecture typical for that era, according to my Art teacher.

With Ryan and Adam keeping me company, I had stationed myself across the street from the main entrance, so the eastern edge of the forest was behind me. A few of my father's men were inside the woods, barely visible in their green tunics and pants. My knives might be in Mr. Weiss' desk drawer, but I had plenty of protection.

Ryan had brought a chair outside with us so I'd have something besides the ground to sit on while I sketched. He and Adam stood on either side of me. I'd been given the fifty-minute class time to work on my drawing, so I didn't have to rush.

I'd been surprised when Adam joined us. He said my father had asked him to keep Ryan company today, but he didn't know why. I made a mental note to ask my dad later.

It was another beautiful late-September day and I was enjoying sitting outdoors with a pen in my hand and a drawing pad in my lap. I'd always loved the smell of dried leaves, that sharp but pleasantly earthy scent. The sun was high overhead, perfect for artwork.

A little while later, a dark sedan drove by slowly, a stranger looking out the window at me. When he spotted my two bodyguards, the car sped up and disappeared around the next corner.

I looked up at Adam. "Coincidence?"

He shook his head. "I didn't like the way that man looked at you. Did you get the license plate number?"

I smiled. "Yep." I had jotted it down in the margin of my drawing. I pulled out my cell, hit speed dial and was speaking to Chief O'Donnell a few seconds later. I described the car, where it seemed to be headed, and gave him the plate number. He said he'd get right on it.

Ryan said, "Lass, I think we should go back inside now. Have you got enough of your drawing done?"

"I think I can finish it from inside."

I turned to Adam. "Will you be out here until school's over for the day?"

He nodded. "I'll wait by your car. I want to see if that stranger's car shows up again."

I threw my car keys at him. "You'll be more comfortable waiting in the car." He caught them, grinning at me.

Picking up my chair, Ryan and I walked back inside. We headed for Art class, which wouldn't be over for another fifteen minutes. I showed my sketch to Miss Burrows and she was delighted with it. "You can finish this in class, Cara. If you're going to this week's football game, you can do some sketching there as well. This will look wonderful in the yearbook."

Ryan and I met Kevin, Patrick, Amy and Neal after the last bell. I collected my knives from Mr. Weiss and we left school. My car was parked half a block away. I'd told the others about the car we'd seen earlier, so we hurried to my car, despite the beautiful weather.

Amy and Kevin were surprised to find Adam waiting for us. Adam tossed my keys to me with a grin. "Thanks, Cara. This was a lot more comfortable than leaning against a tree."

On the way home, Amy asked, "Everyone going to the football game Friday night?"

It was the big game with Greenville, and we all felt we had to go. Sean would be sitting on the bench with Gabe, and I think we were all wondering if Coach would decide to use his "secret weapon."

"Wouldn't miss it," Kevin said with a grin. Next to him, Patrick was nodding, also wearing a grin. Our bodyguards had all become football fans.

"This might be the best game of the season," Amy said. "For sure it will be the toughest. Greenville has an awesome team. Most of their players are the size of tanks!"

After a brief argument with Kevin, we decided to take my car to the game this time, mainly because it was the biggest. It looked so much like the Chief's car, I didn't think anyone would mess with it.

I dropped off Amy and Kevin. When we got home, Adam said, "I communicated with your father earlier, and he feels that Ryan and I should both be with you when you're outside home or school, even on week days." He smiled with those devastating dark blue eyes and asked, "That won't be a problem, will it?"

Naturally, he had let my father know about the drive-by when I was outside school drawing this afternoon. And my father's solution was to double my bodyguard contingent. But it seemed that he'd done that even before the drive-by.

I sighed. I glanced at Ryan and Adam. "It's a good thing I like you guys so much."

Ryan laughed and Adam gave me that familiar amused look.

That night, after we'd finished dinner, I asked my father why he'd sent Adam to school before there appeared to be any threat.

He looked a little embarrassed. "I occasionally have a premonition. It was just a feeling that you might be in danger this afternoon. I don't ignore my feelings anymore. I sent Adam to your school immediately. From what he told me, it might have been a good thing you had two bodyguards while you were outside school today."

He may have been right. We'd never know.

The next day was Friday, and everyone at school was stoked about the game with Greenville. I heard someone mention that Thornewood had beat Greenville only once in thirty-five years, and that was because the entire Greenville team had come down with the flu at the same time. They played, but it was a rather feeble attempt. Thornewood had the victory, but not a very proud one.

I heard several whispers about Coach's "secret weapon" during the day, and it seemed likely that Gabe would finally come off the bench. I asked Sean if he knew what the plan was.

He chuckled. "I think it will depend on how well the rest of the team plays during the first half. But I know Gabe's dying to get on the field and he might get his chance tonight."

"If Gabe's such a good player, why hasn't Coach been using him?"

Sean hesitated, then smiled. "Well, even though Gabe is officially registered as a senior at Thornewood High, his records wouldn't stand up to much scrutiny if someone from another school decided to check him out. Know what I mean?"

"Oh. Because he didn't really transfer from another high school, right?"

"Right. Coach knows that Gabe was only here to act as a bodyguard, the same way he did last spring. The other schools haven't seen Gabe in action yet. Coach is afraid that Gabe's size and speed would raise too many questions."

That made sense.

"By the way, I'll be on the bench with the team, but I'll see you there. And, if we win, celebration at the Grill, okay?"

"You got it."

Much to my surprise, both my parents had decided to attend the game with us. Mom admitted she had always enjoyed the football games when she was in school. Dad had been hearing about the games from Adam, Gabe, and Ryan and had decided to go see what all the fuss was about. We couldn't all squeeze into my already full car, so Mom decided to take her own car.

We had a quick supper of sandwiches and French fries, but when I thought I was ready to go, Mom stopped me and asked me to change my sweatshirt. I was wearing my red Thornewood High sweatshirt in a rare fit of school spirit. Mom shook her head. "You look good in red, but it also makes you stand out too much. Please put on something darker."

Another reminder of my screwed up life. In addition to the constant tension in my neck, my spirits dropped a little, but I told myself to snap out of it. I changed into a black sweatshirt and we all left for the game.

Amy was going with Sean and his dad, and their bodyguards, of course, so she'd promised to save us good seats in the stands. I needed to be close to the top of the stands because I was going to try to sketch the field while the game was being played. My request for the top row in the stands was vetoed immediately. "We'll all stand out too much up there. One or two rows lower will be better."

After I parked my car and waited for Mom to find a parking space, we walked to the stands on Thornewood's side of the field and spotted Amy waving at us from one row below the top of the stands. All in black again, she'd obviously gotten the same advice.

We climbed up and squeezed by the crowd in the stands. There were seven of us, including my parents, so we filled up half the row, much to the annoyance of the other people in that row. But I couldn't help smiling. With Adam so close to me, I wasn't complaining. I forced myself to push away the thought that he was more than a close friend. I really didn't know what to do about my feelings for him. My mother's feelings about our ten-year age difference kept crowding into my brain.

I tried to sketch the field before the players ran out, but there were too many people in front of me. Or maybe I was just too short. And balancing my sketch pad in my hand wasn't working well either. Kevin saw me struggling and called to me, "Hey, short stuff, use your phone and take a picture. You can do the drawing at home." Brilliant. I tried aiming my phone and found I was still too short to get the picture I wanted.

Adam chuckled. "Can I help?"

I handed him my phone and showed him how to take a picture. "Take a few pictures for me, okay? I want one with the field empty, and a few more when the players are on the field." Adam was about six foot three, so he was at the perfect height. I looked further along our row and saw my parents. Mom was wrapped up in my father's arms. They both looked so happy, I looked up at Adam and pointed to them. He grinned and took a quick picture of them.

The team ran on the field and the cheering and whistling began all around us. When the two teams got into position, facing each other, Adam took several pictures. He showed them to me and I knew they'd be perfect for the drawings I wanted to do.

"Hang on to my phone, Adam. If you see a good action shot later, take more pictures, okay? You're at the perfect height. I'll get nothing from down here."

Laughing, Kevin called over, "And that's why we call you short stuff, babe!"

"Very funny, Kevin."

With everyone around us smiling at me, I had to laugh too.

Mr. McKay stood next to my parents, explaining football to my dad. I hoped he'd pick it up faster than I had. I heard Sean's dad say, "Greenville's defense is excellent. Thornewood will have a tough time scoring. It's really a shame Sean's not playing. I think he'd have a better chance of getting past their defense."

By half-time, the score was 14-6, favor of Greenville. We'd managed one touchdown to two of theirs. The cheerleaders were doing their thing on the sidelines, and everyone in the stands was yelling encouragement for our team. The visitors on the other side of the field were doing the same for their team. The noise was so loud, my head started to pound. Crowds would never be my thing.

When the second half started, a familiar figure came off the Thornewood bench. I couldn't see his face through the helmet, but I knew Gabe by the way he moved and by his size. He was as tall as Adam but broader and heavier. And that's when Thornewood's game really began. Gabe wasn't replacing Sean as quarterback. Instead he was the receiver for the bombs Billy Herron threw. Gabe was in the right place every time, caught the ball every time and no one on the other team was able to stop him. The yelling from our side of the field was deafening. I would have given anything for a pair of ear plugs.

Gabe ran two touchdowns in a row, and Thornewood beat Greenville for the first time in thirty-five years, with a score of 20-14.

The stands went crazy. I was sure I'd be totally deaf by the time I got home.

Adam had taken a lot of pictures, several of Gabe running with the ball, with players from Greenville on the ground behind him. And I knew exactly what I was going to draw for the yearbook.

Suddenly Adam aimed the phone at me and took my picture as I looked up at him. He smiled as he looked at it and I grabbed the phone out of his hand. I had to see what he was smiling at. It was the first picture of myself I'd ever seen that had been taken from a foot above me. I realized this was exactly how Adam usually saw me; he was more than a foot taller. I rolled my eyes. In that picture I was smiling up at him, but I looked like a child.

"I'd like a copy of that picture if you can print one for me." I looked up at him and saw that he was perfectly serious.

"Why?" I asked.

He looked amused. "Because you have a beautiful smile."

"Okay, if you really want one." Then I pointed my phone at him and took a quick picture. He frowned and said the same thing I had. "Why?"

I grinned. "Because you're so handsome, Adam."

Seeing that handsome face turn red was gratifying.

As we all climbed down from the stands, my father said they wouldn't join us at The Grill. Mom wasn't crazy about crowds and wanted to go home. He turned to Adam and Ryan and said something I couldn't hear, probably the usual warning about keeping me safe. I just sighed. I hugged Mom and Dad.

"So, Dad, are you a football fan now?"

He smiled but shook his head. "It's an interesting game, but as a parent, I would worry about possible injuries. I think we're fortunate that you don't play football, dear."

Mom chuckled. "I agree. Have fun with your friends. Stay close to your bodyguards. We'll see you later." She kissed my cheek and left for the parking lot with my father's arm wrapped firmly around her.

Amy was still jumping up and down, excited about Thornewood's victory, and Kevin was discussing the plays from the game with Mr. McKay.

When we reached the parking lot, Mr. McKay left us to wait for Sean and Gabe. He promised to drop them off at The Grille if I could drive them home later. I was sure we could squeeze them into my car.

We commandeered the largest table at The Grille. There would be nine of us in total once Sean and Gabe arrived. Gabe would need a little time to clean up so I ordered two burgers each for him and Sean, along with the usual fries and milkshakes.

Their food was ready and waiting for them when they came through the door, all smiles. Gabe received cheers and fist bumps from the rest of the team as he and Sean walked to the back of the restaurant where we were sitting. I had Ryan on one side and Adam on the other, which seemed to irritate Sean. My bodyguards were taking their duties seriously. But I had to stand up and give Sean and Gabe hugs as I congratulated Gabe on his part in winning the game for us.

Grinning from ear to ear, Gabe said, "I can't remember ever having so much fun. Wish I could do this every week, but Coach said he'd only put me in the game when he's desperate." He laughed, shaking his head. "Better than nothing, I guess."

Kevin laughed. "Gabe, with you receiving and Sean at quarterback, we'd be unbeatable. But I think we can all understand why Coach is keeping you mostly under wraps."

Gabe nodded. "Yeah. This is one of the few times I've ever wished I was human."

Ryan, Patrick and Neal were all shaking their heads. They obviously preferred being Elves.

CHAPTER 43

Thornewood's football team was enjoying a winning season, and it was only a week before my parents' wedding when Mom suddenly realized we needed new dresses.

I found her frantically tossing clothes out of her closet one Sunday, finally turning to me with a panic-stricken look on her face. "Cara, you and Amy have been handling all the wedding details so efficiently, I completely forgot this one last detail! I need a wedding dress! And you need a new dress too. We only have a week. What'll I do if we need alterations, or we can't find anything suitable in town?"

My mother was usually so much in control, I had to laugh. This was a side of her I hadn't seen before.

"Relax, Mom. We'll go down to Van Horn's tomorrow. If they don't have anything you like, we'll drive over to Greenville the next day. No problem. Everything will be fine."

She gave me a narrow-eyed look and muttered, "When did you become the mother?"

I giggled. "I'm your maid of honor, Mom. It's my job."

Looking panicky again, she said, "I wonder if your father has given any thought to his clothes for the wedding. Please speak to him about it. He only needs a suit, dress shirt and tie for our civil wedding. He can change into his normal tunic and pants for the Elven ceremony if he prefers."

"Okay. I'll take care of Dad. Just relax now. Maybe a glass of wine?"

When I spoke to my father later about his wedding apparel, he grinned and assured me that Harry Callahan was taking him shopping the next day. "I would never want to embarrass your mother by being inappropriately dressed. Please tell her not to worry."

"I've been telling her not to worry daily. But I'm not sure she's been listening."

After school the next day, I dropped off Kevin and Patrick, picked up Mom and drove to Van Horn's. Ryan and Adam were with us, of course. She was a nervous wreck, even though all she had to worry about was her dress. I did my best to calm her, but the saleslady in the Evening Wear department must have had years of experience dealing with stressed-out brides. She was middle-aged and motherly. Her name tag read "Mrs. Hanson," and she had Mom calmed down in under two minutes. When Mom insisted that she wanted a wedding dress, not a wedding gown, Mrs. Hanson smiled and said, "I think I know exactly what you need, Alicia. Follow me."

The dressing room wasn't big enough for all three of us, so I sat outside while Mom tried on the one dress that Mrs. Hanson had brought in for her. I could hear the rustle of silky fabric as Mom tried on the dress.

"Ahh. This is perfect." Mom opened the dressing room door and stepped out. The dress was ivory satin, full-length, skimming over her curves like a slip. It had slim straps and was cut rather low in the back. Mrs. Hanson handed her a thin silk jacket in the same ivory shade to wear over the dress. It was hip-length and open in the front. The overall effect was breathtaking. I'd never seen my mother dressed like this before. She looked like a queen.

Mrs. Hanson just smiled. "Alicia, I'd suggest one gardenia in your hair. You look beautiful. And make sure your shoes are ivory, not white. We'll just have to shorten the dress about two inches. When's the wedding?"

Mom looked panicky again. "It's this Saturday. Can you do the alteration before then?"

Mrs. Hanson nodded. "Of course. You can pick up your dress Thursday." She turned to look at me. "You'll need a dress too, won't you, dear?"

Mom said, "My daughter will be my maid of honor, so she needs something special too. Cara, I know you're not a fan of dresses, but I'd really like to see you in a full-length dress for my wedding."

I knew this was coming, so I didn't complain. "Okay, let's go find me a full-length dress."

She smiled. "Follow me."

THE DRAGON'S SONG

When it came to a dress for me, Mom had an eagle eye. She went straight to a dress on display. "This would look great on you." Turning to Mrs. Hanson, she asked if it came in my petite size.

"But it's pink! I don't wear pink, Mom. I'll look like a baby." Actually, it was pink and cream, but my dislike for dresses had finally broken loose.

"It's a dusty rose, not really pink, and I think it would look perfect on you."

Okay, it was Mom's wedding, and I wasn't going to argue with her. I'd probably never wear the dress again. Mrs. Hanson brought the dress in my size into a dressing room and I dutifully tried it on.

As usual, Mom was right. The dress fit perfectly. The top reminded me of a silky gypsy-style blouse, the neckline gathered with a narrow ribbon to adjust the neckline either higher or lower, and full sleeves gathered just below the elbow. The full-length silk skirt was flared and belted at the waist. The top was dusty rose, and the skirt and wide belt were ivory. I thought it had a kind of bohemian look and I actually liked it.

Mom and Mrs. Hanson beamed. Mom pulled my hair down from its ponytail, spreading my thick hair over my shoulders. "You have to wear your hair down for the wedding, sweetheart." She chuckled. "Your bodyguards will have their hands full, I'm afraid."

Clearly startled, Mrs. Hanson said, "Bodyguards?" Mom had to explain about my kidnapping and the more recent threats. What she didn't mention was her own abduction.

"Oh, you're that little girl I heard about last spring." I nodded. "Well, I can certainly understand why your parents want you well protected."

At that moment, I caught a glimpse of Adam, who'd been as unobtrusive as a handsome, six foot three inch man could be in a women's dress department. He was staring at me, wide-eyed, as I modeled the pink and ivory dress. I was pleased that I had finally impressed him.

Grinning at him, I said, "What do you think?"

Embarrassed that I'd caught him staring, he simply said, "You're beautiful." He wasn't looking the least bit amused, I was glad to see.

With one eyebrow raised, Mrs. Hanson said, "If that's one of your bodyguards, you're a lucky young lady." Mom just rolled her eyes.

Once we were both dressed, and my new dress carefully wrapped in plastic, we went downstairs to the shoe department and tried on shoes for a half hour. Mom bought ivory pumps with a very high heel that made her legs look fantastic. Since I still hadn't mastered walking in high heels, I found low-heeled ivory sandals that were comfortable. My long skirt would cover them up so Mom didn't complain.

As we left the store, I glanced behind us and spotted Adam and Ryan trailing us, trying not to look obvious. As soon as we were outside, I asked, "Is anyone else hungry? Mom, are you up for The Grille?"

She was finally relaxed now that the stress of finding a wedding dress was behind her. "Sure, I could go for a burger and a chocolate milkshake." She looked at our two bodyguards. "Do I even have to ask if you two are hungry?"

Adam and Ryan were both smiling as we climbed into my car and headed for The Grille.

I was in luck, finding a nice big parking spot in front of the restaurant. Mom smiled. "They must have known you were coming, dear." My lack of parallel parking expertise was no secret.

The Grille was crowded, but we got the last available booth and placed our orders. While we waited for our food, Adam and Ryan described a few Elven weddings they had seen, although Ryan said my parents' Elven wedding ceremony would probably be a little different since it would be held outside Elvenwood and not under the Joining Tree.

"It's a simple but solemn ceremony. Whichever Elder agrees to oversee your vows will probably use his own words. I'm guessing he'll tailor his words to your particular circumstances, Alicia. He won't know you, of course, but he's known Brian from childhood." Ryan grinned. "It will be interesting to see what he decides to say to bless your union."

Adam smiled. "Since it's the wedding of Elvenwood's leader, I think the Elders will ensure that it's a momentous occasion. I also think your backyard will be packed with Elves, some of whom have never been outside Elvenwood before."

Looking panicked again, Mom said, "Cara, please make sure enough food and wine have been ordered. It sounds as though it will be a much larger crowd than I anticipated."

"Mom, I'm sure Amy will have it all under control. Please don't worry." I patted her hand and she took a deep breath. Fortunately, our burgers, French fries and milkshakes arrived at our table, giving Mom something else to focus on. I looked up at Adam and he winked at me, as if to say, *"Don't worry; she'll be fine."*

When we had stuffed ourselves sufficiently, Mom paid the check and we left. As usual, our escorts received a lot of female attention as we walked to the door.

Out on the sidewalk, as Ryan leaned down to open the passenger door of my car for Mom, I heard a sharp crack and Adam threw himself over me and pushed me to the sidewalk. From the corner of my eye, I saw Mom and Ryan on the ground next to the car. I'm not sure I was breathing. The air had been knocked out of me.

I wondered what Mom and Ryan were doing sitting on the sidewalk up against the door of my car. That's when I realized the sharp crack had been a gunshot. For a few seconds I froze, unable to move, although I couldn't really move with Adam pinning me to the ground.

I remembered seeing a police car parked around the corner from The Grille, and almost immediately heard footsteps running toward us. I heard a voice shout, "Stay down. The shot came from the roof of the Post Office." The Post Office was directly across the street from The Grille. Then I heard more than one person running past us.

I shouted, "Mom, are you and Ryan okay?"

Her voice sounded shaky, but she said, "We're okay. Are you and Adam all right?"

"I'm okay, Mom. Adam? Adam, are you okay? Can you move? You're pretty heavy."

He groaned. "I've been hit. Wait for the police. Stay where you are."

From across the street, I heard two more shots, then shouting, then several sirens told me there were at least two police cars converging on the Post Office. Not more than two minutes had passed since I heard the first gunshot.

"Adam, where were you hit?" I reached up and felt his arm. My hand came away covered in blood.

I started yelling. "We've been hit! We need help. Adam's bleeding."

From across the street, I heard the Chief's voice. "Stay down! The shooter is still out there."

I took a few deep breaths, trying to calm myself. "How bad is it?"

Adam gasped. "It's my arm, bleeding quite a bit."

"Don't move. I'm sure they'll get to us as soon as they can." I was trying to reassure myself as well as him.

His mouth was next to my ear. "Sorry if I'm crushing you, love."

Actually, under different circumstances, I might have enjoyed being crushed by Adam. But not if he was bleeding. I sighed. "Don't worry. I don't mind."

I heard a weak chuckle in my ear.

We heard one more gunshot and a shout. "Got him. He's down."

An ambulance pulled up next to my car, and two EMT's ran to us. They lifted Adam off of me and wrapped a tourniquet around his left upper arm. They lifted him on a gurney and put him in the ambulance. I could hear him protesting, saying he was not going to any hospital, that he'd rather see his own "doctor." I was sure he was referring to Kathleen. One of them asked if I was all right because one side of me was covered in Adam's blood. "Yeah, I'm fine. The bullet hit Adam, not me."

I looked over at my car. Ryan and Mom were both sitting on the ground, leaning against the passenger side of my car. Ryan stood, lifting my mother to her feet. She looked at me, half covered in blood, and her eyes got huge.

"I'm okay, Mom. It's Adam's blood, not mine."

Adam argued with the EMTs who thought he needed to be in the E.R. They were taking his blood pressure and temperature. I could hear them sounding surprised that his vital signs were all perfect.

Another ambulance had pulled up across the street. I saw two police leading a handcuffed man to the ambulance. The man was bleeding from the head, but he was on his feet. He looked over at me and gave me a dirty look. One of the cops got into the ambulance with him and they took off, siren on and lights flashing.

I knew then that I had been the target, and if Adam hadn't thrown himself over me, I'd probably be dead. I felt sick, deep inside. I was afraid I might lose my cheeseburger.

The Chief walked across the street, heading for me. Before he reached me, I pointed to the ambulance where Adam was still arguing with the EMTs. Maybe he could convince the EMT's to cut Adam loose.

Another police car pulled up and my father jumped out, running to my mother. I walked over to her and she threw her arms around me. She didn't say a word, just hugged me while my father hugged both of us.

"Dad, we're both okay, but Adam took a bullet in the arm. I think he's trying to talk the EMTs out of taking him to the hospital. I'm sure he wants to come home with us and see Kathleen."

Once he was assured that Mom and I weren't hurt, he strode to the ambulance to collect Adam. Between Dad and the Chief, the

THE DRAGON'S SONG

EMT's were convinced to let Adam get out of the ambulance and leave with my father, who assured them he'd be taking Adam to his own doctor. At least Adam's arm had been bandaged tightly and didn't seem to be bleeding.

Dad looked over at us. "Cara, are you up to driving home?"

"I think so. I'll take Mom and Ryan with me. The Chief can drive you and Adam home." He nodded, taking Adam's good arm and leading him to the Chief's vehicle.

I climbed into my car with Mom and Ryan, groaning when I spotted a bullet hole in the hood. Mom asked what was wrong and I pointed to the hole in the roof.

Once we were all settled in my car, I reached into my pocket for my keys, put the key in the ignition and couldn't remember how to start my car. I sat there, staring at the key in the ignition until Mom said, "What's wrong?"

I laughed, probably sounding slightly hysterical. "I can't remember how to start the car. Isn't that silly?"

Mom said, "Move over, dear. I'd better drive us home." She got out and came around to the driver's side and I slid over to the passenger's side, wondering what was wrong with me.

Ryan reached over the back of the seat and patted my shoulder. "I think you're in shock, lass. Just relax. I'm sure Kathleen can take care of you as well as Adam. It's over. Nothin' more to worry about."

I knew he was wrong. Donald Gaynes was still out there and wanted one or more of us dead.

CHAPTER 44

We followed the Chief's cruiser to our house. As soon as Mom parked my car, my father got out of the Chief's car and rushed to help Mom and me out of my car.

He was frowning, his eyes serious. "Alicia, you're driving? I thought Cara was driving you home."

"Cara is a little more shook up than we realized, Brian. Of course, we're both shook up, but I think I'm doing better than she is. Have you called Kathleen yet?"

He nodded. "If it's all right with you, I'd like to have Kathleen come here. Adam can rest on the couch until she gets here." He turned to me. "Do you need Kathleen's help?"

I shrugged. "I don't know. I think I just need to calm down."

Mom took my hand. "Let's go inside and get the couch ready for Adam."

When we got inside, Mom rushed to the linen cabinet and pulled out a rubber sheet and a soft blanket and spread them over the couch. "It's just in case Adam starts bleeding again when Kathleen cuts that bullet out of his arm." She paused. "Cara, go up to my room. You'll find a couple of men's shirts in the back of my closet. Bring one down for Adam. He won't want to spend all night in that bloody shirt."

I ran upstairs to find the shirt and realized that I was feeling much better since Mom took over and put me to work. Being busy was exactly what I needed. I took the shirt downstairs and Mom asked me to make a pot of coffee. "I'm afraid this will be a long night, Cara. Feeling better now?"

"Yeah, I am." The front door opened and my father came in with Adam. The Chief was right behind them. My father told Adam to sit down on the couch.

Mom asked, "How are you feeling, Adam?"

His eyes looked a little glassy, but he smiled at us. "I'll be fine as soon as Kathleen gets this bullet out of my arm." More serious, he looked at me. "Cara, I hope I didn't hurt you when I pushed you to the ground."

"You saved my life. That's all that matters. That bullet was meant for me."

He nodded, looking suddenly tired.

I heard a knock at the back door and rushed to let Kathleen in. She gave me a hug. "Are you all right, dear?"

"I wasn't hurt. Adam took a bullet that was meant for me. He's resting in the living room."

I led her into the living room and she knelt down next to Adam. After checking him over quickly, she stood. "Alicia, I brought some strong tea to put him to sleep. Would you boil water for me please? I don't want him to wake up when I have to dig out that bullet.

"Brian, I'll need you here in case he has to be held down, so stay close please."

The Chief followed Mom into the kitchen. She started water boiling on the stove and poured coffee for the Chief. "Have a seat, Tommy. I imagine you have questions, but I want to let Kathleen take care of Adam first."

Chief O'Donnell pulled out a chair at the kitchen table and sat down. "There are two police cars in front of your house tonight, and Brian told me he has men stationed behind the house. Ryan's on the front porch as well. Nothing else is going to happen tonight."

I was still standing in the doorway to the living room where I could hear everything that was going on in the house. I wasn't shaking anymore, but I felt my nerves were pulled tight.

Kathleen came into the kitchen with a bag of herbs in her hand. "Put these in boiling water. It will take several cups to put Adam to sleep."

I moved into the kitchen to see if Mom needed my help.

She poured the herbs into the pot and the kitchen was immediately filled with the strong scent of herbs. This wasn't the gentle scent I was used to when I made tea. This was something earthy and slightly bitter. "Let the tea brew for ten minutes," Kathleen said. "That's when it will be at its strongest. Then pour a large cup for Adam. And when he finishes it, pour him another cup. I want him to drink until he can't hold his head up any longer. I'll get his arm ready now. Bring in the tea in ten minutes, no sooner."

"Mom, I'd like to help. I can take the tea in to Adam."

She looked at me and nodded.

I wished there was more I could do for the Elf who had saved my life again. I felt my eyes fill with tears and ordered them to stay where they belonged. Crying wouldn't help anyone.

CLAIRE FOGEL

When I carried the medicinal tea into the living room, Kathleen had already placed several thick towels under Adam. She had stripped the bloody shirt off of him, and washed off the blood all around the bandage on his upper arm and on his chest. Seeing his bare chest made him seem more vulnerable.

I sat down on the floor next to the couch. "Here, Adam. Please drink this down as quickly as you can. Kathleen wants you asleep before she removes the bullet."

He nodded and tried to smile as he took the cup from me. He was paler than he'd been before and there was the sheen of sweat on his face. He'd been leaning back against the arm of the couch, but he propped himself up, drank down the entire cup of tea and handed it back to me, sinking back into the couch.

I hurried into the kitchen, filled up his cup, and returned to the living room. He sat up slowly, took the cup from me and drained it again. He whispered, "Thank you," and his eyes closed.

I looked at Kathleen. She nodded and said, "Adam, can you hear me?"

His voice was hard to hear, but he said, "I can hear you."

She pointed me to the kitchen and I filled his cup with tea again.

This time I had to coax him to sit up and drink. He was about three-quarters asleep, but Kathleen wanted him completely out, so I held the cup to his lips and whispered, "Drink, Adam, please."

He never opened his eyes, but his lips quirked and I heard, "Anything for you, love."

When Kathleen asked him if he could hear her, he didn't answer. His breathing was slow and regular. Kathleen nodded. "It's time to get that bullet out. Cara, dear, perhaps you should wait in the kitchen. He's going to bleed quite a bit."

She had moved a small end table up against the couch and placed the towels and his injured arm on it. Looking up at me, she said, "How well can you handle the sight of blood, dear?"

I didn't know so I looked at my father who was sitting at Adam's feet. "Should I stay?"

He nodded slowly. "I know you feel responsible. Stay with him as long as you can."

From the doorway, Mom said, "I'll be in the kitchen if you need me." I heard her pull out a chair as she sat down with the Chief. I could hear their soft voices as Mom described what she remembered about the shooting.

Kathleen was as skilled with what looked like a scalpel as she was with herbs. And she'd been right; there was a lot of blood. In less than a minute, she held up the bullet she'd pried out of Adam's upper arm and called out, "Here's the bullet if the Chief wants it."

Rushing into the living room, the Chief held out a small plastic bag and she dropped the bullet into it.

Putting pressure on the open wound, she said, "I'll have to stitch him up now, but the worst is over. I'm glad he didn't wake up."

When she started pulling the needle through his flesh, I had to leave the room. My stomach was threatening to embarrass me. When I walked into the kitchen, Mom took one look at my face and said, "Sit down, dear. Kathleen's relaxing tea is in the teapot. I'll pour you a cup."

I sat down and drank the calming herbal tea.

The Chief said, "Cara, I'd like to get what you remember about the shooting tonight. Okay?"

"Okay. All I can tell you is that right after we walked out of The Grille, I heard a sharp crack and Adam pushed me down to the sidewalk, throwing himself over me. It was a few seconds before I realized it was a gunshot. And I had no idea where it had come from. Then I heard someone running past us, then sirens, and you know the rest."

The Chief asked, "You don't remember seeing anyone near the Post Office when you walked out the door?"

I thought about it, but couldn't remember seeing anyone across the street. I shook my head.

"I'm going back to the station now. I'll talk to Adam tomorrow. I think Ryan's still on your porch. I'll see what he remembers. The shooter is in the hospital getting his head patched up. I'll be having a long talk with him in the morning." He got up, thanked Mom for the coffee, and left through the back door.

I poured myself another cup of tea and took some deep breaths, trying to relax. When I looked at the clock, it was only ten o'clock. It seemed much later.

Mom got up and took a cup of coffee in to my dad and asked Kathleen what she could get for her. I peeked into the living room and was relieved to see the stitching was finished. Kathleen was applying a thin paste of something over the stitches. Mom asked, "What is that?"

Kathleen smiled. "It's a mixture of herbs and a special kind of mold, excellent at fighting infection. In your world, I think it's similar to what's called penicillin."

She finished applying the paste that smelled of rotting leaves and damp earth and started wrapping strips of linen around Adam's arm. He was still sound asleep. When she'd finished bandaging him, she stood up and stretched. "I could certainly use a cup of that coffee I've been smelling for the past hour, Alicia." As she left the room, I covered Adam's bare chest with the soft blanket Mom had brought in.

My father joined us in the kitchen. Kathleen chatted with Mom, but Dad was unusually quiet. I think Mom noticed it too.

I took my father's hand. "Come out on the back porch with me. I owe Rowenna a song."

He got up and followed me outside. I could almost feel his nerves humming just under his skin. He started pacing from one end of the porch to the other. I thought maybe if I started singing Rowenna's song, he'd calm down.

Leaning against the porch railing, I began to sing.
"Soaring above clouds,
Across sky so wide,
Almost touching the sun,
Here no reason to hide. . ."

As I sang, I could feel the dragon's magic descending, wrapping itself around us. My father stopped pacing, finally sitting down.

I heard the sound of huge wings coming closer as she flew down, settling herself in the backyard.

"Good evening, Rowenna."

In my head, her rusty voice was alarmed. *More trouble tonight, Cara? There is so much tension, so much anger, in the air around your home. And flashing lights in other parts of town. Did I hear the sound of guns tonight?*

"You know the sound of guns, Rowenna?"

Yes. When there were many dragons long ago, people on the ground sometimes tried to bring us down with their guns. But we flew too high for guns to harm us. Foolish people.

"The evil man we've talked about keeps hiring men to come here and try to kill me, my mother, and our friends. The man shot at me tonight, but Adam protected me and was shot instead. Kathleen, the Elves' healer, is here. She removed the bullet from Adam's arm. He's resting now. He'll be fine."

Her rough voice sounded angry. *Where is man who shot at you?*

"The police caught him. He's in jail."

If I caught him, he would be ash now.

"I'm almost sorry you didn't catch him. But you may get your chance. I'm sure the evil man causing the trouble will try again."

I fly over your town every night, Cara. Call me if you need my help.

"Thank you, Rowenna." I hummed her song again as she rose slowly from our yard and disappeared into the night sky. Her magic swirled around us for a few minutes and then was gone.

CHAPTER 45

Adam slept all night without stirring and spent the next day at our house. Mom had to open the bookstore and I had to go to school, so my father volunteered to stay home and keep Adam company. I'd shown him where sandwich ingredients were kept in the fridge, and he was busy making coffee when I left for school. Nobody would go hungry today.

I found Ryan waiting on the porch, all red-eyed. "You've been up all night, haven't you?" I asked. He nodded.

"I won't be goin' to school with you today. Your father came out earlier and said he'd send someone else. Your principal has already been called, so there won't be a problem. I'll be fine tomorrow."

I heard footsteps on the porch stairs and turned to see my cousin Jason, who gave me a tight hug when he reached me.

"I heard what happened last night. How is Adam?"

"Kathleen took the bullet out last night. I think he'll be fine. He's asleep now."

He couldn't help beaming. "Well, as bad as I feel for your bodyguards, I now get a day in high school with you!"

"Well, let's go. We have to pick up Kevin and Patrick around the corner. Ryan, get some rest. I'll see you tomorrow." He nodded.

As soon as we pulled up in front of Kevin's house, he and Patrick jumped into the back seat. Patrick had obviously filled Kevin in on last night's shooting.

"How are you, short stuff?"

"I'm fine, Kev. Adam took the bullet for me. He's resting at my house."

"At least the police caught the shooter. Have you heard anything from the Chief yet?"

"No. He said the shooter was getting his head patched up at the hospital. The Chief will be questioning him this morning."

"What happened to his head?"

"I think it was more like *who* happened to his head, Kev. I don't think the cops who caught him were too gentle."

Patrick asked, "Did Kathleen get the bullet out?"

"Yes. Adam will be fine once his arm heals."

Patrick reached up and gave Jason a gentle punch. "So you're getting your wish today, right?"

Grinning, Jason nodded. "I'm sorry Adam and Ryan are out of commission today, but I'm really looking forward to filling in for them. You and Gabriel talk so much about all the pretty girls in school, I'm hoping I can meet some of them."

I had to smile. "I have a feeling those girls will be all over you today."

"Really?"

"Yep. You may have to beat them off."

Patrick and Kevin both laughed, but they knew I wasn't kidding. Girls had a tendency to melt when they caught sight of my cousin. Tall and thin, with the face of an angel and a sweet personality, it was easy to fall in love with Jason. But I had to wonder what kind of a bodyguard he'd make. I might have to guard him.

I found a good parking space not far from the school's entrance, and we jogged into the main entrance where Amy, Sean, Neal and Gabe waited for us. Everyone had heard about the shooting.

As soon as I'd handed over my knives to Mr. Weiss and introduced Jason, Sean and Amy started talking at once. It seemed they had both tried to call me last night, but I'd had my phone turned off.

"Sorry, but I had to turn off my phone while Kathleen was performing surgery on Adam's arm. I was helping her, and the last thing I needed was my phone ringing."

Sean looked relieved but he wasn't smiling. "We knew there had been a shooting, but we didn't know whether you'd been shot. It was a long night for us. My dad finally got in touch with the Chief late last night, and he told us Adam had been the only one who got hurt."

Amy hugged me. "Please don't scare us like that again. Sean and I were wrecks for hours last night."

She hesitated. "Will there still be a wedding on Saturday?"

That stopped me. "Uh, we haven't discussed that. I'll talk to my parents when I get home today and I'll call you as soon as I know. But I hope they won't decide to postpone."

Amy nodded. "Yeah, I've already put in a lot of time organizing everything. I don't even want to think about all the phone calls I'll have to make if we're postponing."

The bell rang and we all had to leave for our classes. Sean welcomed Jason to Thornewood High. He'd only met my cousin once before, right after my kidnapping. I looked over at Jason and had to smile at his wide-eyed expression as we walked through the halls to our first class. Almost every girl we passed did a double take when they spotted Jason. Sean and Gabe noticed too and couldn't help grinning.

That was how our day went. At lunch our table was busy as crowds of girls stopped by to ask about the shooting and, of course, to be introduced to Jason. I don't think Jason stopped smiling all day.

When I stopped to think about the bodyguard angle, I finally asked Jason if he was armed. He whispered in my ear, "Of course, cousin. I can throw a knife as well as you can."

That was good news.

When we got home after school, Adam and my father were sitting at the kitchen table drinking coffee. Jason came in with me to say hello and see how Adam was feeling. I made him a sandwich and he went out on the front porch, taking Ryan's normal spot.

My father dropped a kiss on my head and told me that Kathleen would be coming back to check on Adam, whose injured arm was in a sling.

"How's the arm feeling?" I asked him.

He gave me that smile that always turned my heart to mush. "It feels better than it did last night, but I'm hoping it heals fast. By the way, thanks for the shirt and the blanket."

"You look a hundred percent better than you did last night. Have you eaten today?"

My father nodded. "I made sandwiches as your mother suggested. I'm afraid we ate all the ham and turkey, but your mother said she'd be stopping at the store on her way home." He grinned. "I'm trying to talk her into pizza for dinner tonight."

I had to smile. Who knew Elves would go crazy for pizza?

When Mom got home, Conor was with her. He stayed and enjoyed the pizza with us. Despite the fact that last night's shooting was the main topic of conversation, dinner was enjoyable. We were still at the table when Kathleen arrived to check on Adam.

They went into the living room while I loaded the dishwasher and cleaned up. When they returned to the kitchen, Kathleen told us that Adam's bullet wound was healing nicely. She took me aside and handed me a bag of special tea for Adam.

"He won't complain, but I know his arm pains him. Use this tea just for Adam. He won't tell you if he's in pain, Cara. You'll have to ask."

THE DRAGON'S SONG

"I will." Kathleen gave me a quick hug.

Mom got up from the table. "Kathleen, please stay and have tea before you return to camp."

Kathleen sat down next to Conor while Mom boiled water for tea. The conversation returned to last night's shooting. My father was wondering if the Chief had learned anything from the shooter. And that was when the phone rang. Mom answered it, said "Okay," and hung up. "Tommy is on his way over here. He has news for us."

When the Chief arrived, Mom poured him a cup of coffee and he sat down with us. He looked startled when he spotted Kathleen. "Alicia, I didn't know you had a sister."

Mom said, "This is Kathleen, the healer from Elvenwood. She's here to treat Adam's wound." She chuckled. "We're not related."

He shook his head. "You could have fooled me. Well, I moved the shooter from the hospital to the jail this morning. He was more talkative than I had expected."

My father asked, "Has he told you where Gaynes is hiding?"

"No, other than saying he thought Gaynes was out of the country. This man wasn't hired by some middle man. Gaynes contacted him through a site on the dark web and they spoke over the phone. Gaynes was complaining that he didn't think it was such a tough job, but that everyone he'd sent here had ultimately failed to do what he'd been hired for. This shooter, Lawrence Hoffman, has a long history; assault, attempted murder, murder for hire, and so on. He's only been out of prison for a few months. He knows he'll be going back to prison for the rest of his life, and he's blaming Gaynes for not telling him that Thornewood was heavily policed, or that his target was well guarded. He said no one will work for Gaynes now."

Taking a deep breath, Mom said, "That might mean that Gaynes will be coming here himself. He's so insane and bent on revenge, I don't see him giving up, do you?"

The Chief shook his head. "That would be too much to hope for. But we'll be ready. The police presence in Thornewood will be even more obvious now."

He looked at Dad. "This may be the right time for your men to become more visible. Can you make that work?"

"I think we can handle that. Conor, pick the men who are most comfortable in the human world and we'll meet with them. Chief, we'll need you to go over the city map with us. We'll want to place my men wherever the police coverage is lightest."

They agreed to meet at my father's camp early the next morning. Adam asked, "What can I do? There must be something you can use a one-armed man for."

My father, Conor, and the Chief looked at each other. I think they all realized that Adam needed more time to recover. My father said, "If the Chief agrees, we can make this house our command post for the Elves. Adam, you're a telepath. That will make communication easier. You can come to camp with me in the morning, but don't forget, you do need more time to recover."

I could see the relief on Adam's face. When he looked at me, I could also see that he still intended to do whatever was possible to keep me protected. More relaxed now, he winked at me.

This seemed like the perfect time to ask my parents the most important question.

"Are we still having the wedding on Saturday?"

From the look on their faces, that hadn't even occurred to them. They looked at each other. Dad took Mom's hand. "Would you rather delay until that lunatic is behind bars?" he asked softly.

Showing the temperament redheads were famous for, she said, "Absolutely not. I think we've already waited too long. Don't you?"

"You're getting married on Saturday?" The Chief asked.

With a satisfied smile, my father said, "Yes. I hope you'll be there, Tom. There will be a party in the backyard Saturday afternoon. If the police force can spare you for a few hours, I'd like to see you there."

Smiling, the Chief looked at Mom. "It's about time, Alicia. I'll be there."

Mom's cheeks were pink, but she was smiling.

CHAPTER 46

After the Chief, Conor, and Kathleen left, I went up to my room to call Amy and let her know the wedding was still on. I could hear the relief in her voice.

"I'm so glad. Not only because of all the arrangements we've already made, but the window for outdoor weddings will be closing soon. Your parents would have to wait until spring."

"Actually, when my dad asked Mom if she wanted to wait until Gaynes is in jail, her hair seemed to get a little redder! What she said was, 'Haven't we waited long enough?'"

Laughing, Amy said, "Yeah, that sounds like your mom. Tomorrow I'll need you to go to the caterer's with me to make all the final decisions on the food. How's right after school?"

"Sure. You've got everything else under control, right?"

"Yes. I've ordered some tables, a lot of chairs, the china, wine glasses, silverware, and flowers. You did say your mom loves chrysanthemums, and this is the perfect time of year for them. Oh, and one more thing I thought of, but it'll be a surprise. I've already enlisted Sean's help in pulling it off."

"You're not even going to tell me?"

"Nope. But I'll give you one clue. Your yard will look like a fairy tale when I'm through!"

I had to laugh. "Well, that's appropriate."

"Cara, there's one more thing I think I should mention. I think Sean is feeling neglected. Maybe you could give him a call before you go to bed."

I sighed. "I've had too many other things on my mind. I still have to see how Adam's feeling tonight. I have some special tea for him that I think contains something to kill pain. I should make it for him before he turns in for the night."

"What? He's staying at your house?"

"Yep. He's crashing on the living room couch. I don't know how long he'll be staying, but I'm in no rush for him to leave."

"You poor thing, what a burden it must be to have that gorgeous blue-eyed Elf under the same roof." She chuckled.

"Yeah, well, we all have our crosses to bear. Seriously, keeping him down while all this Gaynes stuff is going on won't be easy. I can tell he hates seeing me leave the house without him."

I told her what the Chief had learned from the shooter.

"So you all think Gaynes will be coming here himself?"

"Probably. The Chief is putting more men on duty, and more of my father's men will be out and about in town from now on."

I could hear her smile. "More gorgeous guys for Thornewood's females to swoon over? What a hardship that will be for us."

"I guess that's our temporary silver lining. Right now, I'm just hoping he stays away until after the wedding. I don't want anything spoiling that day for my parents."

I described Mom's wedding dress and my own. Amy did all the oohing and ahhing, as expected. She hadn't decided what she'd be wearing yet, but wanted to make sure she'd be coordinated with Mom and me. Of course she did.

I finally said I had to get back downstairs and make that tea for Adam.

When I got downstairs, Adam was still sitting at the kitchen table with my parents. He looked tired, and when he moved his arm, he grimaced. I put the hot water kettle on the stove and turned the gas on. When the water boiled, I poured it over the special, pain-killing tea Kathleen had given me and handed the cup to Adam.

"Kathleen gave me this tea earlier. It'll help with the pain."

He looked up at me, surprised, and then smiled. "You're too good to me, Cara."

I looked into those dark blue eyes and said, "No. I'm really not."

Tearing myself away from those eyes, I told Mom that I'd be going out with Amy after school the next day to place the final order for the food we'd be serving at the wedding party.

Smiling, she said, "I'm not even going to ask what you two have chosen. I'm sure it will all be wonderful. But be sure to take your bodyguards with you."

"Of course. We'll at least have Ryan, Neal, and maybe Jason with us.

"I've got some homework to do and another phone call to make, so I'll say good night. And Adam, if you need more of that tea, the bag is on the counter. I know you know how to boil water on the stove. No sense being in pain if you don't have to."

THE DRAGON'S SONG

He nodded, his eyes letting me know he appreciated my concern.

I hugged Mom and Dad, winked at Adam, and went up to my room.

Homework could wait. I owed Sean a call.

When he picked up the phone, I heard a relieved-sounding "Hi, Beautiful. I hope you have time to talk. I feel like we haven't really talked in weeks."

"I know. With the wedding and the shooting, there's been too much going on. Sorry."

"Any news from the police?"

"Yeah, the Chief interviewed the shooter and learned a few things." I explained what the Chief had told us and that Thornewood would be covered even more thoroughly now.

"More Elves in town? That should be interesting." He chuckled.

"By the way, I hope I'm invited to your parents' wedding on Saturday. I'll be helping Amy set up your backyard before the party. She's really going all out, you know."

"I know, I know. I think she has a promising future as a wedding planner. I could never have done all of this without her help. I didn't have a clue.

"Actually, you're invited to both weddings, if you'd like to be there. The first wedding will be at City Hall Saturday at Noon. It'll just be our closest friends. In the afternoon the Elven wedding ceremony will take place in our backyard, witnessed by all the Elves who are willing to leave Elvenwood for a few hours. The party will follow."

"You bet I'd like to be there. I think my parents would like to attend both weddings as well. They're always up for a party."

"Um, Sean, has your dad ever told your mom the truth about his Elven heritage?"

"Yeah, he did. She wasn't even surprised. I think she always had a hunch that there was something a little unusual about Dad's family, but since he never talked about it, she never asked." He chuckled. "I think she's ready for anything now.

"Uh, I know I should have asked earlier. How's Adam? How's his arm?"

"Kathleen took the bullet out that night, and he's still in some pain, but I think he'll be fine. He'll just have to take it easy for a while, which is not something he's happy about."

"Is he at your father's camp or back in Elvenwood?"

"Actually, he's here with us right now. He's taken over the living room."

"He's living with you?" He sounded a little outraged. Not that he had any right to be.

"Sean, Adam saved my life. My parents and I want him as comfortable as possible while he's healing. He's also going to help my father with the Elves being assigned in town. Adam's a telepath so he can help with communications."

"I see." I heard a long, drawn-out sigh. "Well, I'm here whenever you want to talk. I'm just glad we're spending time together in school. That's making senior year close to perfect for me." It was time to change the subject.

"How's your nose? When do you get the bandages off?"

"Friday they'll take off the big bandage and replace it with a smaller bandage. The doc says my nose will look great, but he wants it covered up for a while longer. He calls it his 'work of art.'" He laughed. "I'll just be happy it will be straight again, and not on the wrong side of my face."

"Sean, I have a feeling you'll look good no matter what shape your nose is in."

"Thanks. Guess I'll say goodnight. See you in the morning, Cara."

Sean's jealousy was showing, but that wasn't something I had time to worry about. I spent an hour on homework. Then I heard the bell from my laptop; I had new Email.

Sitting down at my desk, I went into my Email program and saw one new message. My heart started pounding. It was from Gaynes Land development. My fingers froze on the keyboard. I didn't even want to open it.

I must have stared at that unopened message for ten minutes before I heard footsteps pounding up the stairs. My father burst into my room, Mom right behind him.

"The Chief just called. Gaynes used his Email account again. Did you receive anything from him?"

I nodded and pointed to my laptop. "I haven't opened it. Not sure I want to."

Mom put her hand on my shoulder. "Tommy's on his way over. Someone in his office is trying to find out where the Email originated. Why don't you bring your laptop downstairs and we can read it together."

I unplugged my laptop and carried it downstairs to the kitchen. Adam was sitting at the table, frowning. "Have you read it yet, Cara?"

Taking a deep breath, I said, "No. I'll open it when the Chief gets here."

Mom poured me a cup of herbal tea and we sat down to wait for Chief O'Donnell.

There was no conversation until the doorbell rang. My father went to the front door to let the Chief in. He came into the kitchen and sat down next to me.

"Okay, Cara. You can open it now. We'll read it together."

I looked up at his calm face and knew that no matter what threats were contained in this Email, the Chief would handle it. I clicked on the message and it appeared on the screen.

"Hello Miss Blackthorne. They say if you want something done right, you have to do it yourself. I'll be seeing you very soon.

Cordially, Donald Gaynes"

My father said, "That's not much of a clue to his plans."

The Chief said, "But we know he's on his way. Cara, we'll be ready for him. At least we know what he looks like. Don't worry. He won't get anywhere near you."

Turning to my father, he said, "Let's plan our coverage now." He pulled out Thornewood's street map and they started making notes of who would be stationed where.

Mom got up and made a fresh pot of coffee. When I looked over at Adam, he was still frowning. He looked over at me and said softly, "You have another friend who needs to know what's going on. Let's go outside."

We both stood and went out on the back porch. Leaning against the porch railing, I began singing Rowenna's song and it was only a few minutes before we heard the sound of wings and felt her magic swirling around us.

I heard her rusty voice before she landed in our yard. *Cara, are you all right?*

"Not exactly. The evil man is on his way here. He sent me a message saying he'll see me soon. I know he means to kill me."

That will not happen, Cara. From the sky, I can see many men in the streets, many vehicles on your roads. And I will be watching from the sky. You must stay with your bodyguards so that he cannot reach you. We will not let anything hurt you.

"Thank you, Rowenna."

You must call me, day or night, if you see this man.

"Okay. I will."

Her great wings lifted and she rose into the night sky, her magic trailing behind her. Within seconds, it was just another normal autumn night on our back porch.

"Let's sit down and talk about this. I know you're nervous and frightened, so we need to be prepared." Adam reached over and took my hand, which always made me feel safer.

"What are you most afraid of?" he asked.

"That he'll kill me, of course. And that he'll kill anyone who's trying to protect me. The man's completely insane. We can't predict what he'll try to do."

"What we can predict is that you'll never be alone and unprotected. There will be Elves near you that you won't even see, in addition to the bodyguards with you. And I'm guessing that Rowenna can get to you in a matter of minutes if you call her."

That sounded good, but I had a feeling that Gaynes would find a way around all those protections.

My parents would be getting married on Saturday, but I was suddenly afraid that I wouldn't be there to see it.

CHAPTER 47

When I left for school the next morning, I found Ryan and Jason waiting on the porch for me. Apparently they'd both been told about the Email I'd received from Gaynes.

"Cousin, you'll be so surrounded from now on, Gaynes will never be able to reach you. You'll never be alone." Jason chuckled. "I'm sure we'll all be getting on your nerves by day's end." As tense as I was, Jason could still make me smile.

I picked up Kevin and Patrick next and found that they were both aware of this new threat. "Short stuff, we'll both be close if you need us."

"I know you will. Last night the Chief told my dad the Highway Patrol would be stopping every car coming into Thornewood, so we should be good."

Luckily, we were able to park directly in front of the school's main entrance. And I'd been happy to see police cars and patrolmen on foot all over this part of town as we drove in. Nevertheless, my nerves were on edge, something Amy picked up on as soon as we met outside the principal's office. She was watching me closely as I handed my knives over to Mr. Weiss. When he went back into his office, Amy whispered, "You didn't give him all your knives, did you?"

I shook my head. Amy didn't miss much. I was wearing my waist holster today under my sweatshirt. It held two more knives. Under the circumstances, I'd decided that my safety was more important than school policy.

Sean asked, "Do you really think you're at risk here in school? There are plainclothes cops patrolling the halls in addition to uniformed police at the entrances."

"I have a feeling Gaynes will get really creative this time. Think about it. He could even dress as a woman and grab me in the rest room. I wouldn't put anything past him."

Gabe nodded. "I wouldn't either. I think you're right to be on guard right now." He looked embarrassed for a few seconds. "Cara, I finally spoke to Gavin. I know how Gaynes manipulated him. I'm afraid if I'd been in Gavin's place, I would have done the same thing. Any one of us would have. So you're right to be suspicious of everything."

That was the longest speech I'd ever heard from Gabriel. Everyone looked at each other, nodding. They all knew he was right.

We left for our classes when the bell rang. I was sure there would be more discussion at lunch.

Surrounded by Sean, Gabe, Ryan, and Jason, I did feel safe. Our teachers didn't even question the fact that our group was a little larger. Between classes, Sean held my hand and that helped too.

At lunch, different scenarios were discussed. Kevin wondered if the police were checking everyone who arrived in town by bus. Sean mentioned that Gaynes might hitch a ride on one of the freight trains that ran through town twice a day. Thornewood wasn't a stop for any passenger trains, so that was ruled out. There was a small private airfield for private planes, another possibility. I wondered if Gaynes knew how to fly a plane.

By the time the bell rang and we left the lunchroom, I was even more on edge.

Amy and I, along with our three bodyguards, drove to the catering office downtown to finalize our food order for the wedding party. Since it was an afternoon party with no sit-down meal, we'd decided on a variety of finger foods. And it gave me something else a lot more pleasant to think about.

There would be tiny sandwiches of all kinds, appetizer-type snacks, fruit kabobs, half a dozen kinds of crackers and cheeses and, at my request, cookies. We also ordered bottles of sparkling water, and Mr. Callahan was taking care of ordering wine and champagne. Amy, of course, was making the wedding cake herself. She promised it would be spectacular!

The catering manager spread out lots of samples for us to try, much to the delight of our bodyguards who always seemed to be hungry. Jason was a huge fan of the little sandwiches. There was ham and cream cheese, chicken salad, tuna salad, turkey with blue cheese, roast beef with Swiss cheese, and even peanut butter and jelly. Of the samples presented to us, not a crumb was left. Amy and I were well satisfied with everything we'd ordered for the party. The deli would have everything prepared Saturday morning. They would deliver and set it up after everyone was back from City Hall.

Amy had arranged for the tables, chairs, and tableware to be delivered Saturday morning. She, Sean, and Kevin would set everything up before we left for City Hall.

Despite all the stress, I was beginning to get excited.

Feeling a healthy sense of accomplishment, I dropped off Amy and headed for home. Ryan sat down on the front porch, pulled a tiny sandwich out of his pocket and grinned at me. "I couldn't resist. These are really good."

I had to laugh. I'd hidden one of those little sandwiches in my backpack too. I was going to let Mom try it, providing I didn't give in to temptation first.

Jason walked into the house with me where we found Kathleen and Adam in the living room. Adam's shirt was off while Kathleen was removing the bandage to check his stitches. A bare-chested Adam had been present in my dreams the past few nights. He really did look great without a shirt. I was still working on my mind control. Sort of.

Jason asked, "How's the healing going, Adam?"

I was trying not to stare, with every intention of continuing into the kitchen, but I stopped to hear the answer and got an enjoyable eyeful.

Kathleen looked up at us and smiled. "We heal quickly, providing there hasn't been too much blood loss. Adam's doing fine, but he needs to keep his arm in the sling while it's healing." She wrapped his arm in fresh strips of linen, tied them off, and stood. "Cara, would you please make some tea for us? Your father went to his camp for a brief visit. I won't leave until he gets back."

Jason helped Adam get his shirt back on, unfortunately, and we all moved into the kitchen. I got the largest teapot out of the pantry and made Kathleen's herbal tea for us, and a small pot of pain-killing tea for Adam.

He said softly, "You don't have to do that for me."

Just as softly I said, "It makes you more comfortable, doesn't it?"

He nodded. "Thank you, Cara. You're very kind."

Jason snickered behind me. Over my shoulder, I gave him a raised eyebrow and a look. There was no more snickering, but that didn't wipe the smile off his face.

Jason started describing the food we'd ordered for the wedding party and admitted he'd had a large part in cleaning up the samples the caterer had put out for us. Kathleen wanted detailed descriptions of everything we'd be serving at the party.

"If I spread the word about all these goodies, I think even more Elves will tear themselves out of Elvenwood and come for the party. I'm afraid some of them are extremely timid when it comes to the outside world. Although, I'm not sure your home can really be considered the outside world, right at the edge of the forest as it is." She laughed. "I hope you ordered enough."

I hoped so too. I'd already learned that Elves loved to eat.

My father returned a few minutes later, sat down and had tea with us. Kathleen had to get back to Elvenwood before it got dark, so Jason left with her and walked her back to camp. One of the men in camp would ride back to the village with her.

It seemed that Jason had been appointed, or had appointed himself—I wasn't sure which—as my second bodyguard until Adam was well enough to resume his duties. In the meantime, Adam was living with us. These were two changes I could definitely live with.

When Mom got home with Conor, she wanted to hear all about the food that was being catered for the wedding party, and I pulled one of the sample tiny sandwiches out of my backpack for her to try. She loved it and praised Amy's experience and good taste. We both knew it was all Amy's doing. I was just along for the ride.

Conor stayed for dinner, which was good because I needed to talk to him. He'd been a kind of mentor/big brother to me since I'd met him in the spring. He'd known me, although from a distance, since I was a baby. He seemed to understand me.

After I'd cleaned up the kitchen, I asked Conor to go out on the porch with me. He didn't ask why, just smiled and opened the back door for me. The only one who looked surprised was Adam.

We sat down on the porch, bathed in the light from the almost-full moon. "Harvest Moon," Conor said. Turning to me, he asked, "What can I help you with, Cara?"

"I'm trying very hard to keep morbid thoughts out of my head, but they keep creeping back in. I don't feel I can talk to anyone else about them. My parents will be terribly upset, and I really don't want to upset them a few days before their wedding. Normally I could talk to Adam, but under the circumstances, he'll just get upset and frustrated because he's injured and can't do much with one arm. My friends would freak if they knew I was afraid I might not live much longer."

Conor nodded slowly as he reached over to hold my hand. "You seem convinced that Gaynes will carry out this latest threat. And, by the way, I can tell how afraid you are. Your hands are like ice." I heard his deep sigh.

"Cara, there are over a hundred men, well, men and Elves, stationed all over town, especially around your house and the route you take to and from school. Every car coming into town is being stopped while the police look for Gaynes. Police all over the state are searching for him. Do you really think he can get inside Thornewood?"

"I know it seems fatalistic, but I do. He's clever the way insane people are clever. He could get here dressed like a woman, or made up to look elderly, or even in a stolen police uniform. The man's nuts, but he's smart. And he wants me dead."

He squeezed my cold hand. "We're not going to let that happen. You have to have more faith in all the people dedicated to keeping you alive and well. Don't forget. You have two advantages he doesn't know about. You're telepathic and can communicate with your father, Adam, Ryan, Jason, and a certain dragon who can reach you in seconds if you run into any trouble. She will kill him, no questions asked. You're extremely well protected, Cara."

He was right, but I couldn't shake the feeling of dread inside me.

When Conor left for camp, I said good night and went upstairs, saying I had homework to do. I hugged Mom and Dad, and reminded Adam to make more tea for himself before he went to bed. He nodded, but his eyes told me he knew something was wrong.

Some meditation in the shower relaxed me, which helped. I was feeling better when my phone rang. It was Sean, of course.

"Hi Sean."

"Hey, Beautiful. You sound tired. Are you okay?"

I didn't know how to answer him. I wasn't okay, but there was nothing he could do about it. And I really didn't want to upset my friends.

"Yeah, I'm probably just tired. There's a lot going on here right now."

"Just two more days until your parents get married. I know you've been worrying about Gaynes, but you have a lot to be happy about right now. When I met you, you hadn't even met your father." He laughed. "The first time I saw him, I thought he looked like a combination movie star/superhero.

"By the way, my parents are looking forward to being at the wedding. Mom insists on being at City Hall too. She's really looking forward to meeting your folks after hearing my dad talk about them. She thinks theirs is an amazing love story. Mom is a total romantic."

His words made me smile. "She's right. It is an amazing love story. I think I sometimes forget about those missing years because they're so perfect together now. So what's going on in your world?"

"Tomorrow I have an appointment after school with Coach. He wants to talk to me about colleges. To be honest, I'm worried about getting the scholarship I was hoping for. I won't be able to play football the entire season, and I think that may hurt my chances. I know Coach has spoken to a few recruiters and I want to know what they've had to say."

"I don't know what your GPA is, but have you thought about applying for other types of scholarships? It doesn't have to be an athletic scholarship, does it?"

"No, of course it doesn't. I just assumed it would be because I've done so well in sports. I hadn't even thought about anything else, but my grades have always been good, so there might be a chance there. That's a really good idea. I'll talk to my dad about it. What are you doing after school tomorrow?"

"I only have one job tomorrow. I have to stop at Van Horn's and pick up Mom's wedding dress. Amy has handled everything else for us. When it comes to parties, she's an expert. Give me a call tomorrow night and let me know how you make out with Coach."

"Okay, Beautiful. Pleasant dreams. See you in school."

"'Night, Sean."

Some of my dreams that night were pleasant, mainly dreams of Adam shirtless. But the others were horrible. In one, Gaynes, dressed like a nun, dragged me into an empty, spooky-looking house with a knife at my throat. He kept raving about making my father pay for not selling him the section of Blackthorne Forest he wanted to develop, which would have made him rich. He kept complaining that everyone had been against him all his life, that no one had ever wanted him to succeed and that no one had ever loved him.

In my dreams, Gaynes captured me in many different ways, kidnapped at school, grabbed at a football game, pulled from my car, and on and on. I don't think my subconscious got any rest at all that night. Which is probably why I was anxious and irritated when I got up in the morning.

I had a bad feeling about today.

CHAPTER 48

Mom treated us to pancakes that morning. She must have sensed my mood. She and Dad talked about the wedding over breakfast and I tried to look cheerful. The last thing I wanted to do was project doom and gloom. Adam wasn't saying much, but he was watching me closely.

When I got up from the table, Mom smiled. "Don't forget to pick up my dress after school, honey. But be sure your father doesn't see it."

"Don't worry, Mom. I'll get it home safely."

My father looked confused. "Why can't I see it, Alicia?"

"It's supposed to be bad luck. I've never been superstitious, but I'm not taking any chances this time."

He smiled and winked at me.

Thankfully, my father seemed to be tuned in to Mom right now, not me. I was grateful. I didn't want him looking into my mind this morning.

Adam thanked Mom for the pancakes and followed me through the living room to the front door. He grabbed my hand as I was reaching for the doorknob.

"What's wrong, love?" His deep blue eyes were full of concern as he looked down at me.

I shrugged. "Bad dreams plus the usual tension, I guess. Don't worry. I'll be fine." I put my hand back on the doorknob. "Ryan and Jason are waiting for me."

Frowning, he whispered, "I wish I was going with you." He wrapped his good arm around me and surprised me with a kiss on my head. "Be extra careful today, all right?"

I tried to smile. "Premonition?"

He shook his head. "No. How about you?"

Shrugging again, I said, "No, just bad dreams. See you later." Opening the door I walked out to the porch. Ryan and Jason were waiting for me.

Adam was right behind me. "Good morning, boys. I want you both close enough to touch her today, no farther. Understood?"

They had been smiling when I opened the door, but they weren't smiling now.

As we ran down the steps to my car, Jason asked, "Did you get another message from Gaynes, cousin?"

"No. Just a bad night. I'm okay."

As we climbed into the car, Ryan was looking at me closely. "You look tired, lass. Maybe you should have stayed home today to get some rest."

"Nope. We have to pick up Mom's wedding dress at Van Horn's after school. That's not something I can put off. I think I'll ask Amy and Neal to come with us. Amy's dying to see Mom's dress." Amy's usual enthusiasm was just what I needed.

I drove around the corner and picked up Kevin and Patrick. When we got to school, Sean, Gabe, Amy and Neal waited for us outside Mr. Weiss' office. I was wearing another sweatshirt with my knife holster underneath, so it didn't bother me to hand over my other knives to Mr. Weiss. Sean and Kevin both noticed that I looked more subdued than usual.

Kevin asked, "Is there anything I can do, babe?"

Since I was more worried about what Gaynes might do outside of school, I asked, "Can you go to Van Horn's with us this afternoon? I have to pick up Mom's wedding dress, and I'll feel safer in a crowd."

He shook his head. "Sorry, Cara. For some reason, my mom's coming home early today. She said she has something important she wants to talk to me about. You can drop us off before you go to Van Horn's, can't you?"

"Sure, Kev. Any idea what she wants?"

"Not a clue, unless she spotted my dad behind the house. He's been really careful to stay out of sight, but who knows?"

Sean said, "You know I'd go with you if I didn't have the meeting with Coach."

Amy had a big smile on her freckled face. "Well, I'm available! Neal and I can go with you. That'll make five of us. Will that help?"

"Thanks, Amy. I know you want to see Mom's dress anyway." Amy could always make me smile. She was so excited about the wedding, you would have thought it was her parents who were getting married.

Sean was especially attentive all day, probably to make up for not being able to go with us after school. "If I could reschedule my meeting with Coach, I would. You seem on edge today. Is there anything you're not telling me?"

"No. I didn't sleep well. That's probably why I'm not myself today. Tired, you know?"

He squeezed my hand. "Well, with three bodyguards plus Amy, you should be fine." Grinning, he added, "I wouldn't mess with Amy for any reason. Anybody who does would have to be nuts."

He seemed satisfied when he saw me smile.

"No worries, Sean. I hope your meeting goes well."

After school, I picked up my knives in the Principal's office and after dropping off Kevin and Patrick, we headed downtown to Van Horn's. I was lucky to find a parking spot near the main entrance, even though the department I needed was located at the rear of the first floor.

Naturally, getting through all the departments we had to pass through slowed us down a bit. Amy didn't want to miss anything, and the store had just begun displaying their new winter fashions. Neal was accustomed to the way she shopped, so he just smiled, taking our slow pace in stride.

Jason seemed fascinated by Amy's ongoing review of all the new fashions. Too much exposure to Amy could make even an Elf fashion-conscious. He seemed as interested in the styles she singled out as she did. I groaned inwardly. At this rate, we might reach the Alterations department by nightfall.

I finally spotted the Alterations desk at the rear of the store. Naturally, there was no one there. Amy, Neal and Jason stopped at the edge of the Men's Sportswear department, only a few feet away, bordering Alterations. Ryan was closer, at the entrance to the men's dressing rooms.

I looked over the desk, hoping for a bell I could ring to bring someone out to help me. Of course, there was no bell. For some reason, my stomach began to tighten up. I'd been on edge all day, and that edge just sharpened.

Calling out "hello" didn't bring anyone out of the workroom either. I felt my muscles tightening. I turned toward my friends and noticed that Ryan was no longer where he'd been. I didn't see him anywhere.

Instantly alarmed, I was about to call out to Jason when I felt something hard pressed into the middle of my back. A soft male voice said, "This is a gun, Miss Blackthorne. If you try to get the attention of your friends, I will shoot each one of them. Now come around the desk and make a right-hand turn into the hallway behind you. Do it quickly."

His voice was so pleasant, it was shocking because his words were so horrible. I quickly turned into the hallway, the gun still pressed firmly against my back. I was now out of sight of my friends. It felt as though he wanted me to hurry, but I walked as slowly as I could, my heart pounding, at the same time sending mental messages to my father and Adam.

Dad - Adam - Gaynes is here in Van Horn's. He's got a gun and he's forcing me away from my friends. Ryan disappeared, and the others didn't see me leave. I don't know where he's taking me.

The hallway seemed to run the length of the building, ending at a door marked "Employees Only." We stopped and Gaynes came around to face me. He held the gun in one hand and a pair of handcuffs in the other.

"Fasten these on your wrists. Do it quickly." He pressed the gun against my chest. I hadn't had a chance to pull one of my knives, not with the gun pressed into my back. And now I wouldn't be able to. If I tried to use *Vox*, I knew he'd pull the trigger.

He pushed the Employees Only door open. It took us outside to the loading dock behind the store. Beyond the loading dock was a wide parking lot and a dark blue SUV, with blacked out windows. The motor was running. I sent another mental message.

Dad, we're on the loading dock behind the store. He has a dark blue SUV parked here. There's no one around, no trucks or cars anywhere.

I looked up at the sky, which had darkened since we entered the store. It wasn't even cloudy; the sky was totally overcast, dark gray. Then I remembered my secret weapon.

Rowenna, the evil man has me captured behind the big store on Main Street. There's a large parking lot in the back that's empty. It's big enough for you. I need your help.

Gaynes pushed me down the stairs, the gun still in my back. At the bottom, I stopped.

"Get in the car, Miss Blackthorne. I won't tell you twice."

There was no way I was getting into his car. I knew I'd never get out alive. I felt cold as ice inside. My heart was beating double time. If I could just reach one of my knives . . .

I walked to the SUV, put one foot up on the running board, bent over quickly and pulled a knife out of my boot. Immediately I whirled around and stabbed him in the wrist. He dropped the gun, looked at me in amazement, then using his good hand, he punched me in the face. Hard.

I saw stars, but stayed on my feet, leaning against the car. He backed away and reached down to grab the gun from the ground with his left hand, and I brought my foot up and kicked him in the head as hard as I could. He went down on his knees and I reached into my other boot for another knife.

Rowenna, where are you? No sooner had I completed the thought, she burst through the gray overcast and sent a burst of flames into the SUV. Gaynes looked up in shock as I quickly moved away from the car. I was done with non-lethal defense. He was only a few feet from where I was standing. I aimed my knife and with both hands cuffed together, I threw it, hitting him in the throat. He fell to the ground. All I heard was a gurgling sound as blood poured from his throat and mouth. I felt both satisfied and sick, at the same time.

I heard sirens and three police cars sped around the corner into the parking lot. Six policemen leaped out, their guns aimed at Gaynes.

I was still on my feet as an ambulance roared into the parking lot, followed by the Chief's car, lights flashing. I looked up but Rowenna had retreated behind the heavy cloud cover. I could still feel her magic wrapped around me. *Thank you, Rowenna. You saved my life.*

I will always protect you, Cara.

Then I felt her moving away as two fire trucks rolled into the lot. Firemen turned hoses on the flaming SUV, putting out the fire quickly.

Suddenly there were familiar arms wrapped around me and I heard my father's deep voice. "Did he hurt you, my Cara?"

The tension suddenly flowed out of my body as my heartbeat slowed. I took a deep breath and leaned into his chest. "I'm all right, Dad. Rowenna was here," I whispered.

"I know, dear. I heard her too."

I looked beyond my father's broad chest and saw Adam standing there, his arm still in a sling, and unmistakable relief in his blue eyes.

"Adam . . ." I waved him over.

"Did he hurt you?"

I pointed to my face, which felt swollen.

My father pushed me away a few inches to look at my face. "Sweetheart, I'm afraid you're going to have a black eye for our wedding." He kissed my aching face and whispered, "It could have been so much worse."

Looking relieved, Adam said, "You did far more to Gaynes than he did to you. Nice work with your knives." He smiled. "Best student I've ever had."

"Dad, Ryan is missing. He may still be in the store. Someone needs to look for him. I know he wouldn't have left voluntarily."

My father looked around, spotted the Chief, and called out, "Tom. We need you."

The Chief jogged over to us. "Cara, do you need an ambulance? I can call for another one." The first one had just taken Gaynes away. I wondered if he was still alive. In truth, I hoped he wasn't.

I held my handcuffed wrists out to him. He shook his head, muttered, "Police issue handcuffs." Pulling a key from his pocket, he unlocked the cuffs and stuffed them in his jacket pocket.

"I just need an ice pack, Chief. But one of my bodyguards is missing inside the store."

Chief O'Donnell called over two of his men. "Search the store. One of Cara's bodyguards is missing. Find him."

I asked the Chief, "Where are Amy, Neal and Jason? They were in the store with me when Gaynes grabbed me, but they never saw me leave. They must be worried sick."

The Chief finally smiled. "They were, Cara. Amy called the station when she couldn't find you. I don't think my men have quite recovered from her call. She and the two boys are out in front of the store in one of the police cars. She said they weren't leaving until you were found. Come on. I'll drive you out to them."

The three of us got into the Chief's car and he drove us around to the front of the store where my friends waited. When she saw me, Amy flew out of the patrol car like a shot.

Throwing her arms around me, she was in tears. "It was all my fault, Cara. If I hadn't been looking at all the new clothes, I would have seen him. We all know we let you down."

Jason and Neal were right behind her, looking guilty and ashamed. But I couldn't deal with them now. "Has Ryan been found?" I asked the closest cop.

He nodded. "We found him in one of the men's changing rooms. He'd been knocked out. We have a doctor in there checking him out."

With that, the last knot in my stomach dissolved. We were all okay. At least until Amy got a good look at my face.

"Oh, Cara, you've got a black eye and a swollen cheek. That really won't go with your new dress. We're going to need a lot of ice and a ton of concealer to make you look decent for the wedding. I'll get some and bring everything over to your house." She grabbed Neal, who looked back and said, "I'm sorry, Cara," and they left for the closest pharmacy.

That left Jason standing alone, looking as though he was ready to face a firing squad.

My father said, "Jason, you and I must have a serious talk very soon." Jason just nodded. He looked at me and said, "Cousin, I will never forgive myself and I don't expect you to forgive me either."

"Jason, we'll talk about it another time. Right now I just want to go home and put an ice pack on my face. Dad, my car's still parked in the other parking lot. I don't trust myself to drive home."

"I'll ask the Chief to bring your car when he stops by this evening to take your statement. I'm sure he'll drive us home." Using his good arm, Adam took my hand and squeezed it.

We walked over to the Chief and my father asked him to take us home. As soon as I was in the Chief's back seat, it hit me. "Oh no! Oh, crap." I put my hands over my face. My head was aching and I had forgotten to do the one thing I was supposed to do today.

My father put his arm around me. "What is it, Cara?"

"Mom's dress. I never picked it up."

I could hear him breathe a sigh of relief. "Sweetheart, we can get it tomorrow. It's not a problem. I'm sure your mother will forgive you."

He laughed softly, patted my back, and Chief O'Donnell drove us home.

Five minutes after we arrived home, Amy came by with the promised ice packs and a lot of concealer, enough to cover at least a dozen black eyes.

We were all sitting at the kitchen table, as I held one ice pack after another to my swollen face. Finally, I just put an ice pack on the table and laid my face on it. Every last bit of energy had finally drained out of me. I felt like a rag doll.

Adam went to the stove, turned it on, and boiled water for tea. When it was ready, he handed me a cup of his pain-killing tea. "This will make you more comfortable."

I looked up at him and saw so much affection in his dark eyes, I would have smiled if it hadn't hurt so much. "Thanks." I lifted my head and drank down the tea. While I waited for the tea to do what it was supposed to, I put my face down on top of the ice pack and closed my eyes.

I didn't even feel my father pick me up and carry me to my room. Not a single dream, thankfully.

CHAPTER 49

When I woke up Friday morning, the sun filled my bedroom, so I knew it was late. I was surprised to find I was still wearing the jeans and sweatshirt I'd been wearing the day before. At least someone had pulled my boots off.

I sat up, trying to get my eyes fully open. When I could focus properly, I was shocked to see blood spatter on my blue jeans. It hadn't been noticeable the night before, but in bright sunlight, the spots were unmistakable.

Pulling off my jeans and sweatshirt, I threw them on the floor. As far as I was concerned, they weren't even fit to be washed. I knew whose blood was on them. They needed to be burned.

There was a soft knock on my bedroom door and Mom stuck her head in.

"Are you finally awake, sweetheart?"

I stood there next to my bed in my underwear, feeling disgusted.

"What's wrong?"

"The clothes I was wearing yesterday. They're covered in blood stains I never saw last night." I looked up at her concerned face. "Can I burn them?"

She came in, closing the door quietly, and walked over to the pile of clothes on the floor. "I'll be happy to dispose of them for you." She rolled the clothes into a ball and put them under her arm. "Why don't you take a nice, long shower and then come on down for a late breakfast. I'm staying home today, and I thought you needed a day off too."

She walked to the door, then turned to me. "Cara, I just want you to know how proud of you I am. And don't worry about your face. I have an idea how we can disguise your bruises." She blew me a kiss and left the room.

Oh yeah. My bruises. I walked into my bathroom with my eyes closed. I was afraid to look in the mirror. I counted to ten and opened my eyes. And closed them again. I'd won my fight with Gaynes, but my face told a different story. One side of my face was red and swollen, and my black eye was every color but black. And this was how I would look for my parents' wedding the next day. I groaned. But then I remembered how much worse it could have been. I shuddered.

I got into the shower and concentrated on my breathing until I felt the tension drain out of me.

After I'd washed my hair twice—just in case I'd collected any blood in my hair—I was beginning to feel human again. Battered, but human. I put on a clean pair of jeans, heavy socks, and my favorite black t-shirt. I combed my hair out and left it hanging down my back. It was long enough. Maybe I could wrap it around my face.

When I got downstairs, Mom stood at the stove and my father sat at the table with Adam, who looked up anxiously when I walked into the kitchen.

He didn't say anything for at least a minute, just stared at me. I stared back, getting lost in his cobalt eyes, as usual. My father cleared his throat, one eyebrow raised, and I poured myself a cup of coffee and sat down with them.

Adam finally smiled. "You survived. Congratulations."

Dad was inspecting my face carefully, his chin resting on one hand.

"I know, I know, I look like I went ten rounds with someone a lot bigger," I said.

Mom turned to say, "All of that will fade, dear, but you got the best of that monster, and that's what matters. Tommy O'Donnell called last night after you were asleep to say that Gaynes survived, but barely. He's in critical condition. Tommy thought you'd want to know that you hadn't killed the man." She and my father exchanged glances.

"By the way, all your friends have called this morning. And your bodyguards are camped out in the backyard. You should go out and see them after you've eaten."

And that's when I realized I wouldn't need bodyguards anymore. It had been so many months, I'd forgotten what a normal life was like. When I looked over at Adam, I could tell that he had realized it too. Whoa. A normal life without Adam? No. He didn't have to be my bodyguard. He was a good friend, and that wouldn't change.

Suddenly relieved, I tried to smile when Mom put a just-baked Quiche on the table.

"For me?" I asked.

Mom laughed. "Well breakfast for you and lunch for the men. You must be starved. You never had dinner last night."

She cut a large slice for each of us and it was totally quiet at the table while we all enjoyed Mom's Killer Quiche. I'd named it months ago when Kevin had dug into a slice and muttered "killer" under his breath. I went back for seconds, ignoring Adam's teasing smile.

After another cup of coffee, I rinsed off my plate and went out the back door to see Ryan and the other bodyguards. When I got to the porch, I stopped short. I couldn't help smiling. They all stood when I walked outside and I rushed down the porch steps and ran straight to Ryan, whose head was decorated with a large bandage.

Grinning at me, he opened his arms and I ran straight into them. After a lengthy hug, I asked, "How's your head?"

"I'll live, lass. The lump on my head isn't as big as yours was last spring. I'm sure Kathleen told you that Elves have exceptionally hard heads. I think my head's probably in better shape than your poor face." He put his hand on my swollen cheekbone. "I should have been able to prevent that, Cara. I'm sorry."

"You don't have anything to apologize for." I looked over at Jason and Neal, standing a few feet behind Ryan. "I can't say the same for everyone, I'm afraid."

They both looked down at their feet, guilt written all over their handsome faces.

Suddenly I was lifted off my feet and swung around, finally set down by a laughing Gabriel. Then he took a good look at my face and stopped laughing.

"I'm sorry. I didn't realize you'd been hurt. You fought the monster and you won! I've always said you're a true warrior, despite your size. You did what a town full of police and Elves couldn't."

He bowed and said, "Congratulations. Well done!"

I looked around the yard and saw Gavin standing just outside the tree line, waving at me. I walked through the yard until I reached the edge of the woods where Gavin stood with Conor.

Smiling, Conor wrapped his arms around me gently. "We're all so proud of you, Cara. You brought down our enemy singlehandedly."

"No, not singlehandedly. I had help." I pointed at the sky with a smile.

"Rowenna was there? During daylight hours?"

"It was totally overcast in town yesterday," I said. "She dove through the clouds just long enough to set his SUV on fire and scare the crap out of him. That gave me a chance to pull out another knife and throw it before he could hit me again."

Gavin's voice was soft. "I wanted to kill him, Cara, but I hear you did some real damage, and he'll never be able to hurt anyone again. Thank you." He bent down and kissed me on both cheeks.

"Gavin, I thought of you when I threw my knife into his throat. If he hadn't survived, I wouldn't have minded."

He nodded and thanked me again, even though I knew he wanted Gaynes dead.

With one arm around my shoulders, Conor dropped a kiss on my head, smiled and said, "I'll see you at the wedding tomorrow." He waved at my dad who stood on our back porch, and walked into the woods with Gavin.

Ryan, Patrick and Gabe were on their way back to camp, all patting me on the back as they walked past me. I walked toward the front of the yard, stopping when I reached Jason and Neal. I didn't know what to say to them.

My father came down the steps and joined me. Facing the two boys, he said, "I want to talk to both of you."

Turning to me, he said, "I'd like to speak to them privately."

"Okay."

Jason and Neal gave me apologetic looks as I left them.

When I was back on the porch, I looked back and saw my father leading Jason and Neal into the woods. Apparently, the expected lecture would take place back at his camp.

When I got inside, Mom was dressed and looked ready to go out.

"Going out, Mom?"

She smiled. "I promised myself a mani-pedi today. Want to join me?"

I groaned. "Normally, I'd love to, but I don't really want to go out in public looking like this.

She nodded. "I understand, dear. I also have to pick up my wedding dress. I called ahead, and Mrs. Hanson will be waiting for me at the front of the store."

I sighed. "Sorry, Mom."

"Not your fault, sweetheart. I'll be back in an hour or so."

She left and I sat down with Adam. My head had started aching, and I got up to get another ice pack out of the freezer.

"Is it painful?" Adam asked.

I nodded. "One side of my face is throbbing."

He got up and put the hot water kettle on to boil. Turning to look at me, he said, "I think you need this tea more than I do."

Just as he poured me a cup of his pain-killing tea, there was a knock at the back door. He got up and let Kathleen in.

She took one look at me, and shook her head sympathetically.

"Have you got anything in your bag of tricks to help this?" I pointed to my face.

"Of course I have, Cara dear. We can't let you go to your parents' wedding looking like you've been in a brawl. Is that Adam's tea you're drinking?"

"Yeah. My face hurts."

"That tea will definitely help you relax, maybe even put you to sleep. Let's go up to your room, just in case you doze off. I have some herbal mixtures in my bag that will take care of that swelling, and maybe start healing the bruises around your eye. I can guarantee you'll look a lot better by Saturday, dear."

Once I was stretched out on my bed, Kathleen spread a mixture of herbs on my cheek that smelled of peppermint and felt soothing and cool.

"Close your eyes, dear. I have another poultice to pat around your eye."

Once my eyes were closed, she began patting something else around my eye very gently until everything but my eyelid was covered. It smelled earthy, and slightly like the pine trees I loved. Between the appealing scents and the coolness I felt on my cheek, I relaxed and fell asleep.

I must have slept for at least an hour. Sitting up, I realized my face wasn't aching at all. I could still hear Kathleen's voice downstairs, so I went to the top of the stairs and called her. I wasn't sure how long this stuff was supposed to stay on my face, and I didn't want to go downstairs with herbs all over my face.

She came upstairs and led me into the bathroom where she proceeded to wash the herbal mixtures off my face gently. Looking in the mirror, I was pleased to see that the swelling on my cheek was almost gone, and the bruising around my eye wasn't nearly as colorful as it had been.

"That stuff is incredible. My face looks better already."

Kathleen smiled. "And I'll leave more of both mixtures for you to apply before you go to bed tonight. Just spread a towel over your pillow. I think you'll look close to normal in the morning and just as pretty as you always look."

I hugged her, and we went downstairs where Adam was making a fresh pot of coffee.

He looked up and smiled when we walked into the kitchen. "Much better, love."

Beaming, Kathleen sat down and had a cup of coffee with us. "Cara will look as beautiful as she always does for her parents' wedding. I'm glad her father sent for me."

His dark blue eyes focused on my face, Adam added, "When she got home yesterday with a swollen face and a black eye, she still looked beautiful, Kathleen. Nothing can ever cover that up."

Kathleen nodded and winked at me while I felt my face get hot. Adam had just paid me a very grown-up compliment and I didn't know how to respond, so I just said, "Thanks."

Mom came through the front door smiling, waving her freshly manicured nails at me. She'd chosen a pearl shade and her hands looked lovely.

"Mom, where's your dress?"

"I hung it up on the coat rack by the front door, dear. Thankfully, the bag it's wrapped in is opaque, so your father won't see it until I'm wearing it tomorrow.

"Kathleen, I'm so glad you waited. I was hoping we could have coffee together. And I see you've used your magic to repair Cara's face." She came closer and ran her manicured fingers over my cheek. "Sweetheart, you look so much better. Kathleen is a magician." She gave me a hug and sat down with Kathleen.

It was late afternoon and the sun was hidden behind the tall trees in the forest. Adam and I went out on the back porch so Mom and Kathleen could chat. I carried out two cups of coffee for us.

"We won't be able to do this much longer," I said. "The weather will soon be too cold." I sighed.

"Oh, that's right. You don't like winter, do you?" Adam asked.

"Nope. Not my favorite season. So many of the trees I love look dead for months. And I can't draw in the woods because my hands get too cold." I sighed again.

He laughed. "Don't rush the season. We'll still have nice weather for at least another month. You'll have time to go into the woods with your drawing pad like you used to."

The Dragon's Song

But I knew it wouldn't be the same. I'd changed too much. I'd be looking over my shoulder for some time to come.

CHAPTER 🍎 50

Mom called for pizza for our dinner so she wouldn't mess up her beautiful manicure. My father and Adam weren't complaining. I was sure pizza would soon show up in Elvenwood's dining hall, if my father had anything to say about it.

After we'd had Kathleen's relaxing tea and I'd cleaned up the kitchen, Adam said he'd be going back to my father's camp.

"Thank you very much for letting me camp out in your living room while my arm's been healing, but I think I should get out of your way now. Tomorrow will be a busy day for the three of you, and I don't want to be underfoot." He smiled. "I'll see you tomorrow."

Mom said, "Having you here has been no problem, Adam. I'm glad your arm is healing. Kathleen told me that your arm will need at least a month before you'll have full use of it again."

I would miss seeing Adam every day and I think he knew it. "I'll walk you out."

He said good night to Mom and Dad and we walked outside.

Adam took my hand. "You won't need a bodyguard any longer. You'll be free to go wherever you want, whenever you want, with no interference from me." He looked a little regretful. "You'll probably enjoy having a normal life again."

"As bodyguards go," I said, "having you and Ryan with me every day has been fun. I'll miss that."

"I'll still be around whenever you need me, you know. I won't be much good in the carpentry shop for a while. Why don't you sing a song for your dragon friend before you go back inside. Without her help, you might not be with us now."

He reached down and brushed my hair off my face. "I'll see you tomorrow, love."

As he walked through the backyard, I began to sing Rowenna's song, and within minutes, I felt her magic swirling around me. It comforted me.

We all went to bed early that night. No one wanted to be tired on Mom and Dad's big day. Mom helped me apply Kathleen's herbal remedies to my face before I went to bed. I was hoping to look more like a maid of honor than a prizefighter by morning. But I tossed and turned all night, constantly waking to imagined noises from outside the house.

I woke up to sun shining through my bedroom windows and real noises coming from the backyard. Looking out my window, I saw men carrying tables, chairs, and numerous boxes into the yard, with Amy directing the operation. She was all over the yard, waving her arms and giving instructions. All she needed was a bullhorn.

Sticking my head out of the window, I called to her and waved. She looked up at me and suddenly covered her face with her hands. That was when I realized my face was still covered with Kathleen's herbs. I ran to the bathroom to wash my face. When everything had been rinsed off, I was delighted to see that my face looked almost normal, with just a little bruising around my eye. From a distance, no one would know that I'd been punched in the face.

I ran back to the window and called to Amy again. This time she looked up and smiled, giving me thumbs up. I grinned, grateful that Amy had everything under control.

After showering and blowing my long hair dry, I threw on my bathrobe and went downstairs, hoping for breakfast. Mom and Dad were already at the table, sharing a huge stack of pancakes.

I hugged them both and asked if they'd be willing to share. Mom laughed. "Why do you think I made so many?" I poured myself a cup of coffee and sat down, helping myself to pancakes.

"I didn't think you'd be cooking this morning," I told her.

"Well, we have to eat, sweetheart. And you haven't yet learned to cook."

I groaned. "Sorry, Mom."

She smiled. "It's fine. We'll get to it eventually, dear. I see Amy's outside, getting the party organized. She must have been up at the crack of dawn. Bless that girl."

"I think she made the wedding cake last night."

Mom rolled her eyes. "She's a wonder."

"What time will we be leaving for City Hall?"

"Our wedding is scheduled for Noon. We'll leave here about fifteen minutes early."

"Am I driving?"

She laughed. "No, dear. We'll be traveling in style. I figure, we're only doing this once, so I ordered a limo."

I looked at my father, who was sitting next to Mom, watching her and smiling. "I told your mother she could have whatever she wanted. She took me at my word." Chuckling, he said, "Getting married in the Elven world is much simpler."

Mom and I helped each other get ready. She used her curling iron on my long hair and arranged it in what she called "Veronica Lake" style, parted on one side with the other side wavy and hanging half over one side of my face. She explained that Veronica Lake was an old-time actress who wore her hair that way in a movie and started a new trend back in the 1940's. It was actually a very sexy look, covering part of the eye that had been so bruised. All I needed was a little of Amy's concealer and you couldn't see any of the damage to my face.

I helped Mom with her hair. She'd pulled it up, off her face, with curls escaping everywhere, and I fastened little pearl clips in her curls. I'd hardly ever seen her wear much makeup, but today she darkened her reddish eyebrows slightly, added gray-blue shadow and mascara, a touch of peach blush, and peach-toned lipstick. When she turned to me, I said, "Wow." I'd always considered my mother pretty, but today she was drop-dead gorgeous.

"Dad will be speechless. You look incredible."

She giggled. "As long as he can say, 'I do,' we're fine."

We were waiting until the last minute to put on our dresses. Mom and I both got dressed in her room so that Dad could use my room. Naturally, she insisted on putting a little makeup on me too. Pink blush for my pale face, a little pink lip gloss, and I was done.

For a girl who'd looked like she'd been mugged two days ago, I thought I looked pretty good.

Dad was already dressed and waiting for us downstairs, so I went into my room and peeked out the window. Amy was still out there, and I could see Kevin and Sean working in the yard too. I had no idea what they were doing. Amy had said something about a surprise she was planning for us.

It was almost time for us to put on our dresses, so I went back into Mom's room.

"Are you two going anywhere for a honeymoon?"

THE DRAGON'S SONG

She shook her head. "No, dear. We both have too many responsibilities at home to go anywhere else. Besides, I've always been a homebody. I love my home, I love to cook, and I'm perfectly happy to stay home with you and your father."

I must have looked skeptical because she said, "Really, Cara. I've never been happier, especially now that Gaynes and his threats are history. And I have you to thank for that, dear." She gave me a gentle hug.

"Is Dad going to be here all the time now? What about his duties in Elvenwood?"

"I think he'll continue to do what he's been doing; part of his time here and part in Elvenwood. He does have a whole village of people to take care of, both physically and financially, so he can't spend all of his time here. I understand that and I don't think I'll mind having some time to myself regularly. You like having your father here, don't you?"

"Are you kidding? Sitting at the kitchen table with both of you is something I always dreamed of. And seeing you two happy together is the absolute best."

She looked at the clock. "It's time to get into our finery, dear." We helped each other into our dresses and heard my father calling from downstairs.

"There's a very large automobile in front of the house, girls."

Mom laughed. "The limo. When your father sees how comfortable it is, I'm afraid he'll want one. He's already hinting about learning to drive."

I giggled. "I know."

I went downstairs first. Seeing my handsome father in his gray suit, pale gray shirt, and silver silk tie was a feast for the eyes. His eyes lit up when he saw me in my pink and cream dress.

"Cara, you look like a fairy queen in that dress. And you're as beautiful as ever."

Mom came down the stairs in creamy satin, looking exquisite, her eyes fixed on my father.

I don't think I've ever seen his eyes look so green, as green as the beautiful forest we both loved. He didn't have to hide anything now. It was obvious that he was madly in love with my mother.

He just stared, finally saying, "Alicia, there are no words."

There was a soft knock at the back door. When I opened it, I found a smiling Conor, resplendent in a light gray suit that matched his silvery eyes.

"Conor, you look wonderful." He held his arm out, I took it and we joined my parents at the front door. He whispered, "I'll be the envy of every young man at the wedding, Cara. You look beautiful."

We followed my parents outside to the waiting limo, where the uniformed driver bowed and opened the doors for us. My father and Conor were both amazed at the luxury inside the limo. Mom looked over and winked at me.

The ride downtown to City Hall took all of ten minutes. When we arrived, and were helped out by the driver, I was surprised to see a small crowd of people waiting for us.

Amy ran up and handed Mom a bouquet of gardenias, and a small bouquet of pink and white miniature roses for me. She had thought of everything. Mom kissed Amy on the cheek and whispered, "Thank you, dear."

I looked around and saw Sean and his parents, Amy's parents, Kevin, grinning at me, Chief O'Donnell actually in a suit rather than his uniform, Arlynn and Jason, and Harry Callahan, holding a camera and taking pictures of everyone. Adam had decided to wait for us at home.

We entered City Hall and headed for Judge Stone's office. He opened his office door and greeted us with a smile. Fortunately, his office was large enough for our friends to join us.

Mom and Dad walked to the front of the room and stood in front of him. I stood next to Mom and Conor was next to my father. Judge Stone smiled at us and began.

"We are here today, in front of witnesses, to join Alicia and Brian in the bonds of matrimony." His eyes twinkled as he said, "I take it there are no objections."

There weren't any.

He looked at my father. "Please repeat after me."

"I, Brian, take you, Alicia, to be my wife, to have and to hold from this day forward, for better or for worse; for richer, for poorer; in sickness and in health; to love and to cherish from this day forward until death do us part."

Judge Stone turned to my mother. "Please repeat after me."

"I, Alicia, take you, Brian, to be my husband, . . ." Her voice shook a little.

When Mom had repeated her vows, the Judge asked softly, "Do you have a ring?"

My father reached in his breast pocket and pulled out a ring that made my mother gasp. He slid it on her ring finger as he looked into her surprised blue eyes, and said softly, "I will love you forever."

The Judge said, "Brian, Alicia, I now pronounce you husband and wife." He smiled at my father. "You may kiss the bride."

My tall, handsome father actually blushed as he put his arms around my wide-eyed mother and kissed her in front of everyone. It was not a brief kiss. Everyone began to applaud.

My parents broke apart, smiling and looking embarrassed, as everyone hugged and kissed everyone else. Judge Stone shook my father's hand and kissed Mom on the cheek, reminding them to sign the wedding register at his desk before they left.

After they signed the necessary papers, we left his office and walked outside, stopping in front of the main entrance so everyone could congratulate my parents personally.

As Mr. and Mrs. McKay were speaking to my parents, Sean found his way over to me, leaning down and kissing my uninjured cheek.

"Cara, you look more than beautiful today. Amy told me you'd taken quite a beating, but you look fantastic. Kathleen must have paid you a visit."

I laughed. "Yeah, she spent most of the day at our house yesterday. I was afraid I'd be at my parents' wedding looking like I'd been mugged, but Kathleen worked her magic."

"I like your hair like that. Very sexy," he said with a grin. I felt my face getting hot.

I said, "Thanks. I'd better say hello to everyone else. I'll see you at home."

Amy and her parents were talking to Mom and Dad so I joined them for a few minutes. Conor was speaking to the McKays and I saw Arlynn hanging back, looking slightly uncomfortable, so I walked over to her.

She smiled when she saw me, hugging me. "You and your mother look so beautiful. I don't think I've ever seen anyone look as happy as your parents do today. I'm very happy for them. This was your dream, wasn't it?"

"More than a dream, actually. For a long time, I didn't think I'd ever have my father in my life." I grinned. "They're not the only ones who are happy today."

"I've never been to a human wedding ceremony. I was fascinated by the vows they made to each other. That was lovely. It put tears in my eyes," she said.

The Chief walked over to us with a big smile. "What a wonderful day this is for you and your parents. I'm glad to see that your face healed up in time. I want you to know that a lot of mouths dropped open when you and your mother got out of that limo. You're both beautiful today." He looked more serious. "Your father is a very lucky man."

He put his hand out to Arlynn. "It's nice to see you again, Arlynn. I was sorry to find that you're not working in Alicia's store anymore. I'll bet her customers miss you."

She shook his hand and frowned. "I wasn't much of a success as a bodyguard, I'm afraid. At home, I'm a baker and I think that's what I do best."

He nodded, giving Arlynn a sympathetic smile. "I have to get back to the office for an hour, but I'll see you both later."

He left and suddenly Kevin was at my side, one arm wrapped around my shoulders.

"Hey, short stuff. I thought I'd have to bring a bag for you to wear over your head, but you look pretty good to me."

Arlynn started giggling, and all I could do was roll my eyes. It was Kevin, after all.

Suddenly, Harry was standing a few feet in front of us, aiming his camera. "Let me get a picture of the giant-killer and her friends," he said, grinning.

I couldn't help groaning. "Great. I have a new name." Harry snapped the picture and went off to find others to photograph.

Kevin was laughing. "Giant killer?"

I just shook my head. "He was no giant, trust me. He was only a little taller than me. And I didn't kill him. But I sincerely hope he's still in pain."

Hugging me, Kevin said, "You did good, babe. You've singlehandedly salvaged our senior year. We're all grateful."

"It wasn't singlehanded. I had a lot of help from our special friend."

"No kidding?"

"Yeah. She swooped down out of the clouds and set his SUV on fire. That was all I needed. I think she would have set him on fire if I'd asked her to."

I looked up and saw Mom and Dad waving at me. It was time to get back in the limo and return to the house for their second wedding ceremony. Since Jason and Arlynn didn't have a ride back, they joined us in the limo and were clearly impressed by the luxurious interior.

THE DRAGON'S SONG

I don't know how she did it, but Amy was already in the backyard by the time we got home. The tables and chairs were already set up, and she and two women from the caterer were setting out covered trays of food while Sean unloaded bottled water and cans of lemonade into metal tubs full of ice. All around the yard, there were pots and tubs of gold, bronze and white chrysanthemums, Mom's favorite flower. Our backyard had never looked so festive.

Jason had rushed into the backyard ahead of us and we could hear his flute playing a spirited tune, which I realized was the signal the Elves were waiting for. Some of the Elves were coming from my father's camp, and the rest had traveled from Elvenwood.

My father dashed into the house, returning a few minutes later wearing the Elven tunic and slim pants I was accustomed to, but in white, not the usual green. He joined Mom in the middle of the yard, ready to greet his people as they emerged from the forest.

Dad gestured to Conor and me and we joined them. Unlike my father, Conor remained dressed in his gray suit, Arlynn on his arm. For the occasion, Arlynn had left her green tunic and slacks at home and was wearing a simple, full-length blue dress that matched her crystal-blue eyes. They made an outrageously attractive couple, and I couldn't help wondering when they would be wed.

Dad also waved Jason over to join me in what I guessed was our receiving line. Jason was also wearing what he called "human" clothes, black slacks and sport jacket over a white shirt. When I realized I was standing next to a boy who was, truthfully, prettier than I was, I had to laugh. Jason looked at me and whispered, "Am I forgiven, cousin?"

He was such a sweet young man, and so sorry he'd become distracted when he was supposed to be a bodyguard, I couldn't stay mad at him.

"You're forgiven. Thankfully, we won't need bodyguards anymore. We can just enjoy ourselves now."

He gave me a blinding smile and kissed my cheek. "Thank you. You are the best cousin a boy could hope for." I took his arm as Elves began walking out of the forest toward my parents.

I loved watching my father's proud smile as he introduced his community of Elves to my mother. Most of them had never seen my mother before and were clearly impressed by her welcoming smile and warmth. I knew most of them by sight and I was happy to welcome them to my home, remembering how welcoming they had been to me months ago.

When Ian and his parents arrived, he made a mad dash for me. I held my arms open and he ran into them. "Cara, I'm really here where you live, and I can finally meet your mother!" Looking over at my dad, he said, "Hi, Uncle Brian!"

The little boy was so excited, even my dad laughed. "Come over here, Ian, and meet my bride. Alicia, this is Cara's special friend. Ian, you can call her Aunt Alicia."

Ian's eyes were big as he took in my beautiful mother in her ivory satin gown. He seemed tongue-tied, so Mom smiled, reaching out to take his hand. "Ian, Cara has told me all about you. Welcome to our home."

Ian's parents joined us, obviously embarrassed by their son's mad rush to me. Dad introduced them to Mom. Doreen, Ian's mom, told Mom what a good friend I'd been to their son, spending time with him every time I visited.

The last to arrive were the Elders of Elvenwood, the village's oldest men. Two of them weren't strangers; they were Sean's grandfather and great-grandfather, both smiling as they walked up to Mom and Dad.

For a few seconds, I wondered where Adam was hiding.

The wedding ceremony would be conducted by the Elder I had met at the practice field not long ago. He was the one who told my father how proud of me they were, and how amazed my grandfather would be. Now that I'd read my grandmother's diary, I thought I understood what he had meant.

It was early afternoon and the sun had been shining brightly when suddenly clouds rolled in, covering the sun completely. Within seconds, I heard ooh's and ah's as tiny lights began to glow from every tree and every bush around the entire yard. There were lights strung along our back porch, lighting up the pots of red geraniums Mom had planted. In Mom's flower garden, the old apple tree was covered in tiny lights, as was the old garden bench that sat under it, and more lights in the rose bushes that were still blooming. This was what Kevin and Sean had been doing early this morning.

The entire back yard looked like a fairyland, totally magical, which was entirely appropriate. This was Amy's surprise and it was wonderful!

CHAPTER 51

After Mom and Dad greeted everyone, the head Elder, Henry Ferguson, led my parents into the flower garden, stopping under the old apple tree. I knew that in Elvenwood, marriages were conducted under the Joining Tree, but here, our old apple tree would serve that purpose.

Everyone hushed as Mr. Ferguson began to speak.

"Brian and Alicia, you stand before us today declaring that you are truly Mated and bound forever by Elven custom.

"Allow me to offer our traditional Elven blessing:

"Now you will feel no rain, for each will be shelter for the other.

Now you will feel no cold, for each of you will be warmth to the other.

Now there will be no loneliness, for each of you will be companion to the other.

Now you are two persons, but there is only one life before you.

May beauty surround you both in the journey ahead and through all the years.

May happiness be your companion and your days together be good and long upon the earth."

He looked at each of them and smiled. "Normally, I would wish that your years together be fruitful, but they already have been. You have blessed our community with an exceptional child, whom we already love as our own. We hope you will be so blessed again."

Looking at my father, he nodded.

My father looked at Mom and said, "Forever, Alicia."

The Elder looked at Mom and nodded.

My mother looked at Dad and said, "Forever, Brian."

Looking out at the gathering of Elves and humans, the Elder smiled. "Please offer your warmest wishes to our Prince and his Lady, Brian and Alicia Blackthorne."

I was the first to wrap my arms around both of them, getting tightly hugged in return. I received a kiss on each cheek from my parents before they were surrounded by our friends. I backed away and was immediately hugged by my cousin Jason who actually had tears in his eyes.

"Cara, I've seen quite a few wedding ceremonies under the Joining Tree, but this one means the most to me. Your father has always been like a father to me, and your mother is always warm and welcoming. Now we're really and truly family."

I hugged him back and smiled. "Yes, really and truly, Jason. Now let's go find Amy, Sean and Kevin, who made our simple backyard perfect for an Elven wedding."

Hand in hand, we walked through the crowd, stopping to talk to everyone, giving and receiving hugs from those we knew best, until we found Amy, Kevin and Sean next to the tables set up for the food. Amy handed us both small glass plates with tiny sandwiches and fruit kabobs. Judging by the empty plates in their hands, Kevin and Sean had apparently been eating since the end of the wedding ceremony. I hoped Adam would get something to eat before my hungry friends ate it all. I hadn't seen him yet, but I knew he was here somewhere.

Once my parents had been congratulated, the guests began to swarm the food tables where the caterer's people were lifting the lids on all the dishes, explaining what each item was. On another table, a young man from the caterer was opening water bottles and pouring lemonade for the guests. At a smaller table, Mr. Callahan had volunteered to play bartender and was serving champagne to the human guests and any of the Elves willing to try it.

Finally, Jason excused himself. "I'll have to leave you now, cousin. Your father asked me to play my flute. Ryan's father, Rob, will play guitar. You can't have a wedding without music!"

He disappeared into the crowd, and it really was a crowd. We had thought that maybe a hundred people from Elvenwood would come, but it looked like a lot more than a hundred to me. I'd never been a fan of crowds so I edged away from the groups at the food and drink tables and tried to find a quiet spot to sit down.

Chairs had been set up around the yard in groups of two and three with small tables to hold drinks. I found one that was empty near the back porch and planted myself, sighing in relief. I felt like I'd been on my feet for hours, so I slipped off my shoes and wiggled my toes in the cool grass. Heaven.

I could hear flute and guitar music from the rear of the yard. It was lovely, sounding like folk music, actually very similar to the dragon's song.

It didn't take long before Sean found me. He was carrying two glasses of champagne. "Mr. Callahan says this is all we get, so we'd better make the most of it." He handed me one glass and sat down next to me.

Smiling, he held out his glass. "Here's to your Mom and Dad, may they be happy forever."

"I'll drink to that. Thanks, Sean." I took a sip of the bubbly stuff and sneezed.

Sean laughed. "Have you ever had champagne before?"

"Only once, and all I had was a sip. Do I have to drink the whole glass?"

He grinned. "If you don't like it, I can take it off your hands."

I took another sip and handed it to him. "I think I'd be better off with lemonade."

He finished one of the two glasses, got up and headed for the drinks table. He was back in no more than thirty seconds with my lemonade and a plate of tiny sandwiches.

As we munched on sandwiches, he said, "I've been to a few weddings with my folks, but this wedding has been incredible. The words the Elder read to your parents were beautiful. My mom actually had tears in her eyes."

"Yes, I thought the ceremony was lovely. And can you believe what Amy did for this party? She did an amazing job. You and Kevin did a fantastic job with the lights. Our yard looks like something out of a fairy tale."

"Speaking of Amy, here she comes." She and Kevin appeared out of the crowd and grabbed two more chairs to sit down with us.

I hugged her. "Amy, this is amazing. The food is perfect, and the lights were a brilliant touch. Where's the wedding cake?"

She grinned. "I'll bring it out in a little while. I just wanted to make sure everyone had something to eat first. It's a big cake, so I'll need someone to carry it out here for me. Volunteers?"

Kevin raised his hand immediately. "I'll be happy to carry it out here for you. Of course, you realize this means I get as many pieces as I want, right?"

She laughed. "Right, Kev."

We were both giggling at that point. Kevin and Sean just looked at each other and grinned.

Through the crowd, I saw Ryan and Lora and waved them over. They were both in their normal green tunics, looking like a matched set.

"Pull a couple more chairs over here, Ryan, and sit with us," I said.

I introduced Lora to Sean. Kevin had already met her at the dining hall in Elvenwood.

"How's your head?" I asked Ryan. I was glad to see the bandage was gone.

"It's all right now, just a bit of a headache."

Sean asked Ryan, "What happened to your head?" He had never heard what had actually gone down at Van Horn's on Thursday.

Ryan looked at me. "Well, Gaynes knocked me out while I was watching Cara. I don't even know what happened after that. Maybe Cara can tell us."

I took a deep breath. "Okay, since you're all here, I'll tell it once. But after tonight, I'll only talk to the police, and only if I have to. The whole thing will be giving me bad dreams for quite a while."

They all nodded, and I told them everything, from the moment I realized Ryan was missing, to seeing the police and fire trucks pulling into Van Horn's loading dock.

Ryan said, "I saw you before you went home, Cara. Your face was a mess. But you look perfect today. How did that happen?"

I smiled. "Kathleen happened. She spent the next day at our house healing my face."

Sean and Kevin were just staring at me, wide-eyed. Amy looked stricken. "Uh, Cara, did I hear you say *dragon*?"

Oops. We'd never told Amy about Rowenna. Her eyes were suddenly too big for her face.

"Um, Amy, why don't we get together tomorrow, and I'll explain."

She nodded, looking a little shell-shocked. "Okay. Come to my house. That way, if I faint, you won't have to carry me too far."

Kevin was trying hard not to laugh, so I gave him a look.

He put his arm around Amy and hugged her. "Sorry, Red. It'll be okay, trust me."

Amy whispered to him, "She said dragon, didn't she?"

I rolled my eyes.

Sean squeezed my hand. "You really took Gaynes down. You're amazing."

Ryan nodded, looking serious. "I should have been able to help you. I'm sorry."

I shook my head. "Ryan, if he hadn't knocked you out, he might have shot you. That's what he threatened to do to the others. I couldn't let him hurt my friends."

Grinning, Kevin said, "I want to hear how you kicked him in the head again."

I gave him a look. "Amy, please give him something to do before I have to kick him."

After she calmed down, Amy took Kevin into the house to help her bring out the wedding cake. "Your last birthday cake was the inspiration for this one. I hope your parents like it."

"I'd better let my parents know the cake is being brought out. Let's go find them."

Sean and I threaded through the crowd looking for Mom and Dad, who were surrounded by Elven couples.

"Sorry to interrupt, but Amy's bringing out the wedding cake," I told the Elves. "This is one of our customs. You won't want to miss it."

The empty food trays had been cleared away and Kevin placed the cake in the middle of the largest table. Amy waited until she had everyone's attention and gently removed the silver dome covering the cake. She smiled at the ooh's and ahh's filling the air.

The cake consisted of three tiers with white fondant icing, decorated from top to bottom with flowers. Roses, daisies, violets, pansies, and ivy twined around all three tiers. It was the most beautiful cake I'd ever seen. My parents were speechless.

Finally Mom said, "Amy, this is a work of art. How can you expect us to cut into it?"

Laughing, Amy said, "I think it will taste as good as it looks. And you have to cut into it so you and your husband can feed cake to each other."

She looked at my father who looked a bit confused. "It's traditional, Mr. B."

Mom was smiling as Amy handed her the silver cake knife. Two pieces were cut from the top tier and my parents fed pieces of cake to each other.

"Amy, you were right. It's delicious," my dad said, grinning.

All smiles, Amy proceeded to cut pieces of cake for all the guests, serving them on beautiful glass plates with silver forks. I thought it was all very elegant. Of course, I should have known Amy would never stoop to paper plates and plastic forks.

Amy kept cutting pieces of cake until everyone had been served. Some of the men, Elves and human alike, had come back to the table for seconds, which didn't surprise me. The cake was fantastic.

Standing next to my best friend, I whispered, "Good job, Amy. Incredible cake."

Grinning, she whispered, "Kevin's had three pieces already, and here comes Gabe for his third piece."

Gabriel bowed to Amy, smiling as he took another piece of cake. "I think I'll have to marry you," he joked. "Neal's loss, my gain, Red." He winked at her and walked away with his cake.

I looked at Amy. "Neal's loss? What did he mean?"

She lost her smile for a few seconds. "I'll tell you about it when I see you tomorrow."

As the food trays were removed, the caterers brought out two silver urns, one for tea and one for coffee. Amy hadn't missed a thing. Guests were finishing their cake and serving themselves tea and coffee. Groups of people sat around the sides of the yard while others walked around chatting.

I was pleased to see Sean's parents talking with his grandfathers. Mr. McKay looked truly happy to be speaking to his father and grandfather after so many years.

Mr. and Mrs. Strauss were talking with an older Elven couple, while Amy and Kevin were talking to Kelly O'Rourke, Kevin's dad. Chief O'Donnell had stayed long enough to have a piece of cake and then left to go back to work. He confided that his job would be a lot easier now, and asked me to thank Rowenna for her assistance. I promised I would.

My parents stood near the front of the yard, talking to Conor and Arlynn when I heard my mother's surprised, "Oh. Hello, Betty." Kevin's mom had stopped by, carrying a beautifully wrapped box.

"I realize I'm crashing your party, but I know you were married today and I wanted to give you this. It's an antique and I think it will look wonderful in this lovely old Victorian house of yours."

Mom said, "This is so sweet of you, Betty. Thank you. I think you already met Brian."

My father bowed. "Miss Sinclair. It's nice to see you again."

Kevin's mom said, "Well, I just wanted to offer my congratulations to you. Kevin's around here somewhere, isn't he?"

They say timing is everything. The crowd behind us parted and Kevin and his father were clearly visible. Betty Sinclair turned toward them and stopped short. "Oh," was all she said.

She saw Kelly standing with Kevin, and Kelly saw her.

Betty shook her head, turned and walked out of the yard.

Mom and Dad looked at each other. My father said, "She didn't know he was back?"

Mom raised an eyebrow. "I guess not."

Kevin and his dad walked up and joined us. Kelly looked acutely uncomfortable.

Kevin put one arm around me. "I'm afraid Mom's gonna have a few words for me tonight, short stuff."

Conor shook his head. "I've heard there's always some drama at a wedding. Kevin, it's not really your problem. The problem is between your parents."

Kelly nodded. "He's right, Kev. If she wants to yell at someone, you can tell her where to find me."

Kevin said, "I think I'd better go home and get it over with. Mom's probably upset. Cara, tell Amy I'll be back early in the morning to pack up everything for the caterer to pick up later in the day. I think she's busy wrapping up all the leftover food, which will probably end up in your kitchen." He grinned. "Although, I did my best to see there wouldn't be too much left over."

Mom started to walk away. "I should help her."

I grabbed her arm. "Mom, don't worry about the food. I'll help Amy put everything away, including what's left of that gorgeous cake. You and Dad just relax and enjoy yourselves while our guests are still here."

Kevin hugged me, Mom, and Arlynn, shook my father's hand and Conor's, and headed for home.

Mom looked worried. "Poor Kevin, caught between two parents who can't stand each other." She took my father's arm and they walked to the rear of the yard where Jason and Rob were still playing music the Elves were enjoying. Ryan's girlfriend, Lora, was singing along with them, and the younger Elves were all seated around them. The sun was going down and the lights in the trees and shrubs created a romantic atmosphere. I saw my father pull two chairs over near Jason and he and Mom sat down to enjoy the music.

After Amy and I finished putting the leftover food away, we joined the group listening to the music. Looking around, I realized I hadn't seen Adam all day. I'd thought he'd be at the wedding, but I never caught sight of him in the crowd.

Finally I spotted him at the edge of the woods, leaning against a pine tree, listening to the music. I stood and circled the group sitting around Jason and Rob, and walked into the trees where I'd seen him.

"I've been looking for you all day. Where have you been hiding?"

He smiled, making my heart flutter a little. I scolded myself severely.

"I've been around. I did congratulate your mother and father right after the ceremony, but I'm not fond of crowds, which is something I think we share." He gave me a rueful smile. "I saw you, flitting from one group to another like a pink butterfly." He chuckled. "You were busy greeting everyone. And I didn't want to get in Sean's way."

I groaned. "Oh, come on, Adam. You wouldn't have been in anyone's way."

Grinning, he said, "I doubt Sean would have seen it that way."

"Well, I missed you today. Did you get anything to eat? You would have loved those little sandwiches."

"I did indeed. They were excellent, as was that beautiful wedding cake. Amy is a real artist when it comes to cakes." He chuckled. "Can you imagine the masterpieces you could create if you just learned to cook?"

I rolled my eyes. He was still laughing. When he stopped laughing, he said softly, "Seriously, Cara, girls dressed in pink, who are as beautiful as you, should never be expected to cook." He looked down at me with so much affection in his eyes, I felt weak in the knees for a few seconds.

"I'll be sure to pass that thought along to my mother." I thought I heard my voice shake just a tiny bit. I felt a sort of tension between us that I wasn't used to.

He took my hand and moved us behind the pine tree he'd been leaning against. The look on his handsome face made my heart start fluttering a little. He seemed somehow unsure as he put his hands on either side of my face. His eyes went to my lips as he slowly bent down to kiss me. My heart pounded as his lips met mine.

Unexpectedly, there was a roaring in my ears. The ground dropped away from beneath my feet. Voices from the party went silent. The earth had stopped revolving around the sun. It seemed that we were completely and utterly alone.

As his lips moved over mine, I felt weak but unbelievably happy. If he hadn't been holding me, I would have fallen. My heart pounded like a hammer.

I'd dreamed of this. Adam was kissing me the way a man kisses a woman he loves. Finally, I reacted by wrapping my arms around his slim waist and pulling him closer. His arms went around my back, caressing me gently. The taste of his lips was intoxicating, even better than fruit punch laced with vodka. I thought I could spend the rest of my life just kissing Adam.

Suddenly his hands were on my shoulders, pushing me away. I looked up at him, shocked at the sudden distance between us, wondering why he'd stopped kissing me.

We were both breathing hard as I reached for him again, but his arms kept me at a distance, a distance I didn't want.

His expression was tormented, guilty, and I didn't understand. I knew he'd liked kissing me as much as I liked it. Why did he look so unhappy?

His hands still holding my shoulders, he whispered, "Cara, forgive me. I shouldn't have let that happen."

"Why?"

"I'm so sorry," he said.

"I'm not."

"You don't understand." He closed his eyes briefly.

Looking over my head, he said, "I think your father's looking for you."

I turned to look into the yard, but my father was by the porch talking to Conor.

When I turned back, Adam was gone.

I thought I heard his soft voice from a distance, "Good night, love."

I stood there and tried to get my breathing and heartbeat under control, missing the feel of his body pressed to mine. I realized that he'd left because he was afraid he'd kiss me again. Which would have been fine with me, but I guessed he was thinking about our age difference. I didn't care about our age difference. It wasn't important. I sighed deeply, closing my eyes, waiting for my heart to stop pounding.

When I felt sure my legs would hold me up, I walked into the yard and returned to my chair next to Amy.

She looked at me and said, "Are you all right? You're really flushed." If I was flushed, it went all the way through me.

"I'm okay."

"Where did you go?"

"I was looking for Adam."

She giggled. "From the look of you, you must have found him. What happened?"

"I'll tell you about it tomorrow, okay?"

"Okay, but come over early. I'll make breakfast for us."

I nodded and smiled. I wanted to keep it all to myself, at least for tonight.

Most of the Elves had already left. I knew those returning to Elvenwood wanted to get back before it was completely dark. The younger men were probably just returning to camp tonight. Amy's parents had just left after thanking my parents for sharing their wedding day.

Sean and his parents had spent a lot of time talking to Sean's grandfathers and to Conor. It looked like a wonderful family reunion for the McKays, who were the last to leave.

Mr. Callahan had finally run out of film and had gone home, promising to have all the pictures he took developed in a few days.

I walked out with Sean and his parents, both telling me they'd had an absolutely wonderful time. They got into their car and Sean kissed me good night before sliding into the back seat.

Adam had been right. When it came to kisses, there were big differences.

When I got back to our yard, Mom and Dad were sitting on the porch, sipping champagne and holding hands.

When I walked up on the porch, my father said, "Why don't you join us."

I yawned. "Thanks, but I'm really tired, Dad. I've got a date with Amy early in the morning. She's making breakfast, so I think I'll go to bed now."

I looked out at the yard, still looking like a fairyland, lights glittering in all the trees.

Mom said, "I think I'll leave these lights on tonight. It's all so pretty, I can't bear to turn them off." My father chuckled, smiling at her.

I kissed them both good night. As I went in the door, I said, "Good night, Mrs. Blackthorne. Good night, Dad." I heard them both chuckling as I went upstairs.

Ralph was already snoring at the foot of my bed. I got out of my dress, pulled on my oversized t-shirt, brushed my teeth, and got into bed. As I lay there, I thought about Adam.

My father had asked me several times if I was in love with Adam. I'd always said I didn't know what it felt like to fall in love. But I knew now.

I was in love with Adam Wolfe.

CHAPTER 52

Naturally, my dreams were full of Adam that night. Nice dreams. Naughty dreams. Great dreams. Needless to say, I woke up early in a really good mood.

I took a quick shower, dried my hair, left it hanging down my back, and pulled on a pair of jeans and my red sweatshirt. There was no longer any reason to avoid wearing bright colors. Adam said I looked good in red. I would wear red often.

Mom and Dad weren't up yet, so I left a note telling them I'd be at Amy's, and left the house quietly. When I peeked out the kitchen window, I didn't see Adam or anyone else out there. I ducked outside quickly to grab one of the pots of mums for Amy.

On my way to her house, I noticed there were no police cars on the streets and no uniformed cops walking through the downtown area. It was, after all, Sunday morning. Thornewood looked like it used to look, peaceful and quiet, a picturesque small town where most people lived peaceful, quiet lives undisturbed by hit men and kidnappers.

As soon as I pulled up in front of her house, she was at the door, waving me in.

"You brought me wedding flowers! Thanks." She gave me a quick hug, taking the pot of flowers out of my hands and setting it on their dining room table. "Mom will love these," she said, grinning.

"I made coffee. Help yourself." She went to the stove where a large griddle was sizzling.

"What are you making us?"

"French Toast and bacon," she said.

"Sounds great." I sat down, pouring cream into my coffee. I could smell the cinnamon Amy's mom always used in her coffee.

While she cooked, I sipped my coffee. "When are you going to tell me what's happening with Neal?" I asked.

She shook her head. "I told you how Neal's parents feel about human girls, didn't I?"

"Yes, but you said he wanted them to meet you, hoping to change their minds."

She brought plates of French Toast and bacon to the table and sat down with me.

"Neal was hoping to introduce me to them at the wedding." She frowned. "They obviously weren't interested. When he led me over to meet them, they simply turned away and said, 'We're leaving now.' And he had to leave with them to take them back to Elvenwood." She sighed. "He gave me back the phone I'd given him and said he was sorry. I'll probably never see him again."

I was surprised. I had thought he really cared for Amy. "Well, if his parents' prejudices are more important to him than you are, it's better to know it now."

She nodded. "It really made me sad, but as you said, better to know now. I'll miss him, but there are lots of fish in the sea, so they say."

I dug into my French toast. "This is delicious, Amy." Amy was the cook I would probably never be.

We talked about the wedding and all the Elves she met for the first time. "Why do you think they're all so good looking? They don't all look alike, but I didn't see one unattractive person there."

I grinned. "Yeah. I guess it's genetic. Like the fact they're all tall, even the women. You can imagine how I felt the first time I visited Elvenwood. I felt like a dwarf."

She laughed. "Well, at least in one way, I'd fit in. One of these days, you'll have to take me to Elvenwood so we can see if the gate will open for me. Wouldn't that be a hoot? Then I could tell Neal where to go!"

"His loss, Amy."

She nodded. "On the bright side, we can really begin our senior year now. Thanks to you, we can start having fun, with nothing to worry about but our grades and our social life!"

We finished eating and Amy poured more coffee for both of us.

"I want you to know I could barely sleep last night thinking about dragons! There's a real, live dragon in Elvenwood?"

I smiled. "Yes. She was a friend of my grandmother's." I described how that tune had been stuck in my head and the research I had to do to get to the bottom of it. When I told her how Jason and I had met her, her mouth hung open.

"So you have a new best friend, right? She just happens to be a fire-breathing dragon." She shook her head. "Your life just keeps getting weirder, my friend." She emptied her coffee cup and sat back, still shaking her head.

"Okay, Cara, I'm dying to know what happened with Adam last night! You were as pink as your dress when you came back."

I could feel my face getting hot again. "Adam's been special to me for a couple of months, more than a friend, you know?" She nodded.

"You've always said he's just a good friend, like Kevin and me, but I had a feeling it went farther than that."

"Yeah. I've really tried not to think about him that way, but those eyes of his make me melt."

Laughing, she said, "I've noticed. He is gorgeous and a really nice guy too. He's always seemed devoted to you and not just as your bodyguard."

I nodded. "We've gotten close, but it's been hard to ignore the age difference because my mom made such a big deal of it. And that's only because my father was so much older when she met him. I guess she's been afraid history would repeat itself with Adam and me. I know Adam's done his best to keep our relationship appropriately platonic. Mom made her feelings about our relationship crystal clear to him." I sighed.

"But last night, something changed. I'm not sure why. Maybe it was just that the time had come, you know?" She nodded, obviously dying to hear the rest.

"I'd been looking for him all day but he'd stayed out of sight. He's not crazy about crowds either, so he was watching me from the sidelines. When I finally spotted him, I went over to him and we talked for a while." I hesitated for a few seconds. "I could feel that something was different, but I didn't know what it was . . . until he kissed me."

Amy smiled. "You don't mean a kiss on the cheek, do you?"

"Nope. It was the kind of kiss I've always dreamed of. I've never been kissed like that before. I didn't want it to end."

"Well, why did it end?"

"He pushed me away. Asked me to forgive him, said he never should have let it happen. He said he was sorry. I said I wasn't. Then he left."

Amy was transfixed. "Oh, Cara, that's so romantic. After all these months, he couldn't resist any longer." She grinned. "And I guess you couldn't either."

"No, I had no intention of resisting. Kissing Adam was . . . well, it was wonderful."

"I've heard him call you 'love.' Do you think he means it?"

"He kissed me the way I imagine a man kisses a woman he loves. There was nothing casual about it, trust me."

Wide-eyed, she whispered, "Are you in love with him?"

I was almost afraid to admit what I was feeling. "I think I am. I never knew what falling in love felt like. I knew I wasn't in love with Sean, even though I like him a lot. But last night I knew."

"Wow. So what happens now?"

"I have no idea. He won't be my bodyguard anymore, but he said he'd be there whenever I need him. I guess I'll be spending more time in Elvenwood." I grinned.

After more small talk, I thanked Amy for a great breakfast and headed for home. Maybe Adam would be around.

When I got home, I found Kevin in the backyard, filling up boxes with plates, glasses and silverware. He'd already stacked up the chairs and tables and taken all the lights down.

"Hey, short stuff. Where've you been so early?"

"I've been over at Amy's. She made breakfast for us."

"Huh. And she didn't even invite her other best friend. I'm crushed. Also hungry."

"Sorry, Kev. If we have any bagels, I can make you a Sunrise Special."

He smiled. "That's okay, babe. My mom is taking me out to brunch this morning."

"Wow! What's the occasion?"

"No idea. I guess it occurred to her that your mom wouldn't be making the usual Sunday brunch today. She has to eat too, although she hardly ever eats at home."

"Thanks for coming over to pack up all this stuff. When are the caterers coming by to pick it up?"

He shrugged. "Sometime today, that's all I know. It's all ready for them."

"Can you stay for coffee? I'll make a pot now."

"Sure. I'd love a cup of coffee."

We climbed the porch steps together and I went inside to put the coffee on.

A few minutes later I brought two cups out on the porch.

"Kev, has your mom said anything yet about seeing your dad last night?"

"Uh, no. That's probably why she's taking me out to brunch today. When I got home last night, she was already in her room with the door closed. I hope she won't tell me she doesn't want me seeing him anymore. I'll never agree to that."

"I don't blame you."

He finished his coffee and looked at his watch. "It's almost ten. I'd better get home. We'll be going out soon. Thanks for the coffee."

I wished him luck and got his usual one-armed hug.

It was a beautiful morning so I poured myself another cup of coffee and made myself comfortable on the porch. Without thinking, I began to hum the dragon's song. It was only a few minutes before I felt the familiar magic swirling around me. Since it was broad daylight, she didn't land but I heard the sound of her broad wings circling above.

You had a large gathering yesterday so I kept my distance. What was the occasion?

"My mother and father were married yesterday, both in the human world and in the Elven world. The gathering was a celebration."

Ah. I am happy for them, Cara. Now they are truly mated.

"I'm very happy, both for them and for myself. This is something I've always dreamed of."

I'm happy for you, child. I dream of my mate returning some day.

I looked up and saw her heading back to the mountains. Slowly her magic faded away.

Leaning back into the comfortable deck chair, I put my feet up on the porch railing and closed my eyes. I was perfectly content here, close to the forest I loved. I could smell the scent of the pines as a soft breeze blew through the trees. The only thing missing was Adam.

I must have dozed off for a while because when I opened my eyes, my father was sitting there with me.

"Good morning, sweetheart. You were out early. Didn't you get enough sleep last night?"

"I'm fine, Dad. Is Mom still asleep?"

He chuckled. "No, she's luxuriating in a bubble bath right now. But I'm glad it gives us a chance to speak privately."

That got my attention.

He looked at me and reached for my hand. "Cara, I have some news that I'm afraid you're not going to like." There was a slight frown on his handsome face.

Suddenly my heart was in my throat, but I didn't know why.

"I got a message from Adam early this morning that he needed to speak to me, so I met him in camp."

My heart was jumping around inside my chest. Had he told my father about the change in our relationship?

He hesitated, so I said, "What is it? What did he want to speak to you about?" He could see that I was unusually tense. It was a definite frown now.

"Cara, Adam has left Blackthorne Forest." He sighed deeply. "He's already gone."

"What? Why? I thought he liked it here." I was trying hard to remain calm, but my voice was suddenly higher than normal and my stomach began to hurt.

"If you still needed a bodyguard, if you were still in danger, I don't think he would have left. At least not now. He took his responsibility to guard you seriously. But the danger is past and your life can return to normal now."

I just stared at him, unbelieving, my heart sinking.

He said, "Before he came here, Adam was a wanderer. He told me he hadn't stayed anywhere very long since he left his home village years ago. I guess he decided it was time to move on, now that you won't be needing him any longer."

I could feel tears in my eyes. Fighting them down, I said, "I do need him. He's one of my best friends." I choked on the words. "How could he leave without saying goodbye?"

Of course, we were a great deal more than best friends. But maybe I was the only one who thought so.

I had a sudden thought. "Dad, he didn't leave because of anything you said to him, did he?" I wondered if it had been something like, 'What were you doing kissing my daughter last night?' Or words to that effect.

"Of course not. I'm very fond of Adam. I hoped he'd make his home with us permanently. What could I have possibly said to make him leave?"

I muttered, "I don't know. He didn't even say goodbye to me."

There was no way I could hold it inside any longer. I jumped up and ran down the steps, through the yard and into the forest. I heard my father calling me but I didn't stop.

I ran until I reached the stream, the place where I had seen my father for the very first time. That spot was full of memories, most of them good.

I couldn't run any farther. My chest was aching, I was gasping for breath, and I couldn't see through my tears. I sank down on the flat rock, pulled my knees up and rested my face on them. Wrapping my arms around my legs, I let it all out, sobbing until my head ached.

Someone sat down next to me and didn't say a word. An arm wrapped around my shoulders pulled me against a chest that smelled like the forest. I knew it wasn't my father. The Elf who considered himself my big brother must have heard me crying. He wanted to comfort me the way he'd done so many times before I ever met my father.

When I finally quieted, he said, "I think I know why you're upset, Cara. I saw Adam leave early this morning. He wasn't happy either."

"Conor, he didn't even say goodbye to me. I thought he cared about me. Was I kidding myself?"

His voice was soft. "I don't think so. I believe he does care about you. I think that's why he felt he had to leave. And I think you know exactly what I'm talking about, don't you?"

I nodded. Conor must have seen Adam and me together last night. We had done something that Adam knew would upset my parents. He had ended the platonic part of our relationship, but then begged me to forgive him.

"Are you ready to go home now?" he asked.

I shook my head. I was in my place of refuge and I wasn't leaving.

Conor sat there with me, saying very little, until the sun set. Then he took my hand and walked me home.

Coming in 2017

THE JOINING TREE

Blackthorne Forest, Book 4

ACKNOWLEDGEMENTS

First, I want to acknowledge the source of the lovely blessing given by the Elder at Alicia and Brian's Elven wedding. It is a portion of a traditional Native American (Apache) Wedding Vow that I came across while searching for something beautiful that I could attribute to the Elves of Blackthorne Forest. I hope no Native Americans will object. I feel there are definite similarities between our Native Americans and my Elves, in that both groups have a tradition of love and respect for the earth.

Secondly, I have to thank my husband for his constant encouragement as well as the new name he bestowed on me: Hemingfogel. Now I simply have to live up to it!

My new Editor, Laurie A. Will, taught me so much as she patiently tried to correct my bad writing habits (dialogue tags, etc.). I think this book is my best to date, and it's largely due to Laurie's influence.

The beautiful cover for The Dragon's Song was designed by my favorite designer, Alexandre Rito, who has been responsible for all my book covers. He always manages to give Blackthorne Forest the mystical look it deserves.

My sincere thanks to Karen Konrad, whose proofreading expertise was appreciated.

A huge "thank you" goes to my readers, especially those who enjoyed my earlier books enough to go to my website -- www.clairefogel.com -- and leave me a message to let me know they liked my books and asked when the next one in the series would be available! I reply to each and every message I receive. I love hearing from my readers. After all, you're the ones I write for!

As always, leaving a review on Amazon makes my day!

ABOUT THE AUTHOR

I started writing not long after I learned to hold a pencil. Writing, writing, constantly writing. I still have the callouses on my index finger to show for it.

For many years I worked in business offices, first as a secretary, then office manager, finally as a marketing analyst. And still writing constantly! Of course, business writing is a horse of a different color compared to the kind of writing I do now. And now I use a keyboard instead of a pen!

I've always loved fiction – mysteries, science fiction, fantasy, romance, and eventually I discovered young adult stories. However, I didn't think I had enough imagination to write one. My husband, Neil, spent years trying to convince me there was a story inside of me, just dying to get out. Finally, in 2011, he convinced me to give it a try.

My inspiration was the Twilight series, a wonderful love story with characters easy to fall in love with. The usual advice to new writers: "Write the kind of story you love to read." That's what I did. I do enjoy vampires and werewolves, but I wanted my story to revolve around a different kind of mythical character. And that's when I began writing the Blackthorne Forest series.

I love series. They give you so much more time to get to know the characters, and to experience their joys and sorrows right along with them. Many of my readers have told me they've fallen in love with the characters in Blackthorne Forest, and one even told me she's joined "Team Adam!" That kind of response to the characters I've created is why I keep on writing.

Book Four in the Blackthorne Forest series will be titled, "The Joining Tree." It follows Cara through high school graduation and into college, as she continues to grow up, balancing her life between the human world she was born in and the Elven world of her father. Her emotional life plays an even bigger part in this story.

I haven't decided yet whether Book Four will be the last in the series. Maybe, but maybe not!

My husband and I live in the mountains of central California with Roscoe, our lovable Boxer. When I'm not writing, I'm washing dishes and picking dry dog food out of the carpet.

You're welcome to visit my web site - www.clairefogel.com - for more information about me and Blackthorne Forest. Leave a message for me; I promise to answer!

Made in the USA
San Bernardino, CA
07 September 2016